Securing Aubrey

Hawthorne Security Book One

Julia Douglas

Hillside Books

Contents

For my husband, who is my real-life book boyfriend.
Thank you for doing all the things so I could make this dream a reality.
Hawthorne Security wouldn't exist without you.

Chapter One

Aubrey

I'm fairly confident I could get away with her murder, Bree mused as she unpacked another box of books and put them away on the shelves framing the fireplace. Some of the covers and pages were bent from being stuffed into the box and driven halfway across the country. Bree frowned. She hadn't *wanted* to hire movers—she wanted to do it herself the way she did everything. Intentionally. Cautiously. Slowly. Her agent, however, had other ideas. When Rae showed up at her house with a group of men she'd hired to pack and move everything, Bree let them because she hadn't wanted to be rude—Rae insisted celebrities didn't pack and move their own stuff. Now, with a few items missing—most notably the teddy bear Nonna had given her the Christmas before she died—and with her beloved books in less than stellar condition, Bree was ready to scream.

Bree took the box cutter from the mantle and sliced through the tape, carefully avoiding her bandaged finger, an unfortunate victim of her aggressive unpacking last night. She sighed heavily, carrying the flattened box into her garage and tossing it onto the pile of cardboard corpses already there, waiting to be recycled and given new life. She walked into the kitchen and poured the last drops of coffee from the pot—the only kitchen item that had made it out of a box. The other boxes sat in the corner waiting to be unpacked and judging her for her taste in takeout and inability to cook anything beyond boxed Mac n' Cheese. Bree shook her head. She really needed more sleep.

Bree walked into the dining room, coffee securely in hand, and sat down at the table. She had forty more pictures to sign and send to her fans, and then she'd be almost free of obligations from the label. She reached across the table to pick up the next picture and bit her lip as she wrote, in painstakingly neat handwriting, *To Skyler. All my love, Aubrey.* Bree methodically tucked the picture into the waiting envelope, careful to preserve the edges of the picture before sealing it. The rest of the autographs went relatively quickly as Bree found her rhythm.

As she signed the last one she let out a deep breath. *Finally.* The anxiety that had been pulsing in her chest since the moment she signed her first contract with the label eased as she sealed the last envelope. She was *free.* Bree let out a shuttering breath, her eyes filled with tears. She hadn't been free in seven years.

Of course, with her father being who he was and her sister's bills still needing to be paid each month, true freedom was still a long way away. But retirement and leaving behind the chaos of Los Angeles was a start. Some people worried about disappearing from the spotlight, but not Bree. She couldn't wait to be yesterday's news. Unfortunately, that seemed like it was still a long way off.

She looked forlornly at the invitation sitting next to her coffee mug. She was cordially invited to be the keynote speaker at a Gala fundraising for families who had lost loved ones to drug or alcohol addiction. The introvert in her wanted to turn it down with a polite but firm thanks but no thanks. The people pleaser felt like she couldn't turn it down. It was a good cause, she was technically available that day, and what was five minutes of her time—and a heap of anxiety—compared to significant financial donations?

Bree sighed and pushed it away. She could deal with it later. Thankfully, the Millers—who were in charge of the event—didn't live in Tennessee. Bree turned her attention to her empty mug instead. More coffee was a requirement if she was going to get the rest of the boxes unpacked.

She grabbed her purse and slipped on her favorite black jacket, which was comfy and stylish. Tessa was a queen. Her former stylist was one of the few perks of being famous that she missed. Well, that and having a chef. Bree grimaced at the boxes still sitting in the kitchen for the last two months, the ones that said "pots and pans," dutifully ignoring them as she grabbed her keys out of the little wooden bowl on the entry table. Eventually, eating frozen meals and boxed Mac n' Cheese was going to get old, but that sounded like a problem for future Bree.

The door closed with a solid thud behind her and Bree locked up—triple-checking to make sure the door was locked. After her last show in Houston, where a note had been left in her dressing room backstage, her paranoia had crept up, slowly suffocating her. She couldn't let it go. Which frankly was annoying—nothing had happened to her. She needed to get over it.

The neighborhood was quiet, the well-kept suburban homes mostly empty on a Wednesday morning. The birds chirped in the trees, unfazed by the clanking coming from the Robinson house. Bree unlocked her car, and Mr. Robinson looked up as it chirped. Mr. Robinson was better than any security camera system. His watchful gaze missed nothing. Noticing Bree, he smiled and waved before ducking his head back under the hood of his 1974 Plymouth Duster. One of these days, he'd get that car up and running, and in the meantime, the occasional backfire seemed to be a part of the rhythm of the neighborhood.

The drive into Rhodes was gloriously boring, traffic almost nonexistent, until she turned into the main square. The park in the middle of town was brimming with booths filled with various crafts from local artisans. From painting to pottery and any other medium one could think of, the Rhodes Annual Artisan Festival brought in some of the best artists from across the state, many of whom fell in love with the small town and decided to make a home there.

The square hummed with energy as tourists flocked to the artisan stalls, enthusiastic smiles and laughter echoing in the breeze. Crowds also meant little personal space and an increased chance of being recognized, which was not a vibe. The best thing about living in Rhodes was the fact the people who lived there really hadn't cared when she moved in several weeks ago. A few of the teens and pre-teens who had listened to her pop music had asked for autographs as their parents fervently apologized, but then the hullabaloo died down, and now it was almost like Bree had lived there her whole life.

Unsurprisingly, finding parking near the festival and the surrounding blocks was a nightmare. The brick storefronts were decorated with banners welcoming visitors to Rhodes and advertising the local businesses. The window displays were intentionally decorated with bright colored art to draw attention and beckon visitors in from the street. After spending a few minutes cruising down side streets, Bree let out a sigh of relief as a spot opened up in front of Willow's Bar and slowly pulled up beside the curb. Willow's would be closed until after five since her daughter participated in the festival with the other junior high school art students.

Bree hopped out of the car and draped her purse across her shoulders, clicking the lock button on her fob until the car beeped back, confirming it was locked. Satisfied the car was secure, Bree looked around and took a deep breath, exhaling slowly. The air in Rhodes was so much crisper and cleaner than Los Angeles. While the beach wasn't down the street anymore, the rolling hills and mountains—and the distinct lack of people compared to L.A.—more than made up for it. Peace was priceless.

Bree spotted the sign for Rhodes Creek Coffee Shop & Bakery and decided her need for coffee demanded a brisk walk rather than a stroll. She raced to the door and held it open as Mrs. Appleman, one of the local elementary school teachers, walked out with her coffee.

"Thank you, Aubrey." The woman said, her smile causing the skin on her forehead and around her eyes to crinkle. Bree nodded, and Mrs. Appleman strolled away, her long skirt swishing as she walked to the corner before disappearing into the crowd of tourists heading to the festival.

Bree's shoulders relaxed as the scent of coffee and pastries surrounded her. Normally a fairly quiet place, the cacophony of voices echoing throughout the space was jarring. Apparently, the tourists also needed a caffeine fix at nine in the morning. Marilee was behind the counter working her magic, and a new guy was at the registers taking the orders. The man working behind the counter was unfamiliar, but he had on a backward blue baseball cap and was wearing an open blue flannel shirt with a plain gray tee under it. He was definitely giving Luke Danes vibes. If this was a new gimmick the cafe was trying out, it was a solid ten out of ten.

"What can I get for you?" He asked, looking Bree up and down before turning his attention back to the screen.

"I need coffee in an IV...stat." She joked. He glared across the counter, and Bree shuffled her feet, a warm blush staining her cheeks. "I'll have a large iced vanilla latte with caramel drizzle, please." She said quietly, tapping her card on the machine and turning down the receipt.

Bree walked over to a table in the back of the restaurant that overlooked the town square. People-watching would be fun today. A few families walked by, bags in hand, as the children pointed excitedly at the different colorful things that grabbed their attention. Movement out of the corner of her eye drew her attention back inside the coffee shop as the decidedly grumpy barista delivered the drink to her table and stalked away.

"Your lack of enthusiasm shocks me," Bree muttered under her breath, stirring the latte so it would be adequately cold.

Her pocket buzzed, and she grinned, taking a sip of her coffee before answering the call.

"I just wanted to let you know that I spent a good portion of my morning contemplating the best way to murder you," Bree said seriously in lieu of a greeting.

"As all good friends and former clients do," Rae said. "Out of curiosity—given the fact I'm like 30 hours away by car—what did I do this time?"

"The movers you hired either did a poor job of packing or lost the bear from Nonna. And as if that wasn't bad enough, they ruined my books."

"I'm sure the bear is in one of the boxes somewhere," Rae said dismissively. "And you have too many books. A few less won't hurt you. Anyway—I have an appointment so I have to jet. I just wanted to tell you to stay off your socials for a bit."

Bree bit back her groan of frustration as her heart fell in her chest. This was why they had butt heads while they worked together in the industry. Rae was singularly focused...on Rae. "Why?" She asked calmly.

There was hesitation on the other end of the line.

"Why, Rae?"

Rae sighed. "There has been a big uptick in followers making inappropriate—or threatening—comments since your farewell tour ended, and it has become clear it wasn't a publicity stunt."

"Like I needed a publicity stunt." Bree scoffed.

"I know that, but the people don't." Rae soothed. "Anyway, just stay off it. And in the event you won't listen—because we both know you won't—make sure to screenshot anything over the top and send it to me and the police department for the file."

"Will do."

"You know, you could come back and call it a spur-of-the-moment decision."

Bree sighed, "You're always trying to pull me back into the rat race. Polite pass."

"Your loss. My ride is here. Gotta run. Ciao, babe."

The call ended before Bree had a chance to respond. She sat the phone down beside her drink, resting her head in her hands. Creepy messages were kind of par for the course. While they shouldn't be sent, it happened often enough that it wasn't as shocking now as it had been in the beginning. The things people would type that they'd never say in real life were astounding.

Bree lifted her head and opened TikTok surprised that her retirement announcement video was still one of her top-viewed videos. That had been posted nearly a year ago—it should have been old news by now. The videos from her farewell tour also gained a lot of traction as some fans shared their sadness that they wouldn't be able to see her in concert again, and others complained angrily because there was no reason for her to step away from the industry. She was just selfish. One of the comments threatened to put an end to her "self-indulgent existence" as soon as the media leaked where she was "hiding from her responsibilities". The vile was unending. Ugh, she should have listened to Rae.

The alarm on her phone rang shrilly in the restaurant as Bree hurriedly swiped at her phone to silence it. When the neighboring tables had quit staring and returned to their coffee or pastries, and the heat in her cheeks had lessened—Bree let out the breath she had been holding. She quickly dialed the only number she knew by heart and waited for Steph to pick up.

"You're two minutes late," Steph joked.

"You were five minutes late last week—" Bree pointed out.

"Fair enough," Steph said with a laugh.

"How are you? How's Adam?" Bree asked, eager for news of her best friend. While she loved the freedom that came from being away from L.A. and the constant hustle and bustle of the city, she missed her friends. She'd kill to be able to grab a cup of coffee with Steph in person and go for a walk to the pier.

"We're great! I can't wait to see you in a few weeks, though. I miss you being in L.A."

"You could always move to Tennessee," Bree tried hopefully.

"If Adam would move, I'd be there in a heartbeat," Steph said loyally.

"That's because you're the best," Bree said.

"And don't you forget it." Steph laughed before hesitating. "Bree, I need to tell you something." She said, her voice uncharacteristically serious.

"What's wrong? Is it Lucy?" Bree asked, concern for the beloved pitbull over-riding her general aversion to anything non-human.

"No, no. Lucy is fine...Just don't be mad at me."

"That sounds promising," Bree said sardonically.

"I saw some concerning comments on your socials and showed them to Adam." Oh boy. Here they go. Bree could imagine Adam's face reading the comment section on her social media accounts. It would be a perfect blend of shock and brotherly-like outrage.

"Okay..."

"And he was super worried about you...like I am." Steph hedged.

"...and?"

"He might have called in a favor to an old friend who owns a security company over in Trenton."

"Steph," Bree groaned, laying her head on the table.

"He's probably going to give you a call. His name is Noah. Noah Hawthorne. He owns Hawthorne Security. Just let him look into this situation and see if there is a threat to you."

"It's not a big deal, Steph," Bree argued. She didn't want to be a bother, and there was nothing he could do for her anyway. She already had a direct line of communication with the police department and reported each and every one of the vile comments or threats made. The last thing she wanted to do was waste his time. Or hers.

"I would agree with you if it was just the comments," Steph said cooly. "But the comments plus the threatening note that made it into your dressing room at the end of your farewell tour indicate that someone wants to get to you."

"The comments and note could be completely unrelated," Bree argued. This was probably the right time to tell Steph about the death threat in the comments before she heard it from someone else, but Bree hesitated. She didn't want to worry Steph with some generic threat from a user with numbers for a name and an animation for a face. It probably wasn't even viable. Weren't there like three things a threat had to include for it to be considered legitimate?

"Aubrey Elizabeth Gray, I will not read about my best friend's death in the tabloids when we could have done something to prevent it. My parents were murdered, Bree. My best friend doesn't need to be." Steph said, her scathing tone effectively bringing Bree back to the present.

"Just lay on the guilt there, Steph. I don't think I got the point…" Bree complained. Steph was a force to be reckoned with when she wanted something.

"Bree," Steph said, gentling her voice. "You don't have to work with him. Meet him. Let him investigate to see if there is a reason for us to be concerned. Just…give him a chance."

"I promise I will be pleasant if he calls." She would pleasantly inform him that his services were not needed. Simple. "I'm gonna go finish my coffee. Same time text week? Your turn to call me."

"Sounds good. I'll even try to be on time," Steph joked. "Love you. Call me if you need anything."

"Love you too," Bree said quietly, picking up her coffee and heading back to her car. Most of the festival attendees would be at the live art demonstration which meant traffic should be at a minimum. A perfect time to head back home before the streets were super busy again. Those boxes—unfortunately—weren't going to unpack themselves.

***

Bree reached her car a few minutes later, taking a much-needed sip of coffee before walking around the hood and groaning. A flat tire. Perfect. Bree opened the car door carefully and set her coffee in the cupholder, carefully protecting the liquid gold from what was sure to be a messy endeavor. She pulled the lever to open the hood and shut the door softly. Bree walked to the trunk, clicking the button on her keys to open the trunk where the jack, spare, and tire-changing tool was. Honestly it probably had a name, but who could keep up with the names for tools outside of a Phillips or flathead screwdriver? The rest were irrelevant. Except when a tire was flat, and she actually needed the weird tool thing.

Bree carted the equipment and spare tire up to the driver's side front tire and looked both ways for traffic before plopping down on the ground. Thank the Lord for a good pair of jeans.

"Hey, Bree. Let me help you," A honeyed voice said. Over to her left was a tall, slim, blonde man leaning against the side of Willow's Bar, his dark, beady eyes watching Bree with interest. Of all the people to stumble upon her it just had to be one of the most entitled, obnoxious boys she had the pleasure of running in the same circles with growing up. Kyle freaking Rhodes.

The hair on the back of Bree's neck rose and she surreptitiously looked around to note the quickest exit. "It's Aubrey. And no...thank you." Bree replied, adding the manners as an afterthought.

Kyle scoffed and took a step closer to her. "Our dads wouldn't like it if I just left you out here with a busted tire. Move out of the way, and let me help you."

Bree hesitated. She wanted to say no. She also didn't want to be rude or cause waves in her new community. While Kyle might have just been the annoying kid she had to see a few times a year growing up, his dad was the mayor of Rhodes now. The indecision pulled her back and forth, tossing her around like waves during a storm. "No, thank you. I've got it." Bree ground out, her pulse skyrocketing as her hands shook. She hated conflict.

Kyle took another small step toward her, and Bree panicked, standing up and clenching the long rod thing in her fist tightly, her heart pounding in her ears. Would he help her? Hit her? Hit on her despite being told she wasn't interested? None of those options sounded particularly appealing.

"Don't be an ungrateful bi—"

"She said she's got it." A deep, gravelly voice said from behind her.

Bree turned slightly to see the newcomer and immediately felt dwarfed by his presence. And a little awestruck, if she was being totally honest. Dark hair, chiseled jaw, tan skin, and height for days. He looked like a character out of a romantasy novel. The only things missing were the bat wings. He looked relaxed, but there was a tension in his muscles that screamed this man wasn't someone you wanted to cross.

"Keep on walking. This doesn't concern you." Kyle said to the stranger, unfazed by the quiet violence radiating off of him.

The man looked at Kyle as though he were nothing more than an obnoxious gnat. "She said no. You seem either unable or unwilling to understand it, so I'll stick around until you get the hint." He said, moving to stand just to the left of Bree. Bree took a slight step away from the stranger, thankful he put himself between her and Kyle the Creep but also wary. She was not about to be one of the women in the movies who were too stupid to live because they trusted the wrong man. Absolutely not.

Kyle waited about thirty more seconds before realizing the man was serious and huffed loudly. "Whatever. I'll see you around, *Aubrey.*"

Bree shook her head, trying to ignore the shiver running down her spine and the hairs still standing on end.

"He's just a creep." She muttered under her breath before squatting back down and loosening the lug nuts on the tires. She got the jack situated to raise the car when the man—who apparently was not planning to leave just yet—cleared his throat.

"I know you told that guy no, but would you like some help?"

"Thanks, but I know how to change a tire," Bree replied, using the lever to lift up the car so she could get the tire off.

"I can see that." He replied. "It's a good skill to have." He looked around the road as traffic began to pick up around them. The demonstration must have ended.

Bree sighed. This was going to be a pain.

"I'm not gonna lie to you, you make me a little nervous sitting on the road so close to traffic. You should have a triangle out so people can see you."

"It's a small town. Slow speed limits. I think I'll survive." Bree retorted, confirming the car was steady before continuing her work. "Besides, cars don't come with triangles to put out when someone has to change a tire. Otherwise, I would."

"If it's all the same to you, I'll just be a human triangle. You won't even know I'm here."

Bree looked at him for a moment, considering his statement. While he didn't give off grade-A creep vibes like Kyle, men were just inherently not trustworthy. That whole man versus bear debate? She'd take the bear every time. But if he wanted to risk life and limb being a human triangle, who was she to stop him?

"If it'll help you sleep at night, knock yourself out. Just stay over there." Bree said, nodding toward the rear of the car.

The man moved toward the back of the car and stepped away from it slightly so he would be easily seen by oncoming traffic, which would hopefully slow down so they wouldn't hit him.

"You mentioned you know how to change a tire. Your dad teach you?"

Bree laughed while removing the rest of the lug nuts. "No, my dad wasn't the type to get his hands dirty."

"Ah," the mystery man said. "Boyfriend?"

"Nope," Bree said, popping the 'p'.

"I've got it. You were on a vacation to Fontenay and driving through the countryside when your tire blew. You were frightened for a moment but determined to find a fix, so you marched up to the Monastery and found a sympathetic Cistercian monk who took pity on you and then proceeded to teach you the proper way to change a tire." He said humorously as the cars slowed down to pass by on their way down the street. Bree found herself begrudgingly appreciative of her human triangle.

"You caught me." Bree deadpanned, lugging the flat tire off before picking up the spare and putting it on. From the corner of her eye Bree watched as the man walked closer, picked up the flat tire one-handed, and put it back in her trunk to properly dispose of later. He returned from the trunk, his eyebrows furrowed and resumed his part-time job as a human traffic triangle while Bree tightened the lug nuts as much as she could by hand before lowering the car back to the pavement.

Bree began tightening the lug nuts with the tire-changing tool thing when the man reached out a hand. "May I?" He asked, observing Bree quietly.

"You might get your suit dirty," Bree muttered, silently drinking in the handsome man in front of her. Why didn't more men dress like that? He looked like he stepped off the cover of a magazine.

He chuckled, the deep, warm sound resonating in his chest. Definitely drool worthy. "I'll take the chance." He said, gently taking the tool from Bree's hand. Bree stood and took a step back, watching as he tightened each of the lug nuts until he was satisfied the tire wasn't going anywhere. "Make sure you get a new tire soon. You don't want to drive around on the spare too long."

"Probably not." She said succinctly, suddenly feeling desperate to get away from the handsome stranger and back to the safety of her new home.

"I'm Noah Hawthorne." He said with a warm smile, walking a couple of steps toward Bree and reaching out a hand to shake hers in a firm, but not painful, grip.

Noah Hawthorne? Freaking Steph.

Chapter Two

Noah watched in confusion as the blood quickly drained from the woman's face. He slowly lowered his hand, concern blossoming in his chest. He looked around in case the guy harassing her was back, but no one was there. Was she okay?

"Noah Hawthorne? As in, owner of Hawthorne Security, Noah Hawthorne?" The woman questioned.

Had they met before? He definitely would've remembered the beautiful woman in front of him. Her dark brown hair was tied back in a plait, and her sharp gray eyes glared at him accusingly. "Yeah. Have we me—"

"Why are you here?" She asked, watching him closely as she rubbed the edges of her shirt between her fingertips.

Confusion trumped any other emotion he was feeling as he focused on the woman in front of him. "I had a business meet—"

"Listen, it doesn't matter. I don't know what Steph told you, but I don't need a babysitter. Please...leave me alone." Nerves laced her voice as though she wasn't used to standing up for herself. Which was not a good thing if people were heckling her like the guy who'd been there a few minutes earlier.

"What—"

"I know that Adam and Steph called you." She said, crossing her arms and jutting one of her hips out. "Tell him that you and Aubrey spoke and mutually decided there was no reason to work together."

Adam? O'Shea? Oh, Aubrey Gray. Oh no.

"You're Aubrey Gray?" Noah asked, furrowing his brow.

"Yes." She said, lifting her chin slightly. "And I'd appreciate it if you'd leave me alone."

Noah sighed. He didn't have the time or energy to figure out her slightly paranoid behavior. If she didn't want security, he certainly wasn't going to force her. His mind flashed back to the slashed tire currently sitting in her trunk. He had one more message to give her, and then he could happily never see her again.

"Listen, your tire—" Noah tried again, his patience quickly fading as she interrupted him again. He just wanted to tell her that her tire was slashed. The damage had caught him by surprise as he put it into the trunk. Someone had intentionally caused it. Did Adam and his woman have reason to be concerned for Aubrey's safety?

"Just stay away from me." She said, backing away from him. She got into her car and quickly engaged the locks. Noah stepped back as she pulled away from the curb, the glare from her stare and her apparent discomfort still cutting into him long after her car had disappeared from sight.

The shrill ringing of his phone stirred him, and he swiped to answer while bringing it up to his ear.

"Hawthorne."

"Hey man, we just got a call from Mike Sullivan over at Mountain River Studios. They're requesting we pull Olsen and replace him immediately, or they will terminate our services." Peter Burke said, his voice low.

"What? They're one of our biggest clients. Did they say why?"

"Olsen couldn't keep his hands to himself."

"I'm about an hour out, but I'll head that way," Noah sighed, ending the call. They were so close to being a big name in the security industry. The right big-name project would help secure the future of the company and, thus, the financial future of his friends and colleagues. His thoughts briefly drifted back to Aubrey Gray—he'd call Adam and let him know that Hawthorne Security was not the right fit to protect her. If they lost Mountain River Studios as a client, he would need a big name, but given her reaction to meeting him, she probably wasn't going to be it.

***

Noah watched closely as Peter and Zach walked Marcus Olsen out of Noah's office. They would make sure he turned in his identification and weapon before escorting him out of the building. Noah leaned back in his chair, his thoughts drifting to that morning. A lingering feeling of dread pooled in his stomach as he recalled the slashed tire and the blonde man who wouldn't leave Aubrey alone.

The last thing he wanted to do was get involved, but Adam was a friend and Noah's gut was telling him Aubrey Gray was in more danger than she thought. And after what happened with Lettie, he always listened to his gut. He wouldn't have the responsibility of another woman's death on his soul if he could help it. He'd give Adam a call and give him a heads-up. Then, he could satisfy his conscience while staying away from her like she asked. He picked up his phone and dialed Adam's business line.

"Adam O'Shea." The deep voice answered on the other end of the line.

"Hey man, it's Noah Hawthorne."

"Noah! How's life in Tennessee treating you?"

Noah laughed. "Much better than life on the coast—that's for sure. Business good?"

"It's unfortunately booming," Adam said, his voice serious. That was the trade-off in working protection details. Business was good—which was good for business. But the business was necessary for unfortunate reasons.

"I hear you, man. Hey, I want to touch base with you on the Aubrey Gray situation." Noah said, working to keep his tone light and cordial despite the anxiety and dread that had been weighing him down all day.

"Have you had the chance to give her a call? I know Steph spoke with her about it this morning, and she wasn't super receptive to the idea. She did agree to be pleasant when you call, though."

"Actually, I happened to run into her this morning while she was changing a tire," Noah said.

Noah could practically see Adam's grimace through the phone. "How did that go?"

"She was...how did you phrase it? Not receptive to me being there."

"She has a thing about men," Adam said.

"A thing?"

"Not my story to tell. But will you still try to give her a call? See if she'll let you look into her situation? I can have Steph work on her from our end also. I wouldn't ask, man, but she's the only family Steph has."

Noah sighed. "I'll try again. Her tire this morning was intentionally slashed."

"Someone slashed Bree's tire?" Adam asked, the unfettered rage clear in his voice.

Noah nodded even though Adam couldn't see him. "Yeah, and I tried to tell her, but she was busy telling me to stay away from her."

Adam sighed. "Thanks for letting me know. I'll tell her."

"Let me try first. Gives me an excuse to call her for you." Noah said.

"Okay. If she won't listen to you, let me know, and I'll give her a call to tell her about the tire. She needs to know about it."

"She does."

"And Noah?"

"Yeah?"

"Take care of our girl. She won't let us come to her, but she's important. To both of us."

"I'll do my best, man. Take care."

"You too."

Noah hung up the phone and rubbed his temples, the throbbing headache he'd had since hearing about losing Claire Reynolds as a client still pounding away. Maybe Aubrey would be more receptive to a phone call since he wouldn't be in her physical space. He doubted it, though. He shook his head and grabbed a few ibuprofen from the desk drawer, tossing them back with a swig of water. He had a feeling he was going to need it for the next call he made.

He picked up the receiver and dialed the number written on the post-it note currently attached to his computer. He had planned on giving Aubrey a call this week. He was going to introduce himself, ask her a little about her and her situation, and try to feel out if she wanted security or if her friends were just being overly concerned. Unfortunately, awful messages were part of being in an industry that thrusts you into the public eye. After meeting her today, he could hazard a guess that she would've turned him down. Albeit more politely, maybe.

The phone rang a couple of times as he waited for her to answer. Unsurprisingly, the phone went to voicemail.

"Hey Aubrey, this is Noah Hawthorne with Hawthorne Security. I wanted to touch base with you about your tire situation. If you could give me a call back at this number, I'd appreciate it. It's important. Thanks." He said, hanging up the phone and resting his head in his hands. The ball was in her court now.

***

As lunchtime approached, Noah's stomach growled ferociously. He really should have stopped to grab something to eat this morning on his way back into town. He clicked open a new tab on his computer to order lunch, pausing as the door to his office slowly crept open. A lone head peered around the corner, an intense look on his face. Theo looked dramatically from side to side to make sure the office was empty before ducking his head back out into the hallway and giving a shrill whistle. Moments later, the door flew open, and four fully grown men tore through the space, making themselves comfortable on the couch and chairs in the office. Eli had a bag of Chinese takeout from the family-owned restaurant down the street and set it down on the coffee table.

"Those are my chopsticks, man. Give them here." Theo argued, holding his hand out impatiently while Peter gave him an exasperated look.

"You don't even know how to use chopsticks," Peter replied, pulling the chopsticks out and making a show of the correct way to hold and use them. "But did you know that 33 percent of the world's population uses them on a daily basis?"

"I could be part of the 33 percent if you give them back. I'm *learning*." Theo countered, grabbing the chopsticks out of Peter's hand and jabbing them aggressively into the bowl. Peter gave a long-suffering sigh before picking up a fork and digging into his food.

Zach observed from his position in the chair nearest to the door and shook his head, chuckling. He looked over at Noah, still sitting at his desk, and gestured to the open chair across from him. "We grabbed you some sesame chicken. How did the meeting in Rhodes go this morning?"

Noah grabbed his water bottle before heading over and picking up his plate of food and a fork. "It went well. They were happy with our security team when we worked with Maria Garzas during her appearance at the festival and let me know that we'll be on the top of their call list the next time she's scheduled to have an event in the area."

There was a chorus of happy grunts and a "Hell yeah!" from Theo before the room quieted again.

"You got back late this morning," Zach mentioned.

"Yeah, there was a woman who had a flat tire. Some jerk was bugging her while she tried to change it so I stepped in until he left." Noah said the memory of Aubrey's small hand tightening on the tire iron as though she'd need to use it to defend herself flashed through his mind while a sickening feeling soured his stomach.

"She get her tire changed?" Eli asked, arching an eyebrow.

Noah nodded. "I offered to help, but she said she could do it on her own. I didn't want to leave her alone there, so I put the bad tire in the trunk and helped tighten the lug nuts, but she wouldn't have needed me. She had it handled."

"That's a good skill to have," Theo said. "Did you get her number?" He asked, wiggling his eyebrows.

Noah barely held in his eye roll. He had no desire to date, and Theo knew it. "No, I was busy being her human traffic triangle, so she didn't get hit by a car."

"Very noble of you," Theo said deadpanned.

"They really should make some sort of cone or triangle standard in vehicles like they do with spare tires. I can't tell you how many times people are on the side of the road and others drive way too close." Zach frowned.

"You could always look her up and send her one." Theo joked.

"Nothing says romance like a traffic triangle." Eli agreed with a laugh.

Noah grabbed the now empty water bottle and chucked it at Eli's head. "Let it go. I was busy wondering who would've slashed her tire. Besides, she was not receptive to me being there."

"Someone slashed her tire?" Zach asked, concern lacing his voice.

"Why wasn't she receptive to you being there?" Theo asked, sounding offended on Noah's behalf.

Noah sighed. "Remember the call we got from O'Shea asking us to look into that friend of his who just moved to our area?" The men collectively nodded. "That was Aubrey Gray. And apparently, she knew who I was, so when I introduced myself, it didn't go well. She 'doesn't need a babysitter.'" Noah said, adding air quotes around the last phase.

"And the slashed tire?"

Noah shrugged. "Don't know. I tried to tell her about it, but she was too busy trying to get away from me after I told her to get a new tire put on her car. I left her a voicemail today, so hopefully, she'll give me a call. Otherwise, O'Shea can deal with it. Anyway, I was going to message you, but since we are all here, I wanted to ask you all about a call I got a few minutes ago. We were asked to provide a security detail for a celebrity meet and greet this afternoon—It starts at four. Whoever they'd hired before backed out at the last minute, and they called to see if we could take it on. I need to let them know in the next half hour. I'm booked this afternoon, but would anyone else like to take the assignment on? It's for an event at a music store in downtown Trenton. There will be a few different artists doing signings and meet and greets. That kind of thing."

"I'm on a tech assignment, and then I am teaching a self-defense class at the gym," Peter said, the only one who didn't have to check the calendar on his phone. The perks of having a photographic memory.

"I'm with the Senator for a meeting between him and one of his more volatile constituents who's been causing a raucous," Eli replied.

"I have a personal matter I'm out of the office for," Zach said vaguely.

"I'll do it." Theo offered.

Zach looked at Theo shrewdly. "You sure?"

"I got it. If anything urgent comes in you can just give me a call. I can operate some of my information systems remotely." Theo replied confidently. Noah hesitated for a moment. Theo was a whiz at all things information systems and technology, and he was their go-to source for any and all information needed while they were in the field. If someone needed him while he was on assignment, that could end up being very complicated.

"I can be on call in case anything comes up, too. It'll just take me a little bit to get there." Zach supplied, watching Noah closely. Apparently, his poker face needed work.

"Thanks, Zach. Alright, Theo, you'll be on the protection detail for the signing event this afternoon. I'll send you details as soon as I get them. The label is sending them over once I confirm." Noah said, relaxing more now that that assignment was out of the way.

There were a few minutes of silence before Eli gave Zach a side-eye. "So...what personal 'thing' are you gonna be out of the office for? You never take time off."

"Did you know when women take leave from work, it's for medical reasons or illness 42 percent of the time, but for forty percent of men, it's usually errands or personal reasons." Peter chimed in.

"I have to look into something back home," Zach said vaguely.

"Is everything okay? Do you need someone to go with you?" Noah asked, mentally trying to figure out how they could coordinate that.

"Nah, man. This is something I need to do on my own. Thanks, though."

"You'll let us know if that changes?"

"Of course."

Noah nodded and turned back to the rest of his friends as Theo started a debate—the benefits of chopsticks versus forks— while giving Peter a pointed look, laughter, and friendly banter going back and forth across the room. Noah sat back and let the warmth settle in his chest as he took in the scene around him—not just friends or coworkers, but brothers. Not by blood but by choice.

***

The clock struck seven, and Noah Hawthorne was still bent over his desk, desperately trying to finish up the day's paperwork so he could go home and grill a steak. And maybe some vegetables. Just so Mrs. Garcia didn't harp on him the next time he saw her. He could reassure her that he was, in fact, eating vegetables...as long as they could be grilled. The door to the office opened, and Noah frowned. It was unlikely anyone coming in at seven p.m. would be bearing good news. Theo's unruly mop of hair preceded him into the room, and he shut the door softly before collapsing into one of the chairs directly across from Noah's desk, his hands busy squeezing one of the little stress balls they kept around the office...mostly to throw at each other when they felt like it.

"How'd the signing go?" Noah asked, furrowing his eyebrows. On the occasions Theo was in the field, he usually liked to go straight home after an assignment and sleep on it before filing any reports. Noah, on the other hand, had to go back to the office and get all of the day's paperwork squared away so he wouldn't have to think about it anymore. Plus, the information was always more fresh the same day. Just a couple more quick forms to complete and file, and then he could go home. A drink and sitting on his deck while looking at the lake and grilling steak sounded heavenly right now.

"It went great. Guess who I ran into."

Feeling particularly ornery, Noah smirked at him and tossed out the name of Theo's current crush, "Cecily Thompson?"

Theo threw the stress ball he'd been squeezing at Noah's head. Noah ducked out of the way, laughing as it flew by. Theo smirked and relaxed back into the chair. "Very funny." He deadpanned. "Actually, I ran into someone who knows you."

Noah raised an eyebrow. "I only hang out with you guys and everyone was in the field today. Kind of narrows the options down a bit. So must've been a professional connection..." Noah thought for a moment.

He shrugged after a few moments, "I don't know, man. Who was it?"

"Miss Aubrey Gray."

Aubrey Gray? Flashes of sharp eyes, a pretty smile, and grit rolled through Noah's head as he replayed the tire change while he looked at Theo thoughtfully. Theo was handsome, funny, and tended to attract invitations from many of the clients he worked with—though he would never accept. There was a strict no-fraternizing rule with clients for a reason.

"How did you meet her? Was she attending the signing?"

Theo looked at Noah as though he'd grown an extra head and paused. "No…" He said slowly. "She was doing the signing. She's one of the celebrities that were there to do the meet and greet."

"I thought she was retired?" Noah asked flatly.

"She is—she said this is one of her last events before she's officially in retirement. She mentioned a couple of endorsement deals she needed to follow through on as well."

Noah nodded, immediately assessing what that could mean for Aubrey—and possibly for Hawthorne Security. If Aubrey was in danger, like O'Shea thought, then she would benefit from their security. As a world-famous celebrity, successfully completing her case could be the bolster the firm needed to go to the next level which would ensure the firm's success and provide financially for himself and his employees.

He wasn't using Aubrey's situation—it would be a mutually beneficial agreement. If she'd agree to it, that is. Noah pushed thoughts of Aubrey Gray to the back of his mind to think over later and clicked through the document he was working on. The sooner he finished, the sooner he could sit on his deck.

"Was the record company satisfied with our services?"

Theo nodded. "I think they were. The woman who hired the original company was out on maternity leave, so I gave our card to her replacement." Theo said.

Noah nodded, his thoughts drifting back to Aubrey. He truthfully had no interest in Aubrey Gray—aside from the possibility of her becoming the client who took the company to the next level. And even that was contingent on whether she could get her on board with following orders if she hired them.

Celebrities who didn't feel the need to abide by the rules set for their protection were a liability to themselves *and* to the people protecting them. He wouldn't risk his brothers for anyone. But if she needed security and could listen to himself or his teammates, then she'd be the perfect client to drive up business. While he wasn't interested in her personally, he was very interested in that.

Theo continued, "Aubrey seemed pretty happy with the event itself until she got a phone call at the end..." He trailed off, appearing lost in thought regarding the call. From the concerned look in his eye, it didn't appear to be a pleasant one.

Concern rose up in Noah's chest as he watched Theo thoughtfully. Aubrey didn't seem to think she was in danger. Despite the blonde man bugging her, the notes O'Shea mentioned, and the slash in her tire which she was currently unaware of. With the addition of the phone call—which could have been unrelated but could be someone harassing her—there was definitely reason to believe she could be at risk. Theo didn't usually get worked up enough to come and give him the info in person, so the call must have been bad. Hmm.

Noah looked up at Theo briefly, frowning, when he realized Theo was still preoccupied with whatever he'd overheard from the call. "Is there something I need to know regarding the call?" Noah asked evenly. If someone was threatening Aubrey, there wasn't much he could do since he wasn't personally or professionally involved with her. He could inform O'Shea, though, and let him handle whatever it was. Noah clicked through the last form, looking up at Theo and waiting for his answer.

"Nah, I just wanted to let you know I met her and give you the overall update. See you tomorrow, man." Theo slapped his leg and stood up, crossing the room in a few steps, and shut the door behind him softly, the click sounding particularly sharp in the otherwise silent room.

Noah sat back in his chair, staring at the door for a few moments. Was Aubrey in trouble? Did she need help? Would she call if she did?

"Not. My. Problem." Noah muttered, submitting the file, jabbing the keys as he typed. Noah's hands had a mind of their own as they opened a new tab and typed Aubrey's name into the search engine to see if any red-flag articles or threads appeared. Photo after photo of her beautiful face flooded the screen. News stories of her retirement, her social media links, and YouTube videos all popped up on the first page of the search. Even after going into retirement, she was still a celebrity—and a pretty popular one at that.

"Get a grip, Hawthorne." He muttered, quickly closing the tabs and shutting down the computer before he could do something stupid like click on one of those articles and fall down the rabbit hole that was Aubrey Gray. He shut the computer down, determined to only daydream about a drink on the deck, a nice juicy steak, and watching the sun set. He certainly wasn't going to be thinking of mysterious notes, slashed tires, or Aubrey Gray.

Chapter Three

Bree sat in her art studio, her hands moving in broad strokes across the canvas to make the seascape come to life in front of her. The ocean was one of the only things she missed about living near L.A. The beach and her friends. She thought longingly of Steph and Adam. They would be visiting Bree in a few weeks to film a video promoting Steph's new fashion line, and Bree couldn't wait. The hours melted by as the painting in front of her changed from broad strokes of color into a seascape showing the depth and beauty of the Oregon coastline. She'd have to go back and visit again.

The last time she had visited the Oregon coast, her life had been completely different. Her mom was happy everyone would be able to go on the trip. Bree's dad had actually taken time off from the law firm and made the trip despite how tight finances had been. Jess had been happy and healthy, practically vibrating with energy as they hiked the trails. The trip had been Jessica's graduation present and it was the first time Bree remembered her being happy after breaking up with her high school boyfriend. It had finally felt like she was getting her sister back. Getting her family back. That was wishful thinking at its finest.

The shrill ringing of the phone made her jump, and she looked at the device guiltily for a moment. She really needed to call Noah back. She had been rude. Plus, maybe what he needed to say actually *was* important. She checked the caller ID and groaned when she saw the name on the screen. Her heart immediately began to race, and she wiped her hands on her jeans before swiping up and answering the call. "Hey, Dad."

"Aubrey," Dad replied, his voice tight. She could picture him standing in the home office, feet shoulder-width apart, and using his free hand to pinch the bridge of his nose to communicate his exasperation, which was already more than evident in his tone. Frustration grew in Bree's chest, and she worked hard to tamp it back down. She was used to being the second favorite child. She'd always played second fiddle to Jess and knew her parents were disappointed that their second and final child wasn't a boy. Nothing was ever enough. Valedictorian. Famous singer. Talented artist. Bree was nothing but pursestrings, but that wasn't Jessica's fault.

"What's up?" Bree asked, working to keep her voice happy and upbeat. If she kept her tone and word choice in check, the call would be short and to the point. Besides, she could understand the strain her parents were under. Between the issues at the law firm and Jess's health, her parents had enough going on.

"The deposit hasn't come in yet, and your sister's hospital bills are due this week."

Bree frowned. Hadn't that check gone through last week? "No worries, Dad. I'll call the billing department and get it taken care of."

"No!" Dad yelled. Bree flinched away from the speaker. "It's difficult enough to have to ask you for money in the first place."

Bree rolled her eyes. *Sure it was.*

"I don't need other people knowing that I can't afford my own daughter's medical treatment. Besides, you have enough going on. Isn't there a party or something we're all supposed to be attending this weekend?" Dad asked.

"It's not a party. I'm hosting a benefit to raise money for families who have a loved one struggling with addiction. I had the chance to meet with a lot of other people on my farewell tour to secure their financial support. It's next weekend, though. Then I'm running up to Chattanooga to grab my mail and visit the museum."

"Your mother and I are not going to some event to raise money for drug addicts. And honestly, Aubrey, your paranoia at this point is embarrassing. Just get a post office box in the town you live in. No one cares where you are."

Bree bristled at his recommendation and decided to just ignore it and focus on the more important point. "It's for *families* who have a loved one struggling with addiction. Like J—"

"Do not start with me, Aubrey Elizabeth." Dad heaved a sigh. "Just make sure the money is in the account. I don't want Jessica's treatment disrupted because of banking issues."

"Dad—"

"Don't 'Dad' me. You should've checked to make sure this was taken care of. Get the money squared away and give me a call Monday." There was a pause as he chastised Bree's mother for interrupting him in the background.

Bree ground her teeth.

"Aubrey, your mother says hello." He forced out. "Call me Monday."

"Of course," Bree replied, not surprised in the least when the line cut out after that. "Goodbye to you too." She muttered, setting the phone aside and picking her paintbrush back up. "How is the new house? How is Rhodes? Any more trouble from Kyle? Need me to call his dad for you? Your mom and I miss you." Bree muttered quickly under her breath, jabbing color onto the canvas with each unasked question. How her mother put up with that man was beyond her, though the large amount of alcohol consumed by her parents could be a factor.

Calls with her dad were always exhausting. Honestly, she didn't want to talk to another soul for at least three to five business days. Bree had loved making music and connecting with people who had similar life experiences or really felt drawn to her music, but singing in front of people and having to meet people was anxiety inducing. Feeling awkward and like you had to plan what you were going to say to people so you sounded normal definitely drained her social battery a little faster than desirable. Only her deep love for Jess and a heavy emotional guilt trip from her dad had kept her in the industry. Once she was financially set, she had been able to step out of the spotlight and into freedom. She was almost done. *Almost.*

The memory of her conversation with Theo about calling Noah poked around in her brain, causing that knot of guilt in her stomach to get heavier and heavier. She jabbed at the canvas and frowned. She shouldn't take her pent-up emotions out on the painting. It's not the painting's fault she couldn't call the man like an adult. *Ugh. Fine.*

Bree forcefully set her brush down and scrolled through the call log on her phone. Before she could chicken out, she tapped on the number Noah had called from and waited anxiously while it rang. Hopefully, he would be gracious—the last thing she needed to deal with right now was another emotionally charged man.

"Noah Hawthorne." Noah's deep voice sounded through the phone.

"Hi, Noah, this is Aubrey Gray. I'm returning your call." She said, holding her breath.

"Ah, Miss Gray. Thanks for getting back to me." Noah said. "I wanted to touch base with you on your tire—"

"I got a new tire." Bree blurted before mentally facepalming. Way to stay cool, Bree.

"Right, I'm glad to hear that," Noah said before continuing as though he hadn't been interrupted. "I actually wanted to touch base with you on your old tire. When I loaded it into your trunk, it looked like the tire had been slashed."

Bree felt the blood drain from her face. No.

"Miss Gray?"

"Umm...sorry. I'm processing. You said you think my tire was slashed?"

"No." Before the pounding fear gave way to relief, Noah continued. "I know it was slashed."

Bree dropped her head to her chest. She didn't need this right now. "I just don't think that could be possible." She argued weakly.

"Why?" Noah asked.

"I didn't see a big gash in it. And I live in a small town. There was a festival going on with a lot of foot traffic. I...I'm just me. Why would anyone want to slash my car tire?"

"The slash wasn't huge—you very easily could have missed it. Small towns have their own share of crimes—and a festival is a great chance for someone to blend in. Normally, small towns know when someone doesn't belong, so it's easier to blend in when there are lots of someones who don't belong." Noah said.

"Still—the only person I've ticked off since moving here offered to help change my tire so..."

"You're also a celebrity."

"Retired." Bree retorted.

"Retired, but still famous." Noah conceded.

"Fair enough."

"Look, Adam and Steph are worried about you. Let me look into the notes they mentioned and the tire and see if anything comes up."

"I just don't think I need security, Noah. It was probably just some teenagers causing trouble or something. The notes have been concerning, but I'm documenting them and have the police department looped in. Mean comments kind of come with the territory of being famous." Bree said. That sounded way more likely than some random person targeting her. She was a nice person—generally. "Also...I'm sorry for being rude to you when we met. I...I don't like being told what to do." Bree said softly.

"Don't worry about it," Noah said.

"I'll let Adam know we connected—and more pleasantly this time," Bree said, a small smile on her face. "And I'll reiterate for the millionth time that I don't need security, so hopefully, he won't bug you again."

"O'Shea is welcome to 'bug' me any time," Noah said seriously. "And Bree—if anything happens or feels off, you're welcome to call me. I'll text you my cell number so you have it."

"I won't use it," Bree warned.

"Fair enough. But at least you'd be able to get in touch with me if you do need to use it."

"Okay."

"Thanks for calling me back," Noah said.

"You're welcome," Bree added softly before ending the call. There. Now, her guilt could chill out. She called. She apologized. They were good. Her phone buzzed with a text message from an unknown number, and Bree opened it up, a smile on her face.

> Even if you never plan on using it—save it.

> Please.

She added Noah to her contacts and tossed her phone onto the table so she could finish her painting. Another hour or so of work and then she could be shoulders deep in a bubble bath re-reading one of her favorite books and all this talk of threatening notes and slashed tires would be behind her. She refused to let this upset her. Retirement was going to be calm and peaceful.

Chapter Four

Bree grinned as she stood on the balcony of the Hunter Museum of American Art. This balcony, overlooking the Tennessee River, was one of her favorite spots to stand and take in the view during her monthly visits to Chattanooga. Taking a final swig of coffee, Bree turned and walked back into the museum, eager to visit the last exhibit before she had to head back to Rhodes. The exhibit focused on abstract expressionist art, which was admittedly not her favorite. There was something to be learned from each form of art, though, so she planned to dutifully read each of the plaques and study each of the paintings even though she'd likely forget them the moment she left. She'd much rather study impressionism.

Bree ambled through the room, studying each painting as she walked by. While most of them were a waste of paint, she paused to look at Helen Frankenthaler's Mountains and Sea. The 1952 masterpiece reminded her a little bit of a young child's watercolor painting, but there was something interesting about the shades of the colors the artist had used. The pastel blue and green drew the eye into the painting, unlike Koenig's Woman Ochre, whose colors felt harsh. The only interesting thing about that painting was that it had been stolen and later recovered. Honestly, it was amazing someone liked it enough to steal. But the Mountains and Sea were softer, and Bree was content to stand there for much longer than she had for the others. Bree moved on and felt she was going cross-eyed as she tried to figure out the appeal of a Jackson Pollock with no luck. To each their own.

A large crowd of disinterested-looking high school students walked into the room, and the noise level rose significantly. The chaperone gave instructions and dismissed the students to walk throughout the exhibit. Bree's anxiety crept up as the room began to feel much smaller than it realistically was. She took one last glance around the room to see if there were any other paintings she wanted to see. As she was looking, she caught the attention of one of the high school girls nearby, who elbowed her blonde friend and whispered excitedly. The other girl whipped her head around and caught sight of Bree, a huge smile on her face.

"Aubrey Gray? No way! Can we get a picture?" She asked excitedly.

Bree started counting in her head, the anxiety threatening to overwhelm her. Her chest was tight, and it felt hard to breathe. "Of course!" Bree said, forcing a smile.

The girls squealed and came to stand next to her, taking a selfie of the three of them. "Thank you so much!" The blonde said before running off with her friend toward a larger gaggle of girls.

Bree turned and walked out of the exhibit, careful not to move too quickly. She didn't want to seem like she was avoiding people or running away...even though that's exactly what she was doing. She moved into the main space of the museum, and the knot in her chest loosened. She could finally take a deep breath. It was past time to go.

"Aubrey Gray?" A woman's voice called from near the visitor's podium.

Bree turned to acknowledge the person speaking and quickly plastered a smile on her face.

"I thought it was you!" The woman said. "I'm Caroline Miller, and this is my husband, Jim.

"It's lovely to meet you," Bree said, shaking each of their hands while her stomach sank. That freaking invitation for the Gala was still sitting in her pile of mail that she had said she was going to deal with later.

"The pleasure is ours." Mrs. Miller replied.

"What brings you to Chattanooga?" Bree asked, hoping it was for pleasure and not for the Gala.

"My wife and I are on the board for the annual gala that raises money and awareness for families who have a loved one suffering from drug addiction. The funds raised at the event go to helping families afford rehab or make their bills while the family's breadwinner is in rehab. It also helps families who may need financial help getting on their feet if their loved one has died from an overdose. We're looking for a venue to host the Gala this Thanksgiving." Mr. Miller said.

"Well, the museum is beautiful. Trenton has some beautiful venues as well. But you really can't go wrong in Tennessee." Bree said. She hesitated before continuing but felt it was important for them to know that she really did care for their organization and understood the importance of it on a personal level. She could do hard things.

Bree took a breath and continued, "Your organization is such a blessing. My family could have benefited from an organization like that." Bree told them warmly. She truly did love the organization and all it stood for. She just didn't want to speak in public or be in the spotlight anymore...at all.

"We think so as well." Mrs. Miller said. "Aubrey, I believe my assistant sent an invitation to see if you'd like to speak at the event. We'd truly love to have you."

Bree maintained her smile on the outside while panicking on the inside. She didn't want to do it. But the people-pleasing side of her wasn't going to let her out of it. She had no other engagements.

"I'm sorry I haven't had the chance to get back to you—I'd love to." She said with a smile, even as her stomach sank and the knot in her chest tightened again.

"We'd love that. Our administrative assistant will send over details." Mr. Miller said.

"Perfect," Aubrey said. They exchanged goodbyes, and the Millers headed toward the abstract expressionism exhibit while Bree made a beeline for the door. Apparently, she was going to give a speech.

Great.

***

Bree's phone buzzed, alerting her to the new message waiting for her as she sat in the Rhodes Creek Coffee Shop watching the sun begin to set. The opening day of the farmers market was a success and the teardown and clean-up portion of the process had begun. A number of people were out helping with clean up, which meant the coffee shop was full of customers, even at seven o'clock at night.

The men at the table behind hers brushed past her on their way out and she felt a shiver creeping up her neck. There wasn't enough space in here. Bree took a deep breath. It's not like someone was out to get her. She needed to chill.

Bree opened the messaging app and responded to a few fans who shared their excitement over seeing her in concert a few months ago and encouraging her on her new endeavors—whatever those were. Bree smiled. Those were the best messages. She honestly loved her fans—they were generally really good, kind, supportive people.

A long, scraping sound—similar to nails on a chalkboard—came from the the door of the cafe and Bree felt goosebumps break out. "Sorry!" One of the workers called out, adjusting his grip on the table he was carrying back into the cafe. Someone cleared their throat impatiently behind the workers. Bree rolled her eyes. She couldn't stand people like that. She turned her attention back to people watching, nursing her iced coffee in her hands.

"Hey Aubrey," a deep voice said from beside her. Bree turned, and her stomach dropped. Five bucks said he was the one clearing his throat behind the construction workers.

"Hi, Kyle." She said, immediately looking for a way out of the conversation. Slimy wasn't the only descriptor that came to mind when she thought of Kyle Rhodes, but it was definitely the kindest one.

"There's an awards dinner coming up in two weeks. I'll pick you up that Saturday at seven." He said, oozing an amount of fake charm that should come with its own government warning label and a set of red flags that could be handed to any woman who was forced to hold a conversation with him.

"I'm not going to an awards dinner—or any kind of dinner—with you, Kyle. Thanks for asking, though." Bree said, attempting to remain pleasant.

Kyle slid into the chair across from Bree.

"I don't recall asking."

"I don't care whether or not you're asking," Bree said with false bravado as her heart raced. She scooted further back to put additional distance between herself and Kyle. "I'm telling you that I'm not going out with you. Ever." Take a breath, he can't do anything—Bree thought, trying to reassure herself. She rubbed her fingers on her jeans anxiously.

"You're going to change your tune one day, Aubrey. And it better be soon." He sneered before getting up and roughly shoving his chair into the table. Her cup rattled, and Bree quickly steadied it before it spilled. She didn't need any more attention on her. She gave a reassuring smile to Marilee, who watched the interaction from the counter, poised to intervene if necessary. Marilee nodded back to Bree and resumed cleaning up.

Bree took a deep breath to steady herself and opened the next message, which contained several pictures. Bree tapped to open the first attachment—she was always cautious when opening pictures. While she loved seeing people enjoy her concerts, some people sent images that she had to report. Then she had to block the person. The first picture was of a garden full of blooming flowers. It looked like the wildflower mix that Bree loved to share on her socials when it was time for gardening. Her home in Los Angeles had the same flowers in the front garden.

Bree opened the next picture excitedly. The blue kitchen cabinets and white quartz counters looked sharp next to the white subway tile backsplash. The gold pulls on the drawers looked exactly like the ones she had picked out when she redid her kitchen in L.A. a few years ago. Even though she couldn't cook, she *could* appreciate a beautifully decorated kitchen.

Bree paused and zoomed in on the picture. Her hands felt sweaty, and the hairs on the back of her neck rose. There, on the side of the island, was a small chip in the paint shaped like the state of Texas. Just like the one Steph had caused when she accidentally smacked her ring on the cabinet. Who was sending her pictures of her old house?

The next picture was her old bedroom a shadow visible in the window but not clear enough to make out any identifying features. The last attachment was a video, and Bree had a feeling she wasn't going to like whatever it was. Bree opened the last attachment—a video—and nausea rose in her throat. There, in what had been her private bathroom, was a masculine hand holding the little stuffed bear Nonna had given her the Christmas before she died. Tears filled her eyes as she stared longingly at the bear on the screen. The movers had left him behind. *Bree* had left him behind. Maybe the person had found him and wanted to return him. Hope flooded her chest. Maybe they were reaching out with pictures to prove they were there and had her beloved bear. She'd ask them to mail the bear back. It was priceless to her and had to be essentially worthless to them. At least sentimentality-wise. If they wanted money or something, she'd happily give it.

The video zoomed in on a small torn piece of paper the bear was holding that said, "How could you leave us behind?" The video slowly zoomed out, and a second hand reached around, twisting the head of the bear around. Bree held her breath. The hand in the video violently jerked the bear's twisted head, decapitating the bear. The tears in her eyes streamed down her face as she buried her head in her hands, hope crashing down around her. Who would *do* something like that? A pair of heels clacked across the floor, and Bree turned her head. Marilee stood next to her, a dish towel thrown over her shoulder.

"Are you okay?" She asked.

Bree shook her head. "I just need to go home." She whispered.

Taking a deep breath, Bree forwarded the message to Detective Ramirez, Rae, and then to Steph as well. She wasn't surprised when her phone rang a moment later.

"Aubrey, you need to hire some security," Steph said in lieu of greeting.

"Whoever it was is clearly in L.A.," Bree argued half-heartedly, her stomach sick and heart aching. Who would do this to her? Bree stood and pushed in her chair, walking toward the cafe door slowly.

"People like that don't just stop, Bree. What if he finds you?"

"No one is going to find me, Steph. I pay Royce a lot of money to keep my information off the internet."

"And the paparazzi?"

"They're not in a small town like Rhodes. Everything I attend is outside of this town, and there is no real connection to me here. It's fine."

"You need to send the video to Noah."

"No. Steph—"

"We can't get to you soon enough if you need help, Bree. Noah can. If you won't hire him, we can at least keep him in the loop."

"Fine. I'll send it over." Bree sighed.

"Are you okay?" Steph asked, her voice softening in concern.

"No. I'm going to head home, though. I was at the coffee shop. Can we talk later?"

"Of course. Call if you need me."

"Will do," Bree said, hanging up the phone as she slid behind the wheel. She locked the car doors and rested her head against the steering wheel while she took several deep breaths to calm the emotional storm raging inside her. It would be okay. The press didn't come to Rhodes, so whoever was tormenting her from L.A. wouldn't be able to find her. It's a big world. They'd give up eventually.

The shadows on the drive home tormented her, her anxiety spiking as the tree branches caused movement in the edges of her vision. Bree took the long way home and made multiple turns to make sure she wasn't being followed. She pulled into her garage, leaving the car running, and the doors locked until her garage door shut tightly behind her. She quickly exited, leaving her mail and packages on the passenger seat, and locked her car before going into the house and locking the door between the garage and house as well. She dropped her purse and slid to the ground, tears welling again as images of her old home and her bear flipped through her mind—an unwanted video reel stuck on repeat in her brain.

Bree trudged into her bathroom, locking both the bedroom and bathroom door behind her. Intellectually, she knew she was safe in her home. But was she? What if the person who sent that video found her? Or the commenter who threatened her life? Was she living on borrowed time?

Bree started the shower and pondered whether it was worth it to sleep in the bathtub so she could stay behind more locked doors overnight. That would probably be excessive. She washed the stress and trauma from the day off and soaked in the warm water for a few minutes while she focused on deep breathing exercises her old therapist had taught her. Once she felt more steady, she turned off the water and threw on her coziest pair of PJs. The material on the sweats was wearing thin, and the shirt was three sizes too big, but that was exactly what she needed.

Bree left her bedroom door locked and curled up on her bed with her favorite comfort read nestled in her hand. She was as secure as she could be for the night, and Poppy was about to kick some craven butt. Her life could wait a few more hours to fall apart. She was done for today.

Chapter Five

Aubrey

The alarm clock cut through the silence of the morning, and Bree groaned, hitting the snooze button and tossing a pillow over her head to block out the sunlight streaming through the sheer curtains on the window. Alarm clocks should come from the factory sturdy enough to be thrown across the room. Or at least come equipped with a less annoying sound option. Forget being a morning person; that's what blackout curtains were invented for.

Reading until after three a.m. was definitely not her best idea. At least not until looking like a zombie became trendy. The video from last night played repeatedly in her head and the only way she had been able to get any sleep was by reading until she literally couldn't keep her eyes open. She needed to get up, though. Zombie or not. The local hotel had hired her to paint a seascape for the lobby, and she needed to get into her studio to work on it.

Bree stayed still for a few more minutes before dragging herself out of bed. She threw on a comfy pair of jeans and a t-shirt before pulling her hair back in a ponytail and slipping on a baseball cap. She unlocked her bedroom door and opened it slowly, listening for any noises in the house that didn't belong. Bree shook her head. She was being ridiculous.

She walked into her kitchen and turned on her coffee pot so it could percolate while she ran out to grab her mail from the day before. She gathered the mail and the newspaper lying on her driveway, waving to Mr. Robinson before hustling back into her house and locking the door securely behind her.

Bree sat on her favorite spot on the couch and sipped her coffee leisurely while she read through the newspaper. Her dad read the paper every day when she was growing up and stressed the importance of being well-informed about what was going on in the world. He seemed to like seeing her read the paper so she had read it every day since she was eight years old.

She turned to the social pages and immediately choked on her coffee, spluttering it all over the crisp pages. Crap. Bree hastily wiped the page with her sleeve, sure her eyes were playing tricks on her. She looked closely at the newspaper and groaned, throwing it aggressively onto the coffee table, and glared at it for a moment before picking it back up.

There was a large picture of Bree at the art museum, a smile etched on her face as she greeted the Millers on the front page of the social pages. The article title "Superstar Aubrey Gray Slated to Speak at Annual Fundraising Gala for Families Affected by Drug Addiction" was in large letters across the front.

The blood drained from Bree's face as she began reading:

Former superstar and social media sweetheart Aubrey Gray has found a meaningful life post-stage in the quiet town of Rhodes, Tennessee. Not one to stay out of the spotlight when it comes to good causes, Gray has already hosted a small benefit to help raise money for families of individuals who struggle with addiction. Jim and Caroline Miller, of the Clarksville Millers, are two of many donors who hold this cause close to their hearts. The Millers both sit on the board of Families Affected by Addiction, which throws the Annual Thanksgiving Gala to raise money to help families whose loved ones need rehab or other financial assistance after facing addiction. It is rumored that this year's gala will be held at The Trenton Center for the Arts in Trenton, Tennessee, at the recommendation of Aubrey Gray and pending the approval of the board. An invitation to the event is highly coveted, and those who will be in attendance are looking forward to hearing Ms. Gray's speech at the Gala.

Bree slammed the paper down on the table and focused on her breathing so she wouldn't burst into tears. They had infiltrated one of the few spaces she felt safe and happy. She expected to run into the occasional fan at the museum but not the press. She read the article again, her heart stuttering in her chest as she took in the first line. *Rhodes.* No. No. No.

Bree struggled to hold back the tears threatening to fall. The sheer weight of the violation was enough to take her breath away. How could they post what town she lived in? How did they even know? What if the person who had threatened her on social media realized where she was from this article? What if the man who ripped the head off her bear found her? What would he do to *her*? Bree held in a whimper. This wasn't supposed to be happening. She had been super intentional about staying out of the news.

Bree grabbed her phone from her pocket as it rang, expecting a call from Rae or Steph, surprised when it was from an unknown number instead. She pressed the side of her phone to silence the call and dutifully ignored it. If it was important, they'd leave a message. The phone rang a second time from the same number. Maybe it was the library checking on the painting she was supposed to get to them later this week. She should get a business line. It also could be the hospital. On the third ring she begrudgingly answered it, not wanting to leave a bad impression on a prospective client or miss a call from the doctor.

"Hello?" Bree said, waiting for the person to speak. Quiet breathing was all that was on the other end of the line and her stomach did a small, anxious leap. "Hello?" She tried again. The line went dead, and she frowned at the phone in confusion, followed swiftly by annoyance. Freaking Paparazzi.

Bree tossed the paper back onto the coffee table and grabbed her coffee. She went out the back door and sat down, swinging slowly on the porch swing while she stared at the lone oak tree in her backyard. She could admit that the buzz around the gala was a good thing, and she was happy to have the opportunity to use her status as a famous musician to bring attention to a cause that oftentimes was swept under the rug because it wasn't something the general public really liked to talk about—or think about.

Her social media accounts had been popping off since the fundraiser and Bree was sure there would be more attention now that the article was released. There was already a flurry of excitement around Bree being in the public eye mixed with some judgement from people who didn't agree with the cause. Which was fine—everyone was entitled to their own beliefs and opinions, and no one was forcing them to donate. Why couldn't they all just agree to disagree? They didn't have to have the same interests, beliefs, or priorities. Bree sighed as her phone vibrated with another notification.

She swiped open the app and frowned when it took her back to the comment threatening her life. The original poster replied to their original comment with a picture of the article from this morning, Rhodes, Tennessee, circled several times. Bree felt the hair on the back of her neck raise.

"Got you." The comment said.

Her pulse quickened and she took a screenshot of the chat to send to Rae for her file and for her own records as well. She reported any threats to law enforcement, the vast majority of them filed away as likely nothing more than the vileness that gets spread on the internet. Filing them at least made her feel like she was doing something. Like if this random anonymous user did decide to come after her she'd at least have some sort of digital trail to prove that it was not a one-time occurrence, but a pattern. Not a crime of passion, but intentional. Methodical. Premeditated.

She shivered. She was watching too much crime TV. Bree flagged the comment in the app and sent it off to Rae before emailing her contact at the local police station. She'd met Detective Ramirez when she first moved into Rhodes and gave him the rundown of her desire to stay out of the spotlight. She also mentioned the threatening notes left in her dressing room and the hateful threats she received on social media. Detective Ramirez told her to go ahead and send any screenshots, and he'd file them away for her so there was always a record. Better to be safe than sorry.

Her phone began vibrating as concerned messages flooded in from Steph and Rae. Bree replied, reassuring them she was okay, and then hesitated, her finger hovering over the share button as she considered sending Noah the video of the bear and the comment from her socials. She quickly dismissed the idea. She already had the police involved—she didn't need to bother Noah, too.

***

Three days later, Bree pulled into her garage after grabbing a latte. She was ready to put the final touches on the painting for the library. She hoped they loved it as much as she did. They asked for the Cliffs of Moher on a foggy day, and playing with the shades of blues, grays, greens, and browns had been a lot of fun. Not only was it fun, but it was shaping up to be exactly what Bree had envisioned.

Bree grabbed the mail and packages she'd tossed on the passenger seat earlier in the week and walked into the house, the blast of AC sending a chill down her spine. Summer was swiftly setting in and it wouldn't be long before the sun would become sweltering. She set down her latte on the kitchen table and quickly sorted through the remaining mail.

Letters were set aside to be answered later, but the packages called to her. While she didn't expect any gifts, she always loved getting them. She didn't get very many presents growing up, so any time a fan took the time to send one she felt the same joy she had when she was eight and Nonna had given her the stuffed bear...memories of the headless bear surfaced and Bree immediately shoved them back down. She didn't have time to break down today.

There were three boxes from her fan mailbox, and Bree took a sip of her latte before opening the first one. She opened the box, a large amount of intentionally layered tissue paper covered the contents. Bree carefully peeled each layer back, suddenly nervous about what she would find. Memories of her poor bear and the threats on her socials were at the front of her mind. She slowly opened the gift layer after layer, her pulse increasing as she peeled back each thin piece of tissue. A pair of gray eyes looked up at her from the bottom of the box, and Bree jumped back, her heart thundering in her chest.

She reached into the box gingerly and pulled out the mirror, scoffing at herself internally. She was going to give herself a heart attack. The mirror was *gorgeous*. It had a black frame around it that really helped the etching on the mirror pop. There were several staffs and the notes to one of her most popular songs, Narcissistic Love. The notes and lyrics flowed beautifully, and the entire chorus was etched into the mirror. She reached inside and pulled out a small envelope holding the card that went with the gift.

Aubrey,

Congratulations on your retirement! I'm so stoked for you. I was in a really bad relationship, and your music helped me through it and gave me the strength to leave

Bree wiped the stray tear from her cheek and tucked the note carefully back into the envelope. She would add it to her rainy day box, where she kept all the kind letters and messages she'd gotten over the years from her fans and friends. Whenever she had a really bad day—especially while she was in the thick of performing still—she would take out the rainy day box and remember that she was making a positive difference. And not just for Jess.

She carefully set the mirror aside and turned her attention to the next box. This one was smaller than the first and more square than flat. She opened it up and found a beautiful glass iced coffee cup with her name on it and a wooden lid that made it super cute. Another kind note accompanied the package, and Bree smiled, setting it aside near the mirror.

Her earlier nerves were gone as she eagerly opened the third box. It was brown and tied with a string that gave it an old-world charm and reminded Bree of her days watching The Sound of Music. Packages were definitely one of her favorite things. Bree eagerly untied the string, anticipation growing as she worked the knot. The best thing about fan packages is you never knew what cool thing would be in it. Coffee mugs, homemade bracelets, music samples, and more. Homemade gifts were her favorite. Bree finally got the knot untied and slipped the string off the package. She slipped her finger along the seam of the paper, gently opening the package and savoring the moment. She loved gifts.

Bree finished removing the paper and opened the box, reaching excitedly through the tissue paper. Her hand closed over something soft and fluffy. She gently pulled the item out of the box and screeched, immediately dropping it as though she'd been burned.

Sitting innocently on her kitchen table was the bear Nonna had given her...minus its head. Bree sobbed and wrapped her arms around herself tightly, the high level of excitement from receiving a gift crashing and burning as horror overtook her. The bear had a note pinned to it and Bree gingerly reached out to grab it. She unlatched the pin and carefully pulled the plain white square of paper off the pin.

Don't worry. We came back to you.

Bree gasped for air, her breaths coming out quickly as sobs wracked her body, terror flooding her veins. She stood quickly from her chair, jumping and crying harder as it fell behind her and clattered to the floor. She paced around the room, trying to get her breathing under control. She was okay. She wasn't physically harmed. The box didn't come to her home address. She was fine. After a few moments, she had her breathing back under control, and the tears flowed quietly down her cheeks rather than the gut-wrenching ugly sobs from minutes before.

This could not be her life. When did her life turn into a real-life episode of Criminal Minds—minus the whole multiple deaths thing? The unfairness of it all crashed into her, sorrow coming in waves. She was supposed to be enjoying a peaceful retirement. Nausea ebbed and flowed with the sorrow. The straight *audacity* of some people. She couldn't imagine what was going through their mind. In what universe would tormenting someone like this be okay? Bree's brain felt as though she were trying to move forward through sludge while the world continued on at a normal pace. She needed to do something. Call someone.

She snapped pictures of the bear and note and emailed them to Detective Ramirez before going into the living room to think. She stared at the table, the horrifying bear sitting forebodingly in the middle of it. This wasn't a harmless message from some nameless account on social media. The pictures that had been taken in her old house. The bear from Nonna. These things were personal.

Bree turned her thoughts to the messages and the gifts and felt a heaviness settle over her. Retirement was supposed to be time to focus on herself. She wanted to be left alone. What would she do if someone broke into her home? Attacked her on the street? What if the person who threatened her online really did come to Rhodes to put an end to her 'self-indulgent' existence? What if the person who beheaded her bear really *was* in town already? What if they were the same person?

She sighed deeply. Maybe it was time to ask for help. She stared at the bear and felt resolve flow through her. She wouldn't cower, but she also wouldn't be too stupid to live. She grabbed her phone and scrolled through the list of contacts, stopping when she came to Noah's name. She could ask for help. Even from someone like Noah Hawthorne. Hopefully, he was in a congenial mood today.

She didn't have the mental energy to deal with an overbearing man right now, but she also didn't have the emotional bandwidth to deal with whoever was harassing her and trying to steal her peace.

Decision made, Bree clicked on Noah's name and waited for the call to connect. The phone rang a few times before a deep voice on the other end of the line answered, and she felt the tension melt from her shoulders for the first time since seeing the article.

"Noah Hawthorne."

Chapter Six

Noah

Noah waited patiently, the phone pressed to his ear as Aubrey gathered her thoughts. After a few moments of silence, he furrowed his brow, leaning back in his chair.

"Hello? Miss Gray?" Noah tried again. When she didn't immediately reply he frowned and debated whether she was in trouble or if she'd called him on accident. Deciding it was likely an accident, he began to move the phone away from his ear.

"Hi," Aubrey's quiet voice said. Noah frowned, straining to hear her.

"Aubrey? Are you okay?" He asked, leaning forward in his chair.

"Sort of?" She said, sniffling before huffing a laugh.

"Did you mean to call me?"

"Yes."

"Okay...how can I help you?" Noah asked, concerned. Last time they spoke she had been adamant that she had no need for security and he was shocked she called him.

"Actually, I... It's just..." She hesitated for a moment. "I'm in a bit of trouble and could use some help."

"Tell me more," Noah said, grabbing a pad of paper and pen so he could take down any pertinent information. Noah waited for a moment and frowned when she didn't continue.

"Miss Gray?"

"Aubrey." She corrected softly. "We may as well be on a first-name basis if we are going to work together."

Noah's eyebrows shot up in surprise. They were going to work together?

"Aubrey," Noah replied warmly, letting her name roll off his tongue. He could work with this. He could handle the woman who was hesitant to hire security. Whatever happened must be serious. She was asking for help even though she clearly wasn't used to it.

Noah decided to try to lighten the mood. Maybe she'd respond well to that. "More tire trouble?" He asked playfully.

Aubrey chuckled quietly. "I wish. It's actually kind of complicated."

Noah waited, letting the silence settle between them.

"There was a threat on my life I need to take more seriously." Aubrey said pensively, "I think I may need to hire a bodyguard for a little bit."

Noah could practically feel his brain stutter to a halt. Was there a type of threat people *didn't* take seriously? "Do you know who is threatening you?" He asked.

"I...can we talk about it in person? I'd feel more comfortable if I could show you." Aubrey pleaded.

Noah released a breath. "Of course. We always meet prospective clients as a team to get information on what's going on and then decide as a collective if our company is a good fit. Are you able to come to our office?"

"Where is the office?"

"Downtown Trenton. I can text you the address when we hang up if that would be helpful."

"That would be perfect. I can be there in an hour."

"Is it safe for you to leave your home on your own, or do you need one of us to escort you in?"

"I think I'm safe to come in on my own." She said hesitantly.

"Listen to me, Aubrey. Two things: First, make sure you're attentive to your surroundings. If you think someone is tailing you or you have any other physical concerns, you give me a call immediately, and I will come to you and escort you to the office. Secondly, listen to your gut. If you step outside and something feels off, go back inside, call me, and I'll come and escort you to the office."

"Thanks, Mr. Hawthorne."

"Noah."

"Noah. I'll see you soon."

"See you soon. Drive safe." He added, his traitorous mind replaying the sound of Aubrey saying his name. He liked how his name sounded coming from her.

As soon as the call ended, Noah picked up his phone and dialed Theo's extension.

"Miss me already?"

"Aubrey Gray called me just now," Noah said, moving the pen and paper back to their designated spot so his desk was clear. He needed to be able to focus. "She's in trouble."

"Fill me in." Seriousness took over the banter from a moment before, and Noah leaned back in his chair, replaying the conversation with Aubrey in his mind.

"I'm not entirely sure. She mentioned there was a threat to her life that she needed to take more seriously."

"Is there a threat to her life she doesn't take seriously?" Theo asked incredulously.

"Apparently—" And he would get to the bottom of that too. Any threat to life and limb should be treated as serious. "She's going to come in to meet the team. She wanted to discuss the threat in person. Meet me in the conference room in about an hour with whoever isn't on assignment. We'll collect information, assess the problem, and determine which contract would be the best fit."

"Sounds good. Need anything right now?"

"Will you let the rest of the team know about the meeting?"

"Sure thing."

"Thanks, man."

Noah ended the call and stared at the ceiling. He felt responsible for Aubrey Gray in a way he hadn't since Lettie and her case had nearly destroyed him. A vision of Lettie's dead body flashed through his mind, and he grimaced. He wouldn't lose Aubrey. He'd get the information and tell her that *all* threats to life and limb should be taken seriously. He wasn't able to protect Lettie, but he wouldn't make the same mistake twice.

***

Aubrey

The drive to Trenton was blessedly uneventful, though Bree obsessively watched her mirrors to make sure she wasn't being followed. On one level, it seemed unlikely that someone would be tailing her, given the fact they sent the *gift* to her public post office box, but what if it was a trap? What if it was meant to lure her into a false sense of complacency, and they actually knew where she was? Bree shuddered. No, she'd take paranoia over being the woman in the horror movie checking out strange sounds in the haunted basement. Man, was she glad her house didn't even *have* a basement.

Bree parked her car and walked up to the average-looking brick office building. Honestly, if the door didn't say Hawthorne Security on it, she could just as easily be walking into a DMV or a bank. Inside the door was a small reception area that was surprisingly well-decorated. The natural light from the big windows brightened the space. There were a couple of white sofas near the windows and a coffee table in front of them, staged with a stack of magazines and a blue vase full of real flowers.

An older woman with short gray hair sat behind the computer at the reception desk and smiled as Bree walked in.

"Good morning! How can I help you?" She asked warmly.

"I'm here to see Noah Hawthorne," Bree said, rubbing her hands on her jeans.

"Do you have an appointment?"

"No, ma'am. But he is expecting me."

"What's your name?"

"Aubrey Gray."

"Have a seat on the sofa, Miss Gray. Mr. Hawthorne will be out to get you in a moment."

"Thank you," Bree said, her heart racing. She could do this. She clutched the box she was holding and walked over to the couches that looked far more comfortable than the couch she currently had. Her home decorator had definitely picked it for its style instead of its function. Bree perched on the edge of the sofa, drumming her fingers quietly against the cardboard box.

A few minutes later, a door to the right of reception opened, and Noah walked out. He spotted her immediately in the small space, his eyes scanning her quickly.

Seemingly satisfied that she was uninjured, he walked over to her and held his hand out. "Thanks for coming in," Noah said.

Bree stood, shifting the package, and shook his offered hand. "Of course."

"Come on back. I'll introduce you to the team, and then we can discuss what's going on. Sound good?"

Bree swallowed nervously. What if they thought she was overreacting? Noah was watching her closely, likely observing all of the expressions crossing her face. Which wouldn't be a bad thing, except her face was a giant billboard for her emotions. If her mouth didn't say it, her face definitely would.

"Yeah. Yeah, that's fine." She said.

Noah led the way to the door and scanned his badge. A dull buzzing sound preceded the click that let them know the door was unlocked. Noah pulled it open, and Bree looked at it warily.

"It's okay. It isn't locked from the inside or anything. We just don't want just anyone able to walk back into our offices or conference rooms, given the nature of our business."

"Fair enough."

They walked down the brightly lit hallway, various portraits of landscapes evenly spaced throughout the hall. Noah guided Bree into a room on the left, and Bree paused, her anxiety spiking. What was she supposed to say? A warm hand rested on her lower back, and she turned to look up at Noah.

"You're safe here, Bree. I'll introduce you to Peter—you've already met Theo—and then you can give us the rundown of what's been going on. No pressure." He said quietly.

Bree walked into the room and set the box she was holding down on the table gently. Noah pulled out the chair at the head of the table and gestured for Bree to sit. Nerves rattled around in her stomach as she sank into the chair.

Noah took the chair immediately to the right of Bree and waited for Peter and Theo to get situated before taking a breath. "You've met Theo," Noah said, gesturing to the man at his right.

Theo waved at Bree, his brown hair looking constantly rumpled. He was skinnier than the other men but still fit. He smiled at Bree and waved a hand.

"Theo is our resident tech expert. He is almost always in the office working behind-the-scenes magic for us," Noah said.

Bree smiled at Theo and nodded her head in greeting.

"This is Peter," Noah said, gesturing to the man across from Theo. Peter nodded at Bree, giving a forced smile—almost like his mouth wasn't quite sure how to smile *and* make it believable. Maybe he was socially awkward like she was. She could empathize with that.

"Peter knows everything about everything. He specializes in corporate protection and takes on our clients who are high-level executives in various companies."

Noah continued, "Zach and Eli are out in the field, but you'll meet them another time. Eli specializes in diplomatic protection, and Zach does protection details and also coordinates with local and national police departments, security agencies, and witness protection."

Bree nodded and waited for Noah to give her the floor. She could do this. She sang in front of crowds full of people, for goodness sake. She could manage a conversation with three adults.

"So tell us what's going on, Bree," Noah said.

"Three days ago, an article was released in a national paper—in print and online," Bree said, pulling the article out of her purse and handing it to Noah. Noah perused the article and passed it on to Theo.

"Okay," Noah said. "It seems like a pretty normal article. What happened?"

"I never told anyone where I live. I have all of my mail sent to a PO box in Chattanooga, and I vary my schedule whenever I pick it up." Bree watched Noah as he processed the information. Theo passed the article to Peter, who read through it quickly.

"The picture in the article was taken at the museum I visit whenever I pick up my mail. I ran into the Millers there and spoke with them, but there wasn't anyone in the atrium with us. Not that I could see anyway. Regardless, anyone who ran the article would assume I lived in Chattanooga since that's where my mail goes, and I'm a member at the museum."

Understanding crossed Noah's face as he furrowed his brow. "The article specifically mentions Rhodes. So someone knows you don't live in Chattanooga."

"Exactly."

"But plenty of people live in Rhodes, Aubrey. Any one of them could've mentioned you live there."

"But how would the journalist have found a random person from Rhodes if they thought I lived in Chattanooga? They're not exactly neighboring communities." Bree said pointedly.

"Fair enough. We can come back to that. So, the article was posted three days ago. Then what?"

Bree hesitated. Maybe she should've sent that video to Noah as soon as she got it.

"Aubrey?" Noah asked.

Bree sighed, "The immediate result was a new social media comment on a threat I received a few weeks ago that I had dismissed."

"A threat you dismissed?" Theo said incredulously.

"Yes. I reported it to Detective Ramirez and sent a copy to my former agent for the file we keep, but then I let it go."

"What was the threat?" Noah asked, his tone lowering dangerously.

"The commenter threatened to put an end to my 'self-indulgent existence' as soon as the media leaked where I was 'hiding' from my responsibilities."

Anger flashed across Noah's face so quickly that Bree would have missed it if she hadn't been staring right at him.

"After the article came out, the same commenter replied to their original comment with a picture of the article and Rhodes, Tennessee circled several times along with a message that says 'got you'. Or something to that effect." Bree said.

"That's a big deal, Aubrey."

"Not really." Aubrey shrugged. "It kind of comes with the territory of being famous."

"Actually, although 41% of Americans have dealt with online harassment, women tend to experience more. And since you were threatened with physical harm—specifically death—it actually puts you in the 'more severe' category of online harassment, which accounts for around 5% of the instances. So it is more of a 'big deal'." Peter countered.

Bree's jaw dropped, and she quickly snapped it shut.

"He has a photographic memory." Theo supplied helpfully. "But he is right, Aubrey. Someone threatening your life *is* a big deal."

Bree could feel Noah's eyes on her and felt the moment he realized she was here for something else.

"You're not here for this threat, though, are you?" Noah asked incredulously

Having Noah's full attention on her made her feel like she walked into class for an exam she'd never studied for. She could try and fake her way through it, but no way was she going to be able to fool anyone. It was like he could see right through her.

"No, I'm not. I received another message that day on my socials. It included pictures and a video." Bree pulled up the pictures and video on her phone and handed it to Noah. Theo scooted closer so he could see, and Peter walked around the table to look on from behind.

"The photos are from my old house in Los Angeles which hasn't been take over by the new owners yet." Bree said.

She paused as Noah tapped on something—she assumed the video—and watched the emotions cross their faces. Confusion, followed by focus—probably looking at the note—, and then surprise.

"Tell me about the bear," Noah said evenly, handing the phone back to Bree.

"It was a gift from my Nonna. I hired movers to pack and move my stuff—well, my agent did—and they left it behind."

"They were inside your home? Adam and Steph have mentioned you've been getting some nasty notes, too...Do you have a stalker, Bree?" He asked, the threat of death and violence clear in the deep tones of his voice.

"I...I don't know. I mean, some level of harassment comes with the job. Not that it should, but it's expected. The notes fell into that category. They were left on my dressing room table, and they were scary, but it wasn't like this." Anxiety rose in Bree's chest, and she rubbed her fingers on her jeans. This meeting was not doing much to soothe her nerves.

"That's helpful information but not what I asked. Do you have a stalker, Bree?"

"I think I might," Bree said softly. "But I'm not convinced he'd come to Rhodes. Or at least I wasn't until they ran a story with my town listed in it." Maybe she should move. Her home was finally devoid of boxes except for the pesky kitchen ones. She loved Rhodes, and she loved her house. She didn't want to go. She took a deep breath and looked pointedly at Noah. "I need to show you something."

Bree gently pushed the box toward Noah. He reached for the box and paused, his gaze meeting hers in question.

"Open it." She said flatly.

Noah slowly pulled the top off the box and took in the decapitated bear lying in the box, surrounded by the wrapping, the note carefully tucked in next to it.

"Bree—is that?"

"The same bear from the video," Bree said with a nod.

"Why do you have it?"

"It was in my mailbox in Chattanooga. I finally got around to opening the packages I picked up last week," Bree said, watching him lean closer to the box to examine all of the items sitting on it. "When I opened the last package, that's what was in it."

"Did you notice anything unusual about the note?" Peter asked.

"Not really. It's a plain white square—like printer paper—and says, 'Don't worry...we came back for you.'"

"And it came to your mailbox in Chattanooga?" Theo asked.

"Correct."

"So this one must have been mailed before the article. I presume your fan mail PO Box is listed in publicly accessible areas." Peter said thoughtfully.

"It is." Bree nodded.

"With the threatening message, the note indicating someone 'got you', and the headless bear, it sounds as though someone—or multiple someones—are going to great lengths to cause problems. Now, what we don't know is whether their goal is to make you uncomfortable or scare you. Or whether they're legitimate threats and your safety could be compromised." Noah said.

Bree's heart sank. She didn't want to do this anymore. Figure out who was trying to scare her or hurt her or worse. She should've just ignored her parents and gone to art school after high school like she wanted. She should've made them figure out their own way to take care of Jess. Panic threatened to bubble up, and Bree shoved it aggressively back down. She could have a breakdown later. Not here.

"You need to install security cameras at your home, Aubrey. Just in case. You also should have security with you when you are out—particularly in crowded areas like the gala you'll be speaking at." Noah said, gesturing to the article.

Bree bristled at his tone and felt her hackles rise. She didn't like being told what to do. But since she was clearly in need of security and security was his speciality she needed to try and work with him.

"I don't want to put up security cameras," She argued. "But, I would like security to and from the last of my collaborations and any errands."

Noah leaned back in his chair, a scowl etched on his face. "You're leaving yourself open to danger, Aubrey."

"What good is a security camera? They don't prevent crime, they just record it as it happens. I don't need people watching my every move." She'd had more than enough of that when she was still in the spotlight. And when she had lived at home. She was finally free to have peace *and* privacy—the pesky article on the gala notwithstanding.

"It could help with identification if the stalker leaves something or comes to your house. It could help us find any cars that routinely go by that aren't part of the neighborhood. No one is going to sit at the office all day and stare at your house." He argued. "But it can help us in the investigation and in proactively keeping you safe."

"We'll revisit the security camera idea later," Bree said primly.

"Fine—we will revisit it. *Soon.* In the meantime, we can figure out a rotation to help with covering you as far as events and errands go. I would also suggest having one of us around if you're going to meet anyone you are suspicious of. That way, we can observe them and the interaction, and we're there to intervene in case things get out of hand."

"Is that likely?"

"It depends. While normally I would say no, someone selling the image to the paper and revealing where you live when you would know that it only could have a handful of people speaks to a certain level of desperation. If it was a large group of people who knew you, knew where you lived, and knew your routines, I'd say it was someone just trying to make a quick buck, and they're less likely to escalate. But, if you find or confront this person or their access to you is cut off—and thus their money supply is cut off—then it could get ugly. I've seen people break over less money than what I'm sure they got from the papers."

A fresh wave of tears threatened to fall as blistering anger and crushing hopelessness ran through her. The picture, taken in her place of refuge, was bad enough. But knowing someone sold the picture *and* where she lived to the press was enough to overwhelm her entirely. Who could hate her that much? Everyone who knew her knew that she liked her privacy and peace. They knew she kept where she lived out of the public eye—especially now that she was retired.

"We can help take care of this Aubrey." Noah encouraged.

Bree nodded and furiously wiped the tears away from her eyes. "So, how much does all of this cost?" She asked, cringing internally at what was sure to be an astronomical number. Security wasn't cheap, and private 'as needed' security—which was what their arrangement sounded like—was likely to cost even more.

"We'll need to know more about your daily schedule, upcoming events, et cetera, before I'm able to provide an accurate estimate. Because it isn't likely to be around-the-clock protection, it will be less than if we planned to provide a 24-hour protection detail. It'll probably be in the realm of \$3,500 to \$5,000 per month depending on travel, events, number of private outings, and the like."

Bree nodded. Expensive, but not more than expected.

"Thanks, Noah."

"You're welcome." He smiled stiffly as though he had to remind his face it was supposed to smile at prospective clients rather than because he actually felt joyful.

"If you could put together a list of collaborations, regular errands, appointments, the gala, and anywhere else where you expect to need private security over the next few months and send it to me via e-mail so I can take a look at the schedule, I'd appreciate it. Then I can send you the paperwork along with a more precise quote."

"Will do," Bree said, picking up the box with her bear and standing. "It was nice to meet you and nice to see you again." She said to Peter and Theo respectively.

"I'll walk you out," Noah said, standing as well.

"Thanks." She said with a grateful smile.

Noah gestured for Bree to walk ahead of him, and they walked down the hall in relative silence.

"Are you comfortable going home on your own, or would you like me to escort you?" Noah asked as they reached the door to reception.

Bree paused. She didn't want to bother anyone, and she hadn't formally hired them, so she really didn't want them to go out of their way—especially all the way to Rhodes. But what if someone was watching her? *Following* her? A shiver crept up her spine.

"I can go on my own. I'm sure it's fine." She said, a forced smile on her face.

Noah didn't look like he believed her, and, honestly, she didn't believe herself either. Noah opened the door, and they walked out into the reception area.

"I'll be careful." She added.

"Text me when you get inside your house," Noah said, leading the way to the front doors. He held the door open for Bree, following her outside as she walked to her car.

"Okay," Bree said, unsure of whether she would or if she'd chicken out from this whole security thing altogether. She unlocked her car and opened the door. Maybe she was making a big deal out of nothing.

Noah leaned against the car door for a moment, his intense gaze meeting hers. "If I don't get a message, Aubrey, I'll personally come by to make sure you're okay."

Bree's heart skipped a beat, and she grimaced. Stupid hormones. She nodded to Noah as she grabbed the door handle.

"I'll text you."

Seemingly satisfied, Noah stepped away from the car. "Drive safe, Aubrey."

Bree's heart stuttered again. When was the last time someone told her to drive safely? Or cared about her safety at all—except Steph and Adam. Man, she missed them. Bree nodded, unable to speak around the knot in her throat, and closed her car door softly.

She would go home and send Noah the information he needed to put together a schedule and quote, and then she could decide if she was going to hire Hawthorne Security. While she didn't want to be too stupid to live, she also didn't want to be the woman who cried wolf.

Chapter Seven

Noah was sitting at his desk, definitely not thinking about Aubrey Gray or the disturbing video he'd seen earlier that afternoon. Watching the bear lose its head left a heavy, sick feeling in his gut. Trouble was brewing, and Aubrey was at the center of it. A quiet ding came from the computer, Aubrey's name popping up on his screen.

Noah opened the message, eager to see what their calendar would look like for the next couple of months. While Hawthorne was rather heavy on clients at the moment, an annoyingly unfamiliar weight of responsibility nagged at him when it came to Aubrey Gray. Like he needed to protect her—though he wasn't totally sure which threat he was protecting her from yet. She seemed to be a little reluctant to let him protect her at all. Whether it was because she didn't want to bother anyone or she was just plain stubborn, he wasn't sure yet.

All he knew was he needed to get her safe and her situation sorted so he wouldn't have to see her again. Then these feelings could go away, and he could get back to his work in peace with a solid win under Hawthorne Security's belt. The accolades from Aubrey's case would surely propel them into the top tier of security services.

Noah's eyes flew across the screen, taking in the various collaborations, meetings, and errands Bree had. It looked as though it was a relatively light travel schedule—a few TV advertisement appearances and some business meetings with different brands or influencers in order to finish up some social media collaborations. Errands were typically done on Tuesdays or Thursdays and she didn't have a lot of social engagements. All in all, it looked like a very doable schedule. Noah sent her back the paperwork and the updated quote, which ended up being less than expected. Always good business when that happened.

He pulled out his cell phone and sent a mass text to the rest of his team and they strode into his office a few minutes later. "We have a new client." Noah said once they'd all settled in their seats.

"Aubrey send over her schedule?" Peter asked.

"Yes, and it looks like we'll be able to accommodate it," Noah said. "She'll need protection at a few work-related events and outings and some regular weekly personal security as well for the foreseeable future."

"Aubrey Gray, the retired superstar?" Eli asked. Every head in the room whipped toward him. Theo looked comically stunned.

"What? My little sister loves her." He muttered.

"What's going on?" Zach asked, sitting on the edge of his seat.

"Someone sold her out to the newspaper. They gave up a picture of her and where she lives." Noah said.

"Sounds like a normal day for a celebrity." Eli pointed out.

"She also received a threatening note at her last performance on tour and a comment on one of her videos threatening her life. When the article came out with where she lived, the original poster commented back with a picture of the article that had Aubrey's location circled multiple times with a new comment saying 'got you.' While she wasn't initially concerned, she received a video of someone in her old house decapitating a teddy bear movers left behind with a note that said, 'How could you leave us behind?' The same bear is now in her possession with a new note that says, 'Don't worry. We came back for you.'" Noah summarized.

"How did the bear end up with her?" Zach asked shrewdly.

"It was sent to her fan mail PO Box." Theo supplied.

A heavy silence filled the room. "Stalker?" Eli asked.

"Could be. One in three women have been victims of stalking at some point in their lifetime." Peter looked up toward the ceiling for a moment. "Forty percent by a current or previous romantic partner and forty-two percent by an acquaintance." He rattled off like he was reading from an encyclopedia. "So it's quite possible that she does have a stalker." He added.

"Aubrey isn't sure it's a stalker, but I'd like to err on the side of caution. We will hope for the best and prepare for the worst." Noah replied.

"If she isn't sure it is a stalker, then what does she want to hire us for?" Eli added.

"General protection. She'd like to find out who might have sold her information but knows that finding out is probably unlikely. She also is concerned after the social media commenter said they'd be coming for her which was followed by the headless bear, though we have reason to believe the bear was sent *before* the article came out." Noah said.

"Our concern about the offender is only a certain number of people know where Aubrey lives and her routines. Not many would be willing to disclose that kind of information to the press." Theo said.

"We know the stats on how likely an offender is to escalate behaviors in these types of situations. She also wants to take the threat to her life more seriously. We're there to help keep her safe." Peter added.

"What do you need from us?" Zach asked.

"I take on our celebrity clients, so I will take on the majority of Aubrey's case. There are a few cases that were on my docket that are not celebrity related that will need to be reassigned in order to make this work. Noah paused for a moment and tried to determine the best way to communicate the deep sense of responsibility he felt for Aubrey's safety. "Aubrey's situation reminds me a lot of Lettie's case." Noah said painfully.

A look of understanding flashed across the faces of each of his teammates, and Zach nodded.

Noah cleared his throat and continued. "Also, there are a couple of events that I can't make, so I will need one of you to fill in on those dates. Otherwise, I think we'll be set."

"I can take the dates you miss." Theo volunteered.

"You don't like fieldwork," Noah said.

"No," Theo shrugged, sitting back in his chair. "But I like Aubrey, so I can make an exception. Besides, everyone else has full schedules, and mine flexes a little more. Plus, depending on where we are, I can pack along my laptop so I can still help if you need it. It's a win-win."

"Thoughts on that plan?" Noah asked the group, making eye contact with each of his teammates. When no one spoke up, he nodded and said, "We'll call it good then. I will get the schedules updated in our calendar app. I'll call you if I need to have you take on one of the non-celeb cases. There are only a couple of them, so it won't be overly taxing. I appreciate you guys."

"No worries, man, that's what a team is for." There was a collective grunt of acknowledgement as everyone trickled out the door. Theo stayed back until the rest had left.

"Anything you need from me?"

"Yeah, actually. Could you look into Aubrey and see what you can find? Any interviews, news articles, social media posts and comments, friends, anything that you think might be helpful or that stands out to you as problematic when you nose around."

"Will do. It may take a while. Eli wasn't kidding when he said she was a superstar. I'm sure there will be a fair number of red flag comments."

"Okay—just let me know what you find out. I'm going to give Aubrey a call and let her know the plan once I have schedules coordinated."

"Sounds good," Theo said before seeing himself out of the office. Noah watched the door close and then turned his attention back to the calendar. He needed to get these details finalized so he could keep Aubrey safe.

***

Noah punched Aubrey's address into his phone and, an hour later, pulled into what appeared to be a quiet, middle-class neighborhood. A frown tugged his face down as he pulled alongside the curb of her little bungalow. There was no fence guarding the front of the home, and it didn't look as though there were any security cameras either. Both would need to be remedied as soon as possible. Noah made a mental note to have Theo look into the right security cameras and locations in order to optimize their eyes on the property. Theo had a knack for figuring out where people would most likely hide and the best way to make sure they were watched in corners they thought were dark.

Noah looked at his clock for the fourth time while he sat in his car waiting for a socially acceptable time to knock on Aubrey's door. He enjoyed the simple things in life. Good friends. A nice handling car. A good steak fresh off the grill. His idea of a good time did not involve going grocery shopping, stopping in at the bank, or mailing literally anything. And yet, while most people considered his job to be glamorous—world tours, being on set, socializing with A-listers—it contained far more of the boring day-to-day stuff than people realized.

The clock on the screen turned to nine, and Noah got out of the car, shrugging on his suit jacket as he walked up to Aubrey's door, steeling himself for what was sure to be an...interesting outing. While Aubrey had asked him to help with her current situation, she definitely seemed reluctant to accept it. Or advice. And would probably rather swim with sharks than listen to a single order he gave—even if it was for her own good. Noah grimaced.

Sometimes, orders given by people in positions of authority were superfluous. Other times, they saved lives. Unfortunately, the only way to mitigate risk was to treat all orders as though they were the life-saving kind. It appeared Aubrey Gray did not ascribe to that idea. But today was a new day, and he was going to be pleasant and patient. He would calmly discuss any changes he thought she should make, and she'd see reason, agree with him, and they'd get the changes made. Today was going to go smoothly.

Noah walked toward the wooden door—a wreath with some greenery, white flowers, and dandelions decorated it, giving it a homey feel. Noah frowned and leaned in closer to determine whether the wreath obstructed the view out of the peep hole which would be a safety hazard. It did seem to create an issue on the peripheries. He leaned in closer to inspect further and found himself suddenly looking at a green shirt instead of a wooden door. He trailed his eyes up and caught Aubrey observing him shrewdly.

"Is there a reason you're hunched over inspecting my door?" She asked, amusement lacing her tone.

She stepped back to let him in and closed the door swiftly behind them. They walked inside, and he found himself surprised at the cozy, well-decorated interior. It wasn't what he expected from a celebrity. But neither was changing a tire. Noah shook his head. He didn't need to think about Aubrey, her house, or her tire-changing abilities. She was a *client*. Nothing more.

"No, your door is solid. But you do need to take the wreath down." Noah said.

"No, thank you," Bree said.

"Excuse me?" Surprise flashed through him. When was the last time a client just outright refused one of his suggestions? Normally they just sucked up to him and agreed to his face. Then they'd go behind his back to do what they wanted. It was annoying but normal at this point. Leave it to the pint-size firecracker in front of him to shake up the routine.

Bree shrugged. "I said no, thank you. I really love that wreath. I think it makes my house feel homey."

Noah took a deep breath and took a small step away from Aubrey. "I hear you. However, it impacts your ability to clearly see who is at your door."

"I love that wreath. Besides, nothing has ever come to my house directly. Every note has been dropped off at a place it was advertised I'd be or mailed to a PO Box that is available to anyone on the web."

"You're being unreasonable," Noah argued, forgetting his earlier resolution to be pleasant and patient.

Bree folded her arms and narrowed her eyes. "You're not the boss of me, Noah. I appreciate your advice and your protection outside of my home, but otherwise, I just want to live my life my way. In peace." She added pointedly.

Noah sighed and ran his hand through his hair. "Okay, but be aware there is a small blind spot." He paused for a moment. While this wasn't the right time to ask her, there may never be a right time, so he might as well get her hackles up all the way. "You know, if you let us install security cameras, then we wouldn't have to be concerned about the blind spot. You'd keep your wreath, we'd be able to see who comes and goes that shouldn't be here. Win-win."

Aubrey huffed out a breath. "For you." She muttered. "Noah, I don't want to hang up cameras. I've had cameras in my space all. the. time. for seven years. I will not willingly hang them up so my every waking moment can be monitored."

"They're just outdoor cameras—" Noah began.

"Noah, please, let's just get this done and get back home. The sooner we are done, the sooner I'm out of your hair."

No argument there. It had been five minutes and already Noah was running low on patience. He walked over to the wooden bowl and picked up Aubrey's keys, double checking the front door was locked before turning to her.

"Are you ready to go?" He asked stiffly.

"Yeah, just let me grab my purse and shoes." She said, opening the coat closet and pulling out a small crossover bag. It was a lot more practical than he expected. She also grabbed a pair of white sneakers and put them on, adjusting the flared bottom of her leggings to cover the sock and tongue of the shoe. Her messy bun was releasing small curly tendrils that framed her face, and if she didn't love to argue with him so much, he could see himself finding her rather beautiful.

They got into Bree's car and sat in silence as Noah backed out of the garage and drove them toward town.

"So fill me in on precisely where you'd like to go today. You mentioned last time we spoke that things might have changed."

Aubrey nodded. "I want to go to the coffee shop in Rhodes, and then we'll be heading to Chattanooga. I need to stop by the post office, the bank, and then the grocery store on the way home." Aubrey paused and seemed to be considering something.

"Is there somewhere else you need to go?"

She paused. "No...Not today." There was an inflection in her voice that made Noah wonder about the undisclosed location, but they quickly arrived at the coffee shop, and Noah was more occupied with making sure their immediate area was safe from any potential threats.

"Wait there," Noah said, hopping out of the car so he could clear the surrounding area and open Aurey's door. He walked to the passenger side and grimaced when he saw Aubrey standing on the curb, waiting for him patiently.

Frustration filled him. "I told you to wait." He said, gesturing to the parked car next to them.

"I am capable of opening my own door," Aubrey argued back.

"Obviously," Noah said, disdain dripping from his tone. "However, if someone wants to get to you or take you out, a great time to do that is when your bodyguard is on the other side of the car trying to get to you."

Understanding flashed across Aubrey's face, a look—almost similar to guilt—settling on her features. "I'm sorry," Aubrey said.

She sighed. "I'm not used to this. I mean, I had security and stuff when I traveled, but that was not because someone was actively trying to harm me. I...I don't do well with orders, but I'll try to do better."

Aubrey tilted her head and looked at him pensively. "Your frustration tolerance seems to be zero. You can't tell me you've never had a non-compliant client before."

"Not from the very beginning. Usually, they do me the courtesy of at least pretending they're going to do—or at least think about—what I say."

"I just save you trouble then. At least I've been honest from the beginning." She shot him a megawatt smile, which took him by surprise. She was teasing him.

"Fair enough. At least I know what to expect from you."

"What's that?"

"Honesty."

Aubrey nodded. "That's a key personality trait, I think."

"I agree with you."

"The world must be ending! Noah Hawthorne agreed with me." Aubrey joked.

Noah rolled his eyes. "The world is most definitely coming to an end." He deadpanned, holding the door open for Aubrey as she walked in.

He followed her closely, his gaze automatically taking in the rear exit by the bathrooms and the door to the kitchens. Both helpful to know in case of an emergency. The coffee shop seemed to be slow this morning, a woman with long gray hair and a long skirt sitting at one of the back tables with a Charles Dickens book in her hands. A few other patrons were scattered throughout the shop, drinking their coffee and either engaging in conversation or working. Kyle Rhodes was at the front of the line, flirting with the barista. Aubrey noticed him at the same time and stiffened visibly. Noah's brows furrowed, and he placed his hand on her lower back, surprised by the warmth and the jolt of electricity that flowed through him at the slight touch.

"Everything okay?" Noah asked quietly, leaning close to her ear so she could hear him clearly.

"Kyle has repeatedly asked me out and doesn't seem to understand the definition of the word *no*." She said quietly.

Anger flared through Noah as Aubrey took a step toward the counter, smiling and greeting the employee before placing her order. Noah tuned her out, looking at Kyle contemplatively. He didn't like men who were incapable of backing off when a woman said no. Tension and nerves rolled off Aubrey in waves. Aubrey didn't seem to be the jumpy type—in fact, she seemed to have a spine of steel that he reluctantly appreciated. The fact Kyle Rhodes caused such a strong reaction was a huge red flag.

Kyle turned as Aubrey thanked the barista and looked her up and down, the look in his eyes giving even Noah the creeps. He wasn't even the one being oggled. Noah stepped closer to Aubrey and lifted his chin slightly, narrowing his eyes. Kyle seemed to notice Noah at that moment, and a grimace twisted his features before he put on his charming smile.

"Bree!" He greeted warmly, moving toward her like he was going in for a hug.

"Aubrey." She replied, stepping back away from Kyle so she was next to Noah instead. Noah took a slight step forward and angled his body slightly in front of Aubrey, boxing her in between him and the counter so her back was covered also.

"Have you given any thought to my invitation from the other night?" Kyle asked as alarm bells sounded through Noah's head.

Aubrey glared at him. "My answer is the same." Aubrey lifted her chin even as Noah noted her hands shaking slightly."

"You should learn how to take no for an answer." She said saucily before placing a warm hand on Noah's back and pressing gently. That was distracting. He got the hint, however, and moved the two of them toward the registers, still keeping his body firmly planted between Aubrey and Kyle.

"You need to learn your place." Kyle hissed, storming closer to Aubrey. "And it's not on your feet." He added in a whisper, a twisted smile etched on his face.

Noah moved toward him, anger radiating off him in waves. "Shut your mouth. That's no way to speak to anyone—let alone a woman. Your mother clearly needs to teach you better."

Kyle bristled, but before he could say anything, Noah was in his space glaring at him.

"Do not *ever* speak to her that way again." Noah countered, his voice dangerously low. "Or I'll teach you that lesson myself."

"Is that a threat? I'm the mayor's son. You can't touch me."

"It's not a threat, boy. It's a promise." Noah said darkly, glowering at Kyle, who finally seemed to realize that he was out of his league.

Kyle turned away from Noah and stormed out, slamming the door behind him so hard the glass panes rattled in the door. Noah rested a hand on Aubrey's back as she blew out a deep breath. He looked down at her in concern. "You okay?"

She nodded.

"Never a boring day in Rhodes when you're around." Noah joked, hoping to bring a smile back on her face. He didn't like the fearful look she had since she first saw Kyle Rhodes. She may be reluctant follow orders, but she was his client which meant she was *his* to protect.

The ride to Chattanooga and the rest of the errands were blessedly boring, and they were able to wrap up at the grocery store with minimal fanfare. Aubrey was only asked to take pictures with two different people and was otherwise left alone.

Noah closed Aubrey's door and pulled his phone from his pocket to enter Aubrey's address. He frowned when he saw several missed calls from an unknown number.

Before he could listen to the voicemail, his phone vibrated, and Theo's face filled his phone screen.

"Hey, Theo." He greeted.

"Trenton General called. Mariela is in the hospital." Theo said without fanfare.

Noah's heart dropped to his stomach. "I'm on my way."

Chapter Eight

Aubrey

Noah's legs bounced nervously as they left the grocery store parking lot. Whatever had been said on the call didn't seem to be good. Bree felt a surprising desire to reach out and comfort him. She didn't like seeing his seemingly unflappable self flustered. She reached out and rested her hand on his arm gently.

"Are you okay? What happened?" Bree asked, concern lacing her voice.

"I need—would you mind if we stopped by the hospital on our way out of town?"

Anxiety filled Bree's chest as she hesitated. She didn't want him to know about Jess. Not yet.

Noah noted her response and exhaled a ragged breath. "Never mind. I'll drop you off first."

"No, it's over an hour back to Rhodes. It would take you forever, Noah." Bree said quickly. "If you need to go to the hospital, let's go. Is everything alright?"

"That was Theo. The hospital called to let me know that Mrs. Garcia fell and was taken to the hospital. She—she is like a second mom to me." Noah said, running his hands through his hair in agitation.

"I'm her emergency contact. I need to go check on her. Make sure she's okay. But I can take you back first." Bree's heart broke a little as worry lined Noah's eyes, and his attention flitted back and forth between her and the road in front of them.

"Noah, let's go to the hospital," Bree said encouragingly. "I can just stay in the car."

"You're not staying in the car, Aubrey."

"Well, you're not going to take an extra two hours—or more—to get to the hospital if you need to be there. I'm a big girl, Noah. I can handle a trip to the hospital." Boy, was that the understatement of the century. Not that Noah knew she frequently spent time hanging out at the hospital.

"Are you sure?"

"Yes," Bree said firmly. "Family is important, and no one...no one should be in the hospital alone."

Noah squeezed Bree's hand and returned his arm to the console. Bree blushed, having forgotten her hand was on his arm, and drew it back to her side of the car.

"Is there anything special she likes? A milkshake, or flowers, or something we could bring?" Bree asked. "When my—" She sighed. Now was not the time to go into the whole situation with her and Jessica.

"Some people like to bring flowers or food when they visit loved ones." She said instead.

"That's a great idea," Noah said.

After twenty minutes and a quick detour for a chocolate shake, they finally arrived at the hospital. Bree's anxiety rose, but she tried to smile reassuringly at Noah anyway as they unbuckled their seatbelts.

"Wait for me," Noah said, distraction and concern evident in his tone as he walked around the car, his head still on a swivel around the parking lot. He must've decided the coast was clear because he opened Bree's door and offered her a hand as she exited the vehicle. She took his hand and he held on to it for a moment as though it brought him comfort and anchored him.

Bree gave his hand a light squeeze, drawing his eyes to hers. "Let's go find her, Noah," Bree said, pulling her hand away from his.

"I don't know where to go." He admitted.

"I do." She said simply, leading him into the main doors of the building. The tall windows created a bright, airy space and lacked the hospital smell that the longer-term care wards seemed to have. The furniture was white and there were accents of light blues and greens placed intentionally throughout the space. All in all, it created a warm, homey atmosphere for people who were going through some of the best—or worst—times of their lives. Bree walked confidently up to the front desk where the volunteer was sitting and smiled.

"Martin!" She said happily, walking around the counter to give the man a hug. At seventy-four years old, Martin Lewis was one of Bree's favorite people at the hospital. His gray hair and blue eyes were full of the wisdom that came with age and a fire that was just his personality. He loved being helpful and had been volunteering at the hospital since his wife passed away a few years ago.

"Aubrey!" Martin replied jovially, giving Bree a tight hug and Noah a side-eye. "Is this your young man?" He asked, raising a brow.

Bree blushed. "No, he's a friend." She said quietly, not wanting to worry Martin with her current situation. "We actually need your help. We're looking for a patient, and we're not sure if she is in the ER still or if she'd been admitted to a room."

"Are you family?" Martin asked, returning to his seat at the computer.

"Noah is. He is her emergency contact."

"Name?"

"Noah Hawthorne."

"*Patient* name?" Martin corrected gently, sympathy written on his weathered face.

"Mariela Garcia." Noah croaked out. "She was brought into the ER a few hours ago by ambulance." He added.

Martin typed on the computer. "She was admitted and is in room 271. Would you like help finding it?"

"I'll get him up there. Thanks, Martin!"

"You're welcome, honey. Glad you're back! It's been nice seeing your face more now that you're not running amok."

Bree laughed. "I was on tour...*working*."

Martin waved a hand. "Pah. Same same. I'm glad you're back now."

Bree waved and turned to look at Noah. "We go this way." She said, leading the way through the pseudo-living space toward the silver elevators.

"You seem pretty familiar with the hospital," Noah said, after Bree greeted a few of the nurses walking through the hall.

"I am," Bree replied.

"Why?"

Bree hesitated. She'd tell him about Jess—but not yet. She had spent so many hours of her life in the sterile walls of this hospital. She knew some of Jessica's nurses better than she knew her own parents. How do you tell someone that? She didn't want his pity. Besides, he had enough going on at the moment.

"I just do." Bree led Noah around the final corner, coming to a stop outside of room 271. Noah looked at her for a lingering moment as though he was trying to see inside her mind and get the answer himself. When it was clear Bree wasn't going to explain further, Noah shook his head and opened the door slowly, pasting a smile on his face that Bree could tell was less than genuine but full of concern.

The room had a small window, two blue chairs, and a lone bed filling the small space. Noah leaned against the door to hold it open, careful not to drop the milkshake in his hand, and nudged Bree gently to walk in ahead of him giving her a soft smile. He followed Bree into the space, closing the door softly behind them.

Bree looked over at the bed. The occupant was a small older woman who looked incredibly frail. Her salt and pepper hair was spread around her, her skin unnaturally pale under the harsh hospital lights. She had an IV and several cords coming away from her, monitoring her vital signs as she rested. Bree felt a squeeze in her chest, anxiety and concern warring within her for this woman she didn't know but who clearly meant so much to Noah. Like Jess meant to her.

"Mrs. Garcia." He greeted warmly, moving the chairs to the other side of the bed so they faced the door. "How are you?"

Mrs. Garcia narrowed her eyes, observing Noah and clocking Bree, who was standing behind him. "What are you doing here?" She asked.

"The hospital called when they couldn't get ahold of Carlos," Noah said.

Mrs. Garcia rolled her eyes. "Ay, I told them not to call anyone. I am fine."

"You don't look fine," Noah said petulantly.

"I know you didn't just tell me that I don't look good, Noah Hawthorne." Mrs. Garcia said pointedly.

Bree chuckled, the small sound drawing their attention to her. Oops.

"Did you bring a young lady to meet me when I am in the hospital in one of these ridiculous gowns?" She asked, glaring at Noah.

"I plead the fifth," Noah muttered. Mrs. Garcia raised an eyebrow. "But…" He said, lightening his tone. "I did bring you a treat." He said, holding the chocolate milkshake toward her.

"Listen, mijo, what do I always tell you?"

"Proper nutrition is key to healing." Mrs. Garcia and Noah said at the same time.

She smiled and patted his cheek as though he were a child.

"Exactly." She said proudly. "But in this case, I'll make an exception." She winked at him and reached for the milkshake before looking back at Bree again. "What's your name dear?"

"Aubrey," Noah answered.

"The girl has a voice, Noah. Let her use it." The woman said spunkily while giving Bree a small wink. "He's a good one, mija. Don't let him get away." She whispered.

Then, loudly so Noah could hear—though Bree had the feeling he heard her attempt at whispering too if the slight blush on his cheeks and his facial expression was any indication—"The doctors are going to do surgery tomorrow, and then I'll be doing some rehab before I can go home, but then I'll be good as new."

Noah smiled at her indulgently. "You'll be back to running a tight ship in no time. I would like to speak with the doctor, though, if you don't mind. Has he come by yet?"

Bree smiled as the two of them bantered back and forth. This softer version of Noah—the one who cared so deeply for his loved ones—tugged on her heart in a way she hadn't expected. Maybe Noah—even with all his bossiness—wasn't so bad after all.

"He has, but his nurse should be able to fill you in." Mrs. Garcia said, her eyes full of love and pride as she watched Noah. "She's probably at the nurse's station."

Noah nodded and looked at Bree. "Will you be okay if I step out for a moment?"

"The girl is fine, mijo. Go." She said, waving him off with her hand.

Noah nodded at Mrs. Garcia, but looked at Bree and waited until she gave him a small smile and nod. He looked relieved as he ducked out to find the nurse.

Mrs. Garcia threw her hands in the air. "You'd think I taught the boy nothing..." she muttered. "Now, my Noah has never brought home a girl before. What exactly are your intentions?"

Bree's heart stuttered. "I'm sorry, my intentions?"

"Yes. Are you dating him? Marrying him?"

"I'm actually just a client," Bree said quietly. "We were out running some errands when we got the call from Theo."

"Hmm. Well, you should see about fixing that. My Noah is a wonderful young man. Thoughtful, considerate, hard-working. You won't find a better husband."

Bree nearly choked. "I—"

She was saved from answering that particular line of questioning as Noah walked back in. He looked between Bree and Mrs. Garcia and seemed to note the slight tension in the room. He raised an eyebrow and walked over to Bree purposefully, resting a hand on her shoulder.

"You okay?" He whispered quietly.

Bree nodded, a light blush spreading across her cheeks as Mrs. Garcia pinned her with a look that clearly said I told you so.

"The nurse gave me the information for your surgery. I'll be here." He said.

"You don't need to—"

"Not an option. I'll be here." He said, walking over to the bed to give Mrs. Garcia a hug. "I love you—I'll be back tomorrow. And you can come stay at my house after if you don't want to rehab at the facility."

"Psh. I'm going to rehab at the facility and return to my home. Thank you for the offer though, mijo. I love you too." She said, patting him lightly on the cheek.

Noah turned to Bree, "Ready to go?" He asked.

She nodded. "It was nice to meet you, Mrs. Garcia. I hope your surgery goes well."

"Thank you, mija. Remember what we talked about." She said with a pointed stare.

"What did you talk about?" Noah asked as a blush stole over Bree's cheeks.

"Just girl stuff, Noah. Don't pester the girl. Now, you two get going so I can get some sleep." Mrs. Garcia said, waving Noah and Bree out the door.

Noah grinned, but took the hint and led them out the door into the hallway.

"Sorry about that," Noah said sheepishly. "Mrs. Garcia has been my neighbor almost my whole life. She lived in the trailer next door growing up and lives down the street from me now. She practically raised me when Mom had to work."

"Don't apologize!" Bree told him quickly. That woman was a firecracker, and Bree loved her already. "She's the best. I would've loved to have someone like that growing up. I think I'd like to be her when I grow up. Broken hip notwithstanding." Bree's heart ached at how true that statement was. Her own mother had spent most of the time absent. She was always either working or focusing on keeping Jess out of trouble. She didn't have much time for Bree.

"Don't let her fool you. She's mellowed with age." Noah said, cracking a large grin. "Come on, let's get you and your groceries back to your house."

Chapter Nine

Aubrey

Noah was going to be here any minute to go for their usual Tuesday errand run, and Bree was a mess. She groaned and looked down at her paint-splattered clothes—unfortunate victims to her ongoing bout of clumsiness that seemed to be marking this entire day. First, she spilled her coffee when she woke up. Then, she was trying to get a painting done and miscalculated how closely she could stand to the palette without bumping it to the ground. The plus side? The splatter did not end up on the painting. The bad news was she now looked like one of those people who run while getting bright colors splashed all over them.

Bree finished wiping up the last of the paint from the floor as the doorbell rang. She groaned as she got up. Bree jogged to the front door and opened it, silently inviting Noah in. Noah walked in quickly, and she shut the door softly behind him.

He took in Bree's appearance and rose a brow quietly. "Decided to go on a color run this morning?" He joked.

Bree laughed, "Not a chance. I'd rather spend my morning with a book and a cup of coffee than be on a run...for fun." Bree gave a fake shudder. She looked down at her clothes and looked at him guiltily.

"Sorry—time got away from me, and then I had this little mishap...I'll need just a few minutes to change."

Noah smiled reassuringly. After being on security detail with Bree for several weeks, he seemed used to the occasional bout of clumsiness which led to them running behind schedule. "No worries, Aubrey. Take your time."

Bree smiled at him gratefully and raced to the bathroom. She took one look in the mirror and grimaced. This was not going to be a quick change, instead she needed a full shower. She turned the shower on and waited for the water to warm up while she went into the bedroom and picked out her third outfit for the day. Laundry this week was going to be a little heavier than usual. She laid the clothes on the bed—a pair of jeans, a soft tee, and some sneakers—and then hopped in the shower to wash away the evidence of this morning's series of unfortunate events.

Fifteen minutes later, she was dressed and headed out to Noah feeling decidedly more human than before.

"Ready to go?" He asked, holding his hand out toward her. Bree looked at him, puzzled. Was she supposed to hold his hand? Listen, they were on the same team, and he wasn't as awful as she thought previously—who could hate a man who cared for someone as much as Noah cared for Mrs. Garcia—but they were not in a hand-holding type of relationship. Though she wouldn't mind that. Hold up.

Bree shook her head internally. She did not need to be crushing on her protection detail. Apart from being cliche—the bodyguard romance trope was popular in the romance novels she loved to read—she didn't need an overbearing man invading her entire life. First, private security was expensive. Second, there was probably some rule about not dating the people they were assigned to protect. Regardless, she didn't need to be daydreaming about Noah Hawthorne and his drool-worthy face. The quiet must've stretched on for too long because Noah lowered his hand and was looking at her in a concerned way.

"Bree, nothing will happen to you. You're safe with me. I just need your keys so I can drive." He said in an encouraging tone.

So he could drive?!? Bree mentally facepalmed. Of course, he wanted the keys she was still holding. "Here you go." She said handing the keys over to him as they walked out the garage door, heat flooding her cheeks while she studied the floor as though it were the most interesting thing she'd ever seen.

"So, coffee first?"

"Yes! Oh, I love you! I desperately need some coffee." The exuberance poured out of her at the prospect of the liquid gold that made the days go smoother...well, when it wasn't being spilled.

"You love me, huh? Let me guess—No coffee at home?" He laughed, pushing the garage door opener and slowly backing the vehicle out.

"Well, I did have coffee this morning, but I ended up with it all over my favorite sweater and jeans instead of with it running through my bloodstream," Bree said as she sighed dramatically.

"It was devastating. My life will never be the same again." She joked with a dramatic flourish, grinning at Noah.

Noah laughed. "I can imagine that would ruin your entire life. I'll send a condolence card at my earliest convenience."

"I would appreciate that," Bree said solemnly.

They backed out of her driveway, and Noah turned the car toward the town center.

"So, normal errands day today?" Noah asked amicably.

"Yes! First, I desperately need some coffee...and maybe a croissant. This week is a Chattanooga trip. I have some mail I need to pick up and hopefully a check to drop off at the bank."

"Endorsement deals pay via check?" Noah asked.

"Nope," Bree said confidently.

Noah looked at her curiously as he turned onto Main Street.

"It's for a small side business I have." Bree shrugged.

Noah looked curious, but didn't press, which was appreciated. No one really knew about her side business selling art, and she preferred to keep it that way. She wasn't looking for notoriety. Being in the public eye for her singing was more than enough. She wanted her art to stand on its own, not go viral because she was the one painting it. She'd much rather paint her seascapes for local libraries and doctors' offices and such. The occasional personal commission came through, but for the most part, it was just small to mid-sized seascapes for offices in Rhodes and the surrounding towns. It was perfect.

"Sounds good. I'm all yours for the day. Chauffeur, coffee date, and designated bag carrier." Noah said with a roguish grin as they pulled into the parking lot in front of the coffee shop.

He had done as Bree requested and dressed down. Having someone accompany her places in a three-piece suit drew unwanted attention and she had enough of that to last a lifetime—or several. She wanted to run her errands in peace and get back home so she could work on her art or read or do literally anything other than interact with people. Noah looked handsome in a suit and tie, but was honestly breathtaking in a grounded, understated way in his jeans and black t-shirt. The way his muscles bulged made him look more like a male model than a security expert, but she wasn't complaining—just appreciating. She could look at him and appreciate his devastatingly good looks without liking him.

"Stay here until I come around to your side." He said in a serious tone.

Bree rolled her eyes. His looks were a ten, but his bossiness definitely backed him back down to a six...or a nine. Whatever.

Noah walked around the car, casually glancing at the scenery as though he were taking it in for pleasure rather than analyzing it. When he got to Bree's side of the car, he opened the door and took a step back so she would be between him and the door when she got out.

Bree stood to get out of the car but her foot caught on the lip of the door. She lost her balance and began to teeter, beginning what was sure to be an embarrassing tumble, when a pair of strong arms wrapped around her. Bree found herself pressed tightly against the car, the cool metal touching her back and Noah's warm body pressed against her front. His arm wrapped tightly around her waist, and he didn't move it as he glanced down.

"You okay?" He asked, his voice a little lower and rougher than normal.

Bree nodded, a hot blush staining her cheeks. "Yeah, I'm good. Thanks, Noah."

"Any time." He said, his roguish grin overtaking his face. A small dimple appeared on the left side of his smile, and Bree about swooned—much to her annoyance. That would definitely not help this situation. Noah removed the arm around her waist and took a step backward so she could close the car door. Of course, she couldn't exit the car gracefully the one time she actually wanted to.

Noah shepherded Bree so she walked closer to the buildings, and he could walk closer to the street as they meandered toward the coffee shop. He walked about half a step behind her, always keeping her within reach, while he looked around surreptitiously. He smiled at her as they walked into the coffee shop, holding the door open for Bree as they went.

"You're quite a gentleman." Bree complimented. Manners were lost on most men her age.

"Thank you. My mom was very big on manners."

"Well she raised you right." Bree said with a small smile. The conversation flowed easily as they moved through the line and she frowned. Grumpy barista was back.

"What do you want?"

Bree sighed. "A large iced vanilla latte please."

"Corbin—you are supposed to be friendly." Lucy griped at her brother, shooing him off from taking orders before turning to Noah with a smile.

"What can I get for you, sugar?" She asked Noah, her southern accent coming through a little extra strong as she looked him up and down, a flirtatious smile on her face. Bree pasted a smile on her face while an unfamiliar sensation burned in her stomach. Lucy had no business flirting with Noah. Bree looked over at Noah to see if he was checking Lucy out as well, but found him to be unimpressed with her attempts at flirting, which felt a lot better than it should.

"I'll have a cup of black coffee to go, please," Noah said, moving ahead of Bree so his back was to the far wall and he was facing the door.

Lucy nodded and leaned over the counter. "Is he taken?" She whispered. When Bree hesitated to respond, Lucy's eyes glittered in delight.

Bree's stomach sank—it's not like Noah was hers, but if Lucy wanted him, she'd likely flirt her way right into his arms. Bree forced a smile, ignoring the voice raging in her head, telling her to claim Noah as her own.

"You'd have to ask him," Bree replied, turning and finding Noah's eyes on her while he waited patiently at the register, the bill already paid. His eyes narrowed, taking in Lucy's facial expression and the tension lining Bree's body.

Noah grabbed their drinks and walked over to where Bree was still standing with Lucy, his body angled toward Bree as his eyes searched hers. "You ready to hit the road?" Noah asked warmly.

Bree nodded and took her coffee from his hand. She would have sworn Lucy's jaw hit the floor when Noah stepped up next to Bree and placed his hand on her lower back. A small trill of satisfaction flowed through her as they turned to walk out of the shop. She appreciated his warmth and strength as they left the building.

"Thank you for my coffee. You didn't have to do that." Bree said honestly. She couldn't remember the last time someone she actually knew tried to buy her coffee or a meal. Her dates were not only few and far between, but also a little lackluster. The last guy hadn't even been able to pretend to be interested in her rather than her money.

"I know. And you're welcome." Noah said simply. "Post office next?"

"Yup. At least we have caffeine for the drive," Bree teased, gently nudging him with her shoulder. Boy, she needed to get a grip and keep her hands to herself. Noah Hawthorne was kind, handsome, and just the right amount of protective, but he was also a little bossy and didn't like when she pushed back on his 'suggestions.' Most of all, he was not hers.

"Sounds good." He said casually, walking slightly behind her, his eyes routinely scanning the area as they walked.

"So, do you live around here?" Bree asked as we walked over to the car. Noah opened her door as he replied.

"No, I live in Trenton."

"Are you a native?"

He laughed. "Nah, my mom and I lived on the east side of the state. I lived in the same trailer park my whole life. How about you?"

"My parents live a few hours from here in Kentucky. I was born at the local hospital out there. I moved to Rhodes after I retired from the industry.

"How'd you end up in Rhodes, of all places?"

"We were doing a show in Nashville, and I saw a sign for the annual art festival, which was going on at the same time. My band and I came up for the festival, and I fell in love with the town and its residents—and their love of art and artists. I told myself that if I retired, this is where I could go. Far enough away from my parents for a little bit of independence, but close enough to be present when I needed to be. A place I could bloom in peace."

"I take it you and your parents aren't close?" He asked, heading south out of Rhodes.

"Why do you say that?" Bree asked, hedging around the question.

"You don't see them and rarely speak to them unless your dad is calling to give you a hard time." Noah frowned.

"Well, no one can accuse you of being unobservant." Bree joked, turning her attention to the countryside as they drove. "It's complicated. Dad pretty much works around the clock. He doesn't approve of my retirement and thinks I should've stayed in the industry."

"And your mom?"

"She's unwilling to take a stance against him. So, she just keeps her head down and stays quiet. Goes to work. Gardens." Bree said with a shrug.

"That sounds tough," Noah said.

Bree shrugged. "It's been that way for a long time. At this point, it just is what it is."

The trip to Chattanooga was uneventful, and conversation flowed smoothly. She gave a quick sigh of relief when they reached the post office. She walked over to her large PO Box—number 107—which was where her fan mail and industry-related mail went. Since she had a few endorsement deals and such to finish, there was never a shortage of communication. Though email was generally preferred by most companies, some still preferred pen and paper. There was a stack of letters and a small package she could open once she got home. She walked over to her second PO Box—number 636—and reached in to grab the envelopes inside. There was a small envelope with an Arizona return address, and her heart leaped in her chest. She bounced on her toes excitedly as she locked the door. It was the payment for her first out-of-state commission piece. She stared at the box in her hand, her body beginning to sweat. Last time she had opened packages...Maybe she'd set it aside until she felt ready to tackle it. She could ask Noah to open the box, but that felt...cowardly. It was opening mail. She was capable of doing it herself—even if she didn't *want* to handle it herself.

"Can we stop by the bank on our way to the grocery store?" She asked Noah, forcing herself out of her head as they exited the post office.

"This is your rodeo, Bree. I'm just along for the ride." He said, his voice infused with heat and humor.

She smiled and bumped his arm gently, his smile warming her from the inside out. They headed to the car, and Noah walked around to open Bree's door for her again. His mom really did raise him right. Once Bree was in the car, he went over to his side and got in, closing the door and starting the ignition.

***

Five hours, an impromptu photo session with some fans who had flagged her down in the store, and a drive-thru hamburger and shake later, Noah and Bree pulled into the garage at her house and walked inside, Noah carrying more than his fair share of the groceries while she looked at him appraisingly.

"If I had known that private security came with a chauffeur, therapist, grocery shopping assistant, and help unloading groceries at home, I'd have hired someone a long time ago." Bree joked, tossing her mail on the counter.

Noah laughed. "We try to keep that information on the down low. Only our favorite clients get that kind of VIP treatment." He teased. Bree smiled, and they chatted about small things as they put away groceries.

Should she invite him to stay for a little bit? Maybe just long enough to get the courage to open up her package. What if he says no? Bree fidgeted with the bags and shifted her weight from foot to foot.

"You okay?"

"Yeah...do you...maybe want to stay for a little bit? We should probably go over the schedule for this week." She added, hoping he'd see her sense rather than her slight desperation.

"Sure—that's a good idea." He said as he put the last of the cold groceries in her fridge.

Bree led him into the living room, water bottles in hand, and flopped onto the couch. Honestly, she was happy to just be still for a few minutes.

"So, other than the TV interview you have on Thursday, do you have anything else this week I should be aware of?" Noah asked a few minutes later.

Bree paused to think and then scoffed. There was no way she was going to remember without looking at her calendar. Her cardinal rule was to make sure she wrote down all appointments, meetings, interviews, signings, tours, travel, et cetera because otherwise she'd for sure forget them the moment she walked through the door into another room. Bree pulled open her calendar app and returned her gaze to Noah who was watching her intently.

"I have a collaboration with my friend Steph on Friday evening. We're supposed to show off her new fashion line and try a new restaurant at one of the ski resorts over in White Mountain. It's a winter vacation-inspired fashion line, so we're getting some footage throughout the lodge."

Noah furrowed his brow and pulled up his phone, typing in it furiously. Guilt settled into Bree's stomach. How could she forget to include that collab on the calendar she sent him? Bree bit her bottom lip nervously. She really didn't need the security around her constantly. Everything had been quiet since the video comment and the bear, minus the altercation with Kyle at the coffee shop. Honestly, there were only improvements since her dad hadn't even called to berate her recently.

"Okay, what time do we leave?" Noah asked, looking up from his phone.

A forgotten Friday collaboration wasn't his problem. It was hers. Bree needed to make the necessary adjustments to her life if she wanted to be as unassuming as possible and remain the VIP client who got driven places and had her groceries brought in. She sighed.

"Noah, I know it's last minute. It's literally the day after tomorrow. I've known Steph forever and I'm sure her boyfriend will be with her making sure she's alright. You know, Adam. I can go on my own."

"Absolutely." Noah agreed. His phone buzzed and he looked down at it, a frown overtaking his face before he typed back a quick response.

"Really?" Bree asked suspiciously. Nothing she knew of Noah suggested he'd have a client go out after dark on their own when there was a risk to them. Even if it wasn't a super high risk.

"No." He said, a hint of a smile on his face.

"It's super low risk." She tried half-heartedly arguing again.

"Low risk isn't no risk." He said firmly. "Is four on Friday too early? It's a couple hours away."

"Four works great. I'll be ready on time—promise."

"Are you going out before then? Do you need a new dress or anything else last minute that would require you to run an unexpected errand?"

"Nope." She said. "I refuse to buy new clothes to attend events. Used to drive my manager completely mad." A hint of pride clear in her voice. "They'd have my stylist sneak new outfits into my wardrobe. It was entertaining if nothing else. Anyway, I'll be home all day working on finishing up a few projects."

"Perfect. I'll be here to get you for the TV interview around nine next Thursday, and then I'll pick you up at four that Friday for the collaboration. But if you need to leave for any reason, give me a call or shoot me a text. Someone will be here to go with you within the hour."

"Yes, sir," Bree said, giving an overdramatic salute. Then she hesitated for a moment, biting her lower lip thoughtfully. "Actually...could you come a little earlier on Thursday? I need to visit my sister."

"Of course." He replied, standing up. "Do you remember your homework from last week? I'm going to give you a pop quiz at some point." He joked.

Bree groaned—she hadn't even started the homework. Noah hadn't been thrilled when she found out that the only number she knew by heart was Steph's.

"I promise I will get your phone number memorized," Bree said with an innocent smile. "Girl scout's honor."

"Were you even in scouts?"

"Nope."

Noah laughed and shook his head. "I better get back to the office. Thanks for lunch—though you didn't have to do that."

"You're welcome—and I know." She said pointedly, mirroring his own words.

"Touché, Miss Gray. Touché. I'll see you Thursday. Lock the door behind me." He said as they rose and walked toward the door.

"Always." Bree replied before adding, "Drive safe."

"I will, Bree. Lock up and call if you need me."

She nodded and locked the door behind him, watching through the peephole as he walked down the driveway and to his side of the car, carefully observing the street. After he pulled away from the curb, she turned to the package sitting innocently on the table, her pulse increasing rapidly. She walked over and carefully sliced through the tape, slowly lifting the flaps of cardboard. Visions of her sweet bear inundated her mind, but she pushed them away. The odds of it being another traumatizing gift were almost zero.

Right?

Chapter Ten

Noah Hawthorne groaned as yet another person cut him off. The traffic to Rhodes was heavier than usual this morning since the Festival of Kites was happening at one of the local parks. Theo gave Noah a heads up so he could adjust his leave time and still make it to Aubrey with plenty of time to chauffeur her to her interview and wherever else she wanted to go. It had been radio silent from her the last few days, and he found his mind wandering to her whenever he had a quiet moment. What was she doing? Was she safe? Did she think about him? Which just left him irritable because she. was. a. client.

Noah pulled alongside the curb and took in Aubrey's unassuming home. Colorful flowers bloomed in the garden, popping against the deep blue-gray color of her house, and it felt very welcoming. Noah hopped out of the car, careful to lock it behind him, and rapped on her door a few moments later. His heart pounded in his chest, and his hands felt a little sweaty as he waited.

The door opened, and her quiet, understated beauty was like a punch to the stomach. Her hair was up in a curly ponytail, and she had just a dash of makeup on that highlighted the natural beauty of her face and made her gray eyes stand out. Noah nearly groaned as he took in the rest of her. Her jeans were practically painted on and showed off her long legs. Her flirty black tank top was modest, but the lace added a level of flirtatiousness that drew him in. Her eyes met his and brightened, a large smile taking over her face.

"Hi!" She said breathlessly, standing aside so he could walk in.

"Hey, Aubrey." Noah greeted warmly, looking around the room and cataloging it. Nothing seemed out of place.

Aubrey disappeared down the hallway for a moment and came back with a pair of black half-boots and an olive green sweater. She sat on the armchair, apparently lost in thought as she slipped her feet into the shoes. Once her shoes were on, she stood and pushed her arms through the sweater, a shudder running through her. Noah furrowed his brow and appraised the situation. It wasn't cold in here—she wasn't the type to blast the AC in the summer.

"Cold?" He asked, concern coloring his tone.

"No, just ready to get this over with," Aubrey replied, picking up the keys and shoving her phone in her back pocket.

"Well, let's make that happen," He said, holding out his hand for the keys. Aubrey dropped them in his palm and they walked toward the garage to get in the car.

"How was your week?" Noah asked, pulling out of the driveway slowly as he checked for oncoming traffic.

"It was fine." She said, adjusting the temperature controls for her side of the car and turning on the heated seat.

"No errands today?"

"No, the label made it very clear that I needed to get this handled, so this is my main priority."

"Okay—just let me know if anything changes, and I'll put it on the calendar." Every other day, he checked to see if they had any new planned security details for Aubrey, but she had nothing. She was home all week, enjoying her time out of the limelight, and he suddenly found himself wishing that she had something going on far more often just so he had an excuse to spend time with her.

"I meant to ask you, what was in the package you picked up last week? I assume nothing bad since I didn't get a phone call." Noah asked.

He had wanted to stay with her to open it, but she didn't seem overly inclined to have him there while she opened it. He saw how anxious she was and had been wondering if she'd had the nerve to find out what was inside the box. Not that he would've blamed her if it was still sitting unopened on her counter. Her last package bugged him, and it wasn't even his beloved bear.

Aubrey blushed and avoided looking him in the eye. "It was a cute jean jacket from Skyler."

"Who is Skyler?"

Aubrey shrugged, "One of my fans. Skyler's always commenting on my posts and sending nice letters or small gifts. It came from the company instead of Skyler, so I didn't realize it was from them at the time."

"Gotcha. So nothing too traumatic then?"

"Nope, it was actually a really nice surprise." She said, locking the front door as they headed to his car.

"That's good—you deserve nice surprises instead of bad ones," Noah said, looking around the neighborhood. He waved at Mr. Robinson and walked Aubrey over to the car. He opened the door for her and took one more look around as she got into the car. Everything looked normal. The quiet suburban street was devoid of most cars since everyone was either at work or school, and the only vehicles parked along the street were the ones he saw every time he was in the neighborhood.

***

Aubrey

"Can you put in the address for where we need to go?" Noah asked as he slid behind the wheel and pulled away from the curb, his eyes focused on the road.

"No need," Bree said with a small smile. "We're going to visit my sister first, and I can get you there. Stay on this road until we hit the 40, and then we're going to take exit 73 for Alpine Road."

Noah nodded and followed her directions, frowning as they pulled into the hospital parking lot.

"I thought we were going to see your sister." He said, confusion coloring his tone as she unbuckled and started to open her door. Noah reached across and pulled the door shut. "Wait there. I'll come around."

After all this time, Bree thought his bossiness would cause her to bristle less often, but she still felt her hackles rise any time he told her what to do. Still, she sat and waited patiently for him to come around. She understood it was for her safety, she just didn't like being told what to do—didn't like having *choice* taken away from her. Even if it was the same choice she'd have made anyway.

Noah walked around the car, surveying the area, and opened her door. "Ready?" He asked, holding out a hand.

Bree took his hand and stepped out of the car, nearly dropping it right away as heat and awareness flooded through her. Butterflies danced in her stomach, and she tamped them down. Noah was not—and could not be—her boyfriend, she internally scolded them. The butterflies didn't care. Once she was steady on her feet, she dropped his hand and smiled at him, closing the car door while bracing herself for the pity and the questions and all the things she was just...too tired to deal with. It was kind of how she felt about life since the messages and threats had escalated. Everything was just...exhausting. Mostly because her now constant anxiety caused her to see shadows and panic over things that either weren't there or were innocent. Like the package with the jean jacket.

They made their way into the hospital, the originally homey lobby area feeling more sterile than it had last time they walked in. Bree nodded to the volunteer at the desk and made a beeline for the gift shop. Five minutes and a bouquet of mums later, Bree and Noah left the shop and headed for the elevator.

They rode the elevator in silence, Noah seeming to pick up on her desire for quiet. She didn't blame him—all of his questions would likely be answered soon enough anyway. They walked out of the elevator and made a right, walking past a couple of public waiting rooms and some private family waiting rooms. Two turns and a nurses' station later, they found themselves in the 300 West unit, where all of the hopeless cases were left to fade away while their loved ones clung on to a deluded hope for recovery.

They walked up to room 363, and Bree knocked twice, more out of habit than anything else, and walked into the room. She looked ahead and froze, her abrupt stop causing Noah to also stop short. His hand braced her hip to steady her. Bree turned toward him and met his gaze, noting the calculated, yet concerned, look in his eyes. He started to step around her, clearly aware of the increased tension, but she put a hand on his arm. Bree looked up at Noah and gave a slight nod and a smile to indicate she was okay. She stood straighter, turning her attention to the unwelcome body in the room while trying to ignore the warm, protective hand still resting warmly on her hip.

"Justin." She greeted cooly.

***

Noah

Noah didn't know who Justin was, but judging by the tone of Aubrey's voice he had a feeling he wouldn't like him much.

A pair of glassy eyes looked up at Aubrey, the bloodshot look in them giving Noah pause. Noah took his hand off her hip and took a small, intentional step in front of Aubrey, so he was between her and Justin.

"What the hell are you doing here?" Justin asked angrily, his voice and blood-shot eyes clearly indicating that he was under the influence of something.

"Visiting my sister. Besides, it's Thursday." Aubrey said, stressing the day of the week as though she were talking to a toddler. "And you're not welcome here any day." She added with the fire and sauciness he'd come to expect from her.

"She's my woman. I can do whatever I want." Justin said, standing up from his chair quickly.

Aubrey stepped around Noah and threw her hands up in the air in exasperation. "She isn't, Justin! She isn't anyone's 'woman' anymore. She isn't even her own woman!" Bree cried out passionately—anger, frustration, and sadness flooding out of her. She threw her hands down in exasperation. "Get out of here, Justin, and don't come back. Especially on Thursdays."

Justin stalked over and got in Aubrey's face. "You don't tell me what to do."

That was more than enough. Noah ground his teeth, working to keep the unadulterated rage under control, mindful to be gentle as he grabbed Aubrey's elbow and pulled her behind him, putting himself between her and Justin. Noah's chest bumped right against his. Invading personal space tended to do one of two things to people. It aggravated them to make the first move, in which case he could hit them back. Or they shied away from the conflict like the cowards they were. Usually, it was the second one. Unfortunately.

Noah pushed further into Justin's space, forcing him to take a step back, and said in a low tone, "Get away from her."

Justin bared his teeth while sizing Noah up, but Noah recognized the moment he decided he wasn't going to engage in a fight. Pity.

"Whatever. You've always been useless anyway." Justin muttered to Aubrey, shoving past her on his way out the door. Anger rose swiftly in Noah's chest and he moved to follow him out the door to give him a piece of his fis—mind.

A soft hand on his arm stopped him as he started toward the door. "Don't. He isn't worth it. He's more bark than bite." Aubrey said, her pale skin and shaking hand belying the light tone she tried to use to convince Noah she was fine. She wasn't fine.

"He bother you much?" Noah asked gruffly.

"No, he isn't usually here. We all have designated days—well, everyone but Justin. No one is here on Thursdays except me." She said.

She patted his arm gently before moving over and taking the seat next to the one Justin had just vacated. "Hey, Jess. How are you? I'm sorry for the scene. Justin and I never did get along, huh?" She forced a laugh.

"I brought my...my friend Noah with me today, and we have some fresh mums for your room. I know they're your favorite." Her voice broke a little, and she stood up, walking across the room and replacing the old flowers near the sink with fresh water and the new ones they had brought.

While she worked on getting the flowers situated, Noah studied the hospital room and the woman lying in the bed. The room was a small, private room, which was great for surveillance because it meant there was one entry and exit point, and there wasn't another patient and their family and visitors to worry about. Kept things more simple but not completely risk-free. Low risk, but not no risk.

The woman on the bed looked to be around the same age as Aubrey. Their features were similar except for the pallor and the hollow look that came with the muscles atrophying over time. He looked over at Aubrey and found her watching him, observing him quietly in the analytical way she did. His heart ached as tension lined Aubrey's eyes and shoulders—she was clearly expecting judgment of some kind. But she wouldn't get it. Not from him. Never from him.

He cast his mind around for a question he could ask that wouldn't be invasive or offensive. Tact in emotionally heavy situations wasn't his strong suit.

"Tell me about her?" He asked. Generic. Way to go, Hawthorne.

"Like what got her here?" Aubrey asked, her posture stiffening slightly. That was actually what he had wanted to know, but not if she didn't want to share.

Noah tried again. "How about what she was like before?"

Aubrey smiled, her shoulders relaxing. "Not many people care to ask that. Jessica is my older sister. She's about three years older than me. We were close enough in age to play together growing up but not so close that she didn't want to push me out of the room when her friends came over."

Aubrey took a breath, watching Jessica as she continued. "Jess loved being social. She was beautiful and loud and extroverted in the best ways and she had the most amazing laugh. She would always tell me stories to cover up the yelling when Mom and Dad would fight, and she attended all of my school events. She was kind of like a second parent for the most part. Until she became a senior in high school and fell in with the wrong crowd. I had been so excited to go to school with her. I'd been waiting for my freshman year to roll around so we could do things together, and while I knew I'd be the nerdy younger sister, we still would be allowed to attend the same events. Instead, she found out her best friend and her boyfriend had been together behind her back, and everyone in her friend group knew about it—except her. Friendship was everything to Jess. It was the worst kind of betrayal, and nothing I did helped. It sent her into a spiral. She ended up making some new friends—ones that hung out with Justin—and they made a habit of making bad choices. Drugs, drinking, racing through town, driving under the influence, partying, just...all of it. I tried to get her to see what was happening—what she was doing to herself and to us—but it was useless. There was no getting through to her at that point. She wanted the friends, loved the attention, and was convinced that she was completely in love with Justin."

"So what happened?" Noah asked, the quiet beeping of the machines keeping Jessica alive, a steady beat to the story being told—possibly for the first time if

Aubrey's demeanor was anything to judge by.

"I tried to get her out of it for years. There was a party during the Christmas vacation while I was home from college that I knew she was going to, and when I found her, I told her she needed to come home. That she wasn't being smart. She wasn't being safe. I told her that this lifestyle would kill her, and I refused to watch her kill herself. I told her I hated her, Noah. That I hated the choices she was making and that it was turning her into a different person." Bree whispered the last sentence, sniffled, and looked up at the ceiling, her throat working hard to overcome the overwhelming emotion.

Tension crept into his shoulders as he fought against the urge to go and comfort Aubrey. First, he didn't know if it would be welcome. Secondly, he was pretty sure that would be crossing all kinds of professional boundaries. He watched as Aubrey pulled herself together. She took a ragged breath in before continuing. Her heartbreak caused an unfamiliar pain in his chest, and the need to do something...anything...to help her feel better became overwhelming. Unable to help himself, he walked over and sat in the chair next to her, gently placing his hand over hers.

"She had been drinking and doing drugs at that party with Justin and his friends," Aubrey said, her voice still choked up. "She...she never made it home that night. I remember being annoyed because I told my parents that she wasn't home, and they blamed me. My dad yelled at me and told me I should've brought her home. Like I was responsible for her. She was my big sister. She was supposed to be getting in trouble for not looking after me. Not the other way around." Bree laughed humorlessly.

"Anyway, a knock on the door came around two in the morning. We thought she was just intoxicated and had lost her keys or something. It wouldn't have been the first time."

Noah had a sinking feeling he knew where this was going. "Who was at the door, Bree?" Noah asked, her nickname falling from his lips unintentionally, but it felt right. *Bree.*

"Deputy Swanson. He'd been a family friend for years. He was working that night and came to tell my parents that there had been an accident. That...that Jessica had been unresponsive, and they had to resuscitate her before the ambulance could load her up and get her to the hospital. He drove us to the hospital. The doctors said the paramedics lost her a couple more times en route but were able to get her back. Some massive surgery later, and this is where she's been for the past seven years. Nothing has changed."

Noah took a deep breath and squeezed Bree's hand, unsure how to respond.

***

Aubrey

"I'm sorry, Bree. That sounds heavy." Noah said, squeezing her hand again while Bree used the sleeve on her other arm to wipe away her tears. She hadn't ever told anyone about the last conversation she'd had with her sister. Of the festering guilt of what she had said accompanied by the sick 'I told you so' feeling in her gut. Telling Noah had been unexpected, but she felt surprisingly...relieved? It felt like a small weight had been taken off her chest. He just listened to whatever she was willing to say. Which was probably why she had shared more than she planned to. He was a good man.

Bree was pretty sure the last conversation she'd had with her sister would haunt her for the rest of her life—even if she was ever able to talk about it and process it outside of sharing it with Noah. She had told Jess that her decisions would kill her, and they had. Jess was brain-dead. The machines were the only thing keeping her alive. It was a cruel torture. For her. For their parents. For Bree. It shouldn't have been this way.

Sometimes, she wished they hadn't been able to revive her en route. At least then they could've properly grieved. Maybe they could've moved on. But no. Instead, they're stuck in this limbo of their parents holding on to hope, her sister wasting away, and Bree alternating between anger that her father guilted her into being the financially responsible party for Jess's care, and guilt over wishing it could just end. Granted, Jess never would've wanted to be kept 'alive' this way. Not a chance. This whole situation was a lose-lose. For both of them.

Bree watched Noah out of the corner of her eye, waiting for the inevitable look of pity. Of discomfort. People didn't know how to communicate with people who were in these situations. Or most situations that involved grief, actually. A meal train for a couple of weeks, some extra conversation at the supermarket or the store, and then everyone felt good about their charity and went on with their lives. Week three, it's quiet in the house—no meals, no company, no distractions—and the family is still there. Grieving. Lost. Uncertain.

It's worse when you technically don't have anything or anyone to grieve yet. When people still count your brain-dead sister as being 'alive' just like you would anyone else. They act like you don't have a right to grieve. It all was heavy and overwhelming, and she generally avoided thinking about it at all costs. Until she had to explain it to someone new and prepare for the onslaught of uncertain sympathy combined with their confidence that she mustn't be grieving because her sister wasn't fully dead.

Noah looked just as comfortable now as he had when he arrived. While he looked momentarily uncertain when Bree first started going down the emotional rabbit hole, he seemed to level out. "You must've been really sad to lose your sister," Noah said after a momentary silence.

"I mean, she's alive," Bree mumbled, giving the traditionally expected answer.

Noah raised an eyebrow. "Is that how you feel, Bree? Or is that how people think you should feel?"

Bree looked at him in surprise as he watched Jessica's even breathing. No one ever acknowledged that she may feel differently about her sister being gone. Bree felt a small seed of affection take root for the man across from her. Noah seemed to see her in ways no one else ever had.

"I did lose her that day, Noah. But if I'm being honest, I lost her long before that." She sighed and stood slowly, walking over to her sister and gave her hand a tight squeeze. "I have to go to an interview now, Jess, but I'll see you next week." She said softly.

Noah and Bree left the room quietly and headed back out to the car. Bree didn't know about him, but she was eager to get the interview over with and get back home. She was already drained for the day.

Chapter Eleven

Aubrey

Bree plopped into Noah's car and buckled up mechanically, her mind focused on the conversation she and Noah had up in the hospital room. She couldn't shake the guilt that dogged her steps whenever she considered that it might be easier to let her sister go than to live in this tension of waiting for something that may never happen. It was tearing her family apart.

Noah frowned. "How are you?" He asked, turning his attention off her and toward the road as he pulled away from the hospital.

"Okay," Bree said, looking out the window as the businesses rolled by, melancholy taking over and settling deep in her chest. A determined look crossed Noah's face as he moved over into the right lane quickly. He turned onto Fifth Street as Bree furrowed her brow in confusion. They were supposed to be heading to the studio in Nashville and the freeway wasn't this way. Noah drove a few more blocks before he pulled into a parking spot in front of a cute white brick building with black shutters and wooden window boxes full of colorful flowers. Bree's eyebrows rose, and a giant grin took over her face.

"We're getting coffee?!?" She asked.

"We are. I noticed your hands were empty this morning." Noah teased.

Bree bounced excitedly while waiting for Noah to open her door before she bounded toward the coffee shop, Noah trailing dutifully behind her. He held the door open and placed his hand on her lower back as she walked into the coffee shop. The warmth from his hand flooded through her, and she missed it when he pulled away.

The line was thankfully short this morning, and they had fresh cups of coffee and croissants in hand and were back in the car in no time. Noah clicked on the country radio station, and Bree felt her mood lighten as they left Trenton in the rearview. She sipped her coffee while singing along to the King of Country—Mr. George Strait—and felt as though her joy just might be contagious if the look on Noah's face was any indication.

They pulled into the station a few hours later, and Bree turned to look at Noah. "Thanks for the coffee and jam session. I didn't realize how much I needed that." She reached out and squeezed his hand warmly.

Noah's voice deepened as his hand squeezed hers gently. "Any time, Bree."

He looked around the parking lot, apparently looking for anyone who might be hiding in the shadows, but it looked pretty normal to Bree. There was a news van in the parking lot and several other employee cars. Nothing out of the ordinary for a work day. Once he was certain no one was lurking, Noah got out of the car and opened Bree's door, offering his hand to help her out of the car.

He held onto her hand a split second longer than necessary, causing butterflies to erupt as their fingers gently twined together. Bree reveled in the warmth of his hand in hers. Noah squeezed her hand gently before dropping it to escort her across the parking lot. His eyes were roving constantly to make sure there was no trouble. When they reached the entrance, Noah opened the door for her, inclining his head to indicate she should go first. Bree nodded her thanks and walked in, immediately wishing she could step back outside into the brief, quiet moment where Noah's hand was in hers.

Instead, she was immediately surrounded by people in her space—touching her, talking to her, and just being too close, though she knew they were just doing their jobs.

"I think her hair should be in a plait—" One of the stylists said.

"She's not a teenager in a YA novel. Her hair doesn't need to be in a plait." One of the other stylists argued.

Another set of hands was pulling at her current wardrobe selection and making tsking sounds to voice their disapproval. "You cannot wear that. I won't stand for it. Maddie! Grab an outfit—something that screams summer with class."

A young woman nodded and practically ran down the hall to the dressing room. She didn't miss this. At all. As the voices got louder around her, she started to feel as though she was being caged in, and panic threatened to overwhelm her. Her breath started coming in quicker, and it felt like the walls were beginning to move in. She couldn't *breathe*.

Mumbled complaints broke up the steady stream of voices around her as a warm body shoved through the crowd and came to a stop next to her. She looked up at Noah in surprise, gratitude filling her. His eyes met hers and softened as he rested his hand on her hip, gently using his body to effectively create and maintain space around them. "You okay?" He asked, his voice rough.

Bree nodded, though she honestly wasn't sure. She just wanted to go home. He seemed to be able to read that on her face and grimaced. He used his shoulders to clear a path and led her down the hall to the room where she would get ready. Once she sat down in the white chair, Noah stepped back into the corner, and she was once again surrounded by people doing the flight of the bumble bee. She smiled and nodded as people chatted around her, messing with her hair and makeup and giving her last-minute talking points, but her eyes were fixed on Noah, who held her gaze with a quiet determination that gave her the strength to sit there. He'd get her out if she said the word. She knew he would.

"Alright, you're ready. Let's go." The public relations lady said when she finished talking through what Bree should say—though Bree'd honestly forgotten ninety percent of it already. She gave one final look to Noah, who gave her an encouraging nod. He would be there. She was safe. With that in mind, she let them lead her down the hall to the final interview of her career.

***

"And, last but definitely not least, tell us about this upcoming gala that you'll be speaking at." The reporter said, leaning in toward Bree as though she were actually interested in what Bree had to say. Though with the number of times Bree'd been interrupted in the last hour, she didn't think the reporter actually cared.

"Thanks for asking—I'd love to talk about that! The Gala will be held at The

Trenton Center for the Arts on a Friday evening in November—the day after Thanksgiving. There will be a lot of celebrities and other notable individuals attending and tickets are available to the general public as well. The building and grounds have been secured for the venue and will be closed that night to the general public, so buying a ticket is a must if you plan to attend.

We are raising money for families struggling with a loved one's addiction, and that will primarily take the form of a silent auction. General donations can be made to the organization as well. I'll be there, and I hope you will be too." Bree said, issuing the invitation to viewers, a genuine smile on her face for the first time. Hopefully getting word out would increase attendance, and thus the revenue, at the event.

They wrapped up and made the requisite small talk while Bree counted down the seconds until she could walk out of this room and get back to Noah. She'd missed him the last few days. She hated the publicity that came along with celebrity life, but if it meant seeing Noah more often, maybe she'd consider taking more endorsement deals or interviews. She shook her head. That was ridiculous. She was an adult, not some lovestruck teenager trying to create an excuse for her crush to walk her to class.

Finally, the news crew indicated Bree was free, and she hustled out to the main waiting area, which was set up like a little living room. There were often security or entourage members hanging out in the space, but today, it was just Noah. He turned when Bree walked in the room his eyes immediately found hers and scanned her quickly. He was always checking her for physical or emotional distress and keeping a pulse on how she was doing. It was kind of nice.

"Ready?" He asked warmly, walking over and standing close enough for her to feel the heat from his body. Their hands hung down at their sides, and their fingers brushed lightly. A shot of pure heat ran through her, and she looked up at him. His eyes darkened, and she had the distinct impression that he felt that same jolt of electricity.

"I am. Let's get out of here." Bree said with a smile. Noah rested his hand on her lower back and guided her out of the recording studio and into the car. The drive home was uneventful, and she found herself wishing she had a reason for him to stay with her longer.

"So what will you do with the rest of your day?" Bree asked as they got out of the car, desperate to add just a few more minutes with him.

He lingered as well, moving far more slowly than normal as they entered the house. "I have a meeting with the guys this afternoon and then I'll go through some inquiries from prospective clients. Probably spend most of it on the phone. You?"

"I have a small commission to finish up so I can send it out next week," Bree said, hanging up her purse and returning her keys to the bowl by the door. She took off her sweater and tossed it on the back of her couch so she could return it down the hall later. Noah leaned on the front door and watched her, a small smile on his face.

"A commission?" Noah asked.

"I have a little side business selling art," Bree said, vaguely surprised when she found she wanted to include Noah more in this aspect of her life which was wholly hers.

"Ah yes—the mysteriously large packages that get sent out periodically. You'll have to show me them sometime." He said, smiling.

"I'd like that," Bree told him, surprised to find that she meant it. Very few people knew—or needed to know—but she wanted Noah to know...everything. The phone in her pocket buzzed and she pulled out her phone, a local number she was unfamiliar with on the screen. She smiled apologetically at Noah before swiping to answer the call.

"Hello?" She said, as Noah watched her carefully. Again with the soft breathing.

"Who is it?" Noah asked, loudly enough that the person on the other end of the line must've heard him.

"Whore!" The male voice spat before hanging up.

Bree pulled the phone away from her ear and stared at it for a moment before bursting into tears.

Noah looked alarmed and wrapped his arms around her, pulling her in close. "What happened, Bree? Who was it?"

"I..." She sobbed harder—the heaviness of the last few weeks settling on her like a ton of bricks. "I..." When she couldn't get anything out, she stopped trying and let the tears flow.

***

Bree rang herself out of tears and was certain she had a dazed look on her face as Noah pulled away from her. He reached out slowly and wiped her eyes with his hand. "Bree?" Noah said softly.

She looked at him, sniffling rather loudly. Embarrassment crept in as her brain processed the fear and anguish.

"Did something bad happen?"

She shook her head adamantly.

"Who was it?"

She shrugged her shoulders, her bottom lip beginning to tremble again.

"You didn't know the caller?"

She shook her head. If she knew who it was, she could report him. Or block him. Or something.

"Was it a man?"

She nodded.

"Did he say anything to you?"

"Yes." She whispered, the man's voice still echoing loudly in her ear.

"What did he say?"

"He called me a whore." She croaked out, her tears silently beginning to fall down her face again despite her attempts to hold them in.

"Has he ever called you before?" Noah asked through his teeth, his jaw ticking rhythmically.

"Yes," Bree said softly.

Noah frowned, "How many times?"

"At least seven." Bree cried. "But he doesn't usually talk. He just...breathes."

"He breathes?"

"Yeah."

"Is it always from the same number?"

"No. It's usually different numbers. Today...today it was from a local area code."

Noah's eyes flew to hers, a look of alarm in them before he schooled his features.

"What? What is it?"

Noah hesitated.

"I'm a grown woman, Noah. Tell me."

He sighed. "A normal...whoever it was could just be getting their rocks off on scaring and tormenting you but given the note, the DMs, and the situation with the press, if it was a stalker then we have to assume local means the stalker could—and likely will—escalate further. It means..." He ran a hand through his hair in exasperation, a tortured look on his face. "It means you could be in more danger than we anticipated." He said evenly.

"You'll keep me safe," Bree said, resting an arm on him reassuringly. "I'm not one of the women in horror movies who is too stupid to live. I may not like you ordering me around, but I do understand when it is necessary. We'll catch him." She said, feeling unsettled by Noah's concern and her own response to it. She would make it through this. There was no alternative.

Chapter Twelve

Noah

The computer cursor blinked repeatedly as Noah stared blankly at the form that needed to be completed in order for Eli to close one of his contracts. Instead of focusing on the paperwork, his eyes had taken on a mind of their own and drifted to the corner of the screen that currently read 1:35. Maybe Theo would need to take a look at the computer to make sure it was functioning properly. It had to have been at least ten minutes or so since the last time Noah had checked the time and it had said 1:32. Just under two hours left until he could leave to grab Bree for her collaboration that evening.

A knock interrupted his thoughts. "Come in," Noah called.

Theo walked in and closed the door behind him with a soft click. Noah's senses immediately went on alert. Normally, they share closed-door information at the morning staff meetings, but Theo hadn't shared anything this morning.

"Hey, Theo. What's up?" Noah asked, putting his computer to sleep and giving him his full attention.

Theo sat in the chair across from Noah's desk and picked up the stress ball that permanently sat on the corner, squeezing it until his fingers turned white. "I want to talk to you about Aubrey Gray." He said, his hands tightening a little more.

Noah furrowed his brow. "What about her?"

"You asked me to take a look into her family, socials, background, and related things."

"I did," Noah said, confusion lacing his tone.

"I haven't been able to deep dive into her parents yet. That's next on my list, but...Have you seen her socials?" Theo asked, making eye contact with Noah.

"No, I haven't."

"Pull up her Instagram," Theo said, gesturing to the phone sitting on the desk, alarm set and ready to alert Noah when it was time to go and pick Bree up.

"Why?"

"Just...do it, please," Theo said, his jaw ticking.

Noah went to Bree's Instagram page, her gorgeous, joyful self smiling right at him. The pictures showed her beauty and radiant joy, but failed to show off her spirit and backbone, which were simultaneously the bane of his existence and two of the things he deeply admired about her. Warmth filled his chest, and Noah smiled at the carefree look on her face. He would pay good money to see that look on her face now. "Okay..." He said, looking at Theo for further direction.

"You see the most recent five to ten pictures?"

"Yep."

"Look at these comments," Theo said as he handed Noah his phone.

Noah scrolled through the screenshots one at a time, nausea, disgust, and rage taking over as he read more and more of the vile messages.

"It's been getting worse. Not only have the comments been coming in more often, but they're also getting more vulgar. More brazen." Theo added, anger lacing each word.

Noah found himself agreeing, his muscles taut as he continued to read. It was message after message of things they think about her. Things they'd do to her. Things they'd like to show her. Some chick named Skyler seemed to adamantly oppose any and all of the creeps, but she was just one of many who tried to keep the people in line who had no interest in wasting the perceived anonymity that the internet provides.

"Find them." Noah ground out, handing Theo's phone back to him while his stomach soured. "Let me know if they pose a threat to my—to Bree."

"Consider it done," Theo said as he stood up to go. "Your Bree, huh?" Theo added cheekily.

"Shut up," Noah said good-humoredly. Theo grinned and headed for the door.

"And Theo?" Noah said.

"Yeah?"

"Order the security cameras, and let's get them installed this weekend. The sooner, the better."

Theo nodded before walking out of the room.

Noah looked at the clock on the computer—1:53—and stood up, ramming his fingers through his hair. He wanted to break something. Specifically the three-dimensional faces of the sick men who had written those things to Bree. About Bree. Noah shoved his chair away from the desk and stormed through the office and down the stairs until he reached the training room. He shrugged off his suit jacket and laid it on the bench before going to town on the nearest punching bag. Every time he hit it, he thought of one of the messages that had been left for Bree. Had she been reading that vile crap?

One of them talked about what they would do if they found her home alone without her bodyguard around—Noah stopped short, the punching bag swinging back and catching him in the stomach. Oof. They knew Noah was with Bree? How would they know that? Did they know where she lived? Panic fluttered in his chest, and his heart raced. What if the offender decided today was the day to show up? Noah wasn't there...Bree was home alone, just like that sicko wanted.

Noah turned abruptly and grabbed his suit jacket, jogging for his office. He threw his keys and computer into his briefcase before practically sprinting out the door. He had to get to Bree. Noah picked up the phone when he got into the car and tried to give her a call, but her phone only rang a couple of times before going to voicemail. He waited for the longest minute in the history of man before calling again. This time, it went straight to voicemail. Fear caused his heart to stutter in his chest as he pressed down on the gas. His girl could be in trouble, and he needed to get there.

Noah drifted around the corner into the neighborhood and raced out of the car, uncaring of how it appeared to Mr. Robinson or anyone else. He pounded desperately on Aubrey's door, praying she was okay and would be able to answer. He'd give her thirty seconds before he kicked in it. That would be quite a sight. Mr. Robinson would for sure be on the phone with the police in that case.

There were a series of light thuds on the other side of the door before a harried-looking Bree answered, a shoe in her hand and one on her foot, cell phone pressed to her ear. Noah walked into the living room trying to dispel the cloud of anger and fear that raged through him. He scanned Bree as she spoke on the phone, checking her for any injuries before letting loose a breath as he realized she was unharmed. Safe. And he would keep her that way. Or die trying.

"Hello?" Bree's exasperated tone drew his attention back to her, a small frown line marring her beautiful face. "Hello?" She said again while trying to slip on her last heel. She teetered and fell backward before he could get to her, landing promptly on her bottom. "Ouch!" She reached for the shoe that was on her foot and chucked it across the room, narrowly missing Noah's face.

"UGH!" Bree grunted, clearly frustrated by whatever was going on with the call. She didn't say anything else before ending the call and chucking her phone across the room onto the chair, where it bounced safely.

"Are you okay?" Noah asked, walking over and offering her a hand.

"I'm fine." She grumbled, a deep blush spreading across her face. She accepted his hand, letting go as soon as she was steadily standing in front of him, her bare toes resting on the hardwood floor.

"What was that about?" He asked.

"Just wondering if whoever sold my picture sold my cell number too." She said, anger lacing every word. "I got another call."

"Did he say anything to you?"

"Not this time."

"Is it the same number?"

"As yesterday? Yes."

"I'll make a note and have Theo look into it. He's also going to be by this weekend to install the security cameras we talked about."

"Noah, I don't want security cameras." She argued. "You can't just order them to be put on my house!"

"You're being unreasonable, Bree," Noah said, anger and relief still pulsing through him simultaneously.

"I'm being unreasonable? This is my life. This is my home. You can't just waltz in here and tell me what to do. We are a team, and we make decisions together. If you want to change something, we sit down and talk about it like adults. Hear both sides, write a pro and con list. *Something.*" She said stubbornly, looking up at him for the first time since her tirade started. Her wrath seemed to pause for a moment as she looked at Noah. Truly looked at him. A frown marred her beautiful face. "You're early." She said, surprise mingling with concern on her face as she continued. "And angry. What happened?"

"Theo popped into my office this afternoon," Noah said.

A look of confusion crossed her face. "Is he okay?" She asked.

"He's fine." Her inherent concern for others—especially those she loved—was one of the things Noah liked about her. "Did you happen to see the comments on some of your last pictures and videos?"

A look of understanding crossed her face. "The new comments." She sighed. "I did, and it's nothing new, Noah. These creeps come out of the woodwork from time to time."

"Theo said it's been happening a lot more frequently. He said it has escalated. The frequency. Bree, the threats." Noah practically croaked out the last word, taking a deep breath and struggling to reign in the violent emotions coursing through him.

"It's not a big deal, Noah. It's just the internet."

Anger flashed through him, temporarily giving him a feeling other than disgust, which had consumed him since reading those messages himself. She read them? He wanted to hunt each slime ball down and rip them to shreds for threatening Bree. For exposing her to such vile thoughts. The blood rushed in his ears, and he felt like his self-control was being torn to shreds by this woman who seemed used to being on the receiving end of unconscionable behavior. Which meant there was someone—dead or alive—who had treated her that way. Who made her feel it was normal. And he wanted to end them. Violently.

"Can I use your restroom?" He asked Bree through clenched teeth, desperately needing a moment to pull himself together now that he knew she was okay and back under his protection.

"Of course," she said brightly, her mood apparently unaffected by the boundless number of creepy men on the internet. "I'm going to go back into my room and finish getting ready. I shouldn't be but five to ten minutes."

"And Noah?"

"Hmm?"

"No cameras. Please."

Noah frowned and headed down the hall, taking a minute to splash some water on his face and take in a deep breath. He needed to chill. Aubrey Gray was a client—nothing more. He couldn't make this personal which meant he couldn't take personal offense. He was always bothered by the crap that people put out on the internet—things they would never say or do in real life because they're behind a keyboard, and they think that it can cover their identity enough to get away with everything.

Ha. Nothing on the internet is anonymous if you know where to look and how to mine the information. But regardless, he needed to present a calm, put-together front. He did not need to look like a raging lunatic who was going to go after every man who dared to threaten his woman. He wanted to protect her. He felt a burning need to keep her safe in his very bones. But Aubrey was not his woman. Even if he wished that weren't true at the moment.

No, that had to be the adrenaline talking. He wasn't looking for a relationship. Though if he was, he'd look no farther than—nope, not going there. He didn't have time for dating. Definitely not a former celebrity. Especially not a client. No way was that going to happen. Not only was it against company policy—a policy he wrote himself—but most women didn't understand the commitment level his job required. They didn't understand the deep-seated need he had to protect. And they didn't trust him to be loyal while on assignment which is what stung the most. All it did was end in heartache for everyone... well, mostly for them. Noah didn't let himself get attached enough for it to be a problem. Not after Sarah.

He walked back out into the living room and did a perimeter check to make sure all of the doors and windows were closed and locked before they left. After confirming that all points of entry and egress were in fact secure, he sat on the couch to wait for Aubrey to be ready.

A soft rhythmic tapping drew his attention to the hallway a while later, and his tongue suddenly felt as though it were glued to the top of his mouth. Noah's pulse raced as he slowly took in the vision that was Aubrey Gray. Her curly hair was down, her face lightly made up, a shy smile on her face. She was wearing a white halter sundress with a pair of wedge sandals that functioned like heels and made her legs look as though they went on for days. Wow.

Noah cleared his throat. "You...you look beautiful." He told her honestly—incapable of stopping the compliment from falling from his lips. A pretty pink blush painted her cheeks and he found himself wondering just how far that blush went.

"Thank you." She said, clearly a little uncomfortable with the compliment which was oddly endearing. Noah couldn't count how many celebrities or other clients he'd worked with who would get dolled up regularly and still riffle around for compliments from their entourage like they were going through a junk drawer.

"I just need to grab my a sweater and my purse and we can head out." She said walking across the room to fetch her things from the coat closet near the front door. Bree grabbed her things quickly and met Noah by the garage door, a soft smile on her face. "Let's go."

Chapter Thirteen

"So, tell me about this collaboration," Noah said, trying to get Bree to talk to him as they got into the car and backed out of the driveway. He wanted to know anything she was willing to share about herself. Everything. Purely as a professional matter—it's easier to protect people when you know their lives inside-out.

Bree sighed, a small frown overtaking her face. "It's been on the calendar for a while, but I forgot to actually add it to the calendar because I talk to Steph so often there was no way I was going to forget it. Steph's winter line is coming out this fall, and she needs some promo photos for it. The lodge over in White Mountain reached out to her because they're opening up a high-end Italian restaurant. They offered to let Steph use their grounds in exchange for trying out the new restaurant so they could gain some traction. So we'll photograph her fashion line with the models and then create content around the updated lodge and new restaurant, including a short live. The goal is to make it seem like people on the other end of the phone are getting an exclusive, insider sneak peek. It makes them feel important, but feels a little like emotional manipulation to me." Bree muttered quietly.

"Sounds like marketing to me." Noah chuckled lightly. "You seem sad about it, though. Are you anticipating trouble?"

"No, I love Steph. She's my best friend. She's engaging, smart, and super down-to-earth. Most importantly, she said there'd be Italian food, and it's my favorite, so she didn't have to ask me twice," Bree said, a light laugh at the end of the statement brightening her overall countenance.

"So what's got you down?" Noah asked.

"It is going to sound ungrateful." Bree hedged, fidgeting with the coat in her lap. Noah wanted to reach over and place his hand on hers to still it. She didn't need to be anxious. Not with him.

"Try me." He said, not sure he'd met a less self-centered celebrity than Bree.

"It's twofold. One…I'm doing some of the modeling." Bree covered her face in mortification. It was kind of adorable.

"You'll do a great job," Noah said seriously. "What's the second thing?"

"I never wanted to be famous or have a singing career." She said softly.

Shock rippled through him. "You didn't want to be a singer? Or famous?" He repeated kind of dumbly.

"Nope." She said, popping her 'p' in the adorable way she did when she was confident about her answer. "So doing things like this collaboration—even though I'm doing it strictly for Steph—is just so far out of my comfort zone. I don't like to use my fame for personal gain, and imposter syndrome is real, even all these years later. I'm just a small-town girl from Kentucky." She shrugged.

"So, how did you end up where you are?"

A heavy sigh from the passenger seat had him drifting his eyes over to her briefly before refocusing on the road in front of them.

"I was on social media just for me," Bree said. "I had a lot of followers because I built a community that was fun. Silly dance routines, updates on the books I'd been reading. Booktok is a fun place to hang out—there are a lot of really fun people. I was just there to socialize since I couldn't really do anything. I was lonely and desperate to connect with people. One day, I filmed myself while I was singing one of the songs I had written and posted it and it went viral. At first, it was fun singing the different songs people requested. My follower count went up, and more people started interacting with my posts so I started earning money from it. Then I was approached by the record label and offered a significant amount of money if I signed with them."

Noah furrowed his brow in confusion. "You don't seem like the type to take a job she'd hate for money." He said slowly, hoping he didn't inadvertently offend Bree with his comment.

She laughed lightly. "You'd be correct. I told them I'd think about it—just so I wouldn't be considered rude. I wasn't going to take it. I told my mom about it, and she and my dad got super emotional, telling me they'd run out of money and were not going to be able to pay Jessica's medical bills and how this amount of money could be life-changing. Life-saving. We wouldn't have to cut off life support from my sister because of our inability to pay. And that meant I couldn't turn the record deal down. I would've been a monster. What kind of heartless woman lets her sister die because she didn't want to take a well-paying job just because of a little introversion and anxiety?"

"So you have been trapped in a world you hate in order to help keep your sister's care afloat," Noah said, understanding dawning on him. It sounded like Bree had too much responsibility for far too long.

"Yep," Bree said.

"That sounds awful," Noah said honestly. "I can't imagine staying in a job I hate—even if it was well paying."

"So security is your dream job, then?" Bree asked, turning her head toward Noah and observing him quietly.

"It was. I really enjoyed working as a police officer after my time in the Corps, and going into private security was a logical next step. There wasn't another security agency in our state, so I started the business and met some of my best friends."

"Was?" Bree probed gently.

"I probably shouldn't be sharing this since you're a client." He told her, laughing lightly, but sobering quickly. That was an incredibly true statement. His mental filters must've stayed behind in the living room along with his jaw which was probably still on the floor after seeing Aubrey.

"I won't tell anyone. And I'll even leave it out of my Yelp review." She said with a wink, humor lacing her tone.

"Does anyone even use Yelp anymore?"

"Nope." She said.

"Well, before this contract, I was starting to fall out of love with celebrity security. There was a level of entitlement and ungratefulness that grated on my nerves. Plus, there were no lines people wouldn't cross. Whether that was our client trying to go against advice, or trying to come onto me after I said no, or someone trying to suck up to me so they could get in with the entourage, it was just never-ending. The lies, the deception, the self-centeredness, the entitled thinking that made people believe they were above the law or above other people. It wore on me. I was ready to take a break—maybe just handle the paperwork side of the business once my current contracts were complete."

"And now...?" Bree asked quietly.

"Now I don't think all celebrities are that way. You reminded me of why I started this business in the first place and challenged my thinking in the best way."

That pretty blush stained her cheeks again and he reached his hand over and placed it over hers, giving a soft squeeze, lingering for just a moment before forcing himself to pull it away.

"I've met some really good people in the industry. Maybe you've just been stuck with the wrong ones." She offered helpfully.

Bree was always looking for the silver lining—when did she think of herself? Of what she wanted? He just wanted her safe.

"Bree, why don't you want cameras at your house? It really would add a helpful layer of security. Even though it is more reactive than proactive, it can help in the investigation." Noah said, trying to get her to see reason.

Bree frowned, and Noah wanted to take back his question. But it was important. *She* was important. He waited and saw her shoulders drop out of the corner of his eye.

"When I got into the industry, I had a hard time making friends," Bree said quietly. "As an introvert, it can be challenging to put yourself out there. Plus, I wasn't interested in the party scene. One of the other singers at the label befriended me. I went over to her house, which had security like I did. A guard at the gate, cameras, the whole nine yards." Bree said.

Noah felt his stomach sink. He had a feeling he wasn't going to like where this story was going.

"She had cameras everywhere. I was desperate for a friend—Steph hadn't moved to California yet. She was still in Witsec, and we weren't in contact. She invited me over for a movie night with some of the other women in the industry. Wine, popcorn, chocolates...I was excited and wanted to fit in. Then the men came over." Bree said, a small shudder moving through her.

"What happened, Bree?" Noah asked, focusing on keeping his voice calm.

Bree took a deep breath as though she were steeling herself against the memories. "I was assaulted. I filed a report, but nothing was done. I was told that it was my own fault for being at the party, and I was intoxicated. That I didn't really fight back." She laughed humorlessly. "For the next year, I would periodically get a text from an unknown number with the video of my assault. I went back to the department, but the video came from burner numbers. No way to track who it was. It kept happening until I changed my number."

"Bree..." Noah felt like he'd been punched in the gut. When Bree pushed back on cameras, it never occurred to him that the reason would be from something so...heinous. He wanted to go find the officers and court that dealt with her report. They should be fired—at minimum. He felt sick.

"So that's why I don't want cameras at my house. I don't want to give anyone the ability to use footage of me—especially in my home—against me. Whether it's for something serious—like being assaulted—or something silly like being clumsy. I know how the internet works." She said seriously.

"I'm sorry, Bree. I didn't know."

"I know. But that's why it's important to make decisions as a *team*. I won't put myself in that position again, Noah. Not unless the threat to my life outweighs the risk of a video being shared. It took years of therapy to come to terms with what happened to me, and it still keeps me up some nights."

Noah nodded and let silence fill the car for several minutes. He wasn't sure how to help her, but he could back off on the camera thing. She knew they were an option and, given the information she just shared, he would need to let her come to him. He still felt cameras were a good idea—but while he knew his team would treat the footage with the utmost care and confidentiality, the idea of anyone having footage of Bree—even if it was innocent footage—made him simultaneously want to hit something and vomit.

"Alright, pop quiz time," Noah said, attempting to bring Bree out of her thoughts. Though this was a non-negotiable—Bree had to have his number memorized.

Bree looked over at him, surprised. "Why do I have to do this again? You're in my contacts."

"Because, as Peter would tell you, 'only forty-nine percent of people in the U.S. have somewhere between two to five phone numbers memorized.' What if there's an emergency? What if you don't have access to your phone or contacts and need to get in touch with me?"

"I don't see that happening," Bree grumbled before rattling off his phone number, a smile teasing the corners of her mouth.

"A-plus! Now keep that information stored in that beautiful brain of yours so you always have it." He said seriously.

"For tonight, though, do you have a schedule of what we'll be doing at this collab?" Noah asked her.

She laughed, and he suddenly found himself wondering what exactly he'd gotten himself into.

***

Aubrey

Noah's words flitted through her mind on the drive up the mountain. From his thoughts on her own accidental trip into stardom to his own cynicism toward working celebrity details. She imagined it was grueling, and adding people who didn't listen to you after pulling long days and putting your own life and reputation on the line for them would be doubly difficult. Guilt swarmed through her as she thought about how difficult she'd initially been with Noah when he'd been trying to keep her safe. It had to have been frustrating for a man like him, who was used to giving orders and having them obeyed.

Noah's eyes were firmly fixed straight ahead as they turned around the last bend of the tree-lined road leading to the resort. They rounded the corner, and the large lodge with pretty lights took her breath away. While there wouldn't be any snow for a while, the owners wanted to get their lodge in the front of people's minds before snow season arrived. In this business, you had to be ahead of the curve, not behind it. Being behind it could mean the difference between a successful launch and failure. Bree really loved the family who owned the lodge—she'd stayed there on one of her trips through this part of the country—so hopefully, the marketing campaign was successful.

They pulled up under the eve and left the car with the valet. Noah walked over and opened the door for her, his warm hand resting on her lower back. Bree smiled up at him, and he smiled down back down at her. They stayed like that for just a moment before the doors opened, drawing their attention inside.

"Aubrey!" An excited voice rang out, and a pair of long arms wrapped around Bree.

"Steph!" Bree said joyfully. "How are you? We haven't talked in forever!"

"It's been like a week," Steph argued playfully.

"That's forever when it comes to you." Bree joked back, warmth flowing through her.

"I couldn't answer the phone and talk to you without spoiling it," Steph replied seriously.

"Spoiling what?" Bree asked, linking her arm through Steph's.

"Want to guess?" Steph whispered conspiratorially as they walked into the lodge.

"You are moving to Rhodes and are going to be my neighbor?" Bree asked, dutifully playing along.

Steph chuckled. "I wish. That town is gorgeous. But nope!" Steph pulled her arm out of Bree's and held out her left hand to show off the shiny diamond resting on her finger. "I'm getting married! Adam proposed to me last weekend." She sighed dreamily.

A large grin took over Bree's face. "I'm so happy for you! Congratulations!! Your ring is beautiful," Bree said excitedly, holding Steph's hand up and examining it from every angle.

"Who's the babe traveling with you?" Steph asked, giving a quick side glance at Noah before returning her attention to me.

"You don't recognize him?" Bree asked, tilting her head slightly.

Steph shook her head. "Should I?"

"He's my bodyguard," Bree admitted quietly, though she would've loved to be able to dish something a little more fun.

"That's Noah?" Steph asked, light shining through her eyes. "Are you going to introduce us?"

"Nope. You've got your matchmaker face on, and I don't need a man. Especially right now."

"Are those internet creeps still giving you trouble? Because I told you, you can always come stay with us."

"Steph, your house is practically Fort Knox."

She shrugged. "But the paparazzi can't get in. And neither can just about anyone else." She said, laughing. She caught sight of her fiancé across the room and squeezed Bree's elbow.

"Excuse me. I'm going to talk to Adam for a minute, and then we can get started. I'm so happy you agreed to do this with me!"

"I'll be here when you get back," Bree reassured her, smiling as Steph walked quickly across the room and flung herself into her fiancé's arm as though it had been weeks since they'd last seen each other rather than minutes.

"Everything good?" A deep, soothing voice whispered in Bree's ear, the scent of coffee and caramel drifting toward her, a warm body close to her back. Her pulse raced, and heat flooded her cheeks. A warm hand came to rest on the small of her back when she failed to answer, and Bree could imagine a small furrow on Noah's brow as he worried.

"It's all good," Bree told Noah seriously. "Steph just wanted to tell me that she got engaged."

Noah watched me quietly. "How does that make you feel?" He asked.

"I'm happy for her. She's my best friend. We don't get to see each other much—our schedules are usually opposite—but we try to get together for coffee or a bookstore trip whenever we're both in the area, and we try to vacation together at least once a year."

"I haven't had a chance to meet Steph. Have you met Adam?" He asked, his voice still close to Bree's ear, causing a hot shiver to run down her spine.

"Yeah—we met last year when we all went on vacation together. He has always been super nice and attentive. They met while she was under his protection when he worked for the feds."

"Really? When he worked for Witsec?"

"Yep."

"Huh. I didn't know that. I knew they met on the job, but I didn't realize she'd been a client. Should she really be an influencer, then? I mean putting her face out there could be dangerous." The disapproval rang clearly in his voice.

Bree shrugged. "Aside from the fact their home is a slightly smaller version of Fort Knox, you'd have to be at least a little crazy to cross Adam because he's got a reputation in the more...undesirable circles of the world. If the term 'morally gray' had a picture next to it in the dictionary, it would be a photograph of Adam's face. Besides, the people she had testified against died in prison. So there's no one looking for her. Adam would never endanger Steph."

"I know—I just..."

"Worry?" Bree asked.

"Yeah."

"I know. You don't have to worry about Adam and Steph, though. They're good. And between Adam and his team, she is well cared for." Bree looked up into Noah's eyes, and he looked down into hers as her breath caught in her chest.

"Bree...you don't have to worry either. I'll keep you safe." His eyes drifted down to her lips, and she cursed the zookeeper in her stomach, who let out the entire butterfly population. They moved infinitesimally closer to each other, Noah's head leaning slightly toward hers. Her heart leaped, and the butterflies went wild.

"Bree!" Steph's voice shouted from across the room. Bree jerked her head back and Noah cleared his throat, taking a small step back and dropping his hand from Bree's lower back. Bree glanced at him before turning her attention over to Steph.

Steph smiled at Bree knowingly across the room. "Time to get started." She said, giving a small eyebrow wiggle.

Bree laughed, trying to ignore her racing pulse, tap-dancing butterflies, and the heat staining her cheeks.

"I'm ready!" Bree called back.

"I bet you are." She said cheekily. The blush in Bree's cheeks burned hotter. Bree walked quickly across the room, hyperaware of Noah's presence. He was like her very own book boyfriend come to life. There to provide comfort because he was always close by, but also capable of violence if the situation called for it. Minus the whole being her boyfriend part.

"Steph, this is Noah. Noah, Stephanie."

"Nice to meet you," Noah said as he reached out to shake Steph's hand, his body still close enough for Bree to soak in some of his warmth.

"Nice to meet you too! Thanks for taking care of our girl." Steph said seriously.

Bree mentally facepalmed. "Anyway," She said, drawing out the word in hopes of changing the topic of conversation. "What are we going to attempt to finish tonight? And most importantly, is word of your engagement out?"

"We want to do some shots of us in my new fashion line just casually around the lodge, showcasing the different amenities. We're trying to give best friends night out vibes. Then you and some of the other models will do some photographs around the lodge. Then we'll set the other models free, and the four of us will have dinner in the new restaurant and film some of that. I can't wait! And no, we haven't made our engagement public yet. Why?"

"Might want to hand over the jewels to Adam then," Bree said with a smile. "And sounds good. I'm all over girls' night out."

"I'll take them over to him. I haven't seen O'Shea in forever." Noah offered, holding his hand out for Steph's ring. Steph smiled at him gratefully and placed the ring in his palm. Noah looked at Bree for a moment before walking over to where Adam was standing. Bree watched as he slapped Adam on the back and handed over the rings, both men smiling and chatting as they watched their women. Well, Adam was watching his woman. Noah was watching his client. Not the same thing. Though sometimes it felt like Noah looked at Bree the way Adam looked at Steph. Like she was the sun.

The next three hours were an interesting mix of fun and grueling as they traipsed around the lodge changing into several different outfits—all equally comfortable and stunning—and filmed in various areas. The food shots were

Bree's favorite because the food was to die for. Ten out of ten would recommend. Bree and Steph chatted for a few minutes before Noah walked over to Bree and placed his hand lightly on her lower back.

"Ready to go?" He asked softly. Bree nodded, gratefully—her social battery had run out ages ago but she so rarely got to see Steph in person that she forged through.

"I'll see you later, Steph! I can't wait to see the footage." Bree said, smiling and waving as they walked out the door, and the valet opened her car door.

"Thanks," Bree told him with a soft smile. He looked into Bree's eyes a beat longer than she expected—as though he were waiting for something—before smiling back at her. A painful-looking scar dissected his right eyebrow.

"You're welcome," he said as he shut her door.

As soon as the car door shut, Bree slumped back in her seat and let out a deep breath.

"You good?" Noah asked, pulling out of the lot slowly.

"Yeah, just tired." She replied, trying and failing to stifle a yawn.

"Why don't you sleep on the trip back?"

"I'm not that tired," Bree argued weakly, another yawn working its way out of her mouth.

Noah laughed. "Alright, Bree. Whatever you say."

She watched the trees fly by in the moonlight as her eyelids got heavier and heavier, the stillness of the night and the quiet hum of the car lulling her into a daze. She closed her eyes for a moment and woke up abruptly when a hand shook her knee.

"Bree." Noah's voice said.

She tried to peel her eyes open but found they were rather opposed to that idea.

"Bree, you gotta wake up. We're home." Noah said, a small smile clearly evident in his voice.

Her eyes shot open at that. They still had over an hour and a half to go. She was sure she didn't...

"How was your nap?" Noah asked.

Fall asleep...She groaned.

"I was just resting my eyes," Bree said cheekily, clearing the sleep from her eyes and hopping out of the car.

Noah's rich laugh vibrated through the space and coursed through her. She could listen to him laugh every day for the rest of her life and never tire of it. She waited for him to get out of the car and clear the house before walking in and dropping her purse and jacket in the closet by the front door.

"Still on for 8 am Monday?" Noah asked, leaning against the front door.

Bree groaned. "Unfortunately. We just need to be at the TV studio by 9:30 to film the commercial. So that should work."

"Sounds good, Bree. I'll see you then. Lock the door behind me." Noah said, his lips drawing in a thin line, his brow furrowed slightly.

"You okay?" Bree asked softly.

Noah sighed. "I'm worried about the people who commented on your posts earlier, Bree. Several of them mentioned trying to get to you while you're at home, and I'm not here around the clock to keep you safe. What if something happens while I'm gone? How did they even know you *hired* security?" An agonized look tore through his eyes as he ran a hand down his face tiredly.

"It was probably someone who saw us together—like Kyle," Bree joked. Her smile fell, and she rested a hand reassuringly on Noah's arm. "I'll be okay, Noah. No one seems to know where I live, and my tech guy has scoured the internet to be as sure as possible."

"Promise you'll call me if something happens. Even if it ends up being a raccoon or something in your yard. I'd rather be called for a hundred false alarms than take a chance and have something happen to you."

"I'll be fine. You don't need to worry—"

"Promise me, Bree. Please."

"I promise. I'll call you if anything weird happens—raccoon or otherwise."

"I'll see you Monday."

"Eight sharp."

"Eight sharp." He smiled. "Lock up." He reminded her once again before stepping outside into the night. Bree closed the door behind him and engaged the locks, watching through the peephole until Noah made it safely into his car and drove away.

Chapter Fourteen

Aubrey

Bree pulled her groggy self out of bed and trudged into the kitchen, eager to pour a cup of coffee before attempting to do anything today. Morning always came quickly when you made questionable choices...like staying up and reading into the night far longer than you should. Bree poured her iced coffee and headed toward the living room, watching as the mail carrier dropped off today's mail. When was the last time she had gotten her mail at home? In all of the chaos of the last few days, she had completely forgotten about it.

She walked outside and grabbed her mail, waving at Mr. Robinson before going back inside to enjoy her coffee. She sorted the letters into piles and tossed the junk mail in the recycling bin. The last item was a brown package. Anxiety flared in her chest as she pictured her headless teddy bear. Surely, no package could be worse than that one.

Bree sat her coffee cup on the counter, turning the package over in her hands. She didn't recognize the name or handwriting on it, which made her a little hesitant to open it. Maybe she should call Noah to come over so he could be there while she opened it. No. With her luck, he'd drive all the way over, and it would be something innocuous like merch to a local business from their marketing people. She was a grown woman. She could open a box.

It was going to be fine. Bree opened the box and gently emptied the contents out onto the counter. There was an envelope and a super cute keychain with a palette and some paintbrushes. She set the keychain on the counter and then opened the envelope curiously. The blood drained from her face as she took in the contents.

It was pictures of her from the last several weeks. Pictures out in public where Noah was next to her—though his face was scratched out of every single one. Pictures of Bree and Noah waiting in line at the coffee shop. A picture of Bree walking out of the hospital after visiting Jess. A picture of Bree with some of her fans in Trenton...If she'd had anything to eat this morning, she was certain it would've made a reappearance. Bree dropped the photos onto the counter, and tears coursed down her cheeks. She pulled out the folded piece of paper and opened it reluctantly. It was short and to the point, legibly scrawled across the piece of white scrap paper.

Stay away from him.

Another sob tore through her throat as her heart rate skyrocketed. A sharp knock sounded moments later, and Bree jumped, sobbing as the crushing weight of fear settled on her. She was going to be sick. Was that him? What would he do to her? Noah would be crushed if he lost his client. He lived and breathed his job.

The knock sounded again and and a frightened sound escaped her. She ran down the hall into her bedroom and locked the door behind her. The shadows outside her window seemed to be larger than normal and Bree's heart felt as though it was going to beat out of her chest. She raced into her bathroom and locked that door as well. There. No windows, multiple locked doors. Her whole body shook as she pulled her phone out of her pocket. She needed Noah.

He picked up on the first ring. "Missing me already?" He teased.

She sobbed harder, relieved to hear his voice on the other end of the line.

"Bree, what's wrong?" He asked. There were a couple of clicks and the sound of jingling of keys through the line as Bree cried.

"Not a raccoon." She rasped out, unable to pull herself together as the images she'd been sent flashed through her mind. *Stay away from him.* Was she endangering Noah by calling him? She froze. Maybe this was a mistake. Maybe she needed to put distance between them so Noah could be safe. Noah would be devastated if something happened to her, but she wasn't sure she'd survive something happening to him—particularly if it was her fault.

"I'm on my way."

"No!" She said quickly. "It might not be safe. You...you need to stay away from me."

"Not happening, sweetheart. I'll see you in an hour. Stay on the line with me."

Bree slumped against the tub and listened as Noah's car started in the background. The soothing engine noises and occasional commentary from Noah kept her grounded while she waited for him to arrive.

"I'm here, sweetheart. Come let me in."

Bree hesitantly left her bathroom sanctuary and walked to the front door. She looked through the peephole and nearly collapsed in relief. Noah.

She yanked the door open as quickly as she could, closing it as soon as Noah was safely across the threshold. Warm hands enveloped her upper arms gently. "Bree?" Noah asked, concern and alarm lacing his tone. "What's wrong?"

Bree shook her head and leaned toward him, collapsing in his arms while she cried. Noah rubbed his hand up and down her back soothingly while the other arm held her tight against him.

"Bree...talk to me. What's going on? Are you hurt?!" His voice was a cocktail of wrath and violence as he held her slightly away from him, assessing her for any obvious injury.

Bree stepped completely out of his arms and led him into the kitchen, gesturing wordlessly at the open package and contents sitting on the kitchen counter. Noah walked over to them, and his whole body stiffened as he went through picture after picture.

"There's no return address or postmark. Where did you get these, Bree?"

"They were in my mailbox when I got the mail this morning. And then someone knocked on my door...loudly...repeatedly." She said quietly.

"Did you see who it was?"

"No...I hid." She admitted, blushing.

Noah lifted her chin so she was looking him straight in the eye. "That was smart. Bree, I'm glad you called." He reassured her. His steady gaze searched hers to make sure she really was as okay as she claimed. Apparently satisfied with whatever he saw, Noah dropped his hand from her face and took his cell phone out, taking pictures of the box, the envelope, the keychain, and each of the pictures. He typed on his phone for a minute before putting it up to his ear.

"Theo, I just sent pictures through. It looks like Bree's stalker may have found her."

Noah pulled the phone away from his ear and looked at Bree closely. "Bree, can we install cameras? Just outside, sweetheart." Bree looked at him helplessly. She didn't *want* cameras. But this package had been in her mailbox. At her home. And whoever sent them scratched at Noah's *face*. She couldn't endanger him. He was too good of a person.

"Who would have access to them?"

"Just my team at Hawthorne Security. I promise you, Bree. Nothing would ever be used against you. It will just give us a chance at catching whoever has been tormenting you." Noah said, a quiet desperation lacing his tone.

Bree nodded.

"I need to hear you say it, sweetheart."

"You can install cameras, Noah. Just outside. And just for Hawthorne. They don't get sent to *anyone* without my say so."

Approval shone in his eyes. "Done." He said to her as he brought the phone back up to his ear.

"Theo, I need you to see what you can find out about the photos and let's move up the camera install. I want it done today." He said.

Bree looked at the photos on the counter listlessly. He could install all the outdoor security cameras he wanted if that meant whoever took those pictures couldn't get to her. Or him.

Noah was quiet for a moment while Theo talked, and Bree just stared at the evidence that she was being followed. Noah hung up and wrapped his arms around her, pulling her in close. "It'll be okay, Bree. We'll find whoever is behind this."

"How would they have gotten these pictures, Noah? Wouldn't we have seen them?"

Noah left one arm wrapped around her shoulder and used the other to flip through the pictures, tilting his head as he thought. "Look at the distortion of color and the compression on these ones." He said, gesturing to the ones of them walking outside. Bree had no clue what he was talking about but looked at them anyway.

"My guess is they were taken from a car with some tint on the windows, given the color, and likely with a telephoto lens. That would account for the compression. There wasn't anything for us to see unless they used the same car repeatedly. Since we didn't see anything suspicious, they could be in different cars. I'm going to go out and look around. Call the police so we can file a report, please, Bree." Then he turned and walked out her sliding glass door.

***

Noah

Noah watched Bree warily. She looked ready to fall asleep standing up, but they almost had everything situated. She had called the police to file a report and called the TV station to reschedule shooting the commercial. They hadn't been happy. But neither was Bree.

The rest of the day passed in a blur of fielding questions from police, turning over evidence, talking with his team, and overseeing the installation of the new security system outside Bree's house. Hopefully an alarm system would be next. He just needed her to agree to it first.

"All done," Theo said, hopping off the ladder Noah was currently holding against the side of Bree's house. Theo walked over to his laptop and punched in a slew of letters and numbers, seemingly pleased with the view the camera provided. He turned to look at Bree who was silently observing while leaning on his truck. "Do you have any questions, Bree?" He asked, shutting his computer and placing it back in his bag.

"Who has access to the system?" Bree asked mechanically. Noah had already told her, but if she needed reassurance from someone else, she could ask anyone. Everyone.

"Just you and us. And you will get an alert on your phone if we are checking in. That way there's transparency and you know we're not abusing the camera system or being creepy or anything."

Bree laughed lightly, the first semi-happy sound Noah had heard from her all day.

"I trust you guys, Theo. I know you're not creepy." She frowned at the last word, a faraway look overtaking her face.

"Thanks for coming out and taking care of this," Noah told Theo, gesturing to the now functional camera system.

"No thanks necessary. That's what brothers are for." Theo nodded his goodbye to Noah and placed a gentle hand on Aubrey's shoulder, whispering something quietly to her that had her nodding before she turned and gave him a big hug. He climbed into his truck and pulled out of the drive slowly. They watched him go for a moment, and Noah turned as Bree swayed. Cursing under his breath, he quickly walked over to where she was and reached out to steady her before deciding to just carry her inside. She was dead on her feet.

***

Aubrey

Bree observed Noah groggily as he lifted her up. Bree considered protesting, but she was so tired. She rested her head against his chest, listening to the rhythmic beating of his heart.

"You don't have to carry me in." She said halfheartedly, even as she nestled into the side of his neck. He always smelled good. Like coffee and caramel. "I can walk." Although she was slightly unsure of that at the moment. Her energy was gone.

"It's no trouble, Bree," Noah said. "I don't mind carrying you."

They got inside and Noah deposited her on the couch gently. He walked into the kitchen and returned with a cup of her favorite iced coffee. Boy his Mama really did raise him well. A look at the clock told her it was probably about time for him to leave for the evening. She reined in her disappointment and tried to be reasonable. The man had been with her for hours today.

"Hey, Bree?" Noah said, coming to sit on the coffee table by the couch.

"Time for you to go?"

"Actually, I was going to ask if you minded if I stayed. I don't...Between the threats on the internet and the photos you got in the mail, I don't feel comfortable leaving you here alone."

Honestly, she didn't want to be alone either, but aside from the fact 24-hour security costs a lot more money, she also lacked extra beds. "That's really nice of you, but I don't have a guest room." She told him softly, kicking herself for that now. Noah...Noah was the first man in her life who made her feel safe. Truly safe. She didn't have to worry about anything when he was with her. It was...novel. And a feeling she didn't want to give up.

"I can take the couch after you go to bed if it wouldn't bother you."

"I don't know, Noah. You'd be really uncomfortable."

"I've slept far more uncomfortable places than this in my life, sweetheart." He replied, a bubble of happiness growing in her chest. She liked him calling her sweetheart.

"Okay, but if it gets to be too much, please go home to your bed and get a good night's sleep. I doubt we'll have to deal with anything else tonight." Bree said, secretly glad that she wouldn't be alone.

"Scouts honor." He said.

Bree raised her eyebrows suspiciously. "Were you even a boy scout?"

"Nope." He said, popping his 'p' like she did.

Bree laughed and sipped on her iced coffee.

"How are you feeling?" Noah asked, watching her closely. "Scared. Then stupid for feeling scared. It's not like I was directly threatened."

"It's okay to feel scared, Bree. It isn't stupid. Those feelings? Those keep you safe."

"It just doesn't feel like it should be that big of a deal. Like other people have it worse, you know?" She asked, her brow furrowed. "I haven't been directly assaulted by whoever this is. I'm mostly left alone."

Noah's eyes darkened when Bree mentioned being assaulted, and he released a deep breath. "No one is going to *touch* you. Never again." He growled.

He paused a moment before continuing. "I was raised by a single mom. My dad bailed when I was young. Mom and I struggled for a long time, but we were happy. We had each other, and she was the best mom." He said, furrowing his brow slightly.

"When I was thirteen, my dad came back into our lives, and everyone said how neat it must be. How glad Mom probably was to have him back. How it was 'nice' that he stepped up and decided to take care of his family." A deep frown overtook his face. Bree reached out and patted his shoulder gently in quiet reassurance.

He gave Bree a small smile and continued. "What they didn't know was that he was a deadbeat at best. He came in and tried to run the house. He belittled Mom and bossed her around like there was no tomorrow. But she wouldn't leave him. She said I needed a dad. Like he could ever be one."

"What happened?" Bree asked, her heart breaking for a young Noah who would've known a peaceful and loving home life before being thrown into a chaotic one.

"He hit her." Noah balled his hands into fists, and his whole body tensed. "He drank too much one night and decided it was a good time to put hands on her."

"Oh no," Bree said, her eyes filled with concern.

"Mom didn't put up with that. She was a fighter. There was no way she'd stay in a relationship with a man who'd hurt her or her child. So when she got away from him, she quickly packed our things. I'd been at football practice. When I got home and found her with a black eye—I finally understood what it meant to 'see red.' I wanted nothing more than his blood. Mom dissuaded me—even though I'd finally grown taller than him—and handed me the stuff she'd packed to take to the car. He was passed out at this point. Or so we thought. Anyway—he put up a fight when we tried to leave, and when he took another swing at my mom, I laid him flat out. Told him we better never hear from him again, or he'd have another thing coming." Noah cleared his throat uncomfortably.

"So, I know how it is to have people telling you to feel or think a certain way. Or for you to feel like you *should* feel a certain way. I wasn't happy to have him back, but initially, I felt guilty for feeling that way. I was supposed to be happy. But I wasn't. I wasn't happy to have him in my house. Everyone else had big opinions about how great it was for him to be home, but no one knew what went on."

Noah finished softly.

"I'm sorry that happened to you," Bree said, squeezing his shoulder and letting her hand linger for a moment.

"It is what it is. But the important thing is to give yourself some space and grace to feel what you're feeling. Give yourself a chance to process it. It's not stupid, Bree. You're going through something scary. It's okay to be afraid. Just know that no one is going to get to you. They'll have to go through me first."

Bree nodded, and they sat in a comfortable, contemplative silence as she finished her coffee. "I'm going to change and get you some bedding for the couch," Bree said.

Noah nodded and she went down the hall to her room. She threw on a night shirt and wiped off any remaining makeup from earlier though most of it had been cried off at one point or another. She brushed her teeth and finished getting ready for bed before grabbing a pillow and blanket from the storage closet in her bathroom.

She walked down the hall toward the living room, the chill of the floor on her bare toes sending a shiver up her spine. She should've gotten him settled *before* she changed for the evening. She walked into the living room, hyper-aware of the cool air kissing her bare legs and the wood floors under her toes. Noah looked up as she entered, and his eyes widened slightly. Bree blushed as he took in her appearance and handed him the bedding. "It can get cold at night. Come and get me if you need extra blankets." She said quietly.

"I'll do that," Noah said, catching her eye with his. "Thanks, Bree." She nodded and practically sprinted back down the hall, her heart racing.

She laid down on her bed and snuggled into the pillow. It had been a long day.

Bad dreams plagued her and when she opened her eyes, a cool draft drifted through the room. The clock on her bedside table said it was a little after two a.m. and she found herself concerned for Noah. She pulled herself out of bed and grabbed a spare blanket in case he was cold. She walked out to the couch and noted his shoulders curving in toward the couch, a furrow on his brow. She gently set the blanket over him, and watched the tension seep out—he looked...peaceful. Satisfied he wouldn't freeze to death, she went back to her room and nestled down into her covers. She fell back asleep, a warmth in her chest despite the difficulty of the day.

Chapter Fifteen

Noah

Noah took a long drag of coffee from his mug before setting it down on the table next to the couch in his office. "Did we get any information from the pictures or notes?" Noah asked, looking at Theo.

Theo shook his head. "My contact at PD said there weren't prints and no sign of who the perp might be."

Noah swore under his breath and grabbed the stress ball from the desk. Maybe he'd squeeze it. Maybe he'd throw it. All he knew was that it had been a full week, and he couldn't take one more day of Bree's listlessness. Of her fear. He missed her spunk and her smiles. He'd even gone over and ordered her to move the mat at her front door, knowing orders get a rise out of her, but she'd just picked it up and moved it to where he indicated. He wanted—no, needed—his Bree back.

"Theo, any info on her dad back yet?" Zach asked.

"The guy is suspicious and definitely hiding something, but whatever he's hiding, he's doing it well. It'll take me a bit, but I'll get there."

"Have we considered the dad as a suspect?" Peter asked. "Roughly 82% of stalking victims know their offender."

"I'm not ruling him out. At best, the man's a narcissist, and at worst, he's responsible for all of this turmoil for Bree. She doesn't think he'd stoop to that level. She says she already gives them money, so why would he? Let's look into Kyle Rhodes, too. He may be involved, he may just be a menace, but let's rule him out." Noah replied, squeezing the ball in his hand tightly. He needed to figure out some way to get Bree's mind off of all this nonsense. Get her away from Rhodes and Trenton and the uncertainty.

"Well I think that's where we're at with our cases for the day. Anything else to add before we head out?" Zach asked.

Everyone shook their head and grabbed their coffee cups, heading back to their own offices and cases.

Noah looked at the peaceful landscape painting on the wall of his office. The view of the open field helped remind him just how small he was in the world when his job began to feel too heavy. He reflected on the painting for a minute before the perfect idea popped into his head. He pulled out his phone and scrolled down to find the number of an old friend who might be able to help bring his vision to life. The phone rang and rang, but eventually a soft, ethereal voice answered.

"Hello?" Juniper said quietly.

"Juni, it's Noah Hawthorne. How are you?"

"Noah!" She squealed in delight. "I'm so good. I haven't heard from you in forever!"

"Sorry about that," Noah said sheepishly, a hint of guilt squeezing his heart. He really should call Juni and Logan more often. He hadn't seen Logan since they were in the Corps together. "I actually was hoping you could do me a favor..."

"Name it."

Noah talked over the details of exactly what he was hoping for and Juni trilled with delight as she agreed to help. Fifteen minutes later everything was set and Noah just hoped it would be enough to pull Bree out of her funk.

***

As the clock struck four, Noah pulled into Bree's driveway and psyched himself up to knock on her door. Suddenly, the idea he'd come up with felt ridiculous, and he wasn't sure she'd leave with him anyway. She had hunkered down in her house, afraid that everyone they passed could be her stalker. Or that he'd be in the wings taking pictures of her. Or that he'd come after Noah. No amount of persuading from Noah had convinced her to leave—much to his chagrin.

He walked up to the door and knocked, making sure he was clearly within sight of the peephole and not obstructed by the wreath, which was thankfully still on the front door. Bree wasn't all the way gone. A few moments passed, and Noah knocked again.

"Bree? It's Noah." He called as he knocked.

Footsteps sounded on the other side of the door. There was a moment of hesitation before the door opened slightly, and Bree's face peeked around the corner. Relief shone in her eyes when she saw him, and she opened the door further so he could come inside. Noah walked in and waited while she shut and locked the door. He turned to look at her and stopped short. Bree was wearing gray sweats and the shirt he'd accidentally left when he stayed over. *His* shirt. A sharp pang of desire shot through him, and he fisted his hands to keep from reaching out and touching her.

"You aren't supposed to be here today," Bree said in lieu of greeting.

"I have a surprise for you," Noah said, watching to catch any micro-expressions that could indicate excitement or fear or anything other than the melancholy that had been etched there for days. Interest flared in her eyes, and he felt encouraged to continue. "Go throw on some jeans and layer on tops." He looked at her bare feet and added, "And some socks and sneakers."

Bree tilted her head, and he waited for the fire. For the pushback. For the 'you don't tell me what to do, Noah Hawthorne.' But it didn't come. Bree nodded and quietly walked down the hall to her room.

A few minutes later she populated fully dressed in blue jeans and a white tank top, a long sleeve flannel in hand, and sneakers on her feet. Bree took a quick detour into the kitchen to leave a light on so it wouldn't be dark when she got home while Noah grabbed her coat from the closet and the keys from the bowl. He opened the front door for her, gesturing for her to step outside. After checking the coast was clear, Bree hesitantly stepped outside and immediately sidled up to Noah while he shut and locked the door.

Noah slipped an arm around her shoulder and led her to the car, quiet worry gnawing at him the entire time. What would he do if he couldn't break her out of this? He wanted to be there for her. To help support her. If that meant adding therapy to Tuesdays or Thursdays, he was all for it. He was confident that she could ask for the moon, and he'd bend over backward to get it for her.

Bree settled in the car, and Noah reached into the backseat to grab the iced coffee he'd picked up in Rhodes on his way there. Bree's eyes lit up and she gave him a small smile. "Thanks." She said quietly, and man, the things Noah would do to keep that smile on her face.

"You're welcome," Noah replied.

Bree kept her head on a swivel as they drove but seemed to loosen up when they left town and it was clear they weren't going into the city either. After about thirty minutes of countryside driving she turned to Noah.

"Where are we going?" She asked, a note of tentative excitement in her voice.

"You're just going to have to wait and see." Noah teased. "How's your coffee?"

"Delicious. And the fact I didn't have to go into Rhodes to get it and wonder if he's there...watching me makes it a solid fifteen out of ten."

Anger flooded through Noah. She shouldn't have to be worried about some creep following her around and taking pictures while she tried to live her life. They drove another hour and a half into the mountains before Noah pulled off on a dirt road leading further up. There was a small area to pull off, and Noah parked there.

"Wait—I'll come around." He said. He walked around the car, appreciating the quiet of nature and the warm, but not hot, weather they had been blessed with. He quickly walked over to Bree's door and opened it for her, offering her a hand to get out of the car. She took his hand, and he squeezed hers gently, releasing it when she was out of the car and steady on her feet.

There was a small trail across the dirt road, and Noah led Bree on the short hike through the woods. She was quiet the entire time, looking around and seeming to appreciate the quiet and lack of people as much as he was.

"I thought about building a cabin in the woods. In the mountains. Away from the hustle and bustle of people." Noah said, breaking the silence.

"Why didn't you?" Bree asked, carefully stepping over some loose rocks.

"I wanted to get my business established first. I knew getting into the industry that security detail is as much about who you know—and who knows you—as it is about how much you know or how capable you are. That meant I needed to be in an area where I could meet with people and network and really get the business moving."

"You've done a great job." Bree offered. Noah felt pride swell in his chest. Bree was good at speaking life into the people around her. She made sure those she cared about knew it. He admired her. He wanted to be honest with her and try to explain how much she meant to him now. It was almost impossible to remember only seeing her as a means to an end rather than the incredibly brilliant woman in front of him.

"Thank you. You know, at the beginning of your case, I saw it as nothing more than a step up for the business. You and I didn't get along. There was no known tangible threat to you at that time. Protecting you was a means to an end."

Bree stopped walking and wrapped her arms around herself, sadness emanating from her eyes. This wasn't going how Noah intended. He quickly continued. "But then we got to know each other. And I learned that you are fiercely loyal, loving, and dedicated. You're smart, and generous, and thoughtful. And when I looked at your case—when I looked at you—I no longer cared about what it could do for the business. I wasn't worried about how failing the case would look for Hawthorne Security. I was worried about you."

"I care about you, Bree. And I'm worried. The last few days," Noah ran a hand through his hair, devastation, and concern flooding through him. "You haven't been you. I know you're scared, but I'll keep you safe, Bree. I'll do anything and everything within my power to keep you safe." Noah said.

Bree walked over to him and wrapped her arms around him tightly in a hug. She held on for a few minutes before pulling away, sniffling slightly, a small damp spot on his shirt where her face had been moments before.

"The last week...it's been awful," Bree said quietly as she carefully traipsed over the rocks. She looked at Noah, and the heartbreak and fear in her eyes nearly drove him to his knees. "I am terrified, Noah. I'm afraid of my own shadow and laugh at myself dozens of times a day when I scare myself unintentionally. I have to laugh, or I'll cry. I don't want to go outside because what if I'm being watched? What if whoever it is tries to get to me? What if you get caught in the middle, and something happens to you? I couldn't bear it."

"Nothing is going to happen to you—or me," Noah said.

"They scratched out your face, Noah," Bree argued.

"Maybe they just thought your face is nicer to look at. Which would be correct." He joked. "They're not going to take me out, Bree. I am cautious and have a great team. We'll be okay."

Bree nodded, and Noah held his hand out her. She slipped hers into his, and they walked the rest of the trail quietly, hand in hand, a contemplative look on Bree's face.

They crested the final hill, and Bree gasped in delight. In front of them was a deep blue lake surrounded by trees with mountains in the background behind it. In front of the lake were two easels with large canvases and paints beside them, ready and waiting to be used.

"It's not the ocean, but it's as close as I could get in Tennessee," Noah told her with a smile.

Bree jumped up and wrapped her arms around him in a tight hug. Noah tightened his arms around her and buried his head in her neck. Relief flowed through him. She liked it.

"How did you manage this?" She asked, practically skipping over to the easels.

"I called a friend for a favor." Noah shrugged nonchalantly.

"This is the best surprise ever!" Bree said, bouncing on her toes, a wide grin across her face. "You're amazing."

Noah chuckled and walked over to the easels as well. "Thank you."

Noah paused for a moment and watched Bree closely as she began turning the white canvas into a masterpiece. "I saw some of your paintings in Rhodes. You've got a gift. How did you get into painting?"

"I really loved art class when I was in school. When I graduated, my parents weren't going to let me go to art school. So I went to college and got my degree in business, but I minored in art. I also found a painter that I really admired—he specialized in landscapes—and I walked into his gallery one day and asked him to tutor me."

Noah's eyebrows rose in surprise. "That seems a little out of character."

"It was. I couldn't believe I had the gall to ask him, to be honest. But I was dying. I wanted to paint, and I wanted to learn from the best. So, I had to step out of my comfort zone. It was one of the hardest things I've ever done. I was pretty sure my heart was going fast enough in that moment to kill me." Bree joked.

"I bet." He said warmly. "Do you want to do art full-time?"

"No. With the money from my tours, sales, and investments, I don't really have to work, but I enjoy it. I love creating things, working through hard problems, and seeing the outcome of that effort. So I'd like to be an artist for my forever career, but without it taking over my every waking moment. A small business would be okay, but I'm not looking to grow it into anything big. I especially love painting seascapes. I'll do some other portrait work or other landscapes when clients request it, but the sea really calls to me."

"You're quite an enigma, Aubrey Gray," Noah said with a slight head shake and a smile. "Do you have any brothers or sisters besides Jess?"

Bree shook her head, "No, Mom was already a bit older when she had us. She said we were her miracle babies. Do you have any siblings?"

"I have a sister. She's married and lives in Florida with my nieces and nephews. I try to visit as often as I can."

"And your Mom?"

"She died a few years ago." Noah's heart clenched as he thought of his mom. She was the best mom anyone could have asked for, and he missed her.

"I'm so sorry to hear that."

"It's funny because you get used to them not being there —like the grief is still there, but it's just not constantly overwhelming—but then something little happens, and they're still one of the first people you want to call. Like the first time I met you. I knew she would've been captivated by your wit and independence. The fact that you not only didn't need my help but didn't hesitate to say so would've been something she found entertaining."

"She sounds wonderful," Bree said, a smile on her face as she worked on painting the horizon line onto her canvas.

"She was."

They talked and laughed together as they painted the landscape in front of them until they couldn't see anymore. Noah turned on his cell phone light, and they took a moment to step back and compare paintings. Bree's painting felt almost like a photograph. The lake was serene, the mountains imposing yet peaceful, and the sun was soft in the sky. Noah's painting looked like he handed a kindergartener a paintbrush.

Bree giggled softly. "I mean, you do have mountains and a lake in the painting." She praised him.

Noah chuckled. He couldn't paint to save his life, and he knew it. But he'd do it every day if she'd laugh like that. "There is a lake and mountains in the picture." He agreed good-naturedly. A chill had set in, and even with the flannel and jacket, Bree was starting to shiver.

"Let's get you home, sweetheart," Noah said, removing his jacket and settling it over Bree's shoulders. They worked together to pack up the easels, careful to set the paintings where they wouldn't get smudged. Bree chatted to him the whole car ride back, the tension dropping from her shoulders, a happy smile on her face.

Today's surprise? A solid win.

Chapter Sixteen

Aubrey

The trip back down the mountain was uneventful, and Bree felt like herself for the first time since those awful pictures had shown up at her house. The trip to the lake was perfect, and she loved that Noah was lighthearted and able to laugh at himself. She'd dated other men who were competitive to a fault and who would've made her feel bad for taking the painting thing too seriously. Instead, he praised her work and seemed happy that she was happy. They pulled into her driveway, and Noah cut the engine. The happiness buzzed in her chest, and she felt like she could float. Noah *cared* about her, she thought giddily.

"Wait for me," Noah said with a smile, hopping out of the car and quickly coming over to her side. He opened her door and offered her his hand, and she felt that familiar jolt of electricity at the touch. This was a man she could fall in love with. For once, that thought didn't scare her. Noah looked down at her and threaded his fingers through hers. They walked up to the porch, the heat from Noah's body reassuring her. She was safe. She didn't have to worry, not when Noah was around.

The door creaked open, the sudden sharp sound painfully loud as it opened up into the dark space. Bree felt anxiety creep up in her chest, trying to suffocate her joy. She didn't like the dark. Hadn't she left the light in the kitchen on? Bree frowned and tried to remember. Well, it either was burned out, or she forgot to turn it on. Either was likely the way her luck was going.

Noah chuckled. "We definitely needed to oil that up. It sounds like nails on a chalkboard." He said, walking over to the table and tossing the keys into the bowl.

He reached to turn on the light when a shuffling sound came from the dining area. Bree felt the hairs on the back of her neck stand up, and her heart raced. Noah threw his hand out in front of her, pressing a finger to his lips to indicate the need for quiet.

Duh.

Bree watched as Noah quickly contemplated the best course of action, clearly torn between investigating the sound and staying with her. It's not like their arrival had been a secret. If someone was in the house, they certainly would've heard the door creak open.

Noah flipped on the lights, immediately grabbing Bree and pulling her behind him so she was between him and the wall. A flash of black sprinted through the space, clearly as surprised to see them as they were to see him. The intruder flung open the back door and disappeared into the night. Noah drew his weapon and took a step to follow the man before turning to look at Bree. She could see the wheels turning in his mind as he lowered the weapon to his side.

"Bree—" he said softly. "We need to go back to the car."

Her heart was still pounding in her chest. She probably would've agreed with anything he said right now. "Okay."

Noah grabbed the keys from the bowl, his eyes fixed on the back door. He took her hand in his, and led her out the front door, not bothering to pause to lock it behind them. The back door was wide open. They raced over to his car and he opened the door for her to get in before walking over to his side, holstering his gun, and getting in as well. He pulled away from the curb and handed Bree his phone. "Call Theo, please." He said shortly, placing a warm hand gently on her knee while scanning the mirrors far more than he usually did when they drove.

"What's going on, Noah? Who was that?" Bree said, her heart thumping along in her chest and confusion clouding her mind. Panic drummed in her chest. Someone had been inside her home. *Inside.*

"I'm not sure. We'll figure it out, sweetheart. Just call Theo, please."

Bree nodded and dialed Theo's number, waiting impatiently for him to answer.

"How'd the 'not date' date go, man?" Theo's voice asked, coming through the car's sound system. Bree noted the word choice through her brain fog and filed it away for later.

"It was perfect. Can you check the security footage for Bree's house?"

"From a specific time period or in general?"

"Tonight from probably four-ish until—" Noah glanced at the clock on his dash, "eleven."

"Anything specific I'm looking for?"

"Someone was in Bree's house."

Bree felt the blood drain from her face. It felt different hearing him say it out loud. More...real? She felt tears roll down her cheeks and wiped them away quickly. She hated crying.

"On it. What else?" Theo said.

"I'm going to call local PD to give them a heads up and see if a unit can meet us out there. Can you and anyone who isn't out on assignment meet us in Rhodes Town Square by the coffee shop in about 90 minutes?"

"Sure thing. I'll also have the info for you by the time we get there." Theo said.

"Appreciate it, brother," Noah said before ending the call.

"Noah—"

"You saw the man run out of your house?"

Bree nodded and took a deep breath, tears still silently falling. She was safe. Noah was there. She had no reason to cry. She told herself over and over. Maybe then she'd believe it.

"Bree, there was also a bouquet of flowers sitting in the middle of your dining room table."

Bree furrowed her brow. What an odd thing to notice. "Okay..."

"There weren't any flowers on your table when we left earlier. Also, your back door had a pane broken."

Her eyes widened. Someone broke into her house and left her *flowers*? Bree laughed maniacally. How was this her life? This was ridiculous.

"Don't worry, Bree. We'll get to the bottom of this." Noah said.

She nodded, not certain she believed him, but too tired to put up a fight.

***

An hour and a half later a black SUV pulled into the parking spot beside them near the coffee shop. The passenger side window rolled down, and Theo stuck his head out and gave Bree a little wave. "All good?" He asked, making eye contact with Noah.

Noah nodded tensely. "Yeah. PD cleared the house within fifteen minutes of us calling. No sign of the intruder. Will you follow us back to Bree's? Zach and Peter in the field?"

Theo nodded, "They're out on joint surveillance tonight."

Ten minutes later, they were back at her house, the black SUV following them as Noah drove. Bree rubbed her hands nervously on her jeans, afraid of what they'd find when they returned. They pulled into the neighborhood, and it looked just as it did every evening—normal, quiet since the majority of her neighbors work tomorrow, and safe. Noah turned off the engine and got out. He walked behind and spoke with Theo and the other guy before shaking his head and returning to her side of the car, opening the door slowly.

"Theo and Eli are here. The others are on an overnight assignment tonight. You've met Theo, but I'll introduce you to Eli. You're safe with both of them." Noah told her as she got out of the car. They walked over to the men, and Bree smiled tentatively at them. The man next to Theo was tall with cropped brown hair, tan skin, and a sleeve of tattoos running down his right arm. Some of them looked like drawings a child might do, while others looked like works of art.

"Hi," the man said, extending his sleeved arm toward her. "I'm Eli Walters."

"Aubrey Gray," She said, reaching out to shake his hand.

"It's a pleasure to meet you."

"You as well." She said, eager for the pleasantries to be over so they could get down to business. Some of her feelings must have been evident in her tone because Noah chuckled a little. Small talk was...challenging. She could do it, but it took a lot of effort.

"Theo, what'd you find?" Noah asked as they walked toward the front door.

"There was a man here, but I wasn't able to see his face. He seemed to know where the cameras were." Theo seemed particularly frustrated, but he couldn't have predicted that.

"Any identifying features?"

"Not that I was able to see. Normal gait, normal clothes. He seemed like he'd just blend in anywhere. Average height, dark hair, nothing noticeable about him."

"Great," Noah muttered, placing his hand on her hip and drawing her to a stop as they arrived at the door. "Wait here with Theo, Bree. Eli and I are going to clear the house."

"The police already came out and did that." Bree pointed out.

"They did, but we want to make sure no one came in while we were out since your back door can't be secured."

Bree nodded and watched as Eli handed Noah a flashlight. Noah and Eli nodded at each other, drew their weapons, and went inside the house. As soon as the door shut, she turned and looked at Theo.

"It isn't your fault that he wasn't on camera, Theo. You can't anticipate every-one's movements."

"I'm one of the best, Aubrey. I always know which shadows these guys are going to lurk in." He said, frustration lacing each word.

"Well, this time you didn't, and that's okay. Besides, he struck at night, which technically means it was all shadows." She tried joking to reassure him.

"Cameras can see in the dark now." Theo pointed out, observing her closely. "How are you?"

Scared. Terrified of being alone. Frightened. "Scared. I keep trying to remind myself not to freak out until there is something to actually freak out about, but that's not going so well." She grimaced.

"Understandably. Do you want to footage sent over to P.D. or should we keep it?" Theo asked, observing her closely.

"That's fine. You can send it to Detective Ramirez." The idea of sending footage out to anyone made Bree feel like she was going to break out in hives, but she wasn't going to sit on evidence. Even if there wasn't anything identifiable caught on tape.

A few minutes later, the door opened again, and Noah re-holstered his gun. "It's clear." He said, guiding her into the house as Theo followed behind.

Bree walked over to the table where Eli was standing and looked at the flowers sitting innocuously on the table, a folded piece of paper in front of them.

"What does it say?" She asked, looking at Eli.

"You can't trust them to keep you safe," Eli said.

Noah practically growled behind her.

Theo walked up and took a look at the note, careful not to touch it. "There also seems to be a piece of artwork printed on the note."

"A famous one?" She asked.

"If it is, I'm not familiar with it. It reminds me of a Picasso...what do you call that? Abstract?"

"Hmm." She said, walking over to look at the note. "It looks like Willem de Kooning's Woman-Ochre." She remembered reading about the painting, but couldn't remember why it had stuck out to her.

"What kind of flowers are these?" Eli wondered aloud.

"Does it matter?" Noah asked, frustration lacing his words.

"It can," Eli said simply.

"These are gardenias," Bree said, gesturing to the large white flowers in the bouquet. "And the little ones are baby's breath. And the last are yellow...carnations?" She looked a little closer at the bouquet and nodded. Those were definitely carnations.

"Bree, we'll need to update the police in the morning. They probably weren't looking for flowers as a sign of a break-in." Noah said, resting his hand on her lower back. It seemed like he was staying as close as he could get right now, and she wasn't objecting. "You'll need to file a report."

Bree nodded and placed the call. Dispatch said deputies would be out shortly to take pictures and collect evidence. How was this even her life right now? The thought of staying here alone—especially at night made her skin crawl. Would she even be safe? What if he broke in again and it wasn't to leave her flowers? Dread pooled in her stomach, and her chest felt tight as her breaths began coming in faster and faster.

Noah rubbed her back and whispered in her ear softly, "Breathe, Bree. Deep breaths." He guided her through the next couple of minutes until the panic faded and she looked at him tears blurring her vision. She wanted to ask him to stay or to take her somewhere else. Anywhere else. But she didn't want to be a burden. Maybe she could just go stay at a hotel. Then maybe she'd feel safe.

***

Noah

"Aubrey," Noah said calmly after the deputies had collected the evidence and their statements, "Would you be willing to stay with me? At my house?"

"Are you sure? I could just as easily stay at a hotel." Bree asked hesitantly.

His gut clenched at the thought. *Over my dead body*, Noah thought angrily. Hotels could be hard to defend properly. Bree wouldn't be as safe there as she would be at his house—in his arms—his brain added unhelpfully. He took a deep breath and tried again. "Just for a little while. Or you could stay with one of my teammates."

"Don't you think you should ask them first?" She asked good-humoredly. "I imagine their wives wouldn't appreciate a random woman coming to stay with them."

"They're not married, but they wouldn't mind. Not if I asked." It would be a favor, but one any of them would do for each other's woman. Not that Bree was his—Noah tried convincing himself.

"I'd rather stay with you, but I *can* stay at a hotel, too," Bree said quietly.

A burst of pride shot through his chest. She'd rather stay with him. "Over my dead body will you stay at a hotel with an unknown person stalking you. You'll stay with me. Let's pack a duffel bag for tonight, and when it's daylight tomorrow, we'll get your bags packed and grab whatever you need for work."

"Oh, since I'm retired, I don't really need anything," Bree said softly.

"You mentioned you had a side job. Painting? We can take whatever you need." Noah said, hoping to be encouraging.

Bree's eyes filled with tears again, and he felt his heart stutter. Did he say something stupid?

"Umm, Bree?" Noah asked, walking toward her hesitantly.

"They're happy tears, Noah. I just...I appreciate everything you have done and are doing for me. You're...you're the best." She croaked.

He brushed the tears away and pulled her into his arms, concerned that everything going on was weighing on her more than she was letting on. "I'm glad they're happy tears, but I still hate seeing you cry." He admitted through the emotion in his own throat. This woman would be the death of him. And boy, it would be the best way to go.

Theo and Eli walked back into the living room, and Noah turned to look at them. "Can you meet us back here around ten a.m. tomorrow? We're going to move some of Bree's stuff into my house."

"Yup," Eli said.

"I'll be here," Theo added.

"Thanks," Noah said. He looked down at Bree. "Your room is safe sweetheart, why don't you go pack what you need for tonight and then we'll head out."

Bree nodded and disappeared down the hall.

"Do you think he'll come back?" Eli asked seriously.

"It's hard to say. I think it depends on why he was here. Bree is supposed to go through the house tomorrow to see if anything is missing so we can add it to the police report." Noah answered.

"It's weird, man. Why is he trying to warn her off of you? Are we sure it's a stalker for Bree and not some chick hung up on you?" Theo mused.

They went back and forth with several different theories until they heard Bree's quiet steps coming up the hall. She looked wiped out. Theo grabbed her bag and Eli made sure the doors and windows were shut and locked—broken pane on the backdoor not withstanding—while Noah grabbed the keys and guided Bree to his car. Once the house was locked up and Bree was comfortably in his car with her bag, Noah waved to Eli and Theo and slipped into the driver's seat. Today had been long, and tomorrow was shaping up to be even longer.

***

The drive to Noah's house was uneventful, but honestly, he could have been driving through a parade of elephants, camels, and the Wizard of Oz, and she still wouldn't have been able to keep her eyes open. Exhaustion sat heavy on her bones, and she was so tired of all of this. Tired of the threats. Tired of the photos. Tired of someone thinking they had the *right* to break into her home—regardless of what they left or intended. Her brain felt full, and her heart heavy.

She closed her eyes until the car came to a stop on Noah's driveway. He pressed the button to open his garage door while Bree looked around surreptitiously. At night, there wasn't much to see. The street was dimly lit, with street lamps evenly spaced out as far as Bree could see. A few porch lights were on, but it was late enough that most lights inside and outside of the houses were off.

The garage opened, and Noah slowly pulled in, waiting until the door shut completely behind them before getting out of the car and walking over to Bree's side. He opened her door and took her backpack, shouldering it gently before reaching his hand in and helping her out. She wobbled slightly, a little off balance, and had to wait for a moment to regain her equilibrium. Noah kept a steady hand on her elbow and guided her to the door. He unlocked it with a key from his key ring, and she raised an eyebrow in question.

"Most people don't lock their garage doors." He shrugged. "Garages aren't that hard to break into, generally speaking. So locking the door between the house and the garage is one pretty simple additional layer of security."

Bree nodded. She saw an episode on a crime TV show once where the killer was getting in using garage door openers and taking advantage of the unlocked door between the garage and the home. She shuddered. She needed to start locking her garage door. One more layer of security between her and whoever was out to get her didn't feel like enough, but it was more than she currently had going for her.

They walked into the dimly lit hallway and Noah locked the door behind them once they entered. "Your room will be just down the hall." He said, walking Bree down and showing her the room and the nearby bathroom. It looked clean and safe which was all Bree needed.

"Thanks." She said tiredly.

"If you need me, my room is down the hall on the left. You also can send me a text or call me. I keep my phone by the bed." Noah hesitated like he wanted to say something else, but stepped back to give her the space to change and get ready for bed.

Bree watched him leave and went through her backpack slowly. Once she found a pair of sleep shorts and a tank, she grabbed them along with her toothbrush and toothpaste and went to the bathroom to get ready for bed.

She laid down and stared at the unfamiliar ceiling a frown on her face. The wind outside seemed threatening and the moans and creaks of the house set her pulse racing every time. A soft knock sounded on her door, and she padded over to it, opening it slightly to confirm it was Noah before she opened it all the way.

Noah stood in the doorway, a pair of gray sweats hung low on his hips and a black t-shirt covering his chest. He had two water bottles in his hands and held one out for Bree. She shook herself out of her stupor, and met his heated gaze. He clearly had noticed her checking him out.

"I thought you might want water," Noah said.

Bree blushed and reached out for the water bottle.

"Coffee would be better." She argued weakly.

"Not at this hour. It would keep you up all night."

"I'm already gonna be up all night." She muttered.

Noah furrowed his brow in concern. "Are you uncomfortable? Would you rather stay at a hotel?"

"No!" Bree said quickly. "No...I just keep seeing that guy crawling out of my house, and every sound the house and wind makes sounds ominous. I'm just freaking myself out."

"Can I help?"

Bree hesitated—she didn't want to be alone. But she didn't want to seem childish, either. It was kind of embarrassing. A heavy gust of wind blew, and Bree jumped. "Will you—will you sit with me until I fall asleep?" She asked.

"Sure."

He walked into the room and waited as Bree got settled into bed before sitting in the armchair nestled in the corner. He picked up a book that was sitting on the side table and opened it. "I'll stay until you fall asleep. You're safe here, Bree."

She nodded and nestled down in the blankets acutely aware of the droolworthy man keeping watch over her. With Noah in the room the noises didn't spike her anxiety and she listened to his even breathing until her eyes closed and she fell into a fitful sleep.

Chapter Seventeen

Noah

"Now, you just have to let me know what to pack and where to find it, and we'll get everything squared away," Noah said as they walked into her house, watching Bree warily from the corner of his eye. "And if you notice anything missing, make sure to jot it down so we can let Detective Ramirez know."

The dark circles under Bree's eyes stood out today, proof of the difficulty she had sleeping the night before. When he asked about it this morning, she just shrugged it off and said she had a bad dream, but Noah suspected it was worse than she was letting on.

Bree nodded. "My art stuff should probably be packed up first," she said quietly.

"Like sketchbooks and watercolors?"

She laughed lightly. "It's a little more involved than that. That's why I don't have a spare bed or bedroom. My spare room is my art studio. Go take a look." She said, sending him on his way.

Eli had cleared the room last night so Noah hadn't had the chance to see it, but when he walked into the art studio, he was immediately captivated by a large picture of a landscape. The early morning sky colors reflected in the water, the soft grasses looking as though they were in motion. There was a small house nestled in the tree line and a child playing on the dock. There was peace and joy and movement, all so beautifully captured. The detail was exquisite. He didn't have to know much about art to know that he was in the presence of greatness. This wasn't a small side gig. Noah turned as Bree approached the room, amazed by her artistic talent.

"Well, what do you think?" She asked, watching him with a curious mix of dread and excitement, like she was looking forward to his reaction, but afraid of what he'd say at the same time. And he understood. This was something private. Something just hers. And she was sharing it. With him.

"It's beautiful. You have a gift, sweetheart." He said, walking over to her and planting a soft kiss on her forehead. She smiled up at him and he looked down at her, watching the way the sunlight streaming through the window danced in her eyes. "So, what do we need out of here?"

The next thirty minutes were spent with Bree telling him what needed to go and where to put it. They had a minor dispute over packing her clothes—Noah told her to just bring it all—and she eventually kicked him out of the bedroom so she could pack in peace. He loaded her things into his car, feeling a mix of lingering apprehension that someone had been in her house and relief that Bree would be coming home with him. Noah went back into the living room with Theo and Eli to wait for Bree.

"Are you sure you want me to stay with you? Long term is different than one night." Bree asked from behind him. "Because I *can* stay in a hotel. I don't want to bother you." She added with a frown.

Before Noah could answer, a loud pounding sound reverberated through the space, jerking their attention to the front door. Noah pushed her gently behind him. "Eli, take her." He said, handing her off to the man standing nearby. Eli nodded and put Bree between himself and the table, Theo taking up the mantle on her right.

The noise repeated, and yells of "Aubrey, open up!" chorused outside.

Bree groaned. "It sounds like Rae." She said quietly.

Noah nodded and made his way over to the door, stooping to peer through the peephole before jerking the door open and pulling Rae in, shutting the door quickly behind them.

Bree was confused. "What's going on?"

"Why don't you tell me?" Rae asked, anger in her voice. Noah stepped around her and came back to the table, positioning himself protectively in front of Bree as Eli moved back slightly to stand on her left.

"I don't know what you're talking about," Bree said, confusion coloring her tone as she moved to stand next to Noah instead of behind him.

"This!" She said, pulling a paper out of her purse and shoving it at her unceremoniously. Bree was getting tired of her attitude.

Bree took the paper and turned it over, feeling the color drain from her face as she took in the headlines and pictures accompanying it. Noah and Bree were splashed all over the front page. Noah pressed against her when she lost her footing getting out of the car the first day. Noah in the wings of the photoshoot she did with Steph. Noah with his hand on her back in the coffee shop. Noah and Bree nearly kissing. Noah, Theo, and Bree installing the cameras outside. The tears that had welled up in her eyes began to run down her face and she let them, not bothering to wipe them away. The article speculated that Noah was her boyfriend and he was the reason behind my unexpected retirement and relocation to "the middle of nowhere."

She was so...angry. Frustrated. Violated. It was an invasion of privacy. Another one. And not just hers. Bree turned her head to look at Noah, whose jaw was ticking. "Noah," She said quietly, tucking into his side as they looked over the paper together.

He looked down at Bree and rubbed her back in a soothing motion. "It's okay, Bree. It's just more speculation."

"So he is your boyfriend." Rae said hollowly. "Aubrey I know I'm not your agent anymore, but it would've been nice to get a phone call or something. Is he the reason you left the industry at the top of your game?" She asked, frustration evident in her tone.

"Can you check the tone? And why are you here anyway? I thought you were going back to L.A.," Bree asked, unable to keep the bite out of her voice.

Rae scoffed, "There was a conference with some big labels over in Nashville, so I thought I'd swing by. Listen, babe. No man is worth giving up the money and fame when you're at the top of your game. Look at you now! Trading nights on the town for nights in this...quaint home. Trading the stage for a paintbrush. You stripped away the most interesting facet of your personality and then whine when you get attention because you're dating a hunk. Give me a freaking break."

Bree stepped back as though Rae had slapped her and nearly collided with the table. Theo and Eli both reached out to steady her. A cacophony of noise surrounded her as everyone began to speak at once.

"What is your problem?" Eli asked, his muscles tensing as he took in the situation.

"You're out of line." Theo snapped, taking a step closer to Rae.

"Apologize," Noah growled out, his hand stilling on Bree's back.

"I didn't leave the industry because of Noah, Rae. I didn't even *know* him. I hated the spotlight. It was a miracle I stayed as long as I did. And whether Noah is or isn't my boyfriend is none of your concern. So back off." Bree argued.

Rae ignored the men and glared at Bree. "You'll get bored of small-town living—hopefully before you completely lose the steam you've built up. Come find me when you get over it, and maybe we'll be able to salvage your career."

Noah and Theo were both vibrating with restrained anger as Rae walked out of the house, slamming the door behind her.

"Wow," Theo said.

"Is she like that often?" Noah asked, clenching his jaw while slowly resuming the soothing rubbing motion on Bree's lower back, the muscles in his hand more tense than before.

"She's always been kind of hot and cold. Normally, I'd attribute it to just her being the way she is, but that was a bit much even for her."

"Has she been acting differently since I started coming around?" Noah asked, tilting his head slightly.

"I mean, she's been a little more moody and distant. Why do you a—Noah Hawthorne! You think Rae is the one who took those pictures and sold my address?"

Noah shrugged. "Why not? She could be trying to distance herself from it by showing outrage that you didn't tell her about something going on with you. Because if she'd been the one taking the pictures, she'd have known."

"It couldn't be Rae. She is probably just feeling pressure from her bosses to sign a big up-and-coming client since they lost me. She wouldn't sell me out, though." Bree couldn't stomach the thought of that.

"What if she was hoping that getting you back into the public eye would encourage you to pick the mic back up?"

"Then she'd be grossly mistaken. I'm never going back."

"We're going to step outside and do a perimeter check to make sure everything is secure from the outside before we all leave," Eli said. Noah nodded, his eyes not leaving hers as a calm Eli and still irate Theo headed out the back door.

"Does Rae know your routines in Chattanooga?" Noah asked pointedly.

"I mean, yeah. She helped me originally set up the box, and I usually text her when I'm going to pick up mail. She knows I stop at the museum, too."

"So it could've been Rae."

"No, it couldn't—"

"It could have been Rae."

Bree nodded hesitantly. "I guess so."

"Has anyone else been acting weird?"

"No, everyone else has been pretty normal. My parents haven't called, but that's not atypical since I sent them the money for the hospital bill for Jess. They usually call more often the closer it comes to being due."

"Hmm," Noah said shortly.

"I need more coffee to get through this day." Bree groaned, her head and heart aching at the thought that her former agent and current friend could possibly be behind all of this.

"How about water?"

"Filtered through coffee grounds?"

"No, plain water."

"Noah..."

"Coffee isn't a meal, sweetheart. You need good nutrition—you've been under a lot of stress."

Bree huffed. "Please?" She tried again with a smile.

"You are trouble, Miss Aubrey Gray." He said, shaking his head and disappearing into the kitchen.

"Only if you try and stand between me and my coffee, Mr. Hawthorne." She joked back at him as she moved to sit on the couch, dropping the article Rae had brought onto the table. His laugh sounded from the kitchen, and her heart filled with warmth, even as she waded through the pain and sadness. Who knew that such opposing emotions could coexist?

Noah came back a few minutes later and handed her a fresh cup of coffee. "Here you go." He said, careful not to let it slosh all over.

She took it from his hand and took a large sip. Heavenly. "So...should we talk about this?" Bree asked, gesturing toward the article sitting on the coffee table.

"What about it?"

"They invaded your privacy too, Noah."

"It's not the first time. Comes with being part of a security detail. I'm just normally in a suit, and they fancy me some sort of wealthy businessman."

"So it doesn't bother you?"

"No. How are you feeling?"

"It was...shocking. First someone was inside my house and then the pictures...It's a lot. But I'm physically unharmed, so I guess it could've been worse." Bree said, attempting to shrug it off.

Noah furrowed his brow. "It's okay that it bothers you, Bree. It was pictures taken of you in private moments. Those don't belong to anyone except you and the person you shared the moment with. It's okay to be angry or feel violated or whatever. Your feelings are valid."

Bree sat back for a moment and tried to sort her feelings. Her head kind of felt like it was full of cotton. "I do feel violated. Those were private moments and they have no business broadcasting them. I went through that before, and it makes me angry that someone thinks they're entitled to share pictures of me and people I care about." She said, anger lacing her tone and sourness filling her stomach.

Noah's eyes softened before darting to the back door as Theo and Eli reentered the space. Eli looked down at the broken door pane.

"We'll get it covered up and get someone out to repair it," Eli said as Theo walked around securing the inside of the house. "We also stopped over and asked Mr. Robinson if he saw anything. He said he didn't notice anyone lurking outside of the house. No unusual cars coming in and out of the neighborhood."

"So he either is coming into the neighborhood on foot or using different cars when he comes through for surveillance," Noah said thoughtfully.

"Or he doesn't do surveillance. Maybe he just got her address and decided to go over. More spur of the moment than planned." Eli suggested.

"We'll have to look into both options. I'll see what I can uncover. Also, I know you wanted to drive Bree's car so she has wheels. So I'm gonna drive your car, and Eli said he'd grab me and bring me back to my house." Theo called from across the room.

"I appreciate it," Noah said as they all returned to the living room, watching Bree carefully while she grabbed her purse.

When Theo and Eli both left, Noah locked the door between the garage and the house and then they hopped into Bree's car and drove. Bree sat quietly, observing him while he drove. He kept his eyes on the mirrors to make sure no one followed them.

After taking a few scenic detours to shake any potential tails, they finally headed toward his neighborhood. It had been so late last night they just went in through the garage and he showed her the guest room and bathroom and they left first thing this morning. Noah normally didn't care much about what others thought, but suddenly he was rather nervous about whether Bree would like his house.

Chapter Eighteen

Aubrey

After an hour or so in the car, they finally came to a small, quiet suburban neighborhood, kids playing at the park and riding bikes on the sidewalk, grandparents sitting on the porches. It felt nostalgic in a way she'd never experienced personally, but read about countless times in books and had seen in different movies growing up. It was homey and looked friendly. She hoped Noah's home was here among these people.

Sure enough, they stopped in front of a modest, but well-maintained home and pulled into the driveway. Noah hopped out and walked around to her side, opening her door and helping her out.

"Come on in." He said, a nervous smile on his face. "You can sit in the living room while I bring your stuff in."

"I can help, Noah."

"You've been through enough the last couple days, Bree. Let me take care of you." He argued as they walked inside, and he led her into a room immediately to the left.

The heaviness of everything that had happened settled, and she fell back against the sofa, all the arguments leaving her.

"Will you be okay?" He asked, eyeing her warily.

"I'll be fine, Noah. You'll let me know if you need help?."

He nodded—though she got the distinct impression that he would not, in fact, let her know if he needed her help—and walked out, giving her a chance to really take in his home. It was a ranch-style one-story that looked surprisingly put together for a bachelor pad. They walked into the foyer, and he escorted her to the living room immediately to the left of the door. There was a slight elevation change, and the long wooden dining table was a statement piece in that area. It was kind of nice. Semi-open where you could be engaged between the living and dining room, but without being in the kitchen—or seeing the kitchen.

There was a secondary living room straight ahead when they walked in and a hallway off to the right where the bedrooms and bathrooms were. It was simply decorated, a lot of wood and dark colors, but the walls were white and the floor was a beautiful light tone that would pair well with all kinds of decorating motifs. She could just see the room filled with accents of light blues, sandy browns, and grays. Like the ocean on a cloudy day. She sighed dreamily. She could make it so beautiful in here.

A rustling from the entryway signaled Noah's return, and Bree smiled as he poked his head around the corner. "All good still?"

"It's been thirty seconds, Noah. I'm good." Bree said. She'd never known a man who was so attuned to others. Noah's innate kindness and thoughtfulness were shown through his patience with her and his deep love and loyalty for his team. They were so lucky to have each other. She'd love to have friends like that.

"I'm going to put your art supplies in the first room on the left. It's been empty, so you can set it up however you'd like. Your bedroom is across the hall."

"Sounds good."

"Do you want to come into the studio and tell me where to put things? I figure it'll be most helpful if you can get them where you want them right away to help you be productive later on."

"I'd love that," Bree said, standing up and making her way down the hall. She wanted to be useful.

The room would be considered small for a bedroom, but was a perfect size for a studio. There was a large window overlooking the lake. Her eyebrows shot up in surprise and Noah rubbed the back of his head.

"The front is modest to look at, and the inside isn't fancy." He said, "But I bought the house for the view."

"It's beautiful, Noah."

"It is." He said, looking at her instead of the view.

Bree blushed.

"So, where do you want the easel?" He asked, bringing the large wooden object in from the hallway.

Bree looked at where the light was in relation to the window. "Can you put it along the back wall? That will give me the best light while I work."

"Sure thing, boss." Noah jested, moving the easel to where she pointed. Over the next ten minutes, they worked on setting up the art studio until she knew she could waltz in and work on her art pieces as though there hadn't been a major disruption to her life. That would come in handy later.

Next, they moved on to the bedroom and guest bathroom. Bree just asked Noah to place her things on the bed so she could sort them later. Once the bags were securely deposited, they made their way back to the other side of the house.

"Want the rest of the official tour?" Noah asked.

"Of course," Bree said, game for anything Noah wanted to show her. They went through the other living room—this one had a large TV over the mantle and giant windows on either side of the fireplace that showcased the gorgeous water view. French doors were to the left of the window, and this family room was open to the kitchen. White cabinets, a butcher block counter that matched the stain of the floor, and a farm-style sink in front of another large window almost made it feel like you were outside.

Noah opened the French doors and they walked outside, a deck off the back of the house leading to an expanse of yard before it slowly dipped down into the lake. Noah had his own dock with a small boat tied to the post.

"Your home is gorgeous, Noah."

"Thank you." He said with pride.

"Is it a three-bedroom then?" Bree asked as they walked back into the family room.

"Four. The room at the end of the hall on the right is my workout room, and the room on the left—next to the studio—is the master."

"Nice."

"It was a solid buy. It needed a little updating when I bought it—the original owners who had lived here were the ones who built it. They took amazing care of it. I just updated it a little bit.”

They settled in and watched some television, talking about their favorite books and movies and just little things until the doorbell rang an hour later, and Noah got up to answer it. Bree felt her heart rate spike, memories of the sharp knocks on her door flooding to the front of her mind. The teddy bear. The pictures. The break-in. The flowers. What if whoever was after her followed them despite Noah’s precautions? What if he found her and Noah was hurt because of it? She really shouldn’t be here.

Noah walked through the kitchen, pressing a few buttons on the oven if the beeps were any indication. She needed to figure out a way to get him to accept her leaving. Maybe she could just fire him? Before she could formulate a plan to leave, Noah appeared near the island with a casserole dish in hand.

He took one look at her and quickly set the casserole dish down on the counter, making a beeline for Bree. “What’s wrong?” He asked, his eyes automatically scanning her for injury before meeting her eyes. “Did something happen? Did *he* call?” Noah asked, his voice low.

“Nothing’s wrong. I’m okay.” Bree said.

“Don’t lie to me, Bree. You look like you’re ready to bolt.” He said, his brow furrowed.

Bree sighed. “Has anyone ever told you that your high level of perception is annoying?” Bree teased. “The doorbell was unexpected. It just reminded me of all the reasons it’s dangerous for you to be around me. I shouldn’t stay here, Noah. What if I bring this psychopath to your door?” Bree couldn’t stand that. She wouldn’t be able to live with herself if something were to happen to Noah or his team because of her.

Noah gently tilted her chin up so her eyes met his. “Let him come,” Noah said, death and violence a promise in his gaze. “He’s not getting his hands on you, Bree. And he’s not going to get to me either. Don’t run away from me. Don’t give him the opportunity to snatch you. Especially because you’re worried for me.” Noah paused, searching her eyes for an answer she didn’t feel she could give him. He must’ve seen that because his grip tightened slightly, agony etched in the lines of his face. Noah reached his other hand around her and pulled her close to him.

"Promise me, Bree." He rasped.

"I promise, Noah."

"Good...good," Noah said, his grip still lightly on her chin. Noah's eyes flickered down to her mouth. The hand on her waist was warm and strong and Bree felt like she was in a romance novel. The air between them practically vibrated with electricity. Noah leaned slightly toward Bree, his eyes moving between her eyes and her mouth. When his lips were barely a breath from hers, a loud beep came from the kitchen.

Noah let out a breath and rested his forehead lightly on Bree's for a second before stepping back from her, letting both hands fall to his sides. "Oven's preheated." He said, walking toward the kitchen.

"Mrs. Garcia?" Bree asked with a grin, a light blush on her cheeks from their *almost* kiss.

He nodded. "Along with handwritten instructions on how to cook it and a fair warning that if I manage to mess it up, she'll whack me upside the head like she did when I was a child because 'the girl needs to eat.'"

Her stomach chose just then to rumble loudly, and Noah laughed. "Man, she is good." He said, walking over to the oven and reading the instructions that Mrs. Garcia had given him. Bree watched as he put the casserole in the oven and set the timer, the paper out of sight.

"How is her recovery going?"

"She's doing great. Her son was able to come and stay with her so she could rehab at home, which means she's giving him a run for his money, and they're both enjoying every minute of it."

They went into the living room and watched television until the timer went off. Noah sauntered into the kitchen to collect the food and dish it up. Determined to do something helpful, she dragged herself off the couch and walked into the kitchen as well.

"Which drawer is the silverware?" She asked as Noah carried the plates to the dining table.

"Top drawer." He said as he walked through the little doorway.

Bree looked down and frowned. There were three top drawers. This is why men weren't allowed to give instructions around the kitchen. Top drawer,, indeed. She opened the first one, though it looked a little too narrow, and found it full of cooking utensils. The drawer next to it was slightly bigger, so she pulled that one open as well.

Stacks and stacks of recipe cards, sticky notes, and stationary filled the drawer, most of it in the same handwriting as the paper he'd shown her earlier. She suddenly felt overwhelmed by a weird mix of warmth and tears. He'd kept all of Mrs. Garcia's notes. He was such a good man.

The next drawer held the silverware-naturally it would be in the last place she looked for it. Which was a weird phrase—who finds something and then keeps looking for it...anyway. She shook herself out of her distracting thoughts and grabbed a couple of forks and some paper towels before heading to the dining table.

"Water?" Noah asked.

"Sure," Bree said with a smile.

Noah frowned and walked over, putting his hand on her head. "Nope, no fever. Must be a changeling. My Aubrey only drinks coffee. She's practically hydrophobic."

"I am not," She muttered, rolling her eyes while giving him a small smile. He thought he was so funny. She chose to ignore the 'my Aubrey' part—though the butterflies in her stomach sure noticed.

"Dinner smells great," Bree said, resting her napkin in her lap gently.

"Mrs. Garcia is a great cook. She tried to teach me growing up, but it's the one thing I never quite mastered. I can grill a steak and some vegetables and make a mean omelet, but outside of that and a cold meat sandwich, there just isn't a lot of cooking happening in this kitchen."

"That's a shame. It's a beautiful kitchen to not get used."

"Do you cook?"

Bree shook her head. "I can't cook to save my life. When I was younger, I would help my mom and Nonna cook in the kitchen. Then we moved away from Nonna, and my mom didn't want to cook with me anymore. She had a lot of work to do—so we often ordered takeout or made something simple. One of the things I miss about being famous was having a chef, but I didn't want someone in my home once I retired."

"I can understand that. How are you holding up?" He asked hesitantly.

"I've been better. But, I am thankful to be in a space I feel safe. Thank you for that, Noah."

He smiled, the action bringing light into his green eyes. "You're welcome, Bree."

Bree took her first bite and practically groaned. It was *delicious*. "I need to see if Mrs. Garcia can teach me how to cook. That is phenomenal."

Noah smiled, "She really is the best."

"Have you heard from your sister lately?"

Noah shook his head. "No, I'll give her a call on Thanksgiving, and she'll call me on Christmas. Holidays are tough—some families pull together once they lose their matriarch, but ours just kind of fell apart." He admitted.

"I can understand that—sort of. Our family wasn't perfect before Jessica's accident, but we were at least together and got along okay. Once Jess was hospitalized, it seemed to just break every body. My mom rarely calls, and my dad calls, but..."

Noah stiffened, every muscle attuned to her. "But what, Bree?"

"He only calls to ask for money or tell me what I'm doing wrong in life."

Noah's jaw ticked. "You don't deserve that."

Bree watched his eyes darken and jaw tick and felt a warmth blossoming in her chest. It felt nice to be cared for. To have someone angry on her behalf rather than just angry with her. She filed away this moment, tucking it in the quiet place in her mind where she could retreat to replay things that made her happy. The space that used to be full of her favorite books, old vacations, friends, and early childhood had been full of Noah the past few months. Noah holding her hand. Noah standing up for her. Noah keeping her safe, which no one had ever done for her. Noah believing her and believing in her. All the things. She'd happily dwell on those. What Bree didn't want to dwell on was her current relationship with her parents.

"Can we talk about happier things? Like...What's your favorite kind of music?"

Bree asked.

"I don't listen to much music."

Bree froze with her fork halfway to her mouth "You're joking."

"Nope, I sit in the quiet with my thoughts or listen to a podcast."

"You know this could be your second red flag," Bree said with feigned serious-ness.

"Second? What was my first?"

"Being bossy." She teased.

"Fair. I think I can argue my way out of this one being a red flag, though." Noah said, his eyes twinkling.

"I don't know, I take music very seriously." Bree hedged.

"If I don't really listen to music, that means you'd always have control over the radio in the car because I really don't care."

Touché. "You've got a fair point," Bree said, shoving the food into her mouth.

"So, really, it's a green flag."

Bree chucked. "Alright, I'll give you that one. The bossy flag sticks, though."

Noah laughed. "When it comes to keeping you safe, Bree, I happily accept the bossy flag."

"I really do need to ask Mrs. Garcia about teaching me to cook," Bree said as they cleared the table and began straightening the kitchen.

"I'll see what I can do," Noah said. "Movie tonight?"

"Pride and Prejudice?"

Noah groaned. "Can't we watch something festive? Like Die Hard? That's a Christmas movie, and it's almost Thanksgiving, so...'tis the season?"

Bree laughed. "What if we do a double feature?" She suggested, wiping down the counters while Noah finished loading the dishwasher.

"Deal. I'll grab the popcorn."

Chapter Nineteen

Aubrey

Three days later, Bree was not only exhausted from interrupted nights of sleep—thank you nightmares—but she was also starting to get a little cabin fever. Noah was at the office for the first time since she'd moved in with him. Normally, he was home, but was constantly busy with virtual appointments and meetings, and while she was used to being alone it was a little strange. She also hated feeling like she was a burden to Noah, though he would never say that she was. Bree sighed and stared at the painting she was working on, waiting for inspiration to strike. It was no use. She couldn't paint when she was like this. Her brain felt as though it were full of cotton—why couldn't she handle stress like a normal person?

The idea that someone was out there, watching her, waiting to get access to her, made her skin crawl. The faceless man had been the star of her nightmares since the break-in, and Bree was tired of the unknown man's hold on her life. She wanted to move past it—she wasn't hurt, nothing was missing—but the lingering feeling of her safe space being violated just wouldn't let up.

She groaned inwardly, sitting her paintbrush down and staring out the window toward the lake. A girl could get used to living with that view. She loved her bungalow, but this view made her reconsider staying in her house. Maybe she should get a new one and have a view like this in her art studio. She filed it away with other things she considered on days she felt like making rash decisions. Most of them never saw the light of day again, and some...like that time she wanted a change and dyed her hair bright pink...have photographic evidence so they can live on in infamy.

The front door opened and she hopped off her stool to go to the main living area to greet Noah. Instead, a man who looked rather tall and imposing in the space, was standing there like he owned the place. Bree stopped abruptly. Her pulse raced and she felt a little lightheaded—Was he an intruder? Was he the one sending the pictures and flowers to her? What was she going to do? Throw a paintbrush at him?

The man turned toward her, and he narrowed his eyes slightly. Several different escape plans—none of them valid—tore through her head, and she tried to glance toward each exit without being obvious.

He seemed to notice his facial expression and relaxed the glare, holding out his hands in a placating gesture. "I'm not here to hurt you. I'm a friend of Noah's. I work at Hawthorne Security."

"You probably shouldn't be here until Noah gets back," Bree said, kicking herself for confirming that she was alone. What a dumb move. Like she hadn't binge-watched Law & Order, Criminal Minds, and the First 48 most of her life. It was official. She was one of the girls in the horror movie that was too stupid to live.

"He's just out back." She said, trying to cover her own blunder.

"Aubrey," the man said, clearly trying to alleviate her suspicions. She took a small step back as the front door opened again, and a familiar boisterous laugh rang through the house.

Theo walked around the corner and quickly took in the sight in the living room. Bree was sure it was quite a scene to look at. The man who claimed he worked with Noah was across the room trying to placate Bree while she stood there looking like a deer caught in headlights.

Theo waltzed past the man and swooped her up in a hug. He gently set her back down and steadied her. "It's been too long, Aubrey." He said jovially.

He didn't seemed alarmed by the man standing in the house, but she had to hear he was a safe person from Theo directly.

"Theo," Bree whispered, leaning closer to him. "Do you know this guy?"

He turned around and laughed loudly. "Nope, never seen him a day in my life." He said with feigned seriousness.

The man looked annoyed and picked up a couple of the throw pillows from the couch, chucking them at Theo.

"I'm kidding! I'm kidding!" Theo said, batting the pillows out of the air. "That's Zach. He's on our team at Hawthorne."

Bree smiled at him apologetically, kicking herself for being so paranoid. Like her stalker was really going to just waltz in the door and take her.

"Sorry." She said sheepishly.

"You've got nothing to be sorry for," Zach said seriously. "You shouldn't just take the word of a random man who walks in your house claiming to know someone you're close to."

"I'm not really close to—"

"You should know that 3.5% of unmarried women are victims of violent or seriously violent crimes, so it wasn't smart to tell him that you were alone. But I think you know that. " Peter added unhelpfully as he walked into the living room.

"You'd think the number of hours I've wasted watching crime TV would pay off, but no. I'm apparently the woman who goes to look in the basement when she hears weird noises while being home alone instead of getting the heck out." Bree joked.

Noah chose that moment to walk around the corner, a bouquet of her favorite wildflowers in his hands and a small smile on his face. "Good thing we don't have a basement." He joked. "Sorry you were startled. I sent a text, but it must not have gone through."

Bree shook her head. "I was trying to work on some art, so I left my phone in my room."

Noah walked over and handed her the bouquet, and she melted on the inside. How did he know what her favorite flowers were? "Thank you! How did you know wildflowers are my favorite?"

He smiled at her softly. "They're the only thing you planted in your garden at home. Observation *is* one of my superpowers." He joked. "And I thought you could use a surprise bouquet that had some positive memories associated with it."

How was this man still single? He was lethal. "Thank you," Bree told him quietly, happiness fluttering in her chest.

He turned from her after a moment and looked at the men gathered. "I'm glad you guys are here. I wanted to run a few things by you."

***

Noah

"Theo?" Noah said, grabbing Theo's attention as Noah walked over to stand next to Aubrey.

Theo halted his conversation with Zach and Peter and came over to where Noah was standing. "What's up?"

"The police just released their official report on the flower situation at Bree's. Can you read through the report and see if there's anything that stands out? Also, call down to the precinct and see what information we can get that might be unavailable to the public. Let's try to figure out where the guy bought them. Maybe he's on film there. I want to know as much as we can. She also has been receiving calls from someone who usually just breathes on the other end of the line and doesn't say anything. I want them found, too. Find out if there's a connection."

"On it," Theo said, grabbing his briefcase and heading over to the dining room table.

"Usually?" Zach asked, his voice serious.

"He heard me in the background last time and called her a name."

"A name?" Peter asked flatly.

"He called her a..." Noah paused, not wanting to repeat it in front of Bree.

"He called me a whore. But he called again after that and didn't say anything." Bree supplied, squeezing his hand reassuringly.

"And has there been any activity from him since those pictures came out?" Zach asked.

"Not so far. The only change was his first calls were from long-distance area codes, and the most recent ones were a local area code." Bree said.

Zach and Peter looked at Noah as they exchanged knowing glances. This was not good. In fact, it was likely going to devolve into very bad unless they got ahead of it. Jealous stalkers could be some of the most dangerous.

A knock sounded at the front door before it opened and the last of our crew came through. "Sorry I'm late," Eli said as he walked in. "There were some issues with one of my diplomatic clients I had to resolve before I could leave."

"No problem, man. Glad you're here."

"So what do we know?" Eli asked. Theo quietly got him up to speed and he looked at Bree seriously. "Aubrey, do you have any idea who could be behind this? Would anyone do this as a joke?"

"No," Bree said defensively, and Noah found himself fighting the urge to step in front of her. He didn't need to shield her from his friends. They'd defend her with their lives if necessary. "I can't imagine anyone in my life doing something like that and thinking it was funny. It's not like I have a lot of enemies."

"I mean, there are the men from social media." Theo piped in from the table.

"And the person who was at the museum who sold the original photo and your address," Zach pointed out.

"And whoever left the photos in your mailbox," Peter said.

"And the guy who just broke in and left flowers inside of your house," Eli added with a frown.

"And Justin," Noah said quietly. Every head in the room whipped around to look at him.

"Who's Justin?" Theo asked.

Bree glared at Noah. It honestly made him just want to kiss her. "It's my sister's ex-boyfriend. He isn't a problem, though."

"Didn't seem like it to me," Noah muttered under his breath. "Justin and Bree got into an altercation at the hospital when we were visiting her sister." Bree winced as he said it, and Noah gently brushed his hand over her arm. "They need to know so they can help, Bree." He whispered to her.

"Your sister is in the hospital?" Peter asked.

"Yes—she's...she's in a vegetative state. But I still visit her most Thursdays. Justin isn't supposed to be allowed in to see her, but apparently, the new staff wasn't made aware." The bitterness in Bree's voice carried throughout the room.

"Bad blood between them?" Peter asked.

"He's the reason she's there." Bree said stoically."But at the end of the day, it was caused by a mix of bad choices and an accident, so it's not like he was violent and intentionally hurt her."

"Okay. We can try to narrow down who might've sold your information and pictures to the press initially. Then we can try and determine if they're the ones consistently harassing you or if we have two problems running loose. Let's go through the different people who know your routines and try to figure out who it might have been."

They all took seats on the couch, Noah sitting as close to Bree as possible while still maintaining some semblance of professionalism, though that was pretty much in the dumpster and on fire at this point. Noah couldn't help placing a reassuring hand on her back or trying to make her smile or the terms of endearment that just seemed to fall from his lips around her. She was like no one he'd ever met and was everything he wanted. Well, she would be if he believed relationships for people who offer security for celebrities or diplomats could work out. There was too much travel, and it required a high level of trust. He didn't want to get hurt again. And he didn't want to hurt Bree—even though it would be unintentional.

"I don't have a lot of friends." Bree began. "So there aren't many people who would've been aware of where I was going and when. Mostly Rae and Steph."

"Not a big socializer?" Peter asked.

"Not at all," Bree laughed, though her hands gently rubbing the soft blanket on her lap belied her anxiety. "I kind of hate being in the spotlight." She admitted.

"You must've hated the job from the beginning. Why did you wait to get out?" Zach asked, puzzled.

"It brought in good money."

"Money isn't everything. Especially if you're miserable. Did you know that there's actually a relationship between being miserable at work and experiencing chronic stress, depression, and anxiety? Then those problems lead to bigger issues like heart disease, high blood pressure, and diabetes. Bad work environments account for somewhere in the neighborhood of eight percent of annual health costs and around one hundred twenty thousand deaths per year." Peter said.

"Is there anything you don't know?" Theo asked, gobsmacked.

Bree ignored Theo and turned her full attention to Peter. "Money *is* everything when it's the difference between your sister being 'alive' and dead." Bree shot back.

There was a heavy silence in the room, and Peter's eyes widened briefly. "I'm sorry," He said. "That must be difficult."

Noah thought of the guilt Bree wrestled with around her sister's situation, and his heart broke for her. He couldn't imagine being in that situation. It made him angry that her father expected her to carry the financial burden of Jessica's hospital stay.

The fact he'd been so quiet lately didn't sit well with Noah either. Men like that had a habit of popping back up when they needed something and usually left destruction in their wake. He wouldn't let that happen to Bree. He'd protect her from the threats—whether they were from her father or someone else.

"It can be sometimes. But I mostly try to stay on the bright side. It's better that way." Bree said, waving a hand dismissively.

"Is...is your sister going to get better?" Theo asked quietly from the dining table.

"No," Bree said. "I don't think she is."

"So why...?"

"Can we move on? Please? My sister has nothing to do with this."

There was a collective grunt of agreement, and suddenly, a pillow came out of nowhere, hitting Zach in the face. Theo roared with laughter and Bree let out a soft smile.

"So Zach, How was your trip back home?"

Zach shifted, "It was fine."

"Did you get to see Kennedy?"

A distinct cloud seemed to settle over his features. "Yeah."

"How—"

"I don't want to talk about it right now." He said quietly and succinctly.

"No worries, man. We're not trying to pry. I know you said you don't need anything, but if that changes, we have your back."

"I know. Appreciate it."

"Let's circle back to the issue at hand," Eli suggested, watching Zach concernedly. "We know that someone sold the photo of you and your location to the press. We don't know who. Have we tried calling the paper and asking for their source?"

Theo laughed. "You know they're not going to give up their source, Zach."

"You never know. Might get a newbie."

"I already tried. No luck." Theo said. "The lady wasn't particularly nice about it either."

"I imagine they get a lot of calls about their sources," Bree said diplomatically. "You probably caught her on a bad day."

That was his Bree, always believing the best in people. "Let's start with the people closest to you," Noah said, moving his attention back to the conversation at hand as well. "Could Rae or your parents have been behind the whole thing?"

Bree paused and looked thoughtful. The men all watched her silently, giving her room to think. "I don't think so..." She said slowly. "I mean I know Rae has always been kind of hot and cold, but she has a successful business. She doesn't need money, though she is trying to sign another big-name client. Same with my parents. I mean, I already send them money and pay for Jessica's hospital bills every month. I can't imagine they'd feel the need to stoop to that level in order to get more money. Especially since usually my dad will just call to ask me and guilt me until I say yes." Bree chuckled awkwardly while the men in the room exchanged dark looks. Bree may have written her parents off, but they wouldn't. Not if he was continually trying to extort money from her through emotional manipulation.

"What about your old manager?" Peter asked, taking notes on his tablet.

"We already asked about Rae," Zach said.

"No, Rae was her agent. I'm pretty sure that's different." Theo said.

"Guys—maybe we let Aubrey answer?" Peter said.

"They are different. You mean Eliana? She's paid pretty well and makes commission. She also has a number of high-profile clients she represents, so she's not getting shafted financially. Plus, I can't think of a reason she'd choose me to provide that information for. She has other clients who are off the grid who haven't been splayed all over the cover of magazines. Some who are bigger names and magazines would pay better for."

Peter made a sound of agreement. "The record label owners?"

Bree shook her head, a look of frustration on her face. "They are making bank off their celebrity clients. I just can't see them doing something like this. They'd be risking their entire livelihoods and the reputation of their studio for what? A few thousand dollars?"

Noah frowned. They were getting nowhere. "How about the other guests at the museum?" He asked Bree, hoping one of them stood out.

"There were some kids on a field trip. I ran into the Millers as I was leaving, and they asked me to speak at the Gala, which I accepted. No one else seemed all that interested in me, to be honest. Other than when I turned down Kyle Rhodes."

"You turned him down?" Eli asked. From what they knew of Rhodes, no one turned Kyle down.

"Yeah, he asked me to an awards dinner, and I said no. He didn't take that well, but Marilee was monitoring from the counter, and he left without issue."

"What do you mean 'he didn't take it well?'" Noah asked, practically growling.

"I mean, men with egos and pocketbooks like his aren't used to hearing 'no' and taking it for an answer. He told me that I was going to 'change my tune one day' and that it 'better be soon'. And then he left." Bree said simply.

"He give you any trouble since then?" Noah asked through clenched teeth.

Bree paused and tried to remember. "No, I think you and I saw him in the coffee shop after that, but he really hasn't done anything. He's a slimeball, but it's mostly entitlement, and thinking his father's position in the community grants him immunity. If he does anything, I'll let you know." A look of determination crossed Bree's face, and Noah brushed a stray lock of hair out of her eyes, his thumb lingering on her cheek and giving a soft caress as it went by.

"So, we effectively know nothing. No witnesses. No suspects. Nada." Eli summarized, sitting back in his chair.

"Essentially," Peter said, closing his tablet and putting it away.

"Sorry I couldn't be more help," Bree said forlornly. "It's one of the reasons the police wouldn't get involved initially. They said it just came with the territory of being famous. They're looking into things a little further since there was a break-in, but maybe they're right." A quiet weight settled over the group as they ran through the information they had—which was admittedly nothing.

"Well, now that we've established we don't know anything, this conversation is far too heavy for me," Theo said, looking around the room. "Cards, anyone?"

***

"What are you doing, Noah?" Peter asked abruptly after Bree disappeared down the hallway to use the restroom. The rest of the team sat their cards down and looked at Noah expectantly.

"What do you mean?" He asked, setting his cards down as well. His friends were watching him warily, as though they were looking for answers on his face to questions they hadn't asked yet.

"Aubrey is a client, and she's living in your house," Peter said flatly.

"She needed somewhere to go after her home was broken into," Noah argued.

"She could've gone to one of the safe houses," Eli said, leaning back in his chair.

Noah felt his chest constrict painfully. "She would've hated that. She doesn't want to give up her life and stay inside the house until this unknown threat is gone. Especially if the threat could just resurface when she did." He argued.

He didn't want Bree to leave. He wanted her here. In his house. In his arms. He was so far gone for this girl, it wasn't even funny. He loved her strength and her ability to really see others. She had the biggest heart. She was kind and funny and beautiful.

"I think you're missing the point here," Zach said, folding his arms across his chest. "You're clearly getting attached to her, and we're concerned that it will influence your ability to keep her—and yourself—safe."

"Aubrey is not a distraction."

"You need to be able to think clearly on the job, Noah. Having someone you're emotionally or physically involved with can cloud your thinking. It can lead to mistakes that get someone hurt or killed." Eli argued.

"Bree is not a liability," Noah said, gritting his teeth. "I hear that you're concerned, but we're not dating. Do I like her? Yes, yes, I do. Do I think she's beautiful? You'd have to be blind to not see how gorgeous she is. But I would *never* risk her safety. Or yours. Or mine."

"But at the end of the day, she *is* a client, and we have a policy in place for a reason. We just don't want anything to happen to you, man." Zach said. A door opened and closed down the hall, and they paused as Bree's quiet footsteps headed back into the main living area.

"We love Aubrey, and if she's it for you, we respect that. As long as it doesn't endanger your life." Eli said.

"Or hers," Peter added.

"I know," Noah said quietly as Bree walked into the room, a small smile on her face.

"You waited for me?" She asked happily.

"Sure did. Always will." Noah said, leveling a stare across the table as he picked up his cards. "You're up, Zach."

Chapter Twenty

Three hours later, after a few rounds of cards, a good dinner, and a lot of laughter, the men of Hawthorne Security left, and it was just Noah and Bree sitting together on the couch in the house. "That was a lot of fun," Bree told him honestly. "I can't remember the last time I just sat around and laughed like that."

"We love getting together. We try and have at least one meal a week together outside of work. Usually, it ends up being a lot more because we're all single, so if we're home there's a good chance we're eating together."

Bree's brows furrowed. "I know it's only been a few days, but you haven't had anyone over or gone anywhere since I moved in."

"I was giving you a chance to settle in—and before you say anything, I wouldn't have done anything differently. Fair warning though, you may find them difficult to get rid of now." Noah chuckled. "Once you're accepted in the fold, you're family. It's kind of like suddenly gaining four older brothers."

"You mean five older brothers?" Bree asked him, raising an eyebrow.

"No," he said huskily, leaning in toward her slightly. His eyes drifted from her eyes to her lips, and his head tilted more toward hers. "Definitely four."

The scent of him overwhelmed her senses in the best possible way and her pulse began to race. She slowly closed her eyes, the warmth from his lips increasing as he came closer—nearly touching hers. Her heart sped up as Noah reached his hand up and cupped her face, drawing her closer to him.

Just as his lips ghosted across hers, a ringtone blared from the cell phone sitting on the coffee table. Noah jumped back from her as though he'd been burned, and she was frustrated. This is why she should leave her phone on do not disturb. It's not like she wanted to talk to anyone anyway. She smiled apologetically at Noah before checking the caller ID. Her dad's name and picture flashed on the screen, and she bit back a groan of frustration. Of course, he'd choose now to call. She debated ignoring it, but she'd feel awful if something happened to Mama or Jess.

"Hello?" Bree said softly.

"Aubrey?" A dark chuckle sounded through the line. It didn't sound like her dad's laugh at all. Then again, nothing seemed like him since Jessica's accident. "So you are alive."

That's a weird way to start a call. "Last I checked I am indeed alive," Bree said uncomfortably.

Noah must've sensed her discomfort because he scooted closer to her and leaned in so he could hear the call as well.

"You wouldn't know it. Your socials have been minimally active for the past week!" He said, anger coloring his tone.

"I've been a little busy, Dad," Bree said defensively. "Besides, now that I'm not in the industry, I don't need to keep them as active." Noah rested a hand on her knee, rubbing it reassuringly.

"Ah yes, you're busy whoring around with some guy. Your mother and I were terribly disappointed when we saw the pictures. We raised you better than that. Let me remind you what your job actually is, Aubrey Elizabeth Gray. Your job is to stay on the front of people's minds. You are responsible for providing care for your sister. You're helping to keep a roof over your mother's head. You don't have time to be slacking off with some guy who probably only has one thing on his mind. Hitting it and quitting it." The sneer came through loud and clear on the line, and Bree's jaw dropped.

What the heck? The blood rushed to her cheeks, embarrassed that Noah was hearing this conversation. Noah continued to rub her leg and reached behind her, pulling a fuzzy blanket down and placing it on her lap. He then reached over and moved her hand over the blanket in a stroking pattern—similar to what she did when she was anxious or upset. She looked at him in wonder. How was this man not married or in a serious relationship? His lack of commitment seemed to be his only red flag. Granted, that was a big one.

"You know what, Dad," Bree said, placing a sarcastic emphasis on his title. Her anger, confusion, and hurt were all-consuming. The weight of the last few days was more than she wanted to carry. "I am not going to carry this family anymore. Perhaps you and Mom will need to figure out a different way to keep a roof over your head. Maybe you and mom..." Bree choked on her tears. "Maybe you and Mom will have to let Jess go and move on."

"You ungrateful, spiteful, brat." Her dad snapped through the line. "When I get my hands on your ungrateful—"

Bree couldn't hear exactly what his next words were because a very still Noah gently removed the phone from her hand and put it up to his ear.

"You will not *ever* speak to her like that again," Noah said clearly in a low voice that threatened violence.

"If it were up to me, you wouldn't speak to her again at all. But that is Aubrey's choice. If you do speak to her, you will not speak to her like that, and you most definitely will not put your hands on her. Put hands on her, and I promise you it'll be the last thing you do." Noah didn't wait for a response; instead, he ended the call and handed the cell phone back to her while draping his arm over the sofa and encouraging her to snuggle in.

Bree burst into ugly tears—the sobbing kind with snot that makes your face all puffy—and leaned into him. What had been a perfect night had turned into a complete disaster. Noah fetched her some Kleenex to mop up the emotional mess and gave her a soft kiss on the forehead. After she calmed down, she thought back to their almost kiss. So close.

"Noah," Bree said, feeling weary, but not ready to go to bed. "Can I ask you something?"

"Anything," he replied.

"Why don't you have a girlfriend?"

His face looked stunned. Apparently, that wasn't what he thought she was going to ask him.

"I mean, you're smart, and you have a good sense of humor. You're thoughtful, and attentive, and protective without being overbearing. You're not hard on the eyes, either. You have a house and a career. You're kind of the perfect catch." Bree said, hoping to come across as casual when she desperately wanted to know the answer.

"Did I ever tell you how I ended up in celebrity protection detail?" Noah asked.

Bree was entirely unsure how those things were related, but she could roll with it. "Nope. You haven't."

Noah looked off into the distance. "I was in the Marines for four years before getting out. One of the guys in my unit was up for discharge before me, and he had moved to Los Angeles to join the police department. He worked his way up pretty quickly. He was charming, good-looking, and had an enormous level of talent. And the ability to tolerate more bureaucratic crap than I ever will. Anyway, when I got out, I wasn't sure what I wanted to do in my life. We had stayed in touch and when I told him I wasn't sure what I wanted to do, he invited me to apply at the police department. I was hired, went to the academy, and got my first beat. I worked my way up, but managed to ruffle some feathers."

She smiled at the idea of a younger Noah taking the world by storm. "I can't imagine your ruffling feathers." She told him teasingly.

He smiled at her and squeezed her hand. "One day, a young woman came into the station while I was there. She was worried about a stalker. She mentioned notes that had been left. Gifts she'd been receiving. Things she found out of the ordinary and that were...unwelcome. Then, the behaviors seemed to escalate. A slashed tire, a photo of her left taped to her apartment door. I went to my boss and told him what was going on. Told him I thought she had a stalker that was escalating. He shooed me off. Told me she was an up-and-coming celebrity who'd been gaining popularity. That rising stars should 'expect' that kind of behavior. A few notes and gifts weren't a threat and the tire and photo on her door could've been done by different people. It could've been unrelated. So I had to go and tell her we couldn't help her. I suggested she look into private security. Maybe a bodyguard. But the waitlists were long."

"What happened to her?"

"Her stalker broke into her home and killed her in April of that year," Noah said. "I had already thought about getting into the protection business, but that was the final nail in the coffin. If law enforcement wouldn't take these threats seriously, I wanted to. And I know the police often couldn't because the perps know the law and how to work within it also. It was just a mix of the perfect storm and bureaucratic complacency. So I quit. Worked in private security for events to get the lay of the land and learn any of the skills I hadn't picked up in the Marines and department, and started up Hawthorne Security."

"I'm so sorry, Noah. That had to be devastating." Bree couldn't imagine someone with his innate need to protect having to sit by and feel responsible for someone getting killed. Especially if he believed he could have intervened.

"So why I'm not in a relationship—" He began, circling back to the question that had started this all.

"I had a bad breakup a few years ago," Noah said after a few minutes of silence. "I was seeing a woman, Sarah, and we'd been together for a couple of years. I thought she hung the moon and figured we'd get married. I asked her to marry me, and she said yes. We were going to get married in the spring. But then we started fighting. Apparently, she thought I'd leave celebrity protection when I 'settled down.' She didn't like the hours, the travel, the days without seeing me. That's what she said, anyway. I found out later her main problem was that I tended to run in circles with some very beautiful, wealthy, and affluent women, and her insecurities led to distrust. I would never cheat on my woman." Noah said adamantly.

"I know," Bree said quietly, squeezing his leg softly in reassurance.

He gave her a small smile. "I tried to explain why I started Hawthorne Security. Why it was important for me to be able to continue working celebrity details. Particularly stalking cases. I could give up the tours and such, but I wanted to stay active in the cases where sometimes around-the-clock surveillance or protection was needed."

"I guess she didn't handle that well?"

"Understatement of the century. We argued, and I had to leave for a trip that afternoon, so we parted angry. I loved her and didn't want to lose her because of my work. I called Zach and asked if he'd pick up my detail for a short time while I went back to sort it all out. Sometimes, big personal issues are hard to keep out of the field, and in that case the best thing to do for your client is call someone else in until it's resolved. So that's what I did. Zach was on assignment that day but flew out to meet us in Colorado the next day, and I took a flight home to work things out with Sarah. When I got to our house, I found her in bed with the male best friend she had told me I didn't need to worry about." He looked down at the ground, clasping his hands together tightly.

"I don't want to get hurt like that again. And on some level, I know she lashed out because she was feeling hurt and abandoned—but..."

"That doesn't excuse it," Bree said, anger on his behalf rising in her chest. "You were both adults. If she had that big of an issue with your career she should've just up and left. There is no excuse for cheating! Like if you don't want to be with me, cool, I wish you the best. Then go mess around while you're single. Like. An. Adult." She huffed out.

Noah laughed lightly, the pain of his past lingering in his eyes. "I agree." Noah paused, an unnamed emotion swirling in his eyes as he looked at Bree. It looked a lot like affection.

Bree waited to see what he was going to say, unsure of how to carry on the conversation. She just wanted him to know she cared about him. She was on his side. And she hoped that Sarah, wherever she was, always got stuck in the slowest line at the grocery store and that she never had a decent cup of coffee again. Good riddance. Heaviness seemed to sit on Noah's shoulders as the two of them sat absorbed in their own thoughts.

"I think I'm going to turn in," Noah said after a few minutes of silence.

"Okay, good night, Noah." She said as they stood slowly.

"Goodnight, Bree." He said quietly, heading to his room.

She walked down the hall and closed her door gently before leaning her head back on their door, contemplating their almost kiss. If only her father had waited five more minutes. She sighed. Tonight, she'd just daydream about how close she'd finally come to feeling his lips on hers.

Chapter Twenty-One

Aubrey

One week later, Bree was seriously considering running away to join one of those anti-technology cults. Between the unending calls for statements from the press when news of the break-in leaked and her financial guy who was handling her portfolio, she also was on the receiving end of no less than five angry phone calls from her father, two tear-filled phone calls with her mother, and three of the weird breathing phone calls where she now waited about five seconds and then hung up. People survived without phones before...She could do it, too.

Bree turned off her phone and headed into the art studio to finish a couple of pieces that needed time to dry so they could be photographed and listed for sale later this week. Now that she was more settled, Noah had been going into the office on the days she didn't need to be out. It was a little strange to be alone after all the time she'd been spending with Noah, but it was also nice to be able to just enjoy the silence. Socializing was really taxing. Even with people she liked.

But sometimes in the silence she'd find herself wondering if every sound the house made was her stalker. If someone was trying to get into the house. If someone was trying to scare her. Sometimes—though she'd never admit it to Noah—she would lock her bedroom door and take a book to sit on the floor in the walk-in closet in her room. Being behind multiple locked and closed doors in a space where she could clearly see everything and no one was hiding helped subdue the anxiety and fear around her stalker still being on the loose.

The other guys from Hawthorne security had been here every other day or so for dinner and brainstorming sessions which mostly turned into banter filled evenings where they all took turns sharing Noah's most embarrassing moments and then throwing each other under the bus for how they all knew them in the first place. It was a loud, fun, warm, and wonderful family. She loved it. She loved them.

Several hours later the front door crashed open and Bree jumped, thankfully managing to keep her wet brush away from the painting.

"BREE!" Noah shouted, his footsteps racing through the house. "BREE!"

He made it to the studio before she could properly stand up. The door opened, and Noah stopped so suddenly it would've been comical in any other situation. His chest heaved, and he rushed over to her, his hands resting gently on her upper arms as his eyes roved her body as though he were checking her over for injuries. Alarm bells sounded in her head as Noah pulled away, but were promptly silenced as he placed a hand behind her head and pulled her toward him with a forceful tenderness before crashing his lips against hers.

All thought stopped completely, and she paused for a moment before kissing him back. He tasted like coffee and his tongue was warm as he swiped it across her lower lip asking for entrance. He didn't have to ask her twice. She opened up for him and felt a little light-headed as he took control of the kiss. He ran his hand through her hair, pulling her closer and guiding her to exactly where he wanted her to be. Her heart sped up, and she wrapped her arms around him, leaning into the strong, solid warmth of his body. She let out a small whimper as he swiped his tongue across hers, and he pulled her closer, his hand fisting in the back of her shirt as he let out a low growl.

They separated for breath and he rested his forehead against hers, both of them breathing heavily, soft bursts of air gently brushing across Bree's face. Once her head was firmly out of cloud nine and she could breathe again without running the risk of needed to be resuscitated, She looked up at Noah, concerned. Bree reached up and put a hand gently on his cheek. "Are you okay?"

He pulled her in for a tight hug. "I'm better now." He said, his face in the side of her neck muffling his voice.

"What happened?"

Noah looked at her, his eyes darkening. "I thought you were kidnapped."

"What?!"

He took a deep breath. "Let's go sit on the couch." Noah wrapped his arm around her and held her close as they walked down the hall and into the living room. He paused when she sat down and looked down the hall. "Your painting stuff is expensive...do I need to wash out the brushes or..."

"They'll keep for a little bit. Noah, you scared me. What's going on?"

Noah pulled his cell phone out of his jacket pocket and pulled up a photograph that showed a printed photo and a folded sheet of paper laying on a desk "Do you recognize this?" He asked.

Bree zoomed in on the photo, and all of the blood drained from her face. It was a photo of her from a couple of years ago in a rather risqué negligee, her hands clearly tied to a headboard. The only reason this photo had ever seen the light of day was because her facial features were nearly impossible to make out due to the heavy shadows that were supposed to give the picture an air of mystery and some universal appeal. It could be any woman wearing the outfit—partaking in the fantasy. It was the one and only time she forgot to research a brand before agreeing to do some content creation for them.

"It's me during a photo session a couple of years ago." She told him seriously. "I made the mistake of taking the name of the brand at face value and didn't do in-depth research before agreeing to it." She grimaced. It was not her finest moment as a businesswoman. First law of business: Always do your research.

She looked at Noah curiously. "You can't see my face in the shadows, though—so how did you know it was me?"

"The birthmark with the freckle next to it on the inside of the right wrist. I've seen you anxiously move your hands around enough to have seen it quite a few times." Noah reached over and swiped to go to the next picture. "Look at the paper."

Bree zoomed in on the paper next, and her heart stuttered.

She's MINE.

Bree dropped the phone as though it were on fire and looked at Noah, suddenly understanding his extreme concern. "Where did it come from?"

"It was in an envelope with my name on it, taped to the front door of the office when I got back from my meeting. I tried calling you immediately, but your phone kept going to voicemail. I thought...I thought he'd taken you."

Bree's heart lodged in her throat, making it difficult to breathe. How did the stalker even know that was a picture of Bree? Noah still seemed to be trapped in his own head, so Bree reached up and touched his face gently. "I'm right here, Noah. I am safe. And I am safest right here with you."

Noah kissed her palm and they sat for a moment, just soaking the moment in and letting the fear and adrenaline get back to a normal level so they could function again.

"Umm, Noah?"

"Hmm?"

"What happened to the original photo and letter? What if it gets leaked to the press or something?"

"I already submitted the originals to the police department. I took a quick photo for our own records before I sent them to the station."

"Oh. Did you see who left it?"

"No. Theo is currently pulling footage from our cameras and asking a few neighboring businesses with cameras if we can see their footage as well. We'll weasel this guy out eventually. Bree...?"

"Yeah?"

"Are you okay?"

"Yes? No? I don't know. My life has been turned upside down and inside out the last few weeks but I've also gained new friends and a temporary great view." Bree said, teasing him about the lake, as she often did. "I...I'd be lying if I said I wasn't scared." She said, her tone serious as she observed him. "Some days, I feel like I'm overly paranoid and going to have a heart attack from seeing my own shadow."

"You're safe with me, Aubrey." He stared into her eyes for a moment before a subtle frown took over his face. "I shouldn't have kissed you." He sighed.

"Why not?"

"Pick your poison. You're my client. You're living in my house under duress. I'm crap at relationships. I didn't ask you first..."

"Listen, I'm not living in your house 'under duress.' Would I be here without my current situation? No. But if I really didn't want to be here, Noah, I would've stayed at my own house. Or gotten a hotel room. Secondly, you're not 'crap at relationships.' You had a bad breakup with a woman who neither understood nor appreciated you. I've lived here for two weeks. I can almost guarantee you'd be a great boyfriend. As far as asking me, I give you leave to kiss me anytime. And you would've stopped if I had resisted or pushed you away or said to stop. You're a good man."

"So...you're picking because you're my client?" He asked, attempting—but failing—to lighten the mood.

Bree stood up abruptly and went into the kitchen to grab her phone. She turned it on, noticing several missed calls from Noah and a couple from an unknown local number. They left a message though, so she'd get back to them later. Maybe she'd ask Noah to listen to them first. She didn't have anything to hide really and she didn't want to listen to multiple voicemails of someone breathing.

She'd ask Noah later. She didn't want to deal with it right now, and he didn't need to either. Especially after the note he'd gotten. Bree stalked back into the living room and sat on the couch furiously tapping away at the buttons so her email app could populate. Why was tech always laggy when you had something important to do?

"Bree?" Noah asked, his brow furrowed in confusion.

She held up a finger. "Give me a minute." She muttered, typing out an email quickly.

Dear Mr. Hawthorne,

Your security services are no longer needed, effective immediately. Your company's services have been adequate, and I look forward to recommending your security services in the future.

Best wishes,

Aubrey Gray

Satisfied with her email, she hit send and waited for the 'ping' to sound from Noah's phone. She put her phone on the coffee table and turned toward Noah. "There's my answer." She replied, gesturing to his phone.

Noah frowned and swiped open his email, reading it quickly before snapping his eyes up to hers, his eyes darkening. He tossed his phone to the side and moved over to Bree's side of the couch. "I'm fired, am I?"

"Effective immediately." She nodded breathlessly. "In writing, via email, per the stipulation of my contract."

Noah's mouth was on hers as soon as she finished her sentence, and tingles traveled through her body. He was delicious. They kissed for a couple of minutes before Noah pulled away and rested his forehead against hers, his hand still cupping the back of her head. "Would you like to go on a date with me, Aubrey Gray?"

The hair on the back of Bree's neck rose as she imagined going out into town. What if *he* was watching? What if he found her? She suppressed a shudder. "I would love to." She said, anxiety overpowering the giddiness filling inside of her. "When?"

"How's tonight?"

"My schedule is looking pretty clear," Bree replied, trying—and failing—to keep the large smile from her face.

"Great. I'll pick you up at seven."

Bree nodded and smiled at Noah as he walked out of the living room. She couldn't remember the last time she'd been this excited to go on a date. Bree's smile fell as she looked down the hall toward her room, an important question floating to the front of her mind. What was she going to wear?

Chapter Twenty-Two

Aubrey

The amount of nerves she had going into this date was unreal. She'd literally been living with the guy for a couple of weeks and had known him for months before that. There was no reason to be nervous. Minus the stalker who could be watching their every move. She dreaded the idea of getting more pictures of herself and Noah in the mail. Would he be watching them? Watching Noah hold her hand or kiss her goodnight? She felt nauseous at the thought and even more unsure of who would be that invested in her.

Bree shook her head. She had ten minutes to get herself together but picking an outfit was proving difficult for a reason she didn't quite understand. She was always a jeans and t-shirt girlie and it was just Noah. He'd seen her in cute clothes. He'd seen her in jeans. He'd seen her in her sweat pants that were two sizes too big last week when Aunt Flo showed up and she ate her heart out on the chocolate almonds he liked to keep around the house. The man had literally seen it all—including bedhead and morning breath. Oy. Yet here she was, standing in a destroyed room, trying to decide what she was going to wear on their first date.

She wanted to look beautiful—like she'd been intentional and put effort into planning an outfit for the date. Noah was worth the effort. So, definitely a dress—no heels. There was one more dress to try on before she tossed it all out the window and decided to never leave the house again. It was a strappy black number she had purchased for a party last year, but never had the chance to wear out of the house because she chickened out of wearing it. It was modest in the front, a scoop neckline that showed a little skin but not much and flared down an inch or two above the knee. The back was where the magic happened. It was cut very low with a few crisscrossing straps guiding the eye down the open back and stopping just above the hip. Enough danger to be sexy, but enough coverage to be at least slightly modest.

Bree slipped into black sandals just as her clock struck seven. Her curls—which she'd set yesterday so they were rocking today—stayed non-frizzy. A light knock sounded on her door and she walked over to open it, suddenly hyper-aware of the mess she'd made getting ready. She opened the door slowly and took in Noah, who looked like a GQ model in his slacks and sports coat.

He looked stunned momentarily before stuttering out. "You look beautiful, Bree."

"Thank you," She said, a light blush creeping into her cheeks. "Let me just grab my purse really quick—"

A soft muttered curse was the only warning before she was pulled back against his body, his arms wrapped around her waist from behind. "Did I say beautiful?" He growled lightly in her ear. "I meant delectable. That dress is absolutely stunning on you."

Bree shivered at the compliment and turned around in his arms. "You're looking handsome too." She told him shyly.

Noah leaned down and gave her a quick kiss, that turned into a slightly longer kiss, before breaking apart. "Nope, we have reservations." He said, mostly to himself.

Bree smiled as Noah placed a hand on her lower back, giddy that she could invoke that kind of response in Noah. It made her feel...desired. She frowned, thinking of the image he'd brought home earlier. Was this showing too much skin? Would her stalker be there watching her and enjoying the dress she picked with Noah in mind? Bile rose in her throat. She could change into something else. She stopped her racing thoughts and took a breath. No. She wasn't going to *let* him win. She was going to wear the dress and look sexy doing it for herself and her date. There was nothing wrong with that.

Feeling a little better after her internal pep talk, Bree grabbed her purse as they walked into the garage. Noah opened her door as usual, but this time the heated look in his eyes sent butterflies scattering through her stomach. "Buckle up." He said, closing the door softly before returning to his side of the car and hopping in.

Noah backed out of the driveway carefully and headed toward town, frequently checking the rearview. Bree observed him quietly, unease still flowing through her. Noah seemed like he was in a rush when he came back earlier. If the stalker found him at work how hard would it be for him to find Noah's home? What if he placed the picture knowing Noah would race home and used that as an opportunity to follow him? What if Noah—in his haste—had been careless?

"Noah…did anyone follow you home earlier?"

Noah frowned. "No. I checked my rearview frequently and made several detours. I would've seen them."

Bree nodded.

"You okay?" He asked, reaching over and placing a hand on her knee.

"Just spooked. If he found you at work what if he finds us at home? How hard would it be to find out where you live?" Bree nibbled on her lip anxiously.

"My home is unlisted. Like you I also take great pains to make sure I can't easily be found. It's not hard to make enemies in my line of work."

An image of Noah bleeding on the ground, a dark shadow standing over him flitted through Bree's mind, causing her stomach to sink and her heart to flutter. Was she bringing danger to Noah's doorstep by being with him? He looked so carefree while driving. Focused, but calm in a way she envied. She probably looked like she was on the verge of a panic attack. Which wasn't far off.

They chatted more about everything and nothing as they drove through town, the smooth cadence of Noah's voice and his confidence doing a lot to put Bree at ease. Noah pulled into a cute little Italian mom-and-pop shop that had recently opened and was the current buzz online. "I love Italian food!" Bree exclaimed, her hungry stomach doing an anticipatory happy dance in celebration of what was sure to be a delicious meal.

"I remember." He said, smiling, offering a hand as Bree got out of the car before lacing his fingers through hers.

They walked into the restaurant, and the hostess smiled as we walked in. "Do you have a reservation?"

"Yes, it's under Noah Hawthorne."

"Follow me." She led them back to the corner of the room where a table with a fancy tablecloth and lit candle waited. Noah pulled out Bree's chair, and he took the seat in the corner where he could have a view of the entire restaurant. The atmosphere of this place was just incredible. "Your waiter will be with you in just a moment." The hostess said before walking away.

Before Bree had a chance to say anything, the waiter was there asking what they wanted to drink and whether they had any questions about the menu.

"Could I get a sweet tea, please?" Bree said.

"I'll have the same."

The waiter nodded and excused himself so they could look at the menus. Bree looked around the room, unsure of what exactly she was looking for. Surely there wasn't going to be some man standing off by himself in a trench coat with a hat low on his brow and a sign reading STALKER hanging around his neck. She was being ridiculous. She turned back to Noah as she opened her menu.

"So, Noah Hawthorne."

Noah smiled indulgently at her.

"Know anything good here?"

He looked over the menu. "I've only eaten here twice since it's newer, but honestly I haven't had anything bad here. Fair warning, I am a creature of habit, so my knowledge extends purely to their pasta dishes."

Bree laughed. "Well, I'm a pasta girlie, so if it's all good that's all I need to know."

"What's your favorite memory growing up?" Noah asked a few moments after they'd given the waiter their order.

"When I was in high school, I had an art teacher named Mrs. Reyes. She was one of those teachers who could command a room just by walking in it, but who still had relationships with her students. She saw me sketching in the quad when I was a freshman and asked if I wanted to sign up for art class the next semester. I wanted to, but my parents wouldn't allow it because I needed to focus on what would help me successfully attain an MBA, and in a moment of borrowed bravery I told her so."

"What happened?"

"She showed up at our front door with a research article in hand waxing on about the benefits business leaders gained from taking art classes. She also pointed out that the state required fine art credits to graduate. My parents relented and let me take art the following year."

"Did you do it your last two years also?"

Bree frowned. "No. My parents wouldn't allow it once I'd satisfied the minimum fine art requirement for graduation. But Mrs. Reyes let me come into her room at lunch and she'd teach me the basics that she could during those times. It was the first time I had someone genuinely interested in me and what I liked. What was your favorite memory growing up?" Bree asked, taking a sip of her tea.

Noah paused for a moment. "Nerf gun wars." He said with a grin.

"Nerf gun wars?"

"Yeah. When I was like I don't know, seven or eight—this was before my sister was born—I would come home from school and there would be a fully loaded nerf gun on the island in the kitchen with a small note that said 'game on'. Mom would be hiding somewhere in the house with her own nerf gun and we'd have a full on battle. I never knew when those days would be—there never seemed to be a rhyme or reason for when there'd be a nerf gun on the counter, but those were my favorite."

"She sounds like a lot of fun."

"She was. She tried to keep our childhoods magical and keep us shielded from the struggles of adulthood despite being a single mom."

The food arrived a few moments later, and conversation dwindled a bit as they tucked in. It was delicious, just as Noah had said.

***

Noah helped Bree stand as they prepared to leave for the evening and she smiled at him. This was the best date she'd ever had. And the restaurant was phenomenal. They walked outside and Noah helped her into the car. Before they left she pulled out her phone and frowned, noticing a few more missed calls and voicemails from that same local number.

Noah got in the car and paused when he saw the look on her face. "What's wrong, Bree?"

"I missed like five calls today from this number."

"Is it him?" Noah asked darkly.

"I don't think so. They left messages, but..."

"You don't want to listen to them?"

"Not really. Does that make me a chicken?"

"No, babe. It makes you human. Want me to listen?"

Bree nodded and handed the phone over to him. He listened attentively, furrowing his brow in adorable confusion from time to time as he listened to all the voicemails. When he listened to the last one, he handed her back the phone and turned to face her.

"Who was it?"

"It was the hospital. I guess Jessica had some complications today, and they weren't able to reach your parents. Apparently, the phone number they had was disconnected, and you were the next point of contact. They want you to come in tomorrow to meet with one of her doctors."

Bree gulped. "Tomorrow?"

"They wanted it to be today, but when it got late, they left another message asking you to come by tomorrow. Billing also called. They asked if you could swing by sometime soon. Might as well stop in tomorrow."

Bree sighed heavily. "It's not going to be good—is it?"

"It's hard to say."

"Will you go with me?"

"Of course."

The rest of the drive home was silent as Bree considered what they could possibly want to talk to her about. Her mind was racing as she contemplated what it could be—maybe her sister had a miraculous recovery and woke up. Maybe she had died. Bree's heart sank. They'd try harder to get in touch with her if Jess had *died,* right? Noah parked the car on the driveway and left the engine running before getting out and coming around to open her door. He closed it gently behind her and escorted her up the front steps, his hand on her lower back the whole time.

"Noah, what are you—"

"I thought you deserved a proper end to our first date—even though we currently live together." He said with a smile.

He stopped in front of the front door and unlocked it, but left it shut. He turned back to Bree and pulled her close to him, his muscular, warm body pressed tightly to hers. The tingling went all the way to her toes, and her stomach swooped.

"Goodnight, Aubrey Gray. I'd like to see you again." He said, his voice husky.

"I'd like that too," Bree said quietly.

Noah leaned in slowly, giving her time to pull away, before swooping down and giving her a good night kiss that heated her up from the inside out. His hands lingered on her waist, tightening as he nibbled her lower lip, and she opened for him, his tongue dancing with hers. He nibbled her lower lip, and she moaned softly while he pulled her even closer. He pulled back after a moment and kissed her again softly.

"Lock the door behind you." He said with a smile.

Bree nodded, her head firmly back up in cloud nine, and carefully made her way into the house, locking the door behind her. She wasn't lying to him earlier—that man could kiss her anytime. She smiled when the garage door opened, Noah moving the car in for the night as he always did. Bree waltzed down the hall to her room, wincing at the storm of laundry that was literally everywhere as she shoved some of it off her bed so she'd have a place to sleep. It was worth it.

Chapter Twenty-Three

Bree and Noah had been sitting in the family consultation room listening to the clock tick for so long that he was about to chuck it out the window. Theo had called on their way to the hospital and said there was nothing on the man who left the pictures. Nothing *new*, anyway. It was the same man who broke in at Bree's. Average height, average build, average, average, average. Frustration was his constant companion. Their perp must have staked out the place pretty thoroughly to be able to avoid Theo's cameras. How was anyone that invisible?

"I can see why Captain Hook hated clocks," Bree muttered under her breath. Noah chuckled as a middle-aged gentleman in a white coat walked through the door.

Noah and Bree stood from their chairs, and the doctor reached out his hand. "Thank you for your patience. You must be Miss Gray." He said warmly, shaking Bree's hand.

"I am."

"And you are?" The doctor asked, turning to shake hands with Noah.

"I'm Noah Hawthorne, sir. Aubrey's boyfriend."

"Pleased to meet you both." He said, sitting down behind the desk and looking at the two of them with a serious expression on his face.

Noah squeezed Bree's leg in a reassuring manner as they waited patiently for the doctor to let them know why he wanted them here. Her quiet look of joy when he had referred to himself as her boyfriend was playing on loop in his mind and was a memory he'd treasure forever. It was quick, but he was all in, and she seemed to be too. Then again, he'd thought that before.

Noah stopped the spiraling thoughts before they metastasized and brought his attention back to the present. The doctor leaned forward and folded his hands seriously. "Miss Gray, your sister has been on the ventilator now for several years."

"Yes, sir," Bree said quietly.

"And in that time, from my understanding, after viewing her charts, she hasn't had any changes in her brain function?"

"No, sir."

"I'm sorry to say that your sister had a series of seizures yesterday that were difficult to control. Her brain was further damaged by the seizures, and she has an infection."

"What does that mean?"

"It means while her recovery before was nearly impossible, now I can say with certainty that she will not recover."

Bree's lip quivered, but she nodded and kept her voice steady. "I understand." She said softly.

"If you have questions you're welcome to check in with Jessica's nurses or we can connect during my rounds." He said, before standing up and walking out of the room.

Bree sat there in a daze, and Noah waited for her to process whatever was going on in that beautiful head of hers. She turned to him about five minutes later, tears filling her eyes. "We can't let her keep suffering, Noah. It isn't right."

Noah reached out to her and pulled her into his arms, tucking her against him securely. He'd never experienced fear like he had when that picture showed up on his door, and he thought Bree was gone. Taken. Being assaulted. They were the longest and worst minutes of his life. Now every time he got to hold her in his arms, he relished it. Though he much preferred holding her while she was happy or just because. He hated seeing her in pain, but he'd hold her through it as well until she could withstand it or get to the other side. He'd forever be her biggest cheerleader. The brief thought of forever didn't send his mind into an automatic tailspin, which was progress.

Noah rubbed his hand up and down Bree's back in soothing motions until she pulled away and looked up at him through tear-filled, red-rimmed eyes. "Thank you for being here, Noah." She whispered softly, her lip still quivering slightly.

"There's nowhere else I'd rather be." He told her truthfully. He held her for a few more minutes while she steadied herself and then stepped away as she went to grab a Kleenex. "Ready for billing?" Noah asked.

Bree looked confused. "I'm not sure what they want with us. We've paid them on time."

"Maybe just some paperwork to sort out." He suggested.

"Maybe," Bree said.

Noah reached out and brushed his hand against hers as they walked and then caught her hand in his as it went by on the next swing. He laced their fingers together, a feeling of warm rightness settling over him. This was his woman, and *no one* was taking her away from him. They reached the elevators and, with the help of a friendly housekeeper, found themselves in front of the head of the billing department's desk.

"Miss Gray, unfortunately, your parents have not returned any of my calls, and you're technically the financial party responsible for your sister's treatment."

"I'm aware, Mrs. Johnson," Bree said respectfully. "I'm happy to help with whatever you need."

"Here is an invoice for the service costs for the last six months." Mrs. Johnson said, handing some paperwork over to Bree. Noah looked over at the figure and his eyes nearly came out of his head like one of those cartoons he watched growing up. The amount was astronomical.

"Yes ma'am," Bree said, confusion still clear in her voice.

"They need to be paid," Mrs. Johnson said kindly.

Bree stilled in her seat, and Noah's heart stuttered in his chest. Did she just say…

"I'm sorry, I'm not understanding. What do you mean they need to be paid?" Bree asked, hysteria creeping into the edges of her voice.

"Miss Gray, no one has paid your sister's medical bill since April, when you made the payment directly yourself."

"That's—that's not possible," Bree said, sinking back in her chair, her cheeks pale and eyes wide. Noah scooted his chair a little closer to hers and wrapped his arm around her shoulder, drawing her close, still reeling from the shock himself.

"Aubrey's parents haven't been paying the bill?" Noah asked Mrs. Johnson. She looked a little disgruntled that he would even ask.

"No, sir. As I said, we haven't received a payment since April."

"But...but...but..." Audrey's breaths started coming in quick pants, and Noah squeezed her shoulder.

"Breathe, Bree. In for four. One. Two. Three. Four. Hold it. One. Two. Three. Four. Out for four. One. Two. Three. Four." He repeated the breathing exercise with her a couple of times until she had herself back under control. She looked crushed.

"You seem rather surprised by this news." Mrs. Johnson said cautiously.

Bree let out a near-hysterical laugh. "I am surprised by this news. I've been giving my father money to pay for Jessica's treatment every month. So I am very freaking surprised by this news." Hurt replaced the hysteria, and Bree looked to be on the verge of tears again.

"So what do we need to do?" Noah asked Mrs. Johnson, hoping that practical steps could help them refocus.

"Getting a good lawyer would be my first recommendation." Mrs. Johnson muttered, though her eyes widened immediately afterward like she couldn't believe she'd said that out loud. Bree laughed, so Noah let it go. Honestly, they probably did need a really good lawyer as a first step. They needed to try to have Bree given Jessica's medical power of attorney. And that started with making sure the bills were paid.

"Mrs. Johnson," Noah said, holding Bree's hand tightly in his own. "Could you make a note in the file that Bree came to see you as soon as she was asked and document our confusion over the lack of payment and the fact Bree said she's been paying her father so he can pay the medical bills?"

"We document everything, but I can make sure to add that in my notes." She said, clicking away at her keyboard a few times until she was satisfied with what she'd written.

Bree looked at him, a question in her eyes.

"That way when you fight for power of attorney they can see that you were not complicit. You showed up when you were asked, were surprised about the money, and the wires you sent to your father will back up the missing funds." Bree nodded quietly.

"Great. Before we take care of the bill, Mrs. Johnson, can we get an itemized bill and is there a cash discount?" His mom always told him to ask. Rule number one: get everything in writing. Rule number two: get an itemized bill. Rule number three: Ask if there's a discount for paying in cash or in full. It's saved him money frequently enough that it was worth asking.

Mrs. Johnson nodded and ran the numbers. It was still insanely high, but Bree and Noah nodded. "I'll call my bank and get that squared away shortly," Bree said softly.

Mrs. Johnson printed a copy the notes from today and an itemized bill of the last six months—He'd need to plant a few trees in the rainforest to pay for that request—and they said their goodbyes with another promise to make payment arrangements shortly. They walked out of the hospital hand in hand, silent until they got into the car.

"How are you feeling, Bree?" Noah asked her as they pulled out of the parking lot. She shook her head, her quivering lip giving away the fact she was overcome with emotion. Noah rested his hand on her knee and drove across town to her favorite coffee shop in Trenton so they could pick up an iced coffee—or two. She could definitely use the pick-me-up today.

Bree smiled her megawatt smile when she noticed where he pulled in and gave his hand a tight squeeze. They walked into the coffee shop, and she smiled at the barista over the counter. "One large iced vanilla latte with caramel drizzle, please." She said with a smile.

"Make that two," Noah said, whipping out his wallet and handing the kid a twenty.

"Thanks," Bree whispered as they dropped the change into the tip jar and moved down to the end of the counter.

"You're welcome, babe."

They grabbed the coffee—both of them actually for Bree—and headed back to the car to head home. It didn't feel like a 'sit in the coffee shop' kind of conversation. When they got back home, Noah sent a quick text to the rest of the guys to let them know there may have been a development and there may not be the normal group dinner this evening, depending on how Bree was feeling. They all sent back a thumbs-up emoji except Theo. Noah's phone rang seconds later, Theo's face flashing on the screen.

"Hey, is Bree okay?" Theo asked, concern lacing his tone.

"I'm not sure—she's been quiet the whole way home. Only drank a quarter of her coffee so far, too." Noah said, frowning.

"Oof. So she's not good at all."

"Not really. Hey, while I've got you, can you do me a favor?" Noah asked. He needed to get information—and get it quickly—but he also needed to stay nearby for Bree.

"Of course. What's up?"

"Will you look into the financials for Bree's parents? Specifically, their finances in the last six to eight months?" Noah had a sinking suspicion that he knew what Theo would find, but the paper trail would confirm it.

"On it. I'll call when I have something."

"Thanks, man. I owe you one."

"The hell you do. Give Bree a hug for me."

Noah hung up and went down to Bree's bedroom, knocking softly on the door.

"Come in," Bree called softly.

Noah opened the door and found Bree looking a little forlorn in her bed—a comfy blanket perched in her lap while her fingers ran over the fabric. He walked over to the bed and sat down next to her, wrapping his arm around her and tucking her into his side. She leaned into him, her hands still moving rhythmically against the blanket. "Want to talk about it?"

She sighed. "Not really, but I guess we should. Maybe we should just get it over with when the guys are here tonight? That way it only has to be dealt with once?"

"We don't have to host if you aren't feeling up to it," Noah told her seriously. "They'll understand if you want some space right now."

Bree smiled up at him gratefully. "I like having everyone here. They don't drain my social battery as quickly as other people. Besides, they're your team. We should tell them."

"And until dinner?"

"I think I'd like to unwind for a little bit. Maybe take a nap."

Noah kissed her forehead softly. "Sounds like a plan. I'll let the guys know, and then we can chat about it tonight. I also asked Theo to look into your parents' financial situation for the last six to eight months. I didn't tell him why, but I figured the more information we had going into this, the better." Bree nodded, and Noah stood up, leaning down to give her a gentle kiss. "I'm going to work in the dining room for a bit. Let me know if you need anything."

"I will." She breathed gently.

Noah walked out of the room, closing her door behind him. He sent a quick text off to the guys letting them know that dinner was a go, but asking them to bring the meal instead so they didn't have to figure out what to cook—and actually cook it—on top of the information bomb that had just been dumped on them.

Pulling out his laptop, Noah spent the next several hours elbows-deep in administrative work for the business while the same question percolated in his head. Where did all of that money go?

Chapter Twenty-Four

Noah's voice drifted into Bree's room from the living area, and she groaned slightly, her mouth feeling dry and her head stuffed full of cotton. She quietly cried herself to sleep earlier and was paying for it now. The overwhelm had dissipated just a little bit, but a heavy sense of foreboding lingered. What on earth was she going to do?

Grief threatened to overwhelm her when she thought of Jess. Her parents weren't going to give up and put Jess out of her misery, which meant this was another task that should've been her parents' responsibility but rested on Bree's shoulders instead. She didn't know how much more weight her shoulders could take before she broke.

She got up and fixed her ponytail before going into the bathroom to make sure she looked semi-presentable. Bree glanced in the mirror and washed off her face, eager to scrub the heavy emotions from the day off her body. Bree walked back into the bedroom and sat on the side of the bed, memories of Jess and her parents playing through her head. Where had they gone wrong? What could she have done differently? She was so tired. Soul deep tired.

Bree took a deep breath, a well of emotion threatening to overwhelm her. It was dumb. It's not like she was in danger at this moment. She needed to pull herself together. There was a soft knock before the door opened and Theo walked in, cozy blanket in hand. He handed her the blanket, and she immediately began rubbing her thumb along it to soothe her anxiety.

"Noah sent me with the blanket and to see if you were up. He said you'd probably like it." Theo mentioned, leaning against the door frame and watching her steadily. "How are you holding up?"

"I'm fine," Bree told him.

He laughed. "I hope you sounded more convincing to Noah if you tried that line. You're not 'fine' Aubrey, and that's okay. You've been through a lot the last several weeks. I mean just the break-in..." Theo paused. "It was scary—hell, I wasn't even there, and I was scared for you."

"But I'm not injured or anything. I was just...startled. And it's been *weeks*, Theo. I should be over it by now."

"Physically, you aren't injured," Theo agreed. "But emotionally, your home—a place you felt safe—was violated with violence. That isn't something that just 'goes away' because you're physically fine."

Bree paused and thought about what Theo was saying. He was right. Her sense of safety did feel like it had been shattered. She couldn't imagine going back to her home and living her life like nothing had ever happened. Any time there was movement she would just be wondering if it was the guy. If he was back to finish the job—whatever the job was.

"When did you get so smart?" She asked Theo, trying to lighten the heavy mood.

"When my home was burglarized growing up." He said seriously, all traces of the light-hearted jokester erased from his face. "I came home from school and found my mother and brother unconscious, the house cleaned out. We got them to the hospital in time—they're fine—but we never felt safe in that house again. We moved pretty soon after. My mom just couldn't rest there."

Bree's heart ached for little Theo. "I'm so sorry that happened to you."

"It was a long time ago. But I did learn from it, and now it can help you. So maybe there is a purpose to the pain we experience even when we're not sure there is at the time. And Bree?"

"Yeah?"

"You know, even though you're not officially a client, you're still under our protection. Nothing is going to happen to you. You're family."

Emotion clogged her throat, and Bree nodded gratefully at him, tears blurring her vision.

"I'm going to head back out with the guys. Come join us when you're ready."

Bree nodded and waited for Theo to close the door softly behind him. She hastily swiped at the tears, hating that she was a crier now. It felt like that's all she did. Once she was presentable enough and was sure she had her emotions under control, she headed down the hallway, following the voices into the main living room.

"Aubrey!" The group chorused when she appeared around the end of the hallway.

Noah got up from the couch and gave her a quick kiss before walking her over to the couch. He helped her get settled and tossed his arm over her shoulder, drawing her into his side.

"Thanks, babe," Bree told him quietly. He grinned roguishly.

"I like that."

"Me saying thank you?" She joked.

"You calling me babe." He countered.

Bree could feel the blush that stole her cheeks and she took the time while he got settled down next to her to cool her jets. Goodness that man was lethal.

Theo whooped from the corner. "You finally made a move? I thought I was going to have to ask her out just to get you worked up enough to ask her out yourself." The group laughed.

"Try it and die," Noah said good-naturedly.

"Noted," Theo replied, a smile still on his face.

"Happy for you, man," Zach said, clapping Noah on the shoulder from his spot next to him.

"Thanks, we're happy too," Noah said, looking down at her and giving her a smile.

"So, not to burst the happiness bubble..." Peter began.

Theo groaned, "You just know how to ruin a moment, don't you?"

"No, he's right. We should talk about this. Bree? You want to share?"

Bree shook her head. Living it once in person was more than enough. She zoned out while Noah updated the group on what had happened at the hospital. From the doctor's prognosis to the issue with the billing department and their subsequent call to the bank to get the debt settled.

There was a collective outraged grumble on Bree's behalf, which gave her a warm, fuzzy feeling inside—a pleasant contrast to the angry bitterness that threatened to overwhelm her when she thought of the missing money. What had he used it for? Why hadn't he used it for Jess's care like he was supposed to? Why was any of this Bree's responsibility? Why didn't her parents care about *her*?

These men, people she'd known for a relatively short time, seemed to deeply care about her. Having people who were one hundred percent in your corner was a strange experience. There was nothing she could do for them—they just wanted to hang out with her because of her. So strange.

"Theo," Noah began, pulling her from her musings. "Any luck on the financials?"

Theo grimaced before looking at Bree apologetically. She tried to give him a reassuring smile, but it fell short—more likely matching his grimace than actually reassuring him.

"I did. It looks like your parents keep separate bank accounts." Theo began.

"They always have," She chimed in. "I never understood why, though. They both contributed to the household financially, so it was a bit odd."

"Well, your mother's statements haven't changed in several years. No new or unusual deposits, no unusual activity, nothing."

"Okay..."

"Your dad's account, on the other hand, shows a slew of unusual activity though one of his accounts we're still trying to get information for. But it looks like all of the money you sent him was put in the account we were able to access, and most of it is gone." Theo said.

"Gone?" Bree asked, her stomach dropping. "It was nearly a quarter of a million dollars. Where did it go?"

"It looks like he might've gotten in over his head with gambling."

"Gambling?" She replied hollowly, her body stiffening as shock settled into her soul. "He spent the money for my sister's care on gambling." There was a violent churning in her chest as her feelings teetered between hollowness and anger.

"Bree?" Noah asked, squeezing her shoulder gently.

The anger won. "He asked me for MORE money a few months ago. He told me the payment hadn't gone through—which I found suspicious—but didn't have time to really look into it. I gave him ANOTHER thirty-five THOUSAND dollars for Jessica's care. Like an idiot." Bree finished in a whisper, her hands fisted in her lap. Betrayal rushed through her, violent and angry and bitter, and a whole host of negative emotions balled up into one overwhelmingly awful feeling.

Theo came over and knelt by her, resting his hand gently on her arm. "You trusted him. That doesn't make you an idiot. It makes him one for abusing your trust."

"I stayed in this career to be helpful. To help support my sister. Instead, I was unknowingly enabling his gambling habit." Bree ground out, devastation washing through her.

"Aubrey. Nearly ten *million* people in the U.S. alone struggle with gambling. And most of them are good at not letting their loved ones know they have a problem." Peter said sternly, drawing her out of her little pity party. "You. Didn't. Know. You didn't know. It's not your responsibility. He is a grown adult. He is responsible for himself. The only thing you can do is change how you move forward."

"And we're here to help." Theo chimed in from in front of her.

"Thanks, guys." She said mechanically, shock, anger, and bitterness still raging through her and making a home inside her chest. The straight audacity of her father. She couldn't fathom doing that to someone. Bree hated borrowing money at all.

"I...I think I just need to step away and take some time. I need to call my lawyer." She paused and looked around at the men gathered around her. "Do I need a different lawyer for contract law than gaining medical power of attorney for my sister?"

"I would think so. But if your lawyer doesn't do it, we can find someone for you." Theo offered.

Bree tried to smile at him though it felt like more of a grimace, "Thank you, Theo. That would be really helpful."

"There's more," Theo said, a serious expression on his face.

"More?" She whispered.

"One of his accounts was an off-shore account in the Cayman Islands. There was a deposit from earlier this year—from National News Daily."

"The newspaper?" Noah asked, an icy rage evident in his low tone.

Theo nodded. "It looks like he got a handsome payout twice. One a little more than the other."

"He is the one who sold the picture and my location?" Bree asked, dumbfounded.

"I'm not one hundred percent certain yet, but I'll know shortly."

"Did he gamble that money away, too?"

Theo hesitated, "Yes. And, Bree...some of it was sent to a private checking account. For Kyle Rhodes."

Bree had no words. None. Noah, however, didn't seem to have that problem. "He *paid* that jerk to bug Bree?" Noah asked, outraged. "What role did Kyle play in all this?"

"I don't know. I'm collecting intel and will let you know when I do."

Noah nodded and reached over to pull Bree closer, his support unwavering.

"Anyone else hungry?" Zach suddenly chimed in from the other side of the room after a few moments of silence.

Bree's stomach growled at once, and her eyes widened. "Apparently, I am."

"Great, we all brought a dish. Let's grab some dinner and take a break from talking about depressing things."

"Avoiding the topic and using food to cope. I like your style." Bree joked, though that felt a little too close to the truth.

Maybe she should see if her old therapist had a spot open. She was super helpful last time Bree needed someone to talk to. A lot of therapists have sliding fee scales, which was super helpful the first time Bree needed help. She didn't have a lot of money at the time, so she didn't think she'd be able to see anyone. The therapist had been a life saver even on Bree's small pre-fame budget.

They went into the kitchen and filled their plates with food—well, Noah filled her plate, asking what she wanted and how much—before going and sitting at the dining room table. Their family meals were the highlights of her week. Just sitting around the table and getting to chat with everyone, laugh, and learn what was going on in their lives made each get together special. They never ran out of things to talk about. Theo was always positively entertaining and watching Zach, who had a very serious countenance, tolerate him and even laugh along was always worth the watch.

After everyone left, she shrunk back into the couch and just sat in the silence for a few minutes while Noah worked on tidying up the kitchen. He returned a few minutes later with a bottle of water and some Dove chocolates in hand. Her favorite. "You're the best." She said dreamily.

"Only for you," Noah replied. "Only for you."

Chapter Twenty-Five

Aubrey

She was not ready for the cold to set in, Bree thought a few days later as she and Noah stood outside the hospital on a blustery afternoon. It was the Tuesday before Thanksgiving, and the upcoming holidays weighed heavy on her mind. "You're sure you don't mind if we go visit Jess?" She asked Noah, his hand held firmly in hers.

"Of course not. Visiting Jess is important, and you know we can always go anywhere you'd like."

"One of these days you'll need to return to the actual office full-time, Noah Hawthorne." Bree teased.

He nudged her shoulder gently. "I can work from anywhere since I'm not taking new active cases right now."

Bree frowned. "You should get back to taking active cases—you used to love them."

Noah shrugged. "They tend to require a lot of travel, and your stalker is still unaccounted for. I'm not leaving you unprotected to chase dollars or reputation."

Bree cocked her head to the side and considered him. "Noah—we may never catch my stalker. Your life can't be put on hold forever."

"My life isn't on hold. I'm building a life with you. Besides, my team has things well in hand. They're good people and great at their jobs. Business is still growing and I've just moved more into a facilitator role for the time being. When you're safe again, I'll consider going back to active cases. Though being home with you definitely has perks." Noah teased. He looked down into her eyes and pulled her in close. "I can be around to protect you and still get my job done. No worries."

"Alright then," She said, smiling broadly. They greeted the nurses at the station as they did every time they visited and headed into Jessica's room.

For the second time there was another person in there visiting on a day that was not theirs. Honestly, with only four people who would visit—three of whom who were actually allowed to visit—you would think the odds of someone else being there at any given time or day would be less. Unfortunately she recognized the back of the man instantly.

"Hello, Dad." Bree greeted as they walked into the room. Noah's hand tightened on hers. She hadn't spoken to her dad since Noah took over the call and hung up on him. Her chest tightened, and tears threatened to fall already. Seeing him aggravated the wound his gambling habit left on her heart. How could he do that to his daughters?

"Aubrey." He said shortly, barely looking her way. "Still whoring around, I see."

"That was uncalled for," Noah said angrily. "Apologize."

Dad laughed. "You know, boy, you have some nerve. You think you're special? My daughter is going to drop you just like she does everyone else in her life when they complicate it or cause conflict or inconvenience her. You'll be nothing but a man in the rearview soon enough. So don't tell me how to talk to my daughter."

Noah stepped into Dad's personal bubble, forcing him to look up slightly to meet Noah's eyes. "I believe that's called 'protecting her peace,' and if I *ever* give Bree a reason to cut me out because I'm not good for her, I hope she does. I hope she does kick me to the curb and leaves me in the rearview because if she does, it would've been my own fault. And that wouldn't be on Bree. That would be on me for being a despicable human being."

Bree's dad looked at Noah disdainfully. "Man, she's done a number on you. You don't scare me, boy." He said, puffing up his own chest. "Aubrey—I need you to send this month's money so I can pay for Jessica's medical bills." He said, gesturing toward Jess, who was lying still on the bed.

"No," Bree said firmly.

He whipped around toward her, his eyes bulging out of his head and the vein in his head throbbing. "What?" He hissed in a low tone, taking a small step away from Noah and toward Bree.

"I said no," Bree repeated calmly, her pounding heart and sweating hands the only things belying her anxiety.

"You would let your sister die because I hurt your feelings?" He sneered, stepping toward her again.

Bree held her ground. "No, I won't give you money because you'll just gamble it all away. None of it was even going toward Jess's care!"

Dad looked like he'd been struck across the face. "What? I wouldn't do that to my family. Do I look like I have a gambling problem, Aubrey? I'm one of the most successful attorneys in the state. Give me a break."

Bree's laugh bordered on hysteria. "Don't play the clueless act with me. I know all about your gambling. About your accounts in the Cayman Islands. How you sold the picture of me and where I lived to the press. I know it all."

"You don't know the first thing—" Her dad said, moving further into her space. Bree was tired. Tired of being lied to. Tired of being used.

"You couldn't even do your dirty work yourself." Bree accused, "You hired *Kyle*? Of all people?"

Dad scoffed. "Please. You can hardly call a few fake accounts, some harmless video comments, and taking a picture of a well-known singer in a public space 'dirty work'. The only thing. I'd consider *dirty* was the tire slashing. That could have ended with someone hurt, but I wasn't involved in that. He did that all on his own. You should have just gotten back in the industry, Aubrey. Enjoyed the fame. The money. The *opportunity*. But no. You ended up a disappointment instead—as usual."

Noah shouldered past her dad and stepped in front of Bree, shielding her with his own body.

"Back off," Noah said. "Or we will call security and have you removed."

"You have no power here, boy. This is my daughter's room, and I'm speaking with my other daughter. They belong to me."

"They're not possessions. They're people. You defaulted on Jessica's payments the last six months. You are the one without power here. And if you ever threaten Bree again, I'll lay you flat. I don't care if you are her father." Noah said, his voice deadly low.

Bree rested a hand on Noah's back gently and peeked around him. "You will be receiving papers this week, Dad. We're taking you to court for medical power of attorney for Jess."

"WHAT?"

"You haven't paid for her bills, and you've drawn this out long enough. She's suffering. It's time to let her go."

"You selfish, ungrateful..." What he was going to say next, she wasn't sure, because Noah's right hook connected with the left side of her dad's face, dropping him like a sack of bricks.

Noah turned to Bree and wrapped his arms around her tightly. "Don't listen to him, Bree. You are... you are everything." He whispered, cupping her face gently.

"What do we do with him?" She asked.

"Leave him there?"

"We could move him to a chair and rest his head on the bed. Then at least he doesn't wake up on the floor." Bree said, trying to be reasonable.

"You're too good to him, Bree. But alright." Noah said, hoisting her dad up and setting him in the chair nearest to Jessica's bed. He rested his head and arms on the bed so it looked like he was sleeping and monitored his pulse for a moment. "He'll be okay. Do you want to say anything to Jess before we head home?"

"Yeah, will you step out for just a minute? I'd like to talk to her alone."

He looked at her dad warily. "Okay, I'll be outside, so just shout if you need me. Otherwise, I'll wait in the hall."

"Thanks, babe," Bree said, watching a soft blush color his cheeks. Noah walked out the door, and she moved to stand next to Jess on the opposite side of the bed from where their dad was.

"I'm so sorry, Jess. I'm sorry about the party and the hateful things I said to you. I'm sorry for not recognizing that you needed help sooner. I'm sorry for all the drama I've brought to your room. First with Justin, and now with Dad. But mostly, I'm sorry for letting you suffer for all these years. I know this isn't what you would've wanted, and I should've fought harder for you sooner. I'll make it right. You'll be in peace soon." Bree pressed a soft kiss to her forehead like she used to when they were kids and took one last look at her before walking into the hall and heading home with her man. It was time to take back her life.

Chapter Twenty-Six

Noah

Bree's scream woke Noah in the middle of the night. She'd been having nightmares since the break-in, and while they'd been less frequent, they were no less frightening. Noah jumped out of bed, bleary-eyed, and walked to her room, knocking softly before opening the door all the way. Bree let out a heart-wrenching scream again, twisting around in her sheets, her body thrashing wildly. He walked over and sat on the side of the bed, careful to avoid her flailing limbs as much as possible. This one was bad.

"Bree," He said quietly, gently shaking her shoulder. "Bree!" He said again, a little more loudly this time. Her eyes flew open, and her terror-filled gaze met his. Her breaths came out in ragged gasps, and tears streamed down her face.

"Noah?" She croaked through the tears.

"I'm here, sweetheart."

"I'm so sorry I keep waking you up. I have these dreams where he takes me away from you, and I never find you again and...and..." choked sobs shook her body. His heart broke at her distress.

"It's okay, Bree. I'll wake up with you a thousand times if that's what it takes for you to feel safe again." Noah pulled her into his arms and held her there until her breathing started to steady.

"Goodnight, Bree." He said softly.

"Noah?" She said sleepily. "Will you stay with me?"

"Bree, I shouldn't—"

"Please, Noah? Please." Her voice broke on the last word.

"Okay, scoot over." He said, slipping in next to her. Noah lifted his arm, and she snuggled up against him, her head on his chest. He moved some of her hair away from his face so he wouldn't suffocate and then stroked her hair. His poor babe. She fell asleep quickly, and he soon found his eyes were also heavy despite the tingling sensation in his arm from keeping his hand in that position. Noah closed his eyes just for a moment, enjoying the feeling of having Aubrey close to him.

He woke up in the morning unsure why it felt as though he had a dead limb. He looked down, enjoying the feel of Aubrey pressed against him, her head and left hand still on his chest. A mental image of a ring sitting on her bare fourth finger flashed through his mind and did strange things to his stomach. He needed to get up.

Noah tried not to disturb her, but the arm she was lying on was no longer taking commands from his central nervous system. Apparently, sleeping like that worked better in fantasy than in real life. Those romance movies should have to pay restitution to all the men who had to chop off dead limbs after having someone lay on it for eight hours. The things they'd do for love.

Noah used his good arm to pull his other one out, shaking it slightly once it was free to try and get some feeling back. Bree's eyes found his, and she blinked awake slowly.

"Good morning, Bree," Noah said, his voice still a little deeper than usual from sleep.

"Good morning." A bright blush spread across her cheeks, and Noah smiled and leaned in for a quick kiss.

"Don't go down the rabbit hole, Bree. I don't mind that you asked me to stay. I enjoyed it."

She nodded warily like she didn't believe him, and he tilted her chin up and gave her another light kiss. She was so beautiful. She climbed out of bed and made it as she did every morning. Noah reached over and pulled her back into him.

She squealed, and Noah smiled, wrapping her tightly in his arms. "Are you feeling okay this morning? You're going to give me a heart attack one of these days." He teased.

"I'll revive you. I've seen a TikTok or two on how to do CPR. I'm sure it'll be fine." She said, trying and failing to keep a straight face.

"I have full faith in you."

"What time is it?"

"A little after ten."

"Noah! I have to get ready."

"The gala isn't until this evening, Bree."

"It takes time to get beautiful."

"You're always beautiful." He said, pulling her close and nuzzling into her neck.

She grinned and snuggled further into his arms under the cozy blankets. "Okay...ten minutes, and then you need to go entertain yourself while I get ready."

"Deal." He said, kissing the top of her head softly.

He could get used to holding her like this.

***

Noah walked toward Bree's room, eager to see how she was since nerves seemed to overtake her earlier. Not that he could blame her. Public speaking was not his idea of a good time. Just as he approached the door, his phone rang, and he swiped up to answer quickly. "Hey, Theo."

"Hey man, we finished going over the venue and checking it over. It is good to go for tonight. It looks like the blueprints are still accurate, and all exits listed are still in working order."

"And the staff?"

"There are a significant number of VIP guests attending, so anyone working the event has been thoroughly background checked. Everyone inside the building has been vetted by two different companies."

"Perfect. We'll meet you guys there around 7:30."

"We'll be here by 6:30 to make sure we've gone over the space again and are ready for when Bree arrives," Theo said.

Noah felt the knot in his gut loosen a little but still had the nagging feeling he was missing something that had the potential to cost him the best thing in his life—Aubrey. He should be concerned about how strong his feelings for her were, but instead he embraced them. She was it for him. He could feel it.

"Sounds good. I'll text you when we leave Bree's with our ETA and route."

After a couple more minutes of working out logistics, he hung up the phone and poked his head in to check on Bree who was restlessly pacing along her bedroom. "What's up, Bree?" He asked, walking over to her and wrapping his arms tightly around her from behind. Bree leaned into him and gave him all of her weight, resting against him. Her body pressed against his caused a heat to shoot through him, and he took a deep breath and tried to think of other things to distract him from the beautiful woman in his arms.

"I don't know what to wear." She sighed. "I can't get away with my usual sweater and jeans at this thing."

"Why not?"

"Noah!" She said, slapping him lightly on the arm.

"What?"

"It's black tie. And I'm the keynote speaker." She said.

"True, but I don't care what you wear. Let them talk. You'll look beautiful no matter what you wear."

"You're such a sweet talker." She complained lightly. "I had a dress picked out, but I didn't like it when I put it on." She grumbled.

Noah smiled at Bree before leaning down and giving her a gentle kiss. "I am one hundred percent honest. Whatever outfit you decide on will look perfect."

"That's super sweet *and* you're not being helpful right now." Bree laughed, ushering him out of the room. "I'll figure it out."

Noah hugged her tightly to him. "I can pick a dress if you want me to. I just don't know that I'm the most qualified..."

"I'll call Steph. I was going to from the beginning. I just wanted to see you sweat first." Bree teased cheekily.

"Well, you succeeded." Noah chuckled. "Do you want to go over your speech one more time before you get dressed?"

Bree looked at him contemplatively. "I don't think so. At this point, I've either got it, and it will go great, or I don't, and I'll cause the whole event to crash and burn."

"You've got this, Bree. You're going to kill it."

She nodded distractedly and leaned up for a kiss, resting her forehead against his for a moment before stepping back.

"Alright, Mr. Hawthorne. Beauty takes time. Get on out of here."

Noah held up his hands in acquiescence, giving her a smoldering smile before he left her to get ready and headed to his own bedroom to shower and trim up his hair. His tuxedo was hanging in the closet, ready to go.

***

Two and a half hours later, Noah paced in the living room, his eye alternating between the clock and his watch. He pulled a little at the bow tie around his neck, the suffocating feeling always on the edges of his mind. This was why he didn't require ties in the workplace. Bodyguards would not be useful if their own ties strangled them. A light clacking sound came from the hallway. He turned to look at Bree, and nearly fell to his knees.

Her hair was curled and up in some sort of complicated, but beautiful, updo that left a sprinkle of curls down to frame her cheeks. Her makeup was mostly natural, but a little heavier than normal, which drew attention to her stunning eyes before dragging the attention down to her lips, which looked perfect for kissing.

She chose the deep green gown that hugged her figure and brought out the color of her eyes. Bree smiled shyly at his reaction and spun in a circle and his eyes caught on the back of the gown which dipped a little lower in the back leaving lots open to the imagination. She looked delectable.

"You're stunning." He breathed as she stopped her twirl.

"The dress is gorgeous. Steph was super excited about this one. And…it has pockets!" She said excitedly, showing him the pockets.

Noah shook his head. "It's not the dress—though the dress is nice. It's you, Bree. You are kind, and warm, and thoughtful, and the goodness shines through you brighter than any star in the night sky. The dress merely accessorizes the inescapable internal beauty of the woman wearing it. You're perfect."

He walked over to her and pulled her to him tightly, leaning down and planting his lips over hers. She smiled, and he licked along the seam of her lips, seeking entrance. She opened for him with a sigh as she relaxed in his arms, and he kissed her long and deeply. Her vanilla scent surrounded him, and he was seriously considering keeping her home all to himself. After kissing her for a few minutes, he pulled away, both of them panting. Bree's eyes flared with desire, and he was sure his did as well.

Noah cleared his throat. "We need to head to the gala before we end up missing it."

Bree blushed and nodded. "Let me grab my clutch and shawl, and we can go."

A few minutes later, Noah walked Bree out to the car, helping her in before heading to his side. He took a deep breath, trying to shake off the gnawing feeling in his gut. They'd gone over the blueprints multiple times and had a plan for just about any scenario imaginable. Likely unnecessarily, but better to be prepared for everything rather than be prepared for nothing. Tonight was a secure event and there would be multiple pairs of eyes on Bree. Everything was going to be fine.

Chapter Twenty-Seven

Aubrey

Bree found it difficult to breathe as they drove to Trenton for the gala. That was partially due to the fact she was going to have to stand in front of a room full of people and give a speech about a topic that was particularly vulnerable for her. But at the moment, it was mostly due to the man sitting next to her looking like he stepped out of a black and white film—debonair with a large dash of danger. Her blood heated, and she ducked her head down to hide her blush, though it would be difficult to see in the car as it got darker.

Jessica always loved the old black and white films. They used to sit on the couch on Friday nights and each have a movie picked out and ready to go. In the days of Blockbuster, you were almost guaranteed to find an old movie in stock, which is probably what started Jess's obsession with them to begin with. Bree's heart ached as she thought of Jess and how they ended up where they were. Jess, in a hospital bed, and Bree on her way to talk in front of hundreds of people. The Bree that Jess had known would have *never* considered doing something like that. Never been on stage. Never taken the risks Bree had in order to take care of her family. Bree frowned as she looked out the window. Life would have been so different.

Maybe her father wouldn't have fallen so deep into gambling. Maybe her mother wouldn't be a shell of the woman she once was. Losing a child did that. It broke marriages and broke people. Thinking of her father's gambling problem made Bree's blood boil. Who did that to their children? To their family? She was working on sitting with the anger and letting herself really feel it, but not hold on to it. Just like her therapist had taught her. Holding on to those emotions didn't make her father suffer—it chained her down.

She took a deep breath and let the emotions sizzle, then she exhaled and let them go. Each time was a little easier, but the sting of that particular betrayal was going to take a while to let go of. As the venue came into view, Bree felt her heart rate quicken and took a fortifying breath. What was five minutes of her time? In a few hours, this would be over—for better or for worse.

They pulled up into the valet line when they reached the venue, and Noah turned to look at Bree. He cleared his throat and turned to fully look at her. "I know you're nervous, and that's okay. It means that this is important to you and you want to do a great job. That nervousness is a strength, not a weakness. You are a strong, smart, fierce woman who is able to take on the world with a mix of compassion and steel that is absolutely irresistible. I will never get enough of you, Aubrey Gray." Bree felt her eyes get a little misty as she watched him reach into his pocket. He pulled a small square out and offered it to her, watching her closely.

Bree reached out and took the square from him—it was a small square of fabric, probably no more than two inches by two inches and made from velvet and some sort of slicky material on the back.

"It's for your pocket." He said, nodding toward the square of fabric as he pulled the car forward. "That way you can rub it to help calm your nerves."

Bree couldn't help the tear that escaped her eye as she clutched the piece of fabric tightly. Noah took her eccentric behaviors that others had mocked her whole life and not only embraced them but encouraged them.

"Thank you," She croaked out as they pulled ahead and put the car in park.

Noah smiled at her softly, his eyes gazing into hers. "You're welcome."

"Ma'am?" A voice interrupted from her right. Bree turned, surprised she hadn't noticed the door being opened, and chastised herself. Way to go, Bree. If the stalker was there, he could come into the ball wearing a bird costume and dancing the Macarena in the middle of the dance floor, and she'd be too wrapped up in Noah to notice.

The valet who opened her door had a forced smile on his face, seemingly irritated at them for taking so long to get out of the car. He held out his hand to her, and she accepted it, a chill moving through her. She let go of his hand as soon as she was steady on her feet and draped her shawl around her shoulders to guard against the chill.

"Thanks, man," Noah said, handing the valet a tip before wrapping his arm around Bree's shoulders.

The valet looked at Noah and raised his eyebrow, which was dissected by a scar. "You're welcome." He said stiffly. "Enjoy your evening."

"You too," Bree said congenially.

The valet smiled at her. "Thank you, I will." He said, walking over to the driver's side and getting in to take it to park. Bree smiled at Noah and tucked in close, soaking in his warmth and strength and just enjoying his presence.

They walked into the hallway and bypassed coat check. It was too cool for Bree to want to give up her shawl. No way. Noah squeezed her shoulder and inclined his head across the ballroom. The rest of the Hawthorne Security team was stationed at each of the immediate exits around the room, along with one or two security guards hired by the event or other individuals attending. Bree felt her shoulders relax for the first time since they left the house. She was safe here. There was enough security here that no one was going to so much as sneeze without security knowing.

They walked to their assigned table and made small talk with their table mates before taking a walk around the ballroom.

"How are you doing?" Noah asked, covering Bree's hand with his own as they walked.

"Other than being convinced I left my notecards at home when I can tell they're in my pocket, I am good. It's a beautiful venue." She said, nodding at the tables decorated with white tablecloths, elegant place settings, and large centerpieces that gave an ethereal quality to the space. The lights were slightly dimmed which gave the room a hint of intimacy.

Noah would probably say it was intimate without compromising the security of attending guests—if she wanted to get the rundown on all things security. Which she didn't. Not tonight. Tonight she just wanted to enjoy being a young woman at a fancy party with her hunky boyfriend and her best friends—minus Steph. She made eye contact with Theo, who made a funny face at her, and she laughed, smiling back at him.

"How long until they start dinner?" Bree asked Noah as her stomach rumbled.

"Any time now. Dinner, speeches, and then dancing."

"You gonna spin me around the dance floor, Noah Hawthorne?" Bree teased, her eyes sparkling.

"I don't know if you can handle me on the dance floor. I'll wipe the floor with you if they put on the YMCA song."

Bree snorted in an admittedly unladylike fashion. "Stop it. I'll pay you to go ask the DJ to put that on later."

Noah chuckled. "I would do it just to hear you laugh." He admitted.

Mr. Miller walked up to the stage and rang a silver bell. "Ladies and Gentlemen, thank you so much for attending the fifth annual Families Affected by Addiction fundraising gala. We are humbled by the attendance and are so thankful for the donations that will provide additional support and resources for families who have a loved one working through or lost to addiction. Please make your way to your tables, and dinner will be served shortly. Thank you." Polite applause rang through the space, and Noah guided Bree to their table, his hand resting gently on her back.

Dinner was phenomenal, and before she knew it the tables were being cleared, and Mr. Miller was back up on stage with the microphone. "Our speaker tonight is a world-renowned singer, two-time Grammy winner, and an avid supporter of the mission of Families Affected by Addiction. While she is no longer active in the music industry, she has been a continual advocate and supporter of our mission. Please give a warm welcome to Miss Aubrey Gray." Mr. Miller clapped his hands together and the rest of the room joined in with enthusiastic applause.

Bree nervously rose from her spot and made her way to the stand, extra watchful of each step up to the stage, anxiety about falling on her face at about a seventy on a scale from one to ten. She made it to the podium and shook Mr. Miller's hand before turning to the audience. She found Noah's eyes in the crowed and he gave her a nod, the rest of the Hawthorne Security Team seated around the table, providing a silent strength she drew on as her nerves raged on.

"Thank you, Mr. Miller. I'd like to thank the Millers and the board of directors of Families Affected by Addiction for inviting me to speak. It's an honor." She paused and took a deep breath. "Addiction is a living and breathing disease that millions of individuals and families suffer from every day. Research says that around seven and a half million children live in households where at least one parent has an alcohol use disorder. Another two million children live in households where at least one parent has an illicit drug use disorder. We need services, not only for the men and women who struggle with addiction, but for the families as well.

"For the parents, siblings, spouses, children, or grandchildren. That's why FABA exists. To help create a space for those who have been affected by these circumstances. These men, women, and children are resilient and brave and deserve the help we can provide. My sister…" Bree paused for a moment, wrestling to keep the tears from her eyes and her emotions under control.

"My sister suffered from an alcohol and drug addiction in her early twenties. A lot of people only saw the addiction. They didn't see the young woman who was vibrant. She loved to laugh and to sing in the car. She loved old movies, was a super protective big sister, and had horrible taste in fashion. She was more than her addiction. Her family is more than her addiction. And that's what we want for the families FABA helps. They are more than their loved one's addiction. Their loved one is more than their addiction.

Let's work together to create and maintain services to offer the possibility of support and change." She wrapped up her speech, her attention fully focused on Noah, who stood behind his chair and clapped enthusiastically as she finished. She paused for a few pictures with the event organizers and stepped down the side of the stage her face flush with excitement and relief that the hardest part of the evening was over.

Noah scooped her into his arms and held her tightly before planting a kiss on her lips. "You were amazing." He said quietly as the live band struck up a waltz. "Dance with me?"

"Always," Bree answered with a smile, taking his hand and allowing him to guide her onto the dance floor. She thought he had been joking earlier about his dancing abilities, but he was surprisingly adept at sweeping her across the floor in an elegant waltz.

"You can waltz!" She said, her eyebrows lifting in surprise.

Noah chuckled. "I told you I could dance."

"You also mentioned the YMCA song in the same sentence, so I don't think that counts." Bree joked.

"I had to learn when I started attending fancy events for work. Most of the time I would be on the side like the others are tonight but occasionally we would need to intervene without causing a scene and that often involved dancing. It's relatively socially acceptable to cut in, which helps break up tension on the dance floor, and if the tension is outside the dance floor, it is always acceptable to ask a lady for a dance. It's a weird skill to find useful, but it's come in handy more times than I care to admit."

"I love that," Bree said enthusiastically. "I can kind of waltz, but only because I was obsessed with Anastasia growing up. I wanted to waltz like Anya and Dimitri."

"I think your reason is better," Noah said warmly, pressing her close to him. Noah twirled her around and pulled her in for a kiss as the dance ended before escorting her to the side of the dance floor. Noah walked with Bree over to where Zach was standing in the back corner and squeezed her waist gently.

"I'm going to use the restroom. I'll find you in a few minutes." He said, planting a kiss on her cheek.

"So...gonna take a turn around the dance floor?" Bree asked Zach, still slightly breathless and warm from the waltz.

"I don't dance," Zach said.

"Fair enough," Bree noted. "Are you having a good time?"

"I mean I'm on security detail, but it seems pretty low-key so far. But you know, low risk—"

"—doesn't mean no risk." Bree finished. "I know, I know. Do you think—"

Her thoughts were interrupted as a low ringing sounded from Zach's pocket. "Hold on a second." He said, resting one hand on Aubrey's elbow while looking at the caller ID. Bree looked over and saw a photograph of a younger Zach with a young woman whose bright blue eyes popped off the screen. They looked super happy. The name Kennedy was over the background. Zach suddenly looked stressed as he was clearly torn between answering the phone or not. The screen went black, and he started to relax, until the screen lit up again, the same low ringtone sounding around them. "Crap. I need to take this. Will you—"

"Go! I'll be fine. I'll just make my way over to Theo." Bree said, gesturing straight down the line of windows to where Theo stood in the other corner talking to one of the other guests. Zach looked uncertain for a moment before she pushed him forward. "Go." He nodded his thanks and swiped up on the call. "Kennedy? Hang on—let me go outside." Zach walked across the ballroom toward the front doors, and Bree stayed still until he was out of sight.

She walked toward the corner where Theo was, desperately wishing she had a fan. The warmth from dancing with Noah and the large number of bodies in the ballroom left her feeling overheated and desperate for some fresh air. There was a pair of double doors that led to the side balcony. She eyed them longingly, the fresh air and fairy lights creating a romantic effect that was hard to walk by. She glanced around and saw that Theo was still engaged in conversation. So was Eli. She hadn't seen Peter yet, but assumed he was working somewhere in the room as well.

Bree was pretty sure this was the balcony that didn't have an exit. Instead, it led to a fenced yard, which meant it was a secure area. The only balcony that had an exit was the northeast balcony, and this one seemed...centered? She slipped through the doors and took a deep breath, inhaling the crisp, cool November air. There were a few others on the balcony, and Bree turned her attention to the stars. She felt like she was in a movie—maybe The Sound of Music or an Audrey Hepburn movie. She could just imagine Noah coming out and finding her, pulling her in close to ward off the chill of the night while they gazed at the stars. Maybe he'd kiss her. Or ask her to dance under the night sky. She walked to the far corner of the balcony to give the others some privacy and to have a little space herself. It was nice to be alone. It had been too long since she was able to just exist. She let out a deep breath.

Bree wasn't sure how long she'd been standing there—though it couldn't have been more than a few minutes since the same slow song was playing—when she noticed the whispers on the deck had stopped. She looked around, suddenly aware she was the only person out there. She glanced around and smacked herself mentally. Being alone on a balcony with a stalker on the loose was a horror-movie level of idiocy. Noah would be fuming.

Bree quickly gathered up her skirts and turned to walk back into the ballroom when she noticed a lone figure standing in the shadows near the stairs.

"I bet you're not supposed to be here." The man said in a quiet, but gleeful tone.

"It's an open balcony." She said, the hairs on the back of her neck standing up as he took a step closer to her. Bree looked desperately toward the doors she'd come out of and subsequently wandered away from.

"That may be true," the voice said again. "But you are not supposed to be here, are you Aubrey?"

A chill went through her even as she steeled her spine "I'm not sure what you mean. I do need to get back to the party now, so please excuse me." She made to walk by the figure, staying out of arms reach.

"Of course." He said, not moving from his spot by the stairs.

She walked quickly by him, peeking out of the corner of her eye. He had a scar on his right eyebrow, but otherwise was nondescript. She knew she had seen the guy before, but her fear-addled mind couldn't seem to come up with where she knew him from. Not a great trait when a stalker was on the loose, she chided herself. She walked by the man and let out a sigh of relief. See? Nothing had happened. She knew she was being para—

She heard a light scrape against the pavement, and then there was a sharp pain in the back of her head. Her vision began to swim, and she touched the back of her head in a daze. She pulled it away and glared at the warm, sticky substance covering her hand. Blood. "This isn't good." She muttered, staring at the blood before feeling her world tilt sideways as everything faded to black.

Chapter Twenty-Eight

Noah

"Hawthorne!" A voice called from the atrium. Noah turned and saw Alan Johnson, one of the senators for Tennessee, waving him over. Noah seriously contemplated pretending he hadn't heard him and making a beeline for the ballroom. He was eager to get back to Bree. Maybe he'd ask her to dance again. The smile on her face lit up the room. Man, he loved that woman. He'd been waiting to tell her until the time felt right.

The museum was a stunning piece of architecture and between the natural wow factor of the museum, the classical music, and the beautifully decorated outdoor spaces, tonight was the night. Noah paused for one more second before letting out a large sigh. Bree was with Zach. She'd be okay while he stopped to find out what the Senator wanted.

Noah turned around and plastered his business smile on his face while he walked over to the group of politicians and their families. "Senator Johnson, it's a pleasure to see you." He said, reaching out to shake the man's hand.

"It's good to see you too. I've been meaning to call down to your office—is Eli still employed at Hawthorne?"

"He is."

"Fantastic. I have an engagement coming up that I could use some additional security for. I'll have my secretary reach out first thing Monday. You know you've got loyal men working for you, Hawthorne. I offered Eli a job to come and work for me, and he wouldn't even entertain the idea."

"I work with the best men in the industry. Eli is definitely one of them." He agreed.

"Great, I'm glad I saw you. We'll be in touch."

"Enjoy your evening," Noah replied, shaking the man's hand again and inclining his head toward the rest of the party. As soon as his back was turned, he let his smile drop and started working his way through the crowd without treading on any toes.

Noah walked toward the ballroom and stopped short when he noticed Zach walking through the crowd toward the room as well. "Zach!" He called, his eyes searching the area for Bree and frowning when he didn't see her.

Zach made eye contact with Noah and worked his way through the crowd quickly and efficiently.

"Where's Bree?" Noah asked immediately.

"I had to take a call. I left her with Theo." Zach said.

Noah let out a breath. Okay—at least she was safe. "What was the call?"

"Kennedy called. I ignored the first one, but she called back right away. I had to make sure it wasn't an emergency."

"Everything okay?" Noah asked as they approached the ballroom doors.

Zach dragged his hand down his face and let out a rough exhale. "I don't think so. I think this case she's working right now is really getting to her."

"Anything we can do?"

"No, but I'll let you know if it changes," Zach said.

They walked into the ballroom, the crowd unconsciously swaying along to the music, a large multitude on the dance floor. Noah watched them for a moment, searching among the dancers for Bree. He wouldn't put it past someone to ask her to dance. She was not only beautiful, but still famous also.

He didn't immediately see Bree or Theo, so Noah walked across the dance floor his eyes scanning the space as he carefully picked his way between the couples.

Theo was in the corner talking with some of the CEOs of a tech company who made software he wanted to get for the company. Eli and Peter were still in their assigned areas, constantly scanning the environment like the other security guards posted throughout the venue. He bumped into the shoulder of a man as he walked by, quickly apologizing. Where was Bree?

Noah made it to the far side of the ballroom and still didn't see her. Maybe she had gone to the restroom, and they just missed each other? But Theo would've been there. Or one of the other men at Hawthorne.

Zach stepped up beside Noah and frowned, looking toward where Theo was. "She was supposed to be over with Theo."

Noah felt his blood pressure skyrocket as he turned to his long-time friend and colleague. "What do you mean she was *supposed* to be? You did hand her off to Theo, correct?" Noah's voice was low and full of the anger he longed to release.

When Zach didn't immediately answer, Noah stalked over to where Theo was still chatting and forced a pleasant smile on his face. "Excuse me, please. I need to borrow Theo."

Theo excused himself from the conversation and moved to stand by the window with Zach and Noah. "What's up?"

"Where is Bree?" Noah asked, a sinking feeling in his gut as he started to fear the worst.

"She was with you," Theo said.

"I left her with Zach while I went to the bathroom, and he said she was with you."

"She was supposed to be!" Zach said defensively.

"What do you mean supposed to be?" Noah asked again.

Zach sighed. "Like I told you—Kennedy called. Twice. It was an emergency. Bree told me to take it outside so I could hear better and said she'd get over to Theo to wait for you. She was walking along this wall to get to Theo the last time I saw her."

Noah's jaw clenched. "And she never made it to you?"

Theo shook his head. "No."

"Noah—" Zach started, but was cut off immediately when Noah lifted his hand.

"I can't talk to you right now," Noah said. "You were supposed to keep her safe. Go and tell Eli and Peter what's going on. We need a grid search of this entire building. Theo, tap into the security cameras and see what we can learn from that. I'll go outside and look. Meet me by the coat room in thirty minutes."

The men nodded and left, and Noah felt terror threaten to paralyze him.

Someone had taken Bree. He didn't know who or where, but he felt in his bones that it was the truth.

***

The security room at the gallery was cramped, with drab white walls, and cheap furniture scattered throughout the space. The security guard was old enough to be Noah's grandfather—if his grandfather was alive—and moved slower than molasses. Noah grit his teeth—his patience hanging on by a thread. Every *second* that passed was too long. There was a ten-minute window where Bree was unaccounted for by the men at Hawthorne. Ten minutes too long. The security guard pulled up the cameras and moved aside so Theo could work his way through them.

"You're going to have to talk to him eventually," Theo said as he began scrolling through the footage.

Noah leaned in, watching each screen in hopes that whatever happened to Bree was caught on film. "Eventually being the key word." He ground out, anger still raging inside.

"I know you're not ready to hear this right now, but we need all hands on deck if we're going to get your woman back."

"We're going to get her back," Noah growled.

"Yes, but we'll get her back faster with our entire team working together instead of being at each other's throats." Theo pointed out, zooming in on one of the scenes in the ballroom. There! Noah watched as he and Bree danced, that beautiful smile on her face taking his breath away. Was she hurt? Was she scared? Was she...alive? No. He wouldn't go down that train of thought. He'd be useless. He had to assume she was alive unless he had concrete evidence that suggested otherwise.

"Noah, if you'd been on assignment—mind you, this wasn't even a formal assignment because she is *not* a client--but let's say it was. If Bree had called you and you ignored the call and she immediately called you back, you can't tell me

237

you wouldn't have taken the call." Theo argued, fast-forwarding the clip a little to see when Noah left the ballroom.

"Of course, I would have answered. But I also would have escorted her to one of you and did a formal handoff so *someone* knew I didn't have her."

"That's fair. Feel the anger—it's okay to be angry or scared. But focus on the bigger picture. We can't let this divide us. We can hash it out later."

"Fine," Noah grumbled. "But Zach and I *will* hash it out later."

Theo nodded and turned his attention back to the screen. Noah watched as people moved throughout the ballroom, and a small movement along the wall caught his eye. "Pull up camera three and zoom in." Noah directed, leaning closer to the screen.

There on camera was Bree, chatting with Zach. Theo and Noah watched as Zach pulled his phone out and ignored the call—just as he said he did. When the phone rang again they could clearly see Bree tell him to answer it and indicate that she'd head to Theo. Noah felt some of his anger dissipate. She was incredibly thoughtful, and he wouldn't expect anything less from her. He did expect more from Zach, but if Bree was the one in trouble—if he hadn't been able to hear her over the noise and needed to make sure she was okay—he could admit to himself that he would've left too.

They watched as Bree made her way along the walls, taking in the decor and dancers, and Noah tilted his head. "She's starting to panic." He said, watching the rise and fall of her chest increase. "She probably had a panic attack."

"Could she be hiding somewhere just away from people?" Theo asked, following Bree closely as she navigated the space.

"I mean, she could be, but I highly doubt it. I think she would've come to one of us and asked to leave."

Camera Bree looked around—like she had contemplated telling one of the men before deciding otherwise—and found one of the balcony doors. Theo switched cameras and they watch as Bree came outside and took a few minutes to gather her wits about her. Her breathing slowed and tension drained from her body as she stood under the stars. She was a vision.

Shadows moved in the corner of the screen and Noah felt the hair on the back of his neck prickle. They were about to witness her abduction—he was sure of it. Noah could tell the moment Bree realized she made a mistake. Her shoulders tensed, and her body language shifted. They watched the rest of the scene unfold in front of them, and Noah nearly released a breath of relief as Bree moved to walk past the shadow. Maybe she was in the museum after all. That hope was quickly squashed as Bree was hit in the head. She swayed for a moment before falling like a sack of bricks. Noah wanted to hurl. Bree was *hurt*.

"Can we get a close-up of his face?" Noah asked.

"No. Too many shadows. But we may be able to reverse engineer the timeline and see if we can catch a clear shot of him coming to or going from the event. He had to originally show up at some point."

"I'm going to stay on this," Theo said, gesturing to the footage in front of him.

"I'll go fill everyone in," Noah said hollowly, opening the secure door to the hallway.

The rest of the team was waiting in the hallway outside of the tiny space. Noah looked up at them, his heart in his chest.

"Aubrey was kidnapped."

Chapter Twenty-Nine

Aubrey

The floor was moving. No. That didn't seem right. She was moving? Bree opened her eyes, taking in the darkness around her—the ground shaking at the same time. A car? A trunk? They hit a bump, her body thumping up and pain shrieking through her head. Flashes of the evening came back. The gala. The balcony. The man in the shadows. Blood on her hands. Coming in and out of consciousness several times over the last...who knows how many hours. Bree's breath came out in panicked gasps.

"Get a grip, Bree." She whispered as she gasped for air. "This. Isn't. Going. To. Help." A soft cry worked its way out of her mouth as they hit another bump. Was he doing this on purpose?! She took a deep breath and worked on controlling her breathing. In. One. Two. Three. Four. Out. One. Two. Three. Four. Over and over again until her mind cleared a little and her focus returned.

Okay, so currently held captive in the back of a car. Not ideal. But almost all cars...all cars?...have a handle inside the trunk. She just needed to get out. Don't let them take you to a secondary location. That was rule number one if you're in the process of getting kidnapped. She needed to act and fast. Her hands were tied behind her back, the ropes cutting into her wrists, but maybe she could get them loose. She pulled them apart and tried to wriggle them around, only succeeding in causing a stinging pain in both arms and tears to run down her face. Great. Kidnapped and snotty. And no longer in her gown? Bree's brain stuttered to a halt. What had happened while she was passed out? How hard had he hit her in the head? Panic fluttered, and Bree stomped it down. She could panic after she got out of this mess.

Bree moved around the trunk backward, letting her hands roam over the interior from behind her back. She just needed to be able to leverage it a little bit...after a few minutes of searching, she fell back on her bottom. This was getting her nowhere. What else could she use? What else could she do? She could kick out the taillight? But would that draw too much attention? Would anyone notice? What was she out if I tried? What was she out if she didn't?

Bree laid back and aligned her feet with where—she hoped—the right taillight was. She kicked over and over again until there was a satisfying pop, and a breeze came in. Bree looked out of the hole, and a new wave of despair crashed through her. It was dark. Which meant he probably wouldn't see her, but neither would anyone else.

Panic threatened to overwhelm her, and the imaginary cotton started to wrap around her brain. No. No, she wasn't going out like this. She scooted her body over to the other side of the car and lined her feet up with the other taillight. She kicked as hard as she could once, twice, three times, and cheered internally when the second one came loose. Now if an officer saw it maybe they'd be more inclined to pull them over.

She sat back and considered what to do next. She needed to get out of this car. It was dark, she had no idea where she was, and she had a head injury. Likely a concussion as well. So, she needed to get out and avoid a head injury while doing so. *Easy peasy.*

If she could find the stupid latch, maybe she could pull it and...then what? Tuck and roll? That sounded like a surefire way to avoid a head injury. She internally rolled her eyes. She definitely needed a better plan than that. If she could get her hands untied—or at least in front of her—maybe she could find a weapon to wield whenever her captor opens the trunk. She tried to remember his face but nothing came to mind other than the nagging feeling that she'd seen him somewhere before.

She could find the latch and then wait for the car to stop and use her body weight as momentum...but he'd have to be leaning over the back of the trunk...it was worth a shot, at least. She couldn't jump out of a moving vehicle. But what about at a stop sign or stop light? There was some chance of her getting run over by another car, which would be a definite setback. Ugh. Why couldn't there be one right answer? A clear path forward. This felt like choosing a favorite book boyfriend...but with a lot higher risk. Obviously. A manic laugh rose in her throat, which she quickly quieted. Her thoughts were running wild ninety miles an hour and entirely unhelpful.

She didn't need to draw attention to herself. How long had they been traveling? How much further did they have to go? Did she have anything valuable or identifiable that she could actually reach and drop out of the back of the car like a modern-day Hansel and Gretel? Bree felt around again and sighed loudly. It was empty.

A spark of hope flared in her chest. Surely Noah and the others knew she was missing by now, and they'd...what? Her phone wasn't there because she had left it in her purse at the Gala. There was no indication of who took her—heck she didn't even know who took her and she was in his car. The hopeful feeling sank just as quickly as it had risen. Noah would find her. And no matter what, she wouldn't be a damsel in distress. Despite the fact she was, in fact, both a damsel and in distress. Eh, semantics.

Bree shook her head clear of the nonsense and the room spun a little. Ugh. Definitely concussed. The night slowly turned to day and they hadn't stopped yet. As the blue light of dawn filled the trunk, hopelessness overwhelming her for the first time.

***

If it was morning, they were at least twelve hours away from home. He must have stopped at some point...or several points...while she was unconscious. As the sun fully rose into the sky, they came into a town and pulled into the gas station. Bree laid down and feigned sleep, listening to see what her captor would do. His door opened and shut, and he muffled a curse by the trunk. Guess he didn't appreciate the remodel of his tail lights.

The trunk opened just enough for him to get to her and he shook her hard.

"Aubrey. Get up."

Bree opened her eyes and got her first good look at her captor, his face coming into sharp relief. The scar dissecting his right brow looked painful, and she vividly remembered having the same thought before. "The valet? From the lodge?" She asked, genuinely confused.

"Don't pretend you don't know who I am." He snarled. "You're finally free of that maniac. Now you can go back to creating music. You're *free.*"

Free of the...Oh, Noah. Years of watching Criminal Minds and other crime TV sank in and she quickly decided that playing along was the best option in this scenario—hopefully those shows didn't fabricate *all* of their information. This would be an awful time to find out.

"I'm so glad you rescued me." She said, though it sounded more like a question than a statement. Bree used her minimal acting skills to make doe eyes at him At least, she hoped that's what her eyes were doing. Her face kind of had a mind of its own sometimes, and now wasn't a good time for that trait to come out.

The valet looked at her suspiciously. "You were happy at his house. Even though he wasn't letting you make your music or talk to your fans. He locked you away." He argued. "But it doesn't matter because I have you now. Though clearly, you don't know how to respect other peoples' property." He glared at her before looking pointedly at the taillights.

"Your parents should've taught you better, but no matter. You'll be riding in the front seat after this. Now, listen *closely.* We're going to go in and use the restrooms. If you talk to anyone, if you make a move that would indicate you're here against your will, I will kill Noah Hawthorne. And Eli. And Peter. And Zach. And Theo. Are we clear?"

Bree gulped and nodded. "Yes." She managed to get out. He reached around her, the smell of body odor and smoke filling the trunk. He was inches away, and her heart rate picked up as he drew a knife out of his pocket.

He looked at her frightened eyes and held up his hands—one of them still holding the knife—in a placating manner. "No, pet. I won't hurt you. I want you to be free. With me." He cut the ropes off her wrists and helped her out of the trunk like the gentleman he thought he was.

"Thanks," Bree whispered quietly, hoping to appease him.

"I wouldn't have left you trapped there with him, Aubrey. Your creative spirit would be snuffed out."

She meant thanks for cutting the ropes, but that worked, too. She walked docilely with him into the store, forcing a smile at the clerk and looking at every security camera in the place. Please actually work. Please actually work. She chanted in her head. At least then maybe Theo could find her. If he knew where to look. But she'd seen enough episodes of The First 48 to know that security cameras were often grainy at best and just as often for show rather than function.

Bree walked into the women's restroom and took her time, hoping someone would walk in. Just when she was beginning to give up hope, the female clerk walked in. Bree took a deep breath while reading her name tag and prayed this would work. "Hi Ashley, my name is Aubrey Gray," Bree said to her in a quiet voice while she washed her hands. "I've been kidnapped and need help."

The girl turned to Bree, her eyes wide. "Are you serious? What can I do?"

"Do you have a phone on you?"

"Yeah."

"Can I use it quickly?"

She nodded and pulled out the phone, handing it to her.

"Where am I?" Bree asked her.

"Close to Lupton, Arizona." She said just as quietly.

Bree dialed Noah's number—a number she was now thankful she knew by heart—and waited impatiently as it rang one, two, three times. *Please pick up.*

"Hello?" Noah's voice asked, his warm timbre filled with worry and suspicion. He sounded tired, too.

"Noah?" Bree whispered back, tears filling her eyes.

"Bree!" He half shouted. "Where are you, sweetheart?"

"I'm at a gas station near Lupton, Arizona. I'm using an employee's phone, but I'm out of time. Noah, it's the valet from the lodge where we did the collaboration shoot. He has a newer white car—I kicked out the taillights, but I'm not sure if he'll get them fixed."

"You need to stay there, Bree. Don't get back in the car with him—"

"I have to Noah. He's armed. What if he takes this out on someone else?"

"Bree—"

"I also think he was using a different name. He told me that I 'know who he really is, so I think he gave a false name to the lodge."

"That's great, baby. You're doing a great job."

"He's putting me in the front seat from now on, Noah. I'm wearing jeans and a dark green sweater with my hair pulled back." Bree felt nauseous, knowing the valet must have changed her out of her gown while she was unconscious.

The sound of a fist pounding on the door interrupted them. Bree looked up, terror in her eyes.

"I have to go, Noah. I...I love you." She whispered. Hanging up before he could reply. Bree looked at the girl and handed her the phone. "Get in the big stall, quickly. And sound like you're violently ill."

Ashley went into the stall and began making retching noises. Bree wished she had time to throw up herself. Her skin felt like bugs were crawling all over it, disgusted at the fact this unknown man had stripped her down and changed her clothes. Noah would find her. She just had to hold on until then.

Bree opened the door and curled her nose in disgust. "Sorry, it took so long." She said, using a smooth tone. "One of their stalls was out, and well—you heard the other." She grimaced.

He looked at her with suspicion before taking her hand and walking out of the store. They walked to the car and he opened the passenger side door for her. She slipped in and buckled up, looking for the cameras around the station hoping that Theo was watching her right now.

He walked over to the gas pump and seemed to be fiddling around with it. Maybe getting a receipt? Whatever it was, it clearly wasn't working. His movements became gradually more agitated and he kicked the pump before walking back to Bree's door and jerking it open.

"Don't. Move. It's not just your life on the line." He said pointedly, slamming the door and stalking back into the gas station. She watched him go and found herself praying that Noah and the guys would be able to intervene and get back in time.

A few minutes later, he walked back out of the gas station, paper receipt in hand, and got into the car. He put the car in drive and pulled out of the parking lot. She casually looked over and frowned as she noticed small cuts along his forearm that hadn't been there earlier. At least, she didn't think they had been there earlier. Bree looked forlornly back at the gas station, hoping that Theo had the chance to find her on one of the cameras before they pulled out and disappeared once again.

Chapter Thirty

Noah

"I've got her!" Theo yelled triumphantly from the dining room table. Noah walked over to where Theo was sitting and watched the live video feed. The perp was standing at the pump, and Bree was sitting in the car looking at each of the video cameras.

"She's making sure she's caught on film," Noah muttered, watching her turn her face fully to each one.

"Smart girl." Zach complimented.

"I've got police en route," Eli said from across the room, holding his cell phone to his ear.

"Will they get there in time?" Noah asked.

"No." Theo said. We watched as the man went back into the store, returned with the receipt, and pulled away.

"Have them put out a BOLO." Zach instructed Eli. "White sedan. Early twenties. Not sure of the make or model. License plate ending in 2R7Y. Two people. 30-year-old woman with brown curly hair pulled back in a ponytail. Jeans, dark green sweater, sneakers. Male, mid-30s, sandy brown hair, green eyes, scar on right eyebrow, wearing dark pants and a light polo."

"On it," Eli said.

"Who is he, Theo?" Noah asked, suddenly feeling that time was not on their side.

"I'm looking—" Theo entered in the new parameters against the other searches they'd done. "Here! Skyler Johnson. 32. Lives outside of Phoenix, Arizona. We have his current address."

Noah walked over and looked at the picture. He slammed his hand on the table. "That's him. That's the valet."

"Is he taking her to Phoenix?" Zach asked.

Theo pulled up a map. "It does look like they're headed that way. The station they stopped at was just off I-10."

"Would he really take her to his house?"

"One way to find out. Either way, we'd be closer to her last known location in Phoenix than we are here. Theo, call Dominic Bianchii—call in that favor we're owed. We need a plane to Phoenix. Grab your go bags. We're leaving in ten."

"We should really get a personal jet," Theo mumbled, bringing the phone up to his ear and placing the call.

The voices around Noah faded as he walked down the hall to get his go bag from the closet. On the way back, he stopped in the doorway of the studio. It was almost as though Bree was there. The smell of paint, the piece she was working on still on the easel, a paintbrush tossed casually on the table next to it. Clean, but positioned as though it had just casually been tossed down. Her speaker still in the corner where she liked it.

"The plane will be waiting for us," Theo said from behind him. Noah nodded. Theo put a hand on his shoulder reassuringly. "We're gonna find her. Or she might find us. She's a smart woman. She'll either find a way to escape or to keep herself safe. She knows you're coming for her, Noah. So let's go get her."

Noah walked out of the room, leaving everything precisely how Bree had left it. Theo was right. Bree was smart and Noah wouldn't rest until he found her. He didn't know what Skyler's problem was, but he did know that Skyler Johnson messed with the wrong woman and it might be the last thing he ever did.

***

Aubrey

If she had to listen to herself sing one more song she'd throw herself out of the moving car after all and save this man the trouble. Concussed or not. Bree grumbled internally as they listened to her last album on repeat for the third time.

The man, who still wouldn't tell her his name because he *insisted* that she knew it and was just being difficult, looked over at her with a frown on his face. "Why aren't you singing, Aubrey? You love to sing."

"Being kidnapped doesn't really put you in the mood for a sing-a-long." Bree said, irritation overriding her fear—and apparently her good sense.

He looked honestly affronted and alternated his attention between Bree and the interstate. "I didn't kidnap you, Aubrey. I *rescued* you. You know, you could be more grateful." He spat, returning his attention to the wheel.

The irritation was about to take over, but she took a deep breath. Her snarkiness was going to get her killed. This man wasn't Noah. He wasn't going to find it oddly endearing. Noah's voice flashed through her mind and she found herself grateful she was able to talk to him—to tell him that she loved him while she had the chance. Even if she didn't make it out of this mess. Even if he didn't reciprocate her feelings. He deserved to know.

"You're right—I'm sorry. The concussion makes me feel a little weird." She admitted placatingly.

"Concussion?!?"

"From when you hit me on the head with the rock." She reminded him in a tone that was far more polite than she thought it should have been, considering *he* was the one who inflicted the concussion. But a girl has to live, right?

"I didn't think I hit you hard enough for that...might need a doctor...medical attention...no...that would draw too many questions..." He muttered under his breath.

"I...I don't need a doctor." Bree said quickly, not wanting him to spiral and decide she suddenly needed to be freed in a more permanent sense of the word. "There's nothing they can do for concussions anyway—just rest and avoid re-injuring it," She reassured him.

"How do you know?" He asked suspiciously.

She shrugged and decided there was no harm in telling him the truth. "I've had one before."

He nodded and gripped the wheel tighter. "We're almost home. You'll be able to rest for a couple of days, and then we can get you back in front of your fans. Your socials will be active again. I can help you manage it, of course, and help keep the creeps and stalkers away."

She didn't miss the irony there. "That would be great. What do you think we should do first?"

"We'll need to produce a counter statement to that farce of a last video you made. The one that said you were done with the label and industry. Hah."

"But I did part ways with the label when I retired, and even if I didn't, my recording studio is back in Trenton."

"I built one for you in the house. We can produce your music together from the comfort of our home. You'll never have to even step outside except for shows and publicity signings. We have a backyard with a big tree you can lay under. And I have a lot of bookshelves—I noticed you have them in your home, and I bought all of the books I could see from your videos so you'd feel at home—" The manic gleam in his eye set her pulse racing and she swallowed past the fear and anxiety.

Play along, Bree. "That sounds amazing." She croaked out. "I love reading."

"I know you do."

They drove for another thirty minutes before they pulled into what looked like a normal subdivision. There were retirees out walking their dogs, a few pre-school aged children playing at the park, and then the car slowed even more as they pulled into a cute two-story with blue-gray siding and neat white trim. While most of the yard was rock, there was a raised flower bed along the front of the home full of fall flowers in bloom.

Bree furrowed her brow. "This is a beautiful home. You live here?"

He nodded proudly, hitting the button to open the garage door.

"You've been in Rhodes for a while, though. How did you keep your yard so nice?"

"I hired a company."

That makes sense. "The flowers are beautiful."

"They're your favorites." He said distractedly as he slowly began inching the car into the garage. As he did, Bree looked over at the garden and found—to her horror—that they were all her favorite flowers. And the house was her favorite color. The garage door slowly closed, and her heart sank right along with it. She had the distinct feeling that she wasn't making it out of this house alive.

Chapter Thirty-One

Noah

Three and a half hours later, Noah and others were exiting the plane in Phoenix and quickly moving through the main terminal so they could get to the front where a car would be waiting for them. They hopped in the car and he turned to Theo who had his laptop open and was crunching away on the keyboard. "Where do we go, Theo?" Noah asked.

"Looks like his last known address was a house in Riverdale. It's about forty-five minutes from here." Theo clicked a few more buttons. "Oh boy." He said.

"What?"

"Check this out."

We all turned to look at the screen he showed them—minus Zach, who was behind the wheel.

"What are we looking at?" Zach asked, signaling to get over a lane so they could get out of the airport.

"It's the guy's house," Eli said, confusion on his face.

"Okay..."

"It's in Bree's favorite color." Noah choked out, looking at the unassuming two-story.

"And the garden is full of Aubrey's favorite flowers," Theo added, looking a little green.

"This guy's level of obsession is way higher than we thought," Zach said, checking his blindspot before hopping on the interstate.

"If he planned his life and identity around Bree and what she likes he isn't going to be willing to let her go. Not without a fight." Noah said.

"Her deciding to step away from the industry was probably the catalyst." Theo reasoned. "If he made her his entire identity, then her suddenly not being on socials or producing more music would leave him feeling adrift. He doesn't know who he is without her. This has the potential to go bad."

"But there is a plus side." Eli chimed in.

"What's that?" Noah asked, staring at the picture of the house as though he could see Bree. Reach her. *I'm coming, Bree.* He thought, desperately wishing he could communicate with her. Reassure her that he was on his way. He wouldn't leave her behind.

He could hear her desperately whispered confession. *I love you.* Like she didn't think she'd have the opportunity to tell him again. He wished she had hung on a moment longer so he could've told her that he loved her too. Her feelings weren't one-sided. She was his life.

"If she is his identity, he is going to be less likely to hurt her as long as she plays along."

"There was blood on the balcony," Noah argued.

"Yeah, but that was probably to gain compliance or get her into the car. As long as she plays along, he probably won't *kill* her."

"I can't believe someone probably not *killing* Bree is the silver lining," Noah muttered, handing the computer back to Theo.

"We'll take what we can get," Zach said.

"Have the local police been informed?"

"Yes, they're getting in touch with our local department and seeing what they can do. They're working to coordinate it. They were waiting on evidence transfer of the video last I heard. They also have to prove she's out of state."

"Couldn't they watch the video from the gas station and interview that employee?"

"The employee never showed back up for work," Eli said meaningfully.

"So he knows that Bree talked to someone." Noah postulated.

"Let's just hope he doesn't know she talked to you," Zach said darkly.

***

The valet unlocked the door to the garage and came around to Bree's side of the car to open her door. They walked into the house, and she was taken aback by the large, warm living space. A fireplace and two-story ceilings immediately captured her attention. Above the fireplace was a signed photograph Aubrey had sent out earlier that year. She walked over to it and read the dedication in the corner. Skyler. His name was Skyler. Memories of different things she'd signed—several in the last six months alone—all made out to Skyler flashed through her mind.

"You like it?" He asked, standing behind her, the warmth of his body making her skin crawl.

"I do. I love getting to connect with my fans in different ways." She said. Which was true. "It looks nice on the mantle." She added—another truth.

"I thought it would help you feel more comfortable here." He said, gesturing to the living space. "Would you like a house tour?" He offered as though she was just another guest visiting his home.

"I'd love one," Bree said, forcing a small smile and hoping it reached her eyes. She looked around the room for ways to escape, but there wasn't anything that immediately stuck out. The kitchen was off to the left, a large island making up the dining space. A glass door to the backyard that had a large tree could be seen, but there was fencing all the way around it. She wondered if there was a gate. Or if she could hop the fence. It looked taller than normal. Now would have been a great time to not be spatial reasoning challenged. Ugh. She turned to look at the entryway and grimaced. The front door looked like it was also locked from the inside with a key. What if there was a fire? She shuddered. That would be an awful way to go.

"This is the living, kitchen, and eating area." He said, gesturing to the open space. They walked down a small side hallway. "Here is the laundry room—" Bree peeked in and noticed a door to the outside that was bolted and locked. It required a key on the inside. Who does that? They continued down the hall, where there was a small bedroom and a guest bath.

"Let's head upstairs." He said, gesturing to the staircase and waiting for Bree to go first.

She nodded, the hair on her neck rising as his body stayed close behind hers. She walked up the steps carefully, keeping an eye out for any way to escape. Who was this guy? The only door so far that hadn't had the same lock seemed to be the garage, but she hadn't exactly had the chance to make sure.

"The first door on the left is the recording studio," Skyler said, opening the door to show a room that had been covered with soundproofing materials. There was a stool and mic in the center of the room and a guitar sitting in the corner, waiting for Bree to play it. The soundboard nearby looked to be a professional quality and a computer—currently turned off—sat on the desk next to it. It was actually a really nice setup for a small home studio.

He backed out and closed the door before moving to the one across the hall. They walked in, and her heart tripped in her chest—what didn't this guy know about her? The room was set up in the *exact* same manner as her art studio at Noah's house. From the art on the wall to the easel placement to where she normally sat her brushes down to dry. Bree shuddered. He had been *watching* her. "Now you can paint too!" He said gleefully. "You'll just be painting for us, of course. You need to focus on your music. But it's a good outlet to have nonetheless."

Bree nodded, unable to form words.

"The last door on the left is mine. It has an attached bath, so we won't need to share right now." He said diplomatically. Bree's blood ran cold. *Right now?* She would *never* share a bathroom—or anything else—with him. She'd rather die first. Skyler continued the tour, oblivious to the internal panic attack Bree was experiencing.

"The door at the end of the hall is the shared bath for all these rooms, so it's just yours. And the room on the right is yours." He said, moving over and unlocking it from the outside with a key. Bree walked in and a tear rolled down her cheek while bile simultaneously rose in her throat. The cream-colored bedspread was gorgeous and inviting—and it looked identical to the one on her bed back at Noah's house. Worse yet, a small teddy bear head was placed neatly in front of the pillows. The stuffing was coming out of the bottom which made it sit strangely lopsided. Devastation swam through her. She wanted to go home. She *wanted* Noah. Bree wiped the tear away quickly. The rest of the room was beautiful. Because it was exactly the same as her room at Noah's house. "It's just like my room at home." Bree croaked.

That seemed to make him angry. "NO! This is your home. I copied *his* rooms so you'd be comfortable while you adjusted."

"Of course. That was...very thoughtful...of you." She managed to get out. She closed her eyes so she didn't have to stare at the room in front of her.

"It was." He agreed, his voice edged with the mania that she was confident would be on display in his eyes—if she cared to look. "It took a lot of planning. A lot of work. A *lot* of trips back and forth while I waited for you. A lot of time spent looking in windows from a distance. Watching. *Waiting.* I paid a lot of attention to you, Aubrey Gray. And how did you repay me for that? For building you a paradise?" He gestured to the house around them. "For *rescuing* you so you could go back to doing what you loved?"

Was this rhetorical? Was she supposed to answer? She teetered back and forth, uncertain of whether to engage or if he was hitting the villain monologue stage.

"You brought someone else into it."

Bree furrowed her brow, confusion etched on her face. "I didn't—"

"Do not LIE to ME!" He half shouted, grabbing a small silver rectangle out of his pocket and slamming it down on the dresser in front of her. "Read it." He said in a calm yet deadly voice.

"Ashley." She read aloud before all the blood drained from her face. The gas station attendant.

"You told her you were in *trouble.* That you had been *kidnapped.* After everything I *did* for you." He slammed his hand against the door. "I couldn't just leave her—risk her going to the police. Risk them taking you away from me. No. So I did what I had to do."

"What did you do, Skyler? Where is Ashley?"

"Dead." He replied. "And it's all your fault. Because you couldn't follow directions. Couldn't do as you were *told*. I knew you were taking too long in the bathroom. I heard you talking to her. 'Go pretend to be sick,'" He sneered. "It didn't take much—keeping my head down and going back into the bathroom where she was still waiting. Afraid to leave. A quick, quiet snap of the neck was all it took for poor Ashley to never be able to help someone again."

Bree gasped, tears filling her eyes as she thought of the young girl who had just been trying to help. "You're a monster," Bree whispered, anger taking over the fear.

"You made me into this Aubrey. *You* did." He looked around the room and seemed to be satisfied that there wasn't anything she could use to escape him. "I need to clean up and rest. You'll be staying in here. I'll see you for dinner." He closed the door, and the lock clicked as it slid into place.

Bree listened for his retreating footsteps and then rushed to the window that overlooked the backyard. She tried to open it, but it didn't work. He had permanently sealed it. It looked to be thicker than your average window. She looked down and considered the height. If she jumped—if she even made it that far once he heard the glass break—would she be able to walk for help after she landed? She probably wouldn't be able to jump the fence, so the gate would have to be unlocked...if there even was one. It was a bad idea. She needed to wait for an opening. It was starting to look like she'd only have one chance.

Come on, Noah. Come and find me. She mentally begged, sagging onto the floor and letting all of the tears of fear, and pain, and heartache pour out of her. She sobbed quietly for a few minutes and then stood, wiping the tears resolutely. She would stay alert. She *would* find a way out of this. Or she would die trying.

Chapter Thirty-Two

Noah

Noah looked at the rest of the team as they parked down the street from the unassuming blue house. "She's in there." He said. He could *feel* it.

"What's the plan?" Theo asked.

"We need to gain access, but we don't want him to get to her first if they're in separate spaces," Eli replied thoughtfully.

"We could try and lure him out," Zach suggested, binoculars pressed against his eyes as he looked from window to window in the house.

"What if he took her with him? Or if he was suspicious of her? Given the dead cashier, we have to assume he's armed, dangerous, and knows she betrayed him on some level." Eli replied.

"She didn't betray him," Noah said angrily. "He kidnapped her."

"But he'll see it as a betrayal. You need to take a step back from this man, or you'll need to sit it out. We can't have you going off half-cocked in there. It could get her killed." Zach said seriously.

Noah took a deep breath and nodded.

"Could we get the authorities to come to the door? Maybe the fire department or the police for a welfare check?" Theo suggested.

"If he sees them, he might turn to murder-suicide. We don't want to escalate the situation." Noah said, rubbing his hands across his forehead. She was so close. They were so close.

"He could have enough supplies in the house to last for weeks or longer. He may not need to leave." Eli said.

"We have to figure out a way to get her away from him *before* we bust him.

Could we figure out what room she's in and extract her?" Theo suggested, weighing all of their previous comments carefully.

"That could work, but we'd need to know what room she is being held in and whether he's with her," Noah said.

"How would we do that?" Zach asked, lowering the binoculars.

"We could involve the neighbors," Eli suggested.

"But what if they're loyal to him and tip him off?" Peter asked, looking up from the blueprints they had grabbed online.

"We could trespass at the neighbors?" Theo suggested helpfully.

"We could wait until dark and split up. One person on each of the surrounding roofs and one in the car. We can monitor each window and see if we can locate the two of them in the house."

"What if he's with her?"

"Then we wait until he isn't."

"If he's hurting her, I'm not waiting. He's a dead man." Noah said, his voice low and threatening while his heart constricted in his chest at the idea of Bree being hurt. Or worse.

"Fair enough. If we have reason to believe something's going on, we'll storm the place early. If we see him being violent, we'll storm the fort. But otherwise we *wait* so we can get her out safely. He hasn't killed her yet, so we're assuming she's still valuable to him." Zach said.

It was a crappy plan. Noah didn't want to wait until dark, but it was wise, and they needed to be wise more than they needed to move quickly, even though every second away from Bree was excruciating. "Okay, I'll take the south roof that looked directly into the back of the house. Theo, you stay in the car and oversee the operation. Eli, you take the east side of the house. Zach, you're on the west. Peter, I want you monitoring the front rooms." The men nodded and quietly turned to observe the house, each in his own thoughts.

Three hours later, the sun had set, and it was dark enough that they could move.

"I'm coming for you, babe," Noah whispered before turning back to the others. "Okay, remember your positions. And be *quiet.* We don't want the families aware that there is something knocking around on their roof. Stay out of sight and— "

"Don't engage until we can make a plan and provide the necessary backup for everyone to get out safely," Zach added, looking at Noah pointedly.

"Zach—" Noah started to argue. He wouldn't wait to move if something was happening to Bree.

"Noah. I know you're the boss and you normally take charge on these things. And I know you're pissed at me right now." He said. "But if you go in there blind with rage and whatever else, you're going to get yourself or Bree killed. Now I know right now you don't care about yourself much, but we do. Bree does. And if it backfired and he killed her instead, you wouldn't be able to live with yourself. So, if you *see* something. You call us. Got it?"

Noah nodded and then hesitated for a moment, working his throat desperately so he could say one last thing. "Bree would want me to say 'be safe' to all of us. So there it is." He choked out. They all nodded.

"He messed with the wrong woman," Theo said. Each man nodded, fierce determination etched on each of their faces.

"Let's get our girl back," Peter said.

***

They split up, and Noah jogged over to the next street, counting houses as he went. Once he came to the house he needed, he slowly walked up the side of their drive, careful to keep out of the way of lights and windows, most of which had the blinds closed. Noah grabbed onto the low point of the roofline and hoisted himself up onto the roof, freezing for a second once he got up, listening intently for any indication that he might have tipped them off. When no sound changes came from inside, He slowly crouched across the roof, hyperaware of keeping each footstep as light as humanly possible. Once he got to the back side of the house, he sat in the nook between the chimney and one of the many angles on the roofline—a lone figure blending with the shadows. He picked up his infrared binoculars and began looking through each window, starting in the bottom left and working his way around.

The giant windows in the back showed the living area and kitchen, which appeared to be empty at the moment, though places were set and there were pans on the stove, so maybe they were getting ready for dinner? Noah scanned the next two windows downstairs, but found no heat signatures. He moved his gaze to the upstairs and peeked into what looked like a recording studio, if the microphone was any indication, and then a room full of art? No. Art supplies. His blood heated, and his blood pressure sky-rocketed. It was an art studio set up exactly like the one they had at home. How long had this lunatic been watching their house? Noah moved on to the next room, and a sound left his throat. *Bree.*

"I found her," Noah whispered into the com.

"Where is she?" Theo asked.

"Top floor. Far right window. Looks like her bedroom at my house."

"Weird way to describe it, but okay. Like size-wise?"

"No, like he copied the furniture, the bedding, the pictures...all of it," Noah reported, the fiery rage in his veins at odds with the severe nausea in his stomach.

Theo swore, and Noah felt himself nodding along. That about summed it up.

"Does anyone have eyes on him?" Noah asked.

"Negative." Peter's reply came through quickly.

"Not here," Eli replied.

"No," Zach said.

"He must be along an interior walkway then," Theo said, the clicking on his keyboard indicating that he was likely flipping through blueprints again.

Noah watched as Bree turned around quickly, her body stiffening.

"I think I found him," Noah said quietly. Sure enough, Skyler Johnson walked into Bree's room and was clearly trying to talk her into something. She shook her head, and he lifted his hand and backhanded her across the face. Icy rage settled in Noah's veins as one thought echoed repeatedly through his head. He was a dead man. Noah needed to get in there. Stat.

"He hit her," Noah said through gritted teeth, watching Aubrey hold her hand to her face.

"Give us a minute, man. We're coming to you."

"No, I need to go in."

"Noah—you're not—"

Noah yanked the com out of his ear and moved stealthily to the tree in the backyard below him. He jumped from the roof to the tree and made his way across the thick branch that hung over the neighboring fence line and into the tree in the backyard Bree was in. He stilled as two bodies made their way into the kitchen and sat at the dining table. Noah looked at Bree—her cheek red where Skyler hit her, and determination flowed through Noah. No one was going to stand between him and his woman. No one.

Chapter Thirty-Three

Aubrey

The pain on Bree's face had turned from the initial sting into more of a throbbing as she sat at the island where he had indicated. She just wanted to go home. She was tired and hurting and over the fear and adrenaline, tired of playing his games. She was not a proficient liar at the best of times, and this was wearing on her already thin nerves. It had almost been twenty-four hours, and she was done.

"I'm sorry you made me do that," Skyler said as he dished up their dinner. "I don't want to hurt you, Aubrey. I want us to be happy together. I can help make all of your dreams come true. There is no me without you. And there can't be a you without *me*." He said, the warning clear as he set down the plate of spaghetti in front of her and waited for her to take a bite.

"Eat." He said shortly. "It's your Nonna's recipe. Just the way you like it."

Nothing was sacred to this man. Bree didn't think she'd ever be able to be in Noah's house or eat Nonna's spaghetti again. A lone tear fell down her face as she obediently picked up the fork to take a bite. *I'm sorry you made me do that*, he had said. She scoffed internally. *Yeah, how dare I refuse to come downstairs with you to eat after you freaking kidnapped me.* Bree's thoughts ran rampant while she forced another bite into her mouth.

A loud shattering sound had her throwing her hands up in front of her face in an attempt to protect it from the glass that was flying into the room from the outside. A loud grunt came from the kitchen and she was abruptly pulled off her chair from behind into a warm body.

There in the doorway, like an avenging warrior, was Noah, dressed head to toe

in black, a gun in his hand and a look of pure rage on his face. "Let. Her. Go."
Noah said, training his weapon on the man behind her.

A glint of silver and the widening of Noah's eyes was the only warning Bree had
before there was a sharp tug at her throat, warm liquid trickling down it.

"Put down your weapon, or I'll do it again," Skyler warned, pressing the
kitchen knife against her throat. The first shallow cut was already stinging.

"Okay—just...Don't hurt her." Noah said, his hard eyes taking Bree in while
slowly bending down and placing his gun on the floor.

"Kick it away," Skyler ordered. Noah rolled his eyes, and Bree found herself
worried that he was going to get himself killed.

"Noah—" She tried, but Skyler yanked her back against him and made another
slice in warning. Bree let out a small whimper, and tears filled her eyes.

"NO!" Noah shouted. "Bree—just—don't talk, love."

Bree couldn't even nod in response as fear flowed through her veins. Noah
looked...frightened.

"There's no way out of this for you Skyler," Noah said, trying to draw Skyler's
attention off of Bree and back on him.

"She's mine. You were trying to keep her all to yourself. You wouldn't let her
do what she loved. She was dying in your house."

"You're right," Noah said, sounding as though he one hundred percent believed what he was saying. "She was dying in my house. I should've listened to her
when she said she wanted to do things and get out of the house. But she's going
to die in *your* house Skyler if you keep cutting her. That isn't what you want, is
it?"

A soft click came from the right, but no one seemed to notice it except Bree.
Both men were too busy facing each other in a standoff where the loser lost their
life and the winner got the prize—her.

"Listen, you can have her," Noah said, holding up his hands in a placating
gesture.

Skyler scoffed. "Like I'd believe that. I'm not an idiot."

"No, man, I mean it. I can see that you care for her. Your house color, the
flowers, the spaghetti. You know her well. She'd be *happy* here." Noah said, taking

a small step toward Skyler.

Skyler loosened his grip on the knife slightly, and Bree could finally take a breath without fear of accidentally slitting her own throat. Noah's eyes met hers, and she saw everything there. Love. Fear. Determination. He wouldn't leave her here. He wouldn't leave her, ever.

"Skyler, we can talk about this. But you have to let her go. Just let her sit on the couch or something. She doesn't need to be in the middle of this. She's a woman you care about deeply. Are you going to let harm come to her while she's under your care?"

"No," Skyler said, clearly affronted by the question. "No, I'm not." He ran his hand down her arm in a caress that made her want to vomit. "You're okay, Bree." He whispered. He forcefully grabbed her arm and sat her on the nearest barstool. She was still easily within his reach, but there wasn't a knife to her throat, and she wasn't directly between him and Noah, so she was counting that as a win.

"Good—that's good. I can see that she's really important to you." Noah said, clearly trying to buy time. For what? "She'll be happier with you." He said, looking directly at Skyler. His eyes flitted behind Skyler for a brief second.

"I know she—" Skyler began as Noah abruptly dropped to the ground.

"NOAH!" Bree screamed as he fell, fear flashing through her.

Skyler's confusion mirrored hers as a loud boom sounded in the room, making Bree's ears ache and her head spin.

There was a moment of silence before the ringing started. It was quiet at first and gradually grew louder as the other sounds around her came back into focus. Skyler fell forward onto the ground, a bullet hole taking up residence in the back of his head. The blood oozed around him, and while she didn't want to look, she couldn't look away. Her body was shaking, and she could hear her breath coming out in sharp pants as she stared.

A pair of hands wrapped around her arms, and she froze, slowly moving her gaze away from Skyler's dead body and tensing from the touch. Noah lifted his hands up in a placating manner. "It's me, Bree. You're safe now." He said, moving to stand in front of her to block her view of Skyler, but still not touching her.

Bree looked at Noah as she tried to make her brain move through sludge and process what he was saying. She looked at the empty space where Skyler had been standing. Eli watched her, the gun still in his hand, arm resting at his side. He gave her a small nod and re-holstered his weapon before he turned on his heel to open the front door. "Key," Bree whispered to Noah.

"What, sweetheart?" Noah asked, leaning a little closer.

"He'll need the key. To get out the front door." Her teeth chattered, but she wasn't cold. "On the ring." She said, nodding down toward Skyler's dead body.

"He already opened the front door, Bree," Noah said reassuringly.

She must've looked confused because he added, "Eli is a master at picking locks. It's come in handy countless times."

Eli nodded and walked over toward them, and crouched down a little so he was on Bree's level. "Don't give him another second of your life, Aubrey. He brought this on himself."

She nodded and looked back at Noah, who was hovering close to her. "Noah?" Bree asked, tears streaming down her face as it finally sunk in that he was *there*. She was *safe*. She threw herself at him, sobs coming out of her as he wrapped his strong arms around her and nuzzled his nose in her hair, his breath gently stirring the strands that never seemed to stay in place.

"Bree." He held on to her tightly as the scene around them changed. The front door opened and the room filled with sounds of other people coming into the house. Bree turned her head and watched Theo, Peter, and Zach. They took in the dead man in the living room with about as much interest as she would give the weather channel.

"Did you call the police? EMS?" Noah asked, clutching her to him tightly.

"Sure did. They're en route. Put some pressure on that slice on your arm, Noah. Looks like it may need stitches." Peter replied, staring pointedly at the gash on Noah's arm.

"That's what happens when you crash through a window instead of waiting for your team," Eli added, raising an eyebrow.

There was a panicked flutter in Bree's chest. "But you guys shot him." She said as her brain finally started functioning again. "Won't you get in trouble? You'll go to jail. You can't go to jail for me."

"Relax, Bree," Noah said softly. "No one is going to jail. You were kidnapped, and he was holding you at knifepoint. It was self-defense."

"And you breaking through the window?"

"You were here under duress. And if they slap me with a trespassing charge, I'll take it. You're alive and safe, Bree. I'll take whatever they want to throw at me."

Zach rolled his eyes. "As romantic as that is, no one is slapping you with anything, Noah." He paused as the sound of sirens blared through the open door. "Let's give statements and get out of here."

***

Several hours and a hospital trip later, Bree found herself tucked into Noah's side on the plane back home to Trenton. The doctor said the cuts were superficial and her concussion would just take some time to heal. Other than being in shock, she was perfectly fine. The shock had mostly worn off by the time they made it to the hospital, and the police had arrived to collect their statements. Turns out that them having reported all of the incidents along the way saved Eli and Noah from charges. They had made all the necessary police reports which corroborated their story.

Bree nestled into Noah's shoulder, content to listen to the banter of the men as they headed home, but her eyes began closing of their own accord, desperate for the rest that had eluded her since her kidnapping. Now that she was safe, her body was ready to sleep.

Chapter Thirty-Four

Aubrey

It had been a week since her rescue, and bright lights still bothered her. Her doctor said concussion symptoms can last for weeks to months after the fact, which left Bree feeling particularly grumpy. She and Noah had been staying at a hotel since his house triggered bad memories for her, and her house was overrun by paparazzi who were looking for the scoop on her kidnapping. Vultures.

They checked out of the hotel and stopped in at the cafe to grab some coffee on their way to the hospital to talk with Jessica's doctor. The walk through the doors was harder than ever, the weight of Jessica's care now firmly on Bree's shoulders since the lawyers had called to let her know she'd won power of attorney. When they reached the doctor's office, she reached out and knocked, Noah's hand warm and supportive on her back.

"Come in." Dr. Matthews called.

"Aubrey, Noah." He said, greeting them as they walked in. "How can I help you?"

"I umm...I was recently given power of attorney for Jess and...and I was wondering if your opinion has changed at all. Since last time we spoke."

The doctor gave a grim nod of understanding, compassion, and honesty written on the planes of his face. "I'm sorry, Aubrey. I have to say that in my medical opinion, nothing has changed, and it is extremely unlikely it ever will. Your sister has been gone for a long time. The machines are just keeping her body alive."

The crushing weight of despair slammed into Bree like a freight train, and it felt hard to breathe. Her sister had been her best friend growing up—an anchor in a household that was tumultuous at best. But her sister was gone, and admitting that...it was harder than she imagined. She took a deep breath and found solace in the warmth of Noah's hand around hers. Solid. Unfailing. "I'd like to...I'd like to end life support interventions." Bree said, her heartbreaking further as flashes of life with Jess flitted through her mind.

"You don't have to make that decision today." Dr. Matthews said.

Bree paused and considered what the doctor was offering her. More time to think. More days to come by and bring her sister's favorite flowers to her bedside. More time to engage in one-sided conversation in the hopes that maybe she hears. Maybe she'll get better. Maybe something could be different. But nothing would be different. Keeping her here...keeping her here for more flowers and stilted bedside conversations would be selfish at best. Cruel at worst.

Bree shook her head, her eyes filling with tears despite her resolve to stay strong and not break down. "She's suffered long enough. I...I wouldn't want to be left that way. Not if there was no chance of me getting better. And Jessica...Jess wouldn't have wanted that either." Noah's hands rubbed up and down her back in silent support as the doctor and Bree worked out logistics. They'd come back tomorrow afternoon to say their goodbyes.

"Thank you, Dr. Matthews. For everything." Bree said, reaching out to shake his hand.

"I'm sorry I couldn't do more." He replied, shaking her hand kindly.

Noah and Bree got up and left the office, intent to visit Jess before tomorrow. "I'd like to sit with her for a while," Bree told Noah softly. "I...I'm not ready yet."

"We can stay as long as you'd like," Noah said, guiding her gently through the halls though she knew them like the back of her hand. Still, his support was all that kept her from running from the building. From falling to the ground and pulling out her hair, screaming about how unfair this was. How horrible it was. His support...it was everything.

They walked around the corner and into Jessica's room, for once empty aside from the two of them.

"I'm so sorry you've been stuck here for so long, Jess," Bree said through her tears as she sat next to her and cradled Jess's hand in her own. "I'm sorry for the fight we had before your accident and for not standing up to Dad for you. For letting them drag this out for you for so long. I love you. We love you." Bree sat down and let the tears fall, holding Jess's hand and listening to the steady beat of the heart monitor she was attached to, the soft whirring of the ventilator constantly running in the background.

"What are you doing here?" A sharp voice said from the doorway. Bree's dad's arms rested around her mother for the first time in a long time as they looked at Noah warily.

"I was here to see Jess, but we're going now," Bree said as she stood, already tired. Noah stepped up beside her, his hand a solid support on her back. "But before we do...I wanted to let you know that Jess will be taken off life support tomorrow."

Bree's parents stepped back slightly as though they'd been slapped. "You don't get to have a say in what happens to *our daughter*." Her dad spat.

Noah moved quickly, putting his body slightly in front of hers, violence etched in the lines of his face. He would fight for her and it made Bree love him all the more. But this wasn't his fight. Bree tapped him lightly on the back and stepped around him. "I'm not debating this with you. I *am* letting you know that Jess will be removed from life support tomorrow afternoon if you'd like to be here." She said calmly. "I'm sorry for your loss." Bree looked up at Noah and nudged his shoulder. "Let's go, love."

Noah looked down at her and nodded, reaching out and taking her hand in his. They walked around the bed and headed for the door. Her dad stood in the way, and Noah stepped closer to him, invading his space just like he had with Justin. "She's being far kinder than I would," Noah said quietly. "And I have no qualms about sitting you down *again*. So back off."

Warmth flooded through her as she fully appreciated the man by her side. She had always longed for a champion—someone to stand in her corner and stand up for her when she couldn't. Now that she had learned to stand up for herself, she didn't need him in that capacity, but still found herself exceptionally grateful that she didn't have to fight every battle alone. Noah squeezed her hand gently in reassurance, his eyes trained fully on her dad.

Dad looked like he was going to object before Mom came over and placed her hand on his arm. "It's enough, Charles. Our *girls* have been through enough."

Dad stepped out of the doorway, and Noah and Bree walked out—Noah's body remained tense until they stepped outside into the fresh air. "I couldn't do what you just did. I just want to hit something."

Bree shrugged. "They're losing a daughter too. And it doesn't do me—or you—any good to take our feelings out on them. It's time to let it all go. I don't care if they like me or what I do for a living or who I'm dating or where I live. I don't really care about the reasons they had for keeping Jess on life support so long or pushing the financial responsibility to me. I don't even care if my mom knew about the gambling—though since they often fought about finances growing up, I'm sure she does. I just don't care anymore. They can live their life, and I can live mine. I have you. And Theo. And Eli and Peter. And Zach. I'll be okay. And they will, too. One day."

Noah shook his head. "If you say so, babe."

"I think I'd like to go back to my house too."

"But the paps—"

Bree blanched as she thought of the paparazzi who'd frequently been hanging out in front of her home since the story broke about her stalker and subsequent kidnapping. One of these days she was sure they'd get bored and move on to greener pastures. Thankfully, her life was too boring to interest the tabloids for now. "We'll handle them. But I'm not letting them run me out of my home. I worked hard for that house, and I love it. My little bungalow. But you can come and visit—sometimes." Bree said, smiling at him cheekily.

"Oh, I can visit sometimes, huh?" His chuckle filled the parking lot as he wrapped a warm arm around her. "Only if sometimes is most days ending in -Y."

"I suppose I'm amenable to that." She laughed.

Noah opened the car door for her and watched her closely. "I love you, Aubrey Gray."

Her heart leaped in her chest, and she smiled at him. "I love you too, Noah Hawthorne," Bree said, leaning in for a kiss. His lips moved expertly over hers, and she leaned into him as his hand rested on her left cheek. He smiled into the kiss before pulling away, gently caressing her cheek. They'd get through this.

She would get through this.

✳✳✳

The next afternoon, Bree stood in a silent vigil with Noah at her side as the nurses prepared to end Jess's life support. The soft whirring of the machines and comforting beeps indicating she was alive grounded Bree to the spot when it felt like she would be adrift in her grief. The hospital room door opened, and her mother walked in, dark circles under her bloodshot eyes and tears streaming down her face. She walked over to where Noah and Bree stood, careful to stay out of the way of the bustling staff. A few minutes later, Dr. Mathews walked in and looked at the threesome standing watch over Jess. "Will you please step out for a moment? I'm going to remove her breathing tube, and we'll get the alarms turned off. I'll call you back in shortly."

Noah nodded for the women, and Bree felt him shepherd them gently out into the hallway.

"Is he coming?" Bree asked her mom quietly, both of them painfully aware of which *he* Bree was talking about.

Mom sniffled. "I'm not sure. He's here somewhere, though."

The three of them stood in the hallway, the dinging of call lights and quiet chatter from the nurses and families in other rooms a familiar cacophony yet painful as their time here came to an end.

Dr. Matthews appeared a few moments later. "You can go back in now. I'm so sorry for your loss." He added, shaking hands with Bree, her mom, and Noah before walking down the hall. Bree couldn't imagine having his job. They walked back into the room where a nurse was checking over the last of the equipment. She smiled softly, one of the soft apologetic smiles where they aren't sure what to say, but want you to know they understand you're grieving, before walking toward the door.

"Press the call light if you need anything. Stay as long as you'd like." She added, ducking into the hall quietly.

Jess's chest rose and fell rhythmically, and without the tubes and beeping machines, Bree could almost imagine Jess was just asleep. The hospital room door opened, and her dad walked in, his eyes flickering between Jess and his wife.

Mom sobbed and walked over to him, clinging to him as tears fell down her face. Bree shifted uncomfortably, and Noah wrapped his arm around her shoulder. They waited in silence as Jess's respirations slowed down before stopping altogether. Her chest settled one final time, and a loud wail came from across the room, startling Bree in Noah's arms. Bree's mom fell to the floor, sobs shaking her body as she rested a hand on Jess's leg. Dad rested his hand lightly on Mom's shaking shoulders as though he was uncertain how to comfort the distraught woman.

The wails pierced the quiet room for several minutes until quiet sobs took over, and Bree felt tears trickling down her cheeks. She hurriedly wiped them away, not wanting to break down in front of anyone—especially not her parents. After a moment, she stood and walked over to Jess, smoothing back her hair gently. "Goodbye Jessie," Bree said softly, her voice catching on a barely suppressed sob.

She took Noah's hand and walked carefully around her grieving parents, her anxiety lessening as they stepped out of the hospital and into the fresh air.

"Bree?" Noah asked concern etched on his face. Bree shook her head, unable to put the emotions weighing on her into words. Grief. Relief. Sadness. Joy. Freedom. Devastation. All warring for a place in her scarred heart. She sent up a silent prayer and felt a quiet peace. She would heal. And one day, she would see her sister again.

"Let's go home," Bree said softly.

Noah wrapped Bree tightly in his arms and pressed his lips to her hair gently. "I love you, Aubrey Gray."

"I love you, too." She said, nuzzling into him before stepping into his car and into their future.

Chapter Thirty-Five

Epilogue: One Year Later

Aubrey

"Aubreeeeeey, we're gonna be late!" Theo called from her living room as she finished putting on the last swipes of makeup. It wouldn't take as much time if she did it more often. She chided herself internally, giving one last glance in the mirror. Bouncing curls, light, neutral makeup. All good things, all good things. Noah was being nominated for a public safety award after handling an incident last month and she couldn't be more proud of him.

Her own small business providing support and finding and sharing resources for families affected by addiction—now expanded to include gambling and other addictions outside of drugs and alcohol—had been growing like crazy the last year. Soon, she'd need to bring on help to manage the research and consulting load. But her business kind of felt like her first baby, and finding someone to trust to help manage it was more than she could bear at the moment.

A memory of Bree and Jess playing in their backyard when they were little crossed her mind, and she felt her heart squeeze painfully. The grief of losing Jess hadn't gone away. Some days, it was barely there, just a light kiss of the wind in moments that she would have loved to share with her sister. Some days, it was a category five hurricane, and it was all Bree could do to hold on to the present moment...and to Noah.

Bree grabbed her wallet and phone and shoved them into her pockets before slipping into her trusty black sneakers. She walked out and did a little spin, laughing as Theo gave an encouraging round of applause like any good big brother would do. Exasperated with just enough 'she's adorable' to make it tolerable.

"I'm ready," Bree said, skipping over to him.

"Perfect. We can—" Theo's phone dinged, and he looked down to read the message quickly. "Ah, can you go start the car? I need to make a quick call." He said, frowning.

"Sure." She said. Bree walked over to the key bowl and picked up her keys. She walked out to the driveway to start her car only to find that it had a flat tire.

"How is this my luck?" She muttered under her breath, thankful she always budgeted extra time to get places. Bree opened the car door and placed her homemade coffee in the cupholder. She definitely didn't want to spill a drop of that. She needed the caffeine for all the socializing she was going to have to do today.

She shut the door softly and pushed the button to open the trunk where her jack, spare, and the tire-changing tool were. Did it have a name? Probably. Did she know its name yet? Nope.

She loosened the lug nuts on the tires and had just gotten the jack situated when a pair of men's dress shoes appeared in her field of vision.

"Would you like some help?" A deep voice asked in a tone that hinted at bemusement. *Noah.*

"Aren't you supposed to be at City Hall?" Bree asked, looking up at him and appreciating how delectable he looked in his suit.

He smiled at her as though she was missing her cue. "Would you like some help?" He asked again pointedly.

"Thanks, but I know how to change a tire," Bree said, using the scissor jack to lift the car up so she could get the tire off.

"I can see that," Noah said. "It's a good skill to have. Your dad teach you?"

She laughed at that while eyeballing the car and making sure it was both high enough and steady. "No, my dad wasn't the type to get his hands dirty."

"Ah," Noah said. "Husband?"

"Nope." Bree said, popping the 'p.'

"Fiancé?" He asked.

She laughed, "Nope. Noah, You're off scrip—"

Bree turned to look up at Noah and found him on one knee in front of her, a ring box in his hand.

"Aubrey Elizabeth Gray, you had my heart the moment you told me a Cistercian monk taught you how to change your tire."

"You said that." She mumbled, a giant smile on her face.

"Semantics." He said with a wink. "You are the love of my life, and I want to spend every day of the rest of my life with you. Would you do me the incredible honor of becoming my wife?"

"Yes!" She said, throwing her arms around his neck. Her heart raced, and a huge bubble of joy overwhelmed her as she nuzzled into him. He wrapped his arms around her waist and pulled her in tightly.

"I love you, Bree." He said, his voice warm and deep in her ear, sending delicious shivers down her spine.

"I love you too, Noah," Bree replied.

Noah pulled away slightly and took her left hand in his, carefully slipping a beautiful silver band with a solitaire diamond over her ring finger.

A chorus of whoops came from various places around her house and she laughed as Theo stuck his head out the front door and Eli and Zach populated from one side of the house. Peter stood up on the roof and gave Noah a thumbs up.

"I got it!" He said, waving a camera around in the air and losing his footing momentarily. Bree breathed a deep sigh of relief when he was steady again. "I'm okay!" He called.

Noah kissed her hand and pulled her close. "Let's get this tire aired back up and get down to City Hall. Then I'm taking my fiancée on a date. How does Mexican food sound?"

"That sounds perfect," Bree said. "Come on y'all. Let's get this over with."

"Wait, how come you're not buying Mexican food for all of us?"

"Yeah, we're all going to this shindig. It's all or nothing, man."

"You know we could just follow you and show up—"

Noah sighed. "Fine lunch together. But dinner is just with Bree. "

The guys high-fived and got to work airing the tire back up on the car.

"They're incorrigible," Noah grumbled.

"And you love it," Bree said, nestling into him. He squeezed her shoulder affectionately.

"I do." He said with a smile and shake of his head. "For some reason, I do."

Acknowledgements

Wow, I am so excited about the release of Securing Aubrey! There are so many people who had a hand in making the first book of the Hawthorne Security series a reality. First and foremost, I owe everything to God. That he would sacrifice his son, Jesus, for us so we could be made right and have a relationship with him is something I will forever be in awe of. I couldn't do anything apart from Jesus. If you have questions about God or salvation or need prayer, my inbox is always open. Please feel free to reach out.

Secondly, I'd like to thank my husband and our two kids, who have been staunch supporters throughout this process. I couldn't have written, edited, re-written, and re-edited without their unfailing love and support. They gave me the time and space to complete the writing process and also pulled me out of my writing cave sometimes to remind me there's more to life than working—like losing to them at cards. I love all of you so very much.

Third, I'd like to thank my parents and sisters. You guys have always been the loudest cheering section around, and I appreciate each of you. Thank you for the moral support, the babysitting, and, of course, the iced coffee deliveries. Y'all are the best!

Last but not least, this book would not be nearly as good without the help of my team. I want to give a shoutout to my outstanding developmental editor, Caroline Acebo. Caroline was such a wonderful resource and legitimately the most kind, joyful, positive person to work with. She's the best! Another shoutout to the team over at Books and Moods, who designed the cover. They were great with all of my questions and the design changes as the book evolved from the first draft to its final iteration. Lastly, I'd like to give special thanks to my beta readers,

Kianna, Nancy, Joanna, and Ashley. You guys are all amazing, and I appreciate you very much!

About the author

Julia's novels are enjoyed for their intriguing plots, heartfelt romance, and wholesome themes, making them a perfect escape. When she isn't weaving tales of love and suspense, Julia enjoys her cozy life in the suburbs with her real-life book boyfriend (her husband) and their two amazing children. You'll often find her reading a book, running her kids to their activities, or trying to figure out what to make for dinner.

Follow her on social media or visit her website to stay updated on her latest releases and author events.